CW00523389

WAR

OF THE

GOD QUEEN

DAVID HAMBLING

War of the God Queen
Copyright © 2020 David Hambling

All rights are reserved. No part of this book may be reproduced in form or by any means without prior written consent of the author.

No part of this publication may be reproduced, distributed, or transmitted in any form or by any means, including photocopying, recording, or other electronic or mechanical methods, without the prior written permission of the publisher, except in the case of brief quotations for critical reviews and certain other non-commercial uses permitted by copyright law.

Visit the Shadows from Norwood Facebook page –
www.facebook.com/ShadowsFromNorwood
for more about the story behind War of the God Queen and the world in which it unfolds.

Contents

For the Merton gang: a group of really determined women can do anything

Visit the Shadows from Norwood Facebook page for news, special offers, articles, location photographs, maps and more about the world of Harry Stubbs

www.facebook.com/ShadowsFromNorwood

"He who cannot give an account of three thousand years is living from hand to mouth."

—Johann Wolfgang von Goethe

"They were able to undergo transformations and reintegrations impossible for their adversaries, and seem therefore to have originally come from even remoter gulfs of cosmic space… The first sources of the other beings can only be guessed at with bated breath."

—HP Lovecraft, *At the Mountains of Madness*

The Handmaidens

Miss Jessica Anne Merton BA, trainee architect, abducted Dulwich, London 1927 (See *The Dulwich Horror of 1927*)

Mlle Marie-Therese Varlin, communard organiser, abducted Paris, France 1871

Ms Izabel Bethânia Viana Telles Veloso , professional video gamer, abducted Sao Paulo Autonomous District, Brazil 2104

Lady Timi of the mercantile family Telgedi, abducted Budapest, Hungary 1562

Lu Zhu, physician and ob-gyn specialist, abducted China, date uncertain

Rachel bat-Joseph (alias), student Cabbalist, abducted Middle East in Year 3997 Hebrew (236 AD)

Vana Baker's daughter , brewer and baker, abducted Numidia (Algeria, North Africa) c. 600 AD.

Illi, hunter, abducted North America vicinity of Newfoundland c 1600 AD.

Noora, potter, abducted Arabia c. 900 AD.

Inzalu, villager, abducted Malaysia, date uncertain

Lalit, court attendant and musician, abducted India c. 250 BCE.

PROLOGUE

Dulwich, South London, 1928

IN FICTION, CHARACTERS ROUSE ONE another in the middle of the night by tossing pebbles at bedroom windows. In reality, if someone wants to wake another person, they bellow and bang drunkenly on the door, until the neighbours shout at them and someone looks out to see what's the matter.

I am a light sleeper, and the commotion woke me at once.

"Bill!"

I could not see the man at all until he took a few paces back from the door, but only one person in the world had ever called me Bill. The streetlamp illuminated a bush hat over a khaki outfit, accompanied by an overstuffed kit bag. A second man, similarly dressed, was seated, head lolling, on a low garden wall. The first man shaded his eyes to peer up at me, and I recognised him at once. I had not seen Crispy since our university days, almost five years ago. And I could easily guess the identity of his companion.

"Bill! I've got to talk to you!"

I could have told him that it was the middle of the night or that it could wait until morning. That would have been futile, though. Crispy

1

did not sound sober or calm. A shouted argument was not going to win me any popularity with my landlady, the other lodgers, or the rest of the street.

"I'll be down directly," I said, already donning my dressing gown.

My sleep was rarely peaceful, and now that I was wide awake, I had little chance of returning to the land of Nod. Conversation even with Crispy was preferable to insomnia. I could not imagine what he wanted, but people rarely wake their friends at three in the morning to give them good news. I slid back the bolts, turned the key, and after cautioning the two of them to silence, ushered my old acquaintances upstairs.

"Well, this is cosy," Crispy said, taking in my compact apartment before dumping his kit bag in a corner.

"Like university digs," Bunny, his companion, said, stacking his on top of it. The room was crowded with the three of us and the bags.

"Aren't you going to offer us a drink then?" Crispy asked.

"You've got a bloody nerve," I said.

"I suppose I have." He rubbed his jaw, which sported two days' worth of stubble. Beneath it, his fair skin was sunburned. He was careworn; young Crispy was already halfway to being middle-aged. Not that I looked any better myself. "Sorry, I've been through the mill lately. Perhaps it is a bit thick, but I want some answers."

"I dare say." I placed the sherry decanter and three glasses on my desk. I could not smell drink on his breath, so his agitation must have been from some other cause. A glass or two might sooth him.

Both men made the same disgusted face when they saw what was on offer—nobody in their set drank sherry, which was fit only for maiden aunts. When I hesitated, though, Crispy waved me to go ahead and pour.

Crispy and Bunny had been boon companions for as long as I had known them. The Honourable Wordsworth Patterson-Kelly was universally known as Bunny on account of his prominent front teeth, which, along with his receding chin, gave him a decidedly rabbit-like appearance. Crispy—actually Crispin Something-Something—had more or less adopted Bunny, who would have been lost at Oxford without him. Most such relationships fade after a term or two, but Bunny's chronic lack of confidence meant that he was only comfortable beside his friend.

If Crispy bought a new bicycle, grew a moustache, or took up badminton, Bunny did the same. I doubted Bunny lacked ideas of his own, and he may have been the brighter of the two, but he lacked self-belief. A look at Bunny's family—known for violence, drink, and harsh discipline—suggested causes for his condition, but no cure. Crispy had enough self-belief for two, further bolstered by having Bunny to back him up, like a one-man chorus of approval. Some said that Crispy only let Bunny knock about with him because Bunny's family was loaded. That was totally inaccurate. Plenty of men kept a loyal hound as a favourite companion, and no Labrador was ever more loyal than Bunny.

They were a harmless enough pair, slightly comical in their almost-matching outfits, swelling the crowd or helping the party go with a swing. The two of them belonged to a great many dining clubs in Oxford and were always in demand. They rarely said anything clever or funny, but the two of them laughed so easily and so heartily at everyone else's efforts that the company was inspired to ever-wittier sallies, and the party began. When they left, as they always had other invitations, the average IQ in the room may have increased a few points, but the fun left with them, and the evening was suddenly flat and sober.

"Bill the Brainbox Blake," Crispy said, raising his glass. "Your very good health, sir."

"Cheers, William," Bunny added.

"Cheers," I said.

They each took a good swallow in unison.

"We have to talk to you about your girl," Crispy said.

"What girl?" I honestly had no idea who he was referring to. It had been a long time since anyone could be described as "my girl." Perhaps the best candidate was poor Sophia, now raving and shut away in an institution. Sophia had once been a close friend, and more than a friend. But she was never "my girl."

"You know," he said. "That Jessica. The brainy one. Jessica Merton."

Her name was a stab in my heart. I had not thought of Jessica for a long time. The last I had seen of her was when the ground literally opened up and swallowed her. Jessica's was one of the many deaths in what had become known as the Dulwich Horror. That dreadful incursion into our world had been repelled, but Jessica's life was part of the price we paid.

I had been too wrapped up in myself and my studies to appreciate Jessica until it was too late. Taking things for granted was easy when life ahead was an endless vista of parties and outings. Memories of our long walks, always perfectly in step, while earnestly discussing architecture or history and those vigorous tennis games—Jessica played to win, and her overarm serve was ferocious—were jewels left on the beach by a tide that would never return.

Her body was never found in the ruins. Jessica had been officially declared dead while I was still in hospital, the only survivor to be dug out of the rubble.

"Jessica—" I practically choked on the name. I cleared my throat, composed myself, and tried again. "Jessica is no longer with us."

"That's what they told us," Bunny said.

"She was a rather serious girl, wasn't she?" Crispy said. "Intense. Not given to practical jokes."

I shook my head. Jessica's sense of humour sometimes ran to whimsy, but practical jokes were beneath her.

"Obviously not," Bunny said.

"I know," Crispy said. "I told you she wasn't the sort."

"You can talk in riddles all night if you want to," I said. "But I'd really prefer a coherent story. Let me get you started. You've been abroad, somewhere hot. What does Jessica have to do with it?"

Crispy finished his sherry with another gulp. "We went treasure hunting, Bunny and I, looking for ancient tombs that hadn't been plundered."

Howard Carter had a lot to answer for. Hundreds of young men must have been inspired to follow in his footsteps, looking for Pharaonic treasures or imperial hoards to uncover. In most cases, though, the would-be Carters were a couple of thousand years too late. Local robbers had invariably been there before them, tunnelling in with pick and shovel. Three feet of stone wall was not much deterrent when a year's wages were on the other side.

I must have looked sceptical, and Crispy forestalled my objection. "You see, we had a method. We only went to the places where the local thieves had been deterred by rumours of curses or demons or black magic."

Bunny nodded earnestly.

"A curse won't stop a man who's starving," I said. "Maybe it stops three in four of the more superstitious of them, at best. Even if there's only one robber every decade, that's two hundred over the millennia. Enough to pick any tomb clean. Doesn't help the odds of finding an intact tomb."

"He's always ready with the arithmetic," Bunny said. "Mr Blake has a head for numbers."

"And that's where he's wrong," Crispy said firmly. "A lot of learned men tried to tell us the same thing when we were preparing the expedition, and a fat lot they know. If they tried something other than sitting on their over-educated arses, they might discover something."

Premonition flashed through me, lightning revealing the path through a dark forest. "Of all the people, it had to be you two."

Neither of them ever looked likely to do anything much in life. Nobody expected more from them than pottering around in a family firm or occupying an undemanding post in the colonial administration. They were just the types expected to find in some far-flung corner where the real work is done by efficient flunkies whose sole shortcoming was not to be born British. Or maybe they would serve their turn as MPs in the family seat. In the race of life, Crispy and Bunny were also-rans.

"It was our method," Crispy said. "Bunny's method, as a matter of fact. And those greybeards know nothing… ever hear of the Burned City?"

I shook my head.

"Hah! Down Mesopotamia way. And I thought you knew everything, Bill. Wandered over half of North Africa and the Middle East before we ended up there."

Waves of memory were carrying him off. I waited, and in due course, Crispy took up his tale.

"It's a godforsaken place. Nothing but sand and dust. Hot as hell in the daytime, cold enough to freeze your bones at night. The people, they're not civilised. Not as you or I understand it. They'll cut your throat and rob you as soon as look at you." He looked up to check that I was following him. "Well, maybe we did look like a pair of simpletons, fresh out of England, not a clue how to put up a tent or ride a camel. Don't speak a word of Arabic…"

"I think they speak Farsi there."

"Exactly," he said. "But we found the place. A Hungarian fellow, Professor Stein or some such, got there first and was carrying out an excavation. Digging all these trenches in straight lines and right angles and shouting at the natives. He was surprisingly friendly, though I think we were a disappointment to him. Oh, there it is." Crispy had been going through his many pockets and came out with a piece of stone the size of a wine cork. It was an amber carving of a woman's face. The hairstyle was different, but the line of her jaw, the nose, the cheekbones, all brought back her appearance. "Looks like her, doesn't it? Jessica, I mean."

"There's a resemblance," I said.

"We found it there. The long and the short of it is that they have these caves. Stein wasn't interested in them, but according to tradition, they are haunted by demons—and the tradition still runs strong. The locals wouldn't even discuss them! So of course, we had to take a look. In the end, Stein showed us the path, just a goat track really. There's a rocky outcrop with a cave leading down."

"An entrance to the underworld," Bunny added. "Like the one by Lake Avernus in the Aeneid and Acheron in the Odyssey. Or Cape Tenaron in the Peloponnese was where Orpheus went. The gates of hell."

Crispy shook his head. "It had a peculiar quality of sound. Outside, there was nothing, but inside, there was this whispering noise. Just air currents or maybe water way down below, but we could tell at once why it was supposed to be haunted. There were carvings around the cave mouth, but what they were, I couldn't tell you. We went down single file, stooped, even then it was a tight squeeze. At times it was more like a tunnel than a cave. They must have enlarged it over the years…" He went over to his kit bag and took a thick brown envelope from a side pocket.

"Klein had a camera," Bunny said. "Photographed everything—terribly methodical chap. We borrowed it to take pictures of the chamber."

"What chamber?"

"The big chamber at the bottom with all the carvings," Crispy said. "Here, you'll need a magnifying glass to make out the text."

"I can't read Farsi," I said.

"Have a look." He passed me the photographs. "The letters are about an inch high."

I turned on the goose-necked desk lamp and held the wad of photographs close to the bulb. The black-and-white images were far from perfect. Bunny and Crispy must have struggled with their borrowed photographic equipment. I couldn't guess how long it had taken those two bumblers to set up the tripod and how much flash powder they'd gone through learning to use it.

The first image showed part of an underground chamber, the raw stone carved into smooth walls and symmetrical niches. There were inscriptions on the walls, and in the second photograph, the carved text was quite legible with aid of the glass.

"We rubbed sand into them," Crispy said. "To make the letters stand out better against the dark stone."

I struggled to make out the writing. The alphabet was completely unfamiliar. It looked like a simple type of cuneiform, all V's and W's, half of them upside down or sideways. But one section was in bigger letters—the Roman alphabet. It was written in English. The first line almost made me drop the picture.

My name is Jessica Merton. I was born in London in England in the year 1903 AD. The incised letters recalled so many notes Jessica had written to me, the same short *S* and slanting *T*. And then she was there again, in my mind's eye, tall, serious, and attentive. All the more beautiful because Jessica never in her life realised how beautiful she was.

I shot a look at Crispy then recalled his question about Jessica and practical jokes. What must he have thought when he read those words, thousands of miles from home?

"Of course, it can't be dated." Crispy lined up the next six photographs on the table in front of me. "It could have been carved a month ago by a bored soldier. And obviously, it looks like a practical joke. But keep reading—we did. There's a sort of Rosetta Stone explaining how to translate the text into English. See, these are the letters, and then there's a list of vocabulary."

"So it should be possible to translate it," I said, already picking out the words in the first line.

"It took an age, and we had to guess at some of the words, but this is ninety-nine percent accurate at least." Bunny placed a thick pile of handwritten papers in front of me. "You can translate it yourself or write to Professor Stein, or do whatever you want. But this is what she wrote. I think you had better read it."

PART ONE: ARRIVAL

CHAPTER ONE: BRAVE NEW WORLD

My name is Jessica Merton. I was born in London in England in the year 1903 AD. Here, I am called Yishka-from-Heaven.

I leave this for future generations, so that they will know of the war that was fought and what happened here. Stories are inevitably already distorted and embellished by the ignorant and those who want to exaggerate certain elements from tribal, political, or religious loyalties. If nothing else endures, let these words be my legacy.

I came here by the intervention of a demonic being, a nightmare alien intruding into my own dimension. The knowledgeable call it Cthulhu; what lies behind the name, what it is, and where it came from are, I believe, beyond the grasp of human minds. In any case, several of us confronted an emissary of this being, and an abyss opened up and swallowed me. I was lost to the world I knew.

I fell an immense distance through the darkness, farther than it should be possible to fall. At first, I screamed, from surprise and the sensation of falling, thinking I was about to die or be horribly injured at any moment. The air rushed past me. Time always seemed to stretch out at moments of crisis, but I kept falling. Eventually, I stopped screaming. Paralysing fear was pushed aside by survival instinct and a need to understand what was happening.

I happened to know that the tallest building in the world was the Russ Building in San Francisco and that it would take about eight seconds to reach the ground if I had jumped from it. I did not know how deep the Grand Canyon was, nor the extent of the world's deepest mine, but I had been falling for far, far too long.

I started counting the seconds. "One, one thousand. Two, one thousand. Three…"

I reached sixty seconds, and I was certain this was not a fissure in the ground but something quite other. When Alice fell down and down the rabbit hole, that was a benign and childish magic. She fell for miles and miles and expected to land in Australia. I had been thrown into a pit to dispose of me.

I turned in the air, terrified but at the same time exhilarated and curious. This was not an infinite space. I could sense the walls close around me. Luckily, they were smooth. Any projecting rock would have been like a stone pillar in the path of a speeding car.

The light above had disappeared, and I was falling through utter darkness. My eyes were adjusting, and I thought I was seeing things when shooting stars started to punctuate the pitch black. They were lanterns or torches set into recesses letting into the shaft. They all gave off the same flickering blue-green light resembling glow-worms rather than candle flames. The cavity through which I was falling was smooth, contoured stone, more like a channel worn by water than a mineshaft. It widened out, becoming cavernous as the walls disappeared into a vast space. I caught sight of balconies, terraces, peculiar turrets, and fancifully crenelated walls. My first thought was this was the outskirts of hell and that the architecture resembled a twisted version of Gustave Doré's illustration of Dante's *Inferno*.

My second thought was that if the disturbance had been caused by the Cthulhu's city of R'lyeh breaking through into our world from another dimension, then I must be falling through R'lyeh itself. Before

I could fully form the thought, I had plunged onwards through an opening in a wide courtyard and into the apparently infinite abyss below.

I later developed a theory that R'lyeh, under the control of its unseen ruler, stretched out like the roots of a tree. It extended through the natural cracks and interstices of the world, reaching into accessible times and places. It was a genuine eternal city in that it existed outside of our sort of time, but it could only manifest at certain specific intervals. Later experience confirmed this.

The light above me disappeared a second time. I fell miles through the dark, until another, more wholesome light glimmered far below. Perhaps it was the way the light moved, the sound, or the smell. Maybe it was just intuition, but I knew there was water down there.

A fall onto anything solid would be fatal. Water might be a different matter. Like Alice, I was not falling as rapidly as the laws of physics should have dictated. My descent was governed by the distorted rules of R'lyeh, but I was still travelling at considerable speed. It did not occur to me until much later that the being drawing me down there wanted me alive.

I had always been an excellent swimmer, and high diving inspired no fear for me. I had seen stunt divers jump off bridges. I could survive if I adopted the correct posture.

I entered the water like an arrow, with a terrific shock. I felt myself plunging through the water, my ears popping. A second later, my arms then my body collided with the sandy bed. This second impact was hardly noticeable above the stinging in my hands, arms, shoulders, and forehead.

All I could think was: *I'm alive.*

I swam briskly to the surface, shook my head, and took several deep breaths as I examined my surroundings. I had lost my glasses during my fall, but I was not completely blind without them. I was in a pool perhaps twenty feet across, in the middle of a cave the size of a church hall. The cave mouth opened out into a rocky hillside and green fields beyond, crops waving in broad daylight.

I was startled as something splashed down next to me, kicking water in my face. It was my handbag. I took it, frog-kicked to the edge, and pulled myself out, water streaming from my clothes. The pool was cool rather than cold, and the air was noticeably warm.

A minute before, when I had fallen down the rabbit hole, it had been the middle of the night. Here, it was broad daylight. Either I had fallen all the way through the Earth, or I had been displaced in time as well as space. I pushed the thought aside.

An ugly, coarse-looking man padded into the cave, drawn by the splashing. His long hair was unkempt, and his only garment was rough tunic. He looked into the water, puzzled. Seeing me, he grunted. He did not look friendly. Already, this Wonderland had an ominous tone.

"Where is this?" I asked.

The hirsute creature did not respond but roughly grabbed my arm. I was not one to tolerate beastly behaviour and slapped him at once with my free hand. My slap was full force, hard enough to make his ears ring. He swayed, blinking. Letting go of me, he took half a step back, a hand to his stinging cheek. Before he could recover from his surprise, I was running out the open cavemouth and had gained a lead of several steps on him before he started after me.

The heat and the light hit me at once, but I did not pause. Focused entirely on getting away, I did not hesitate, running off down the shallow sloping path. The dirt track took me past rows of dark cavemouths. Shapes stirred deep inside some of them as I passed. Some caves were cages with crude wooden bars. Faces looked out at me from behind them—frightened female faces.

The man from the cave was chasing me, but he was losing ground. He was not built for running, like an old, fat hound chasing a gazelle. I would have stopped and tried to free the captives, but he was pounding close behind me.

As I looked back, I almost ran into another man, this one carrying two buckets with the aid of a yoke. He was as startled as I. He had the same boorish look as the first, who was shouting to his companion, but I was already well past before he had a chance to seize me.

The path plunged into long grass that reached my shoulders, and something buzzed past my ear. I sensed it was dangerous, and I later found out it was a sling stone. A luckier cast would have ended my flight then and there. I ran, taking care to stoop and stay as low as I could. After a few minutes, I stopped to catch my breath and look around. There was no sign of a pursuer.

I always carried a spare pair of glasses in my handbag, and I donned them. Even with my corrected vision, the tall grasses through which I walked were unfamiliar. Bright-yellow blooms, which I had assumed to be dandelions, peeped out from behind the grasses, along with bursts of tiny blue flowers at ankle level. I did not recognise either. Other than the rocky outcrops behind me, the scenery was almost featureless. The grass ranged from shoulder high to waist high, and a solitary skeletal tree was the only landmark on a smooth horizon.

I continued on, walking briskly. Danger was still close behind me. The hot sun was rapidly drying out my wet clothes. I was not in England—of that much, I was sure. I could not begin to guess where I might be. A few minutes later, some ruined buildings gave a hint. They were low, mud-brick affairs. The brown bricks were crumbly, flat, and obviously sun-baked rather than fired. The buildings were an ancient pattern reminiscent of parts of Egypt. This was more like North Africa or the Middle East than Europe.

I had not seen the man in the cave in good light; the one with the yoke had looked vaguely Mediterranean, but too hairy and too dirty for me to be sure. I had only caught a brief look at the captives. They were all women, mainly dark haired, some with lighter or darker skin than others, all miserable. Two of them had been visibly pregnant, which struck me as especially sinister. Male captors and female captives did not seem like a promising combination. I had no doubt that I would have been penned up with them if I had been less fleet of foot.

Everything about the situation was impossible, but after accepting the idea of a monstrous being from another dimension threatening Dulwich, my current situation seemed simply more of the same. I had been flung across the world by this extra-dimensional being. Now I had to find my way back, but going back the way I had come was out of the question. So I continued in more or less a straight line. Birds flew up from the grass and sang sweetly before descending again—larks, just like the song larks at home.

Drumbeats on the ground warned of the rapid approach of horsemen, several of them. Running would have been futile. I could have hidden in the long grass, but boldness seemed the better strategy.

"Hey!" I shouted and waved.

They had already seen me, and seconds later, I was surrounded by a semicircle of six mounted men. They reminded me of American Indians mounted on war ponies without saddles, wearing open leather vests. But they wore breeches more reminiscent of Tartar horsemen than native Americans. One had a necklace of animal teeth, which again made me think of the American plains.

The riders seemed curious rather than hostile. The points of their leaf-bladed lances were aimed into the air rather than towards me. I took that as a good sign. I stood upright, my arms folded and chin high, trying not to betray the terror I felt. Appearances could be deceptive, but the men did not give the same repulsive impression the slavers did. I was, however, aware of my vulnerability as a woman alone facing a group of savage men—and of how their eyes lingered on my damp clothes clinging to my body.

The oldest among them, clearly their leader from his bearing, cleared his throat and spoke gruffly in an unfamiliar language.

"I do not understand you," I said, slowly and clearly. "Do you speak English?"

He cocked his head then carried out a rapid interchange with the man next to him. All of them looked similar enough to be brothers or at least cousins. The youngest could be no more than fifteen; the leader was a grizzled veteran of perhaps forty-five.

I tried speaking in French, Italian, Latin, and scraps of other languages I knew. All to no avail. They tried, too, calling out haltingly in different but equally unrecognisable tongues. After that, they started talking amongst themselves. I did not like the way they were looking at me and grinning as they spoke. Lewd remarks crossed all language barriers.

There was a colloquy between the leader, whom I would later come to know as Old Harsis, and his second-in-command. Old Harsis was the most experienced of the warriors of this party. The others deferred to his wisdom. I later found out that Old Harsis's wisdom was contained in a small but endlessly repeated stock of proverbs of the "look before you leap" and "better safe than sorry" variety. This cautionary approach was a balance to the nomad warrior's natural recklessness, and Old Harsis's longevity was a testament to his wisdom.

I owed my life to Old Harsis's caution. He warned the others against doing anything hasty that they might later regret, whatever their impulses might be after finding a young, helpless woman from another tribe. His words, though few and repetitive, carried weight. There was less grinning and more curiosity.

Old Harsis issued a command, and the youngest of them dismounted and led his horse to me. The first thing that struck me was the boy's height. I was taller than some men at home, and I towered over him. Few of the warriors, even the full-grown ones, were above five feet six. I later came to know that this fresh-faced youth was Damki, and he was the most junior member of the fighting force.

Damki held up the reins and kept repeating a phrase. I grasped that he was asking me to mount. Unlike many of my friends, I had never been overly fond of horses. Having friends who were horsey types meant I had spent some time around stables and had ridden a little. Ponies could be a mean, cunning breed, but maybe the ones at home were all spoiled. This one was placid enough. I patted his nose, and after hoisting my skirt, I mounted in a strenuous and ungainly, but effective, movement. This provoked comments from the men: not the laughter, which I had expected, but surprise, as if none of them had ever seen a woman on a horse before.

Damki climbed up behind another rider. Then we set off at an uncomfortably fast pace. I hoped the horsemen were taking me to the nearest white settlement or trading post.

I scrutinised the other riders on the way. They were a dark-haired and brown-eyed people, with light-olive complexions. They might equally have been Greek, Moroccan, or Persian. All were simply dressed to the point of raggedness, down to their uncured leather boots. Everything about their equipment was primitive to the point of being archaic. It was clearly a hunting party; some had strings of dead birds slung over their shoulders, and others bore goatskin bags dripping with the blood of fresh kills.

There were still lancers in the British army, and people still hunted with boar spears, but the men's spears had a rough, home-made appearance. And they were tipped with bronze rather than steel. The wildest tribesmen in the hills had a few old rifles, so the band's weapons surprised me most. Even Old Harsis did not have so much as a rusty flintlock pistol. It made me wonder just how poor the people were or how far from civilisation they lived that even weapons had not reached them.

The party was in no hurry, and we made several diversions for game, most of them unsuccessful. When some animals broke from the grass, the men galloped off in wild pursuit. One of them scored a kill with his spear: a wild piglet. Without dismounting, he leaned over and picked the carcass off the ground, half-sitting on it to keep it in place behind him. When we encountered guinea fowl, two of the men unslung short bows and let fly. One of the birds was killed cleanly; the other flapped about on the ground before one rider stabbed it with the point of a spear and held it up for the bowman to take his prize.

The hunters joked amongst themselves, clearly at ease. There were some curious stares in my direction, but the men were more intent on outdoing each other in bagging the next game animal. The landscape was a rolling grassy plain, which hardly varied, with only the occasional stand of trees, or low rise. Otherwise, it seemed we were going around in circles. Once, we came upon a steep gully about twenty feet deep and the same across. Invisible from thirty yards away, it would have been a deadly obstacle to an unwary rider. We trotted a mile downstream to where the banks flattened out. Without me, they would probably have just jumped their horses over it.

After a time, we stopped for the horsemen to make a small fire and barbecue a dozen small game birds on wooden skewers. To be polite, I took the one that was offered to me. It was undercooked, and the meat was stringy. I picked at it while the others tore into theirs. Damki alone noticed me discarding the half-eaten bird while the others wiped their greasy hands on their breeches and mounted up, but he said nothing.

I was surprised when, without warning, we reached our destination—a cluster of hide tents. The horsemen slowed to let me take the lead as we approached. Old Harsis called out to the sentry. A small crowd gathered to meet us. I dismounted and was faced with the lean, wiry man whom I later knew as Amir.

Amir's position six paces ahead of the others, as well as his comparatively rich clothes, marked him as leader. Two leather straps studded with bright metal discs crossed his chest, insignia suggesting a military commander. A smile never far from his lips, Amir was good-looking in a Latin-lover style. And there was something behind those eyes when he met my gaze, energies beneath the surface. He might have been uncivilised, but he was no fool.

As the others maintained a respectful distance, Amir approached this new prize, with the delighted look of a small boy finding a new bicycle under the Christmas tree. He walked around me and shot questions to Old Harsis, all the while looking me up and down in an indecently frank manner. He did not force my mouth open to look at my teeth, but his gaze had much the same effect. He spoke to me in soft murmuring tones.

"I do not understand," I said. "Does anyone here speak English?"

Amir looked confused then made a sort of bow. He continued to smile and make calming sounds, as to a nervous horse. The crowd pressed closer, but they still kept back at arm's length. Amir casually cuffed a small boy who tried to touch my skirt and drove the rest back with an imperious wave. One old woman sniffed at me ostentatiously, like a dog. After a long inspection, and once it was obvious dialogue was impossible, two women came and led me away to a tent with rugs on the floor. A few small cushions were the only furnishings.

The timid, silent female servants brought me food, drink, and water for washing. The food was flat bread with strips of rather gamey meat—goat, the staple diet. Completing the meal was a little pot of sour cream, like the yoghurt that had become fashionable in some circles.

With some ceremony, one of the girls kneeled down to present me with an infusion of herbal tea and waited anxiously until I showed that I approved by smiling. After that, I managed to explain to the girls by signals that they were to leave me alone.

I was simply dying for a cigarette, but there were none to be had. I had smoked my last one in the tense hours before our struggle with Cthulhu's emissary. Instead, I sat alone and had a good cry, letting all the pent-up emotion go. I was in a strange land, far from home, without a friend. I had no idea what to do. But I was alive and in one piece, and I had escaped immediate danger. I offered up a short but heartfelt prayer of thanks.

I took the mirror from my handbag and looked myself in the eye. "Now then, Jessica, pull yourself together. Nothing so very terrible has happened to you, and it won't so long as you remain strong. You are a modern woman, not some fainting Victorian maiden. Show these heathens you're an Englishwoman."

A short time later, one side of the tent was raised to reveal an open area. They had created a sort of courtyard, almost a paddock, for me. This was my garden, my outside space. The nomads used their tents mainly for sleeping and lived in the open air, but I was to have as much seclusion as I wanted.

What struck me most at first was the stench. My tent was in the upwind section, and the rest of the camp was suffused with the stink of human and animal filth, mingled with butchery, rotting meat, and campfire smoke. Most of the tents were goat hide; only those of the higher-ranking families were made of woven black goat hair.

I came to appreciate that I was not a prisoner, but if I wanted to venture beyond my own precincts, an armed man—the youth Damki—would accompany me. I was an honoured guest, not a captive, or human plunder found on the plains. Amir did not want to offend or frighten me, but I was wary of his intentions. I did not guess then that the nomads thought I was from heaven, though they could hardly have given me a more reverent reception. To be strictly accurate, I was an angel, a messenger rather than a divine being in my own right, but the nomads' theology did not make such fine distinctions. Whatever I was, I was to be looked after.

Damki stood guard by my tent. None could enter without permission. After a while, I felt able to take up the offer of going out, and we went on a walk around the encampment. He seemed almost afraid to look at me.

The camp was larger than I had at first realised, but it was a miserable sight. Amir's band comprised about one hundred fifty adults in extended family groups. The children did not stay still long enough for me to count but ran around in groups or hid in odd corners. About half the women, many of them several years younger than me, carried babies on their hips. Seeing some of the little ones made me want to weep. There was real poverty in England, of course, but this was something else. The marks of disease and malnutrition were everywhere.

There was not the least trace of the modern world, not a machine-woven blanket or so much as a needle. The poverty was not quite absolute, though the nearest things to luxury were the embroidered cushions in my tent. The nomad women wove cloth, prepared hides, and pounded grain in stone bowls. Beyond a few copper cooking pots and their tents, they were practically without possessions.

As I toured the camp, the people gazed at me curiously, as though I were an exotic animal that Amir had captured. When I stared back, they made a gesture—a salute? obeisance?—and turned away.

The people were quite uniform to my eye. Even when I came to know them, I had trouble telling some of them apart because they were all so closely related. The majority were first or second cousins to each other. Some women from other bands had been brought in to leaven the mixture, while surplus daughters had been exported, but this was generally a close-knit group, a family of families.

A word which seemed to follow me around the camp. I caught it occasionally in conversations when they thought I was out of earshot: the word was "beraish."

I indicated to Damki that I wanted to walk beyond the bounds of the dismal encampment. He grasped his spear more tightly and followed me. It was approaching dusk. Volleys of barking greeted us as we stepped out, and we were surrounded by dogs, sniffing eagerly, tails half-raised. They checked me momentarily, but I remembered to show no fear and walked slowly onwards, being careful not to look them in the eye. They were semi-wild, like farm dogs. I did not recognise the breed, but they had short, curly tails. I guessed, correctly as it turned out, that they went with the nomads on hunting expeditions, and that was why they were excited to see someone coming out. I later found out that they were also goat dogs; they were not used for herding but mingled with the goats and protected them from wolves and other predators. They were noisy and excited by the smell of a strange human but wagged their little tails happily enough when they decided I was not an enemy.

The grassland stretched in every direction, with no roads and no haze of smoke to mark other settlements. Brown hills lined the northern horizon, with the hint of purple mountains beyond, but the skyline was otherwise blank and, to me, entirely alien. The one thing that cheered me was when night fell and the stars came out. They were bright, not the haze-dimmed stars of London, but more importantly, I recognised the constellations—the Great Bear, Orion, and Cassiopeia. I could even see the pale band of the Milky Way winding across the sky. If nothing else, I knew I was on Earth, and in the northern hemisphere.

Three horsemen rode by, silhouettes waving their spears, dead animals slung over their horses' necks. They whooped happily to Damki, who replied in more subdued tones. He was on duty.

A pale half-moon rose, bestowing a silvery sheen on grassland. Damki was growing increasingly restive, and I reluctantly returned to the camp. In the night, I could hear the activity all around. The sound of every crying baby, screaming child, and domestic argument echoed through the camp. I could hear Amir, another man, and the two women who had served me talking quietly in the next tent. One woman nearby wailed piteously for half an hour before she gradually subsided into sobbing. She did this on every subsequent night, as well. Later, there was snoring from all directions.

There were not enough cushions for a mattress, but I took two of them for a pillow. I lay awake for hours that first night, gripping a small knife I had filched at dinner. I hoped that Amir was a gentleman, but I could not rely on him. I wondered again and again if I should have made a run for it while outside the camp. The nomads had horses and dogs, though, and would surely have caught me. At least I was safe here from wild animals. If not from wild men. I expected Amir to appear at any minute and try to seize me. He never did.

I must have drifted off to sleep, because I was woken by dogs barking and goats bleating. A minute later, two or three men were shouting—the sort of wordless yelling used to chase off an animal. After that, the noise died down, until there was just snoring again. I sighed and rolled over, still holding on to my knife. I had survived the first day. Tomorrow, I would start my efforts to get home.

CHAPTER TWO: THE CAMP OF AMIR'S PEOPLE

I WOKE WITH ACHES AND pains all over from the hard ground. My first action after breakfast and ablutions was to gather armfuls of dried grass for bedding. My two attendants watched me, puzzled, then eventually started helping. I later found out that only invalids and the elderly slept on straw beds. The nomads did not see why a healthy young woman would want a pallet. As with so much else, I smiled and gestured, and they did not seem to mind.

I wanted desperately to get back to civilisation, but nothing offered any clue where to go or how to get there. I could do nothing here until I spoke at least a little of the language. Studying it became my full-time occupation, all day and every day.

The women who attended me were not, in fact, servants, but Amir's sisters, Aruru and Puabi. The nomads had no servants, an admirably egalitarian arrangement, if inconvenient. Everything anyone wanted, they had to do themselves. Although perhaps it would be truer to say that the women were all servants and the men were all masters. And the children, the few old enough to be useful before being declared adults, were servants to everyone, when they could be found.

Amir had assigned his sisters as my companions, on top of their other duties of looking after him and his brother. As far as I was concerned, their top priority was teaching me the language, though I was happy to learn while carrying out chores. I had never milked a goat or pounded grain, but I did my best. They worked steadily but without enthusiasm. Finishing one chore early only meant starting the next one sooner.

I started by picking up an object and getting them to say its name. Gradually, we moved on to verbs and adjectives. I also managed to discover the rough meaning of that word "beraish," which was dangerous or unclean, being applied equally to rotten meat and evil spirits.

Aruru was wary, obedient but withdrawn. Communicating with her was difficult. Puabi was more forthcoming, though perhaps not so clever and more inclined to go off at a tangent. Everything I said confused Puabi. She could not grasp why I did not understand so much of everyday life, but had no curiosity herself.

When the sisters were fed up with my incessant questioning, I had Damki collar a few children. I played with them, teaching them new games like Simon Says and Hopscotch in exchange for conversation. After two weeks of hard work, I could communicate in pidgin. After that, I improved rapidly.

Neither of my female companions was in awe of me in the slightest. While Amir might have regarded me as a being from heaven, to the sisters—and most of the rest of the band—I was simply a strange woman Amir favoured. So I had to be tolerated on that account. None of them displayed any interest in who I was or how I had come to be there. Nor had they much interest in the wider world.

"Where from?" I asked, indicating the copper pot in which goat stew was simmering.

Aruru shrugged. I might as well have asked her where stars came from.

"Some men made it," Puabi said, as though I might have thought cooking pots grew on trees.

"What men? Men where?"

"I don't know. Somewhere."

"Other nomads?"

"Of course not! Traders bring them from somewhere. Along with all the other things."

The sisters had never heard of metal ships, railways, armies of white men with guns, or guns at all. The colonial powers had stamped their imprint in every corner of the earth. Even where they had not set foot, they were known. And trade goods, tools, and cloth travelled ahead of them into every jungle and mountain range and river delta.

The nomads had metals such as bronze, gold, silver, copper, lead, and tin, but that was all. Knives and scissors of Sheffield steel had travelled the globe and were traded up the Congo, the Orinoco, and the Mekong, in places where no white man had ever been. The nomads, however, still used bone needles and bronze axe-heads. Some of their hunting arrowheads were flakes of stone. I could not find so much as a stamped brass button, a tin mug, or a scrap of machine-woven fabric.

I could not accept the obvious conclusion. I had told myself that, perhaps, after a blow on the head, I had wandered about in state of mental fugue for weeks, not knowing who or where I was, and that I had come back to my senses after landing in that pool. Fugues and other types of amnesia were increasingly well-documented. My friends had many conversations about self, identity, and responsibility in these states. Exactly how I had come to be in a far-off land was a mystery, but I did not need to invent magical portals to explain it.

It was not just Aruru and Puabi. Nobody here knew of the modern world. There were occasional outsiders, other nomads, traders, and pilgrims. All of them were equally ignorant of the things I asked about.

Daniel, my mathematician friend, had assured me that, according to Einstein, travelling through folded space-time to other eras should be as easy as walking through a door. That had given rise to many convoluted discussions—chiefly amongst my male friends—on causality and time travel. Inevitable, the conversations turned to the well-worked conundrum of whether they would have killed the Kaiser as a child or warned Archduke Franz Ferdinand about the impending assassination attempt. Daniel had also insisted on the extra-dimensional nature of the thing we had faced in Dulwich. I wondered what had happened to Daniel.

Eventually, though, I was forced to accept that I was stranded in the past, lost in that broad swathe of history we called the Bronze Age. It was the era from something like four thousand to one thousand years before Christ. I could be anywhere in it, or rather any*when*.

Perhaps it should have occurred to me that I might as well be in the remote future, millennia after our civilisation had crumbled into dust. Perhaps I should have been looking for the ruins of my own culture. In actuality, it made precious little difference. I was far from home, amongst a primitive people, and I somehow had to make my way back.

I was like Hank, the engineer in Mark Twain's comic novel *A Connecticut Yankee in King Arthur's Court*. Except rather than being a rugged he-man with a convenient knowledge of gunpowder, metallurgy, electric dynamos, and eclipses, I was a woman whose education had nothing to do with engineering. I was in a society where females were chattel. Hank had no difficulty outwitting the dull and superstitious medievals around him and enlightening them with his modern ways.

Even Robinson Crusoe had a chest of tools, a few muskets, and ammunition when he was washed up. He managed to make a comfortable place for himself in primitive surroundings and triumphed over cannibal tribesmen. I did not have the skills or the equipment of Hank or Crusoe. I could not expect my situation to lead to jolly adventures like theirs.

I gave up thoughts of immediate escape and devoted myself to my language lessons. In the process, I learned about the daily life for the nomads.

Where were the men? I wanted to know. The men had gone out hunting, Aruru told me. They hunted like this—miming a bow—or like this—throwing a javelin. What did they hunt? Aruru went through a series of charades, using fingers to indicate horns and miming bounding along in great leaps or grunting like a pig. I learned the names for the different types of gazelles, antelopes, hares, and pigs. The game birds were easier; she could show me the partridges, pheasants, and ducks which had been brought back. Sometimes, we drew pictures in the dust. Not much of a substitute for pen and paper, the strategy was surprisingly effective.

The men also hunted foxes, wolves, and lynx, both for the pelts and because they were a threat to the flocks. Amir had a gorgeous leopard-skin cape, a trophy taken by his grandfather, but leopards were exceedingly rare.

Fighting was more important even than hunting. The warrior's main preoccupations were raiding their neighbours' herds of goats or horses and fending off raiders who might attack their own. Raiding was their great sport, the aim being to grab a trophy without being caught. There were rarely fights when the groups met. Usually, the stronger side simply chased away the weaker, shouting taunts and insults. Sometimes the pursuers caught the slowest member of the other party and made an example of him—pinning his body to the ground with wooden stakes for the buzzards and taking his horse as a trophy.

Aruru and Puabi were proud of their brother's prowess. Nobody could ride faster than Amir, and nobody could beat him at spear-fighting. Amir's brother, Nergal, was a near copy of Amir, but with fewer smiles and less talk. He hardly spoke to me, confining himself to polite nods. But he watched and listened. Nergal was not as strong and brave as his brother, but his sisters thought he was very cunning.

"On a raid, Nergal pretends to ride slowly and draw off the enemy warriors, then when they get close, he puts on a burst of speed and leaves them behind," Aruru had said. "So the others get away easily. It always works."

The children were everywhere, and when not busy with chores, they were as active as children always are. Little boys banded together and hunted imaginary antelope, hurling reed spears, or fought each other in spear battles. Little girls pretended to dig up tubers then stir imaginary pots or nursed wrapped-up bundles of grass.

Either the nomads had little idea of history, or my two teachers were ignorant of it. They could only tell me two things about the past. There had been a plague or epidemic called the Great Dying. This killed many people and annihilated entire clans, back in the time of their father. Some time before that had been the Time of Monsters, which they talked about in hushed voices as though it were something too awful to mention.

I learned their proverbs. "The wind dries the rain" fairly described how quickly the effect of the infrequent rain showers disappeared. It was a favourite, a general-purpose expression to mean that all things pass.

"Chew the root too long, and it gets bitter" reflected their desire to keep moving on.

"One man, one horse, one spear; one woman, one tent, one pot" encapsulated their social order. Women ranked as somewhat less desirable possessions than horses.

I thoroughly exasperated both Aruru and Puabi with my persistence, but I squeezed as much of the language out of them as they would give. I practised as much as I could with the children and sometimes sat with other women—though they were nervous of me—to give my brain more to work on.

As my facility with the language grew, Amir would drop by to listen to my conversations with his sisters. Then, he started joining in. I was acutely aware of his interest, and I repeatedly probed them about it.

"He says heaven sent you to help him fight the Spawn," Puabi said. "He wants revenge for our father. He died last year."

"Spawn?"

Puabi chided her sister. "We should not talk about the Unclean."

29

I did at least gather that Amir's father had been killed near to where I had been found. The Spawn were associated with the slavers I had escaped from. It was bad to talk about them because they were *beraish*.

"What are these creatures?" I asked with a chill of foreboding.

"Amir will tell you," Puabi said, with a small shudder.

"And Amir wants me to help with his revenge? Is that all he wants from me?" I asked.

The two of them looked at each other and giggled. I blushed.

"Only revenge," Puabi said. "It is all he thinks of."

It was worse than being Robinson Crusoe; I was supposed to be John Carter, Edgar Rice Burroughs's ridiculous army officer transported to Mars to battle strange creatures. Of course, John Carter was a superlative swordsman, tactician, and a natural leader. Like Hank and Crusoe, he was ideally suited to his exile. I was a non-fighting woman whose military knowledge consisted of being forced to work through with Caesar's Gallic Wars in Latin and having two war-obsessed brothers with battalions of lead soldiers.

I got on well enough with the sisters, but our relations never made it beyond the formal. Amir turned out to be my best and most dedicated language tutor. The whole idea of teaching was alien to him, but he was an intelligent man. He found that shouting louder and louder and repeating the same meaningless phrase over and over was no good. Once he understood this, he was surprisingly good at breaking down expressions into baby talk I could understand.

Amir seemed as pleased as I was when I mastered a new verb tense or a concept, which he took as a credit to his teaching skills. Once I was able to carry on a conversation, we had many pleasant evenings around the campfire. Amir and I talked, with occasional interjections from Aruru and Puabi, while Nergal listened from the shadows. Others must have been listening nearby too; with no wireless, newspapers or magazines, they were starved for novelty. He would not talk of the unclean creatures, though. It was not yet the day for that.

The language lessons overlapped with my attempts to find out more about the surrounding world and its people. Unfortunately, Amir was almost wholly ignorant of what lay beyond the immediate bounds of his band's territory. There were cities in the hills to the north, and there were villages and larger settlements on the coast to the south, but they did not interest him. It was significant that in their language, the nomads called themselves the People, their language was just Language, their roaming grounds were just the Land. They did not see themselves as one people amongst many.

Amir thought I could help him, that I would convey some great wisdom to him. Of course, I had any amount of knowledge that the nomads lacked. But the precious degree I had worked so hard to win was in architecture. Ironically, I had found myself amongst people who did not have buildings. It was almost comically useless.

I had not even brought any useful accoutrements of the twentieth century. The contents of my handbag were precious little help. If I had known I was coming here I might have packed a revolver, if I had one—and even a steel-bladed knife might have seemed miraculous here. I would always be grateful for my spare glasses, and they should have been another wonder from the future to these people who did not have glass. The children wanted to touch them and try them on, but the adults were completely indifferent. If I had been farsighted, I could have used the lenses to start fires, but near-sightedness meant that I did not even have that small miracle to hand.

My other possessions were less useful. A coin purse, my house keys, and a handkerchief—all belonged to another century. The compact mirror and lipstick, never used, which my friend Sophie had insisted I carry. At least the address book with a pencil was useful. I used the blank pages to jot down vocabulary, though my writing became ever more miniscule as I tried to save space. A dry-cleaning ticket provided a little more writing space.

My watch had, surprisingly, survived both the fall and the dunking in water and seemed to be keeping good time. If I had arrived in the seventeenth century, or even the fourteenth, it would have been the wonder of the age. Such precise timekeeping would have been astonishing. But to a people who had no clocks and no use for them, it was just an oddly decorated wristband.

Amir noticed how I kept looking at my wrist and did not understand my explanation.

"The time is always what the time is," Amir said. "What else could it be?"

The confusion was because the nomad's expression for time meant where the sun was in the sky. Morning, noon, or evening were obvious for everyone, even if the sky was cloudy. Only someone who lived in a cave and never went out would need an artificial means of telling the time.

"Do your people live in caves?" he asked.

"Not exactly…" I could have explained to him the benefits of being able to time the boiling of an egg, but that would hardly interest a warrior chief. I dropped the subject.

I had one genuine weapon which might be of use, a weapon which was psychic rather than physical. But I was reluctant to use it. Driving out devils by invoking the devil was a risky practice, and black magic was not something to be trifled with.

Damki, my youthful bodyguard, became nervous when I spoke to other men. He was perhaps worried that Amir would be jealous. He would not talk to me himself but answered everything with "You must ask Amir, Lady."

When I addressed the men, I felt like a duchess trying to strike up a conversation with coal miners. They melted away at my approach or laughed nervously when I tried to ask them questions. When I eavesdropped on their conversations, they were speaking about horses, hunting, or fighting. It was their trade, and it was all they knew.

I decided the men were, like the wolves that roamed the grasslands, only comfortable when they were in a pack. Their awkwardness reminded me of rugby players who are so boisterous as a group and so tongue-tied on their own. I could recognise a few of them by sight: Old Harsis, of course, and his nephew Young Harsis, the ox-like individual who was Little John to Amir's Robin Hood. I knew a few others, as well, like Igmil, who was the best rider, and Alshu, who was the best archer.

When the men were not eating and drinking or collapsed in a state of exhaustion, they practised throwing javelins from galloping horses at a straw dummy or the ancient sport of tent pegging—spearing a target on the ground from horseback. Sometimes, they sparred on foot with spears, reversing them and striking with the blunt ends. There was laughing and shouting beforehand as they worked themselves up, but the bouts themselves were as serious as any sporting contest and more bruising than most.

As his sisters boasted, Amir was by far the best with a spear, and he practised twice as often as anyone else. He was far more inventive. He blocked or parried with neat circular movements or swung his spear like a quarterstaff, moving so quickly that his opponents could not follow.

Back in England, Amir could have been a champion athlete. Puabi explained that, as the band's leader, he had to be strongest in battle. He might also be called on to fight duels with leaders of other bands to settle issues of property or territory, or even face challenges from within the band. His skill with a spear was literally a matter of life and death. Kings here did not appoint champions to do their fighting for them.

I needed some exercise myself besides walking and riding, and I asked Amir if he could show me how to use a spear. If I was a goddess, perhaps I could be a war goddess, a Boudicca leading the nomads in battle. Amir was shocked.

"A woman may not use a spear," Old Harsis told me. "It is unclean even for her to touch it."

When a boy achieved adulthood, he was given a spear and rode with the warriors; when a girl married, she was given a cooking pot. The symbolism was laughable, but it reinforced the social division between the sexes.

"One man, one spear—" Amir reminded me.

"I've got it," I said.

If I was a goddess, I was a domestic one. And I would need to find other forms of exercise.

Every week or so, the entire camp upped sticks and moved. The tents and other possessions were loaded onto horses or dragged behind them in an arrangement like a North American travois. Wheels might have been impractical, but dragging looked backward to me. The men, women, and children walked alongside the horses, surrounded by barking dogs, with the goat herds bleating protest behind until they reached the new campground.

The nomads measured distances in horizons: the distance to the horizon was about four miles everywhere. Several hours travelling took us a distance of two horizons, the prescribed distance according to Old Harsis, where we pitched camp again. The nomads always set up their tents in a particular arrangement, centred on Amir's large goat-hair tents with each family getting its allotted space around them according to rank.

Old Harsis was a hero. As a young man, he had been captured by enemy warriors. They had staked him to the ground, ridden their horses over him, and left him for dead. His own people had mourned him and were overjoyed when he hobbled into camp two weeks later. This brush with death, and his subsequent caution, gave him a reputation for wisdom and a knowledge of the ways of heaven. Apart from a few mumbled phrases, though, there was little sign of any religious sensibility amongst the nomads.

"Do you truly believe I am a goddess?" I asked Amir one evening.

Amir stroked his beard before answering, a pose he sometimes struck to give him time to think and lend his eventual utterance weight. At last, he said, "Yishka, if you are not a goddess, then I forswear religion."

He placed his hand on his heart and bowed for emphasis. Rudolph Valentino could not have done it better. Amir could not pronounce my name. "Yishka" was as close as any of them could get to "Jessica." I probably mangled their names just as badly.

I kept revising my estimate of Amir's age. When I first met him, it was his air of seniority and command that had impressed me, and I would have guessed he was in his thirties. Afterwards, in private and close up, he looked barely more than twenty, his face unlined and unformed. Amir was a man, though, and a leader, but that did not stop him from behaving childishly at times. When one of his men fell off his horse, Amir acted the event out for me twice, laughing all the way through. He would have loved Laurel and Hardy.

The nomad religion had been effectively erased by the Great Dying a generation before. The priests said the plague was a punishment from the gods, but even when the People did everything the priests told them, the Dying continued. Some of the priests had died of the plague themselves; others had been driven out for their failure to placate the gods or had fled from shame and religious doubt. The plague burned itself out soon afterwards, leaving the nomads with god-stories and traditions, but no fixed dogma or rituals.

Amir believed in me because he needed to believe. His world had been cracked by his father's death, and he was responding in the only way he knew. He was on a quest for vengeance which could not succeed without divine assistance.

One religious concept they had clung on to was *beraish*, which applied to anything taboo or forbidden. The nomads were a profoundly practical people, and this was one of their few words which was more spiritual than prosaic.

I had a peculiar dream during this period.

I dreamt of chatting with my friends. Sometimes it was a picnic in the park, a boating trip, or in a restaurant, and sometimes we seemed to switch between different places. Always, I was explaining how the nomads had somehow mistaken me for a goddess, and everyone was hooting with laughter.

"*But which goddess?*" *William asked.* "*Surely you must have been steel-eyed Athena, mistress of wisdom?*"

"*More an angel than an actual goddess,*" *I said.*

"*Sounds topping,*" *Daisy said.* "*I hope they brought you oodles of sacrifices.*"

"*Libations,*" *William said, raising a glass.* "*Drinkable sacrifices.*"

"*How perfect,*" *George said.* "*They obviously couldn't tell you were* 'Non angeli, sed angli.'"

"*She's a lot more angelic than you are, George,*" *Sophie said.* "*Though I suppose you could pass as a fat cherub if you had wings.*"

"*George is more of an imp,*" *Thomas said.* "*But I think we can agree Jessica is definitely an angel.*"

"*But, Jessica,*" *George said,* "*how did you get all the way back from there?*"

Daniel started to say something, but his face was swallowed up in flames, and I knew it was a dream. That was when it always ended, and I woke up.

The grasslands had looked dull at first. I began to appreciate they were an ocean, ever changing. The grasses were never still. Sometimes it was a restless, random stirring. Sometimes long, regular waves followed each other. Never entirely still, the air might subside to a faint whisper or accelerate to hurricane force, whipping up with stinging sand. The sky was huge, far bigger than at home, and clouds sailed across it like fleets of schooners. Sometimes black storms rolled over, bringing sudden downpours and outbursts of thunder and lightning, but it never rained all day as it did at home.

The days were hot. The women and children took a siesta in the afternoon. It was dry, too dry; I suffered from nosebleeds, so my handkerchief was useful for something. The wind was brisk in the morning and evening but slowed to nothing in the heat of the afternoon. Clouds were rare; every sunset was a gory mess. The dawn was scarcely less bloody, but over quickly.

I still had trouble getting more than two words out of Damki. He had been assigned guard duty because he was too young for other tasks, but he took a stubborn pride in following me around and standing in a protective stance by my tent for hours. Amir might have given him the job because he was a spare part, but Damki had taken the role as an honour.

I was getting quite used to Amir, but relations with his brother took an alarming turn when I had been with the band about six weeks. He slipped into my tent one morning while I was going through vocabulary in my notebook.

"Good morning."

I practically jumped at the man's voice. For a moment, I thought it was Amir—he had the same eyes and mouth—before I recognised Nergal. I had hardly exchanged two words with Nergal, and he smiled when he saw my confusion.

"What are you doing here?" I demanded, standing up and trying to sound commanding instead of scared. "Nobody is allowed in here."

"It is time for us to talk. Before, you could only speak like a child. Now you have grown up, and I can talk properly to the goddess. You are a goddess, I understand?"

My grasp of the language was imperfect, and Nergal was making no effort to make it easier for me. I understood him as much by his manners than the actual words. I did not reply, but looked down at him from my full height.

He smiled again and looked appraisingly around the tent. "Amir has given you good quarters. I wondered where these cushions with the gold thread had gone! As comfortable, I trust, as the place you came from?"

"Amir has been generous and has treated me well," I said. "I do not think he would be pleased to know his brother has visited me without his permission."

"You certainly talk like a goddess! But you should be grateful to me, you know. I was the one who told Amir that heaven would send a sign. Otherwise... he might have acted differently. You would be just another female captive. I am the one who keeps reminding him you are a goddess; he might forget otherwise."

When he spoke, he was completely different to his brother. Amir was strong, brave, and gallant; Nergal was none of those. But I suspected he was a great deal cleverer.

"Thank you," I said stiffly.

Nergal smiled broadly and made himself comfortable amongst the cushions. He picked a nut from a bowl and regarded me benignly. Amir was never so casual in my presence.

"It was gracious of Your Divinity to arrive when you did," Nergal said. "We needed a miracle. 'Heaven supplies miracles'—one of our sayings. It was difficult for Amir to keep the support of the others in his mission of vengeance, but with heaven on his side, he is much more successful. Old Harsis says there is no precedent for revenge except against men… but he cannot deny heaven."

"Your brother is a great leader," I said. "If anyone can fight the Unclean, it is Amir."

"Revenge is a grilled bird, which I can pick up, take a bite or two, and toss aside," Nergal said, throwing an empty shell away to illustrate the point. "Amir has to eat it all, bones and feathers, too, even if it chokes him. He is honourable… but not clever."

"He is honourable," I said.

"Amir cannot fight the Spawn without the help of heaven," he said through a mouthful of nuts. "I would like to know what help you have brought. I do not think you can summon lightning as they say, can you?"

I did not reply. If I could call thunderbolts, I certainly would have done so then.

"Come, sit down next to me," he said. "Amir thinks you are clever, and for once, I think he is right. We should be allies. I know about women, but I want to learn about goddesses."

Nergal was full of himself, all too much like some of the overconfident young men I had met at Oxford. Their strength comes from the fact that women are too indecisive to oppose them, and they take first one liberty then another, until there is no stopping them.

"Amir's brother will always be my ally," I said.

He laughed. "Amir finds you enchanting. He is easily distracted by new things, for a time. But he gets bored. When we were boys, we found a wolf cub separated from its mother. He fed it goat milk and looked after it for weeks. But he lost interest… and the dogs killed it." He smirked most unpleasantly.

"I'll remember that," I said.

"It would be very good for you to be my ally. I would like to add the voice of heaven to my voice. And I find you pleasing."

He rose to his feet and moved closer, first one step and then another. I did not retreat. Nergal's leer was disgusting. I would have been scared if I had not been so angry.

"Where did you come from, truly?"

"I fell from the heavens."

He exhaled slowly. His breath was unpleasantly hot. "If you say so, it must be true."

Nergal kept his face a few inches from mine, as if waiting to see what I would do. He had to tilt his head up to do it.

I made myself into a statue. I was not going to swoon for his pleasure. "If you try to touch me, I will give you a slap you will not forget." I wished I had my knife, but it was still under my bedding. "And Amir will not be pleased when I tell him." I glared until, at last, he looked away.

"The goddess is in a bad mood." He smirked again.

He seemed pleased. I was in his power, and he could take me when he wanted. But for his own pleasure, or to disconcert me, he would wait. "I look forward to meeting you alone again." Nergal made a low, ironic bow and ambled out.

I did not stop trembling for some time afterwards.

Amir was not one for intrigues. If I told him about Nergal, he would fly off the handle and probably challenge his brother to a duel or something. Whatever happened would weaken Amir's position. Nergal had the low cunning of a political operator who would have thought of all the possibilities. I did, however, make sure I had always kept my purloined knife ready to hand by day, as well as by night. If Nergal ever threatened physical rather than verbal advances, I promised myself I would slice off any body part he tried to touch me with.

Chapter Three: Place of Monsters

I settled into a sort of life, but it was temporary. I was neither happy nor unhappy. I never had the feeling of exploring a wondrous new land or of getting to know people. My initial anxiety had worn off, and I was beginning to trust Amir. I was well aware, though, that he could easily change his mind about me, and I would be a slave or worse. My position here could not be a permanent one.

My sole desire was to get home. That would mean getting back to the cave with the pool where I had first arrived. As far as the nomads were concerned, the place was unclean. Damki shook his head violently whenever I suggested a ride in that direction. It was the Place of Monsters.

I knew the Monsters preoccupied Amir, and that many parties were sent out to watch the place rather than hunting or raiding. Their reports often put him in a bad mood, but he would not explain to me.

One evening, he was in a worse temper than usual. The evening meal was goat stew seasoned with a local variety of rosemary. Aruru, like many amateur cooks, had decided that if a little seasoning was good, more would be better.

"This tastes bad," Amir said after the first spoonful. "Is the meat spoiled?"

"An enemy's goat always tastes better," Nergal said in a placating tone. Unfortunately, this only reminded Amir that he had been watching the Place of the Unclean instead of catching game, which was why we had to slaughter the tribe's own goats.

"I can't eat this." Amir threw his bowl on the ground.

"Don't waste it," Nergal said.

"I'm sorry," Aruru said.

Amir scowled. After a second, he stood up, took Aruru's bowl, and threw that on the ground, too, scattering brown stew across the dirt. She burst into tears.

"How dare you!" I shouted, standing up myself.

The scene was instantly frozen. If I had been thinking, I would have remembered that nobody ever talked back to Amir, that he was the supreme leader with the power of life and death. But I had spent two hours helping Aruru prepare the stew, stirring and stirring it so it did not stick and burn in the thin copper pot while the meat softened.

Aruru and Puabi looked terrified, anticipating an explosion. Nergal was watchful. Amir was caught between anger and bemusement.

There was no sense in trying to back down now. "You are supposed to be a leader, not a spoiled child," I said, quiet but resolute. "Whatever happens out there, you should not take out on your family. Apologise to your sister."

"Never serve me stew like that again," he told Aruru then mumbled, "Sorry." He turned and walked away.

Aruru was trying to recover pieces of meat and vegetable from the ground. "Take this," I said, passing her my bowl. "I have to talk to Lord Amir."

I found him gnawing on a strip of dried meat. His mood had subsided; he offered me some, but I declined. My jaws were not strong enough for that stuff.

"You need to tell me what it is that's bothering you," I said. "I think I speak Language well enough now."

"Well enough to tell me off in front of my family. Eloquent even." He flashed a smile. "You are right. I should not put this off any longer."

"This is about the slavers and the monsters," I said.

"They tricked Tena, my father," he said. "So he would let them go to the place. The place is forbidden. Unclean, you know? They said they just had to see it, for penance. They brought him gifts. Tena did not know they were the people of Tulu, the Unclean. Keepers of slaves. They went into the caves, and they did not come out. And they made their evil magic, and they bred monsters… from women."

That was the gist of it. Women were kept there. There were strange women from unknown tribes, and the women gave birth to monsters.

"Strange women," I said. "You mean women like me?"

"Not as beautiful as you," he said. "Not as tall, not as wise, not as strong. Not with metal around their eyes. But women who look different to us, not like People."

"And these women… they give birth to the monsters?"

"Yes."

I was shaken to the core, but a part of me was not surprised. This was all too much what I had been expecting. I had been brought here for a purpose. I had not fallen here by accident. I had not survived the fall through infinite space because I was a good diver, but because other forces had wanted me to survive. I had been brought here to breed monsters for that alien-devil-thing.

Back home, a lifetime away, I had participated in a lively conversation about *The War of the Worlds* in which my friends mocked the idea that aliens from Mars would consume human blood as HG Wells suggested. The consensus was that nothing which evolved on Mars could survive the temperature, pressure, and radiation of our planet or breathe our air. And even if they did, their metabolism would be totally different to ours. For some reason, proteins were important: they would have different proteins. Humans would be indigestible, at best, and most likely highly toxic. As for the busty females in flimsy spacesuits menaced by lustful aliens on the covers of magazines read exclusively by teenaged boys, it seemed a mating between a man and an octopus was more plausible.

There was another way of looking at it. An alien being which did not belong on our world would have to adapt. The easiest way to do this would be to borrow the form and structures of animals already living there, modify them, and fold them around its own alien core. Like a shipwrecked sailor who builds his shelter out of whatever comes to hand, it was using human material to house its essence. Or, in this case, its brood.

The Place of Monsters had been deserted for generations. Two years ago, a wandering holy man had warned Amir's father that there was an evil alignment of the stars, but had not told them where the danger lay. A few months later, the bad men came and tricked their way in.

After Amir's father was killed, a watch was set on the place. The scouts reported that there were captive women. No slave caravan had been seen arriving, and the source of the women was a mystery. It was as though they had grown out of the earth, conjured by the Tulu's people. As I guessed, I was not the only one to fall down the rabbit hole from another time and place.

"What are these monsters?" I asked.

"They are monsters," Amir said. They were not just dangerous animals like wolves, snakes, or scorpions, but unclean, unnatural things. They came out of the water and lived on land. They were like many snakes together. He sketched in the sand with the tip of a knife, but I could not understand his drawing, which seemed to consist entirely of wavy lines.

"Bigger than a man, smaller than a horse. Or maybe like a horse. It is difficult to say. Sometimes you do not see them. They change. They hunt both in the day and at night, by the light of the moon and the stars, or even when it is dark." He looked at his sketch and curled his lip. "When I was a boy, I did not think the old stories were real. I thought they were noises and shadows and fear, like the phantoms that children run away from. But the monsters are real."

"Yes," I said.

"They killed my father," he added tonelessly, looking at the ground. I was silent, and after a minute, he continued.

"My father led raids against the Tulu men. Not for glory, but to kill them because they are unclean. They threw stones at us from their slings and hid deep in their caves. My father made a big raid with every spear, to kill them all. But in the deep cave, there were monsters. He held them back long enough for the others to get away, but they killed him. Now there are many monsters. They roam out farther every day. I will kill them, every one of them. You will help me, just like the goddess in the old stories."

"I will try," I said. "But I need to understand what is happening."

There were strong echoes here of events in Dulwich, of strange births under the influence of otherworldly beings. The ancient Greek myths of Leda, Danae, Europa, and the rest being seduced by multi-formed Zeus might have a grain of dark truth in them.

"We cannot kill them," Amir said. "Not without help from heaven."

The people looked to the gods to save them, and as far as Amir was concerned, I was the divine saviour. He had prayed for signs from heaven, and I had appeared on cue. Not a goddess exactly, but heaven's appointed messenger. To Amir's way of thinking, my unusual appearance and obvious alienness were proof positive that I had been sent from above.

Pretending to be a god was an old trick when Cortez encountered the Incas. I never tried to deceive Amir, and he ignored my attempts to explain that I was just a woman. At first, I assumed he was being crafty, that he wanted to use me to help win over his people. His insistence, though, even the face of my own denials, gradually changed my mind. He believed I was from heaven; he needed to believe I was from heaven.

Old Harsis had said I was from heaven, because I did not fit into his rigid scheme of classification any other way. Nergal agreed I was from heaven, because it suited his purposes, whatever they were. It did not matter to Amir that I refused to accept the pedestal he wished to place me on. He thought I was being coy for some reason and that I needed to be persuaded to help him.

Robinson Crusoe, with his musket and pistols, easily rescued the grateful Man Friday. I had no weapons and was reliant on this band of Man Fridays for my everyday survival. I would help them however I could, but my help did not amount to anything.

"You must see the creatures," Amir said. "When you have seen, you will help us. We will go tomorrow."

I was eager to go back. I still imagined it might be possible to sneak into the cave where I had arrived and climb my way back home while Amir's men distracted the slavers.

The party set out before dawn. Amir decided to bring four men with spears: Damki, Old Harsis, Igmil, and Sabian. Young Harsis, their strongest warrior, was left out because he lacked the requisite stealth. We dismounted some distance from the place, and Damki was instructed to stay with the horses while we continued stealthily on foot. We crouched as we followed Amir down a trail he had scouted the day before.

As we drew closer, Amir gestured for complete silence. The men moved like cats, communicating through hand signals. Amir led us out of the grass to a narrow goat path zig-zagging up to a rocky prominence. It was an excellent position to observe the Place of Monsters. The cave from which I had emerged was no more than a hundred yards away, clearly visible in the early-morning sun.

The place was different to how I remembered it. There was more activity. I had arrived during the heat of the afternoon when the occupants were sluggish. Now men trudged down the paths on their errands, one half-leading, half-dragging a female captive down a path,

WAR OF THE GOD QUEEN

another carrying water in the other direction. Others appeared to be guards or sentries.

I saw details I had missed earlier: the remains of thick pillars sprouting out of the rocky ground and the wide paths. And there was so much water, a stark contrast to the arid grassland. Low aqueducts, showing signs of recent repair, fed a series of terraced oval pools that could have been fishponds. Shallow depressions in the rock were the ghosts of other pools from long ago.

My eyes sought out the entrance where I had arrived. It was the largest cave by far, with eroded statues in bas-relief around it. Beside it were many smaller cavemouths, cells excavated out of the rock face, each holding one or two women behind wooden bars. I counted twenty captives, and there might have been more out of sight.

"There is one," Amir said, pointing to a cavemouth, his voice a low murmur an inch from my ear. "This is the Spawn of Tulu."

The creature lingered in the shadows as if sniffing the air, then it emerged.

I had visited an art gallery in Paris once—how long ago that seemed!—to see an exhibition of the astonishing and scandalous pictures of Max Ernst. Surrealism was new, and the artists took a rather childish delight in obscenity and sexual matters. But the painting that struck me most was his *Celebes*, which depicted a monstrous creature, part machine, part elephant, part nightmare, in a scene that might have been underwater. An aura of destruction hung about it, one of Ernst's many pictures inspired by the War.

It must have been *Celebes* that gave me the sense of déjà vu when the monster emerged.

There was something of an elephant about it, not in its size but in its ponderous movement and its appendages—very like elephant trunks. My first impression was of a crab the size of a small car. It had feelers, eyestalks, and complex lobed antennae, all of which emerged from its surface or disappeared back into it like the appendages of a snail. Tentacles waved and weaved as it held them clear of the ground.

It did not move like a crab though but lurched with slow, stiff steps on a single leg, like a woman shuffling along in a fashionable long dress too tight around the knees. The Spawn combined the traits of an octopus and a slug, and it was even more repulsive than the combination suggests.

In addition to raising itself up on its leg and shuffling slug-like, the creature had another gait, dropping down and crawling along with its tentacles as though swimming. It looked like a mass of pythons swarming over the ground. This was even slower, but allowed the creature to remain almost flat as it stalked prey. The thing seemed also somehow less than solid, like an inflated balloon or a grounded airship limping along. Like a sunset or a ballet, it could be described, but I doubted whether anyone could understand such things without directly witnessing them. Everything about the Spawn seemed abnormal. It was a different kind to all other living things: unnatural and unclean.

I gazed in horrified fascination as the thing made its way down to one of the pools and dabbled with two tentacles as though testing the temperature. A man walked by, giving it a wide berth. The thing reached into the water and hauled out something that squirmed and writhed: a smaller version of itself, which it placed on the bank. The smaller thing turned around, shook itself like a dog, then slithered back into the pool. Amir had already explained about the creatures' life cycle. They were born in the water before they crawled out onto land. They started small, no larger than a guinea-fowl, and got bigger and bigger.

The way back to my home seemed plain enough. I had to get back to that chamber where I had arrived and somehow climb back up the stone shaft, all the way up to the modern age, London, and home. Getting in without attracting attention would be impossible. Amir said that the Spawn were sensitive to the slightest vibration and could detect footfalls from a hundred paces off. It would take an army to fight past them, and there were at least a dozen of the slavers to contend with, as well. If I could get to the chamber with the pool, I would be faced with an ascent of several thousand feet of chimney— quite a feat for a team of seasoned mountaineers with full equipment, and not something I was about to try with hostile strangers below.

We watched the Spawn for half an hour. One of the things killed a tethered goat brought by a slaver. It wrapped its two thickest tentacles around the poor beast's neck, cutting off the frightened bleating. The goat was still thrashing as the monster started tearing it apart with horrible ripping sounds, throwing the pieces into a pool for its young. One tentacle tore off a stray scrap of flesh and conveyed it to the creature's own body. An opening briefly appeared, lined with rows of jagged teeth, and vanished again.

In outline, the Spawn was nothing like the horror I had glimpsed in Dulwich, but they were certainly cousins. They might not have looked out of place in an aquarium or scaled down to the size of insects, but those crawling things were monstrous in the true sense of the word— portentous things, brimming with dread. Perhaps there was some innate human reaction to things which are truly alien, like the frisson one feels when seeing a squid or looking into the eyes of a spider. Something in humans' blood warns us that these are beings from another order entirely.

After a time, Amir tapped me on the shoulder and signalled that we should return. I followed him back down the steep path, and we had almost reached flat ground when Amir suddenly froze.

"Watch out!" he hissed.

The Spawn seemed to materialise out of the ground in front of us. It had the chameleon's gift of matching the colour and texture of rock, sand, or grass. I found out later that after two minutes in one place, they were almost impossible to see, even when I knew where to look. As soon as the creature moved, the illusion disappeared, but it was still hard to make out its form, as though it were made of smoke and shadow.

The narrow path was the only way down, and the Spawn blocked the way. Its tentacles fanned out like flower petals opening as it sensed us. Then it shifted colour to the shade of old leather, suddenly appearing in sharp relief.

I shouted the incantation I had so diligently memorised in the British Museum, the spell supposed to repel evil things. It'd had some effect Dulwich, but this creature was immune. It lumbered forwards, its foot—or feet—undulating beneath it.

The warriors levelled their spears at the creature, keeping a good distance back as the tentacles wove like snake charmers' serpents. I soon discovered why: two tentacles shot out, extending to twice their normal length to grab at one warrior's legs, as quick as a snake. He yelled and struggled madly to escape the tentacles' grip. The other men responded immediately, stabbing at the limbs with their big-bladed spears.

Some of the tentacles had flattened tips, like the blades of an oar, for grasping. Others were thin and flexible. They coiled and stabbed forward like snakes.

Amir landed a solid blow, transfixing one tentacle and pinning it to the ground. Other spears stabbed at the same point, and the thing was severed, writhing like a dying snake. The Spawn hardly seemed to notice and continued to flail and strike with its other tentacles. I watched the severed section, which had landed uncomfortably close to me. As soon as it stopped moving, it fell apart into a purplish mush. The smell was disgusting—rotten eggs and ammonia were the most obvious components, but the combination reached into my stomach, making it heave.

A tentacle wrapped Igmil's spear and yanked it from his grip, but Sabian and Old Harsis stabbed at the creature's body, inflicting gaping wounds. Amir snicked off an antenna with a sweep of his spearpoint. The wormlike thing squirmed about on the ground before dissolving into jelly.

A narrow tentacle flicked around Sabian's knees like a whip and wrapped round. He grunted as he was hauled off his feet, sending his spear flying. Sabian screamed and grabbed hold of rocky protrusions as he was dragged towards the creature. The others tried to stab at the tentacle holding him, but the air was full of tentacles, all moving independently, batting away their spears or wrapping around and pulling them away.

Amir swung his spear, using the edge like an axe, but it was too late for Sabian. A second tentacle had hold of him, and his grip gave way. He was still screaming as his body disappeared, but the creature wrapped him with all its remaining tentacles, seeming to ball up like a hedgehog around its victim, muffling his screams. Then the screaming stopped. I could hear popping and cracking sounds as the man's body gave way.

The men plunged spears deep into the Spawn and twisted. It was no more solid than an octopus, and its flesh offered little resistance. I could not tell if they were trying to kill it or to end Sabian's suffering. It ignored the wounds torn into its sides, entirely intent on its prey.

"Back!" Amir ordered, and the warriors sprang away just before the creature's tentacles burst outwards again, lashing blindly in all directions.

We rushed past the Spawn. Amir had shrewdly used a spear and the one Igmil had dropped to pin it to the ground through its broad single foot. When I glanced back, it was feeling for the spears and pulling them out. It would not be stuck for long, but from what I had seen, the things could not move faster than a slow walk. However, we were running at speed.

When we reached Damki and the horses, we mounted up and raced away at a gallop. I clung on for dear life; I had not practiced riding enough. It would be ironic to escape such a monster only to be thrown to my death from a pony. But with my fingers camped onto its mane and my knees digging into its flanks with all my strength, I somehow stayed on.

When we got back to the camp, I realised others had been injured. Old Harsis was missing part of his scalp. Igmil's shoulder had been dislocated when the spear was twisted from his grip. Those injuries were barely worth speaking of, though, as far as the warriors were concerned. I insisted on washing the scalp wound, and I would have stitched it up if I had the nerve. Igmil would not let me touch his shoulder, but thankfully, some of the others helped. With some cries of pain on his part and laughter on theirs, they got it back in its socket.

"I'm so sorry about Sabian," I said to Amir. I was still in shock from the encounter, which was as unreal as my plunge down the abyss which had brought me here. My reality was becoming unglued; I needed to talk about concrete things, to make it real again. "I never really talked to him."

"Sabian, a good warrior, was son of my father's sister and my mother's cousin," Amir told me. He was quiet, but far from despondent. "He was brave—you saw he never hesitated."

"Was he married?" I asked.

"Of course," Amir said. Virtually every adult was married. Amir and his siblings were rare exceptions: the plan had been for the sisters to marry the leaders of other bands to cement alliances. They were currency being kept in the bank. Then Amir would have to find a wife for himself and Nergal, but domestic matters had been put aside until the creatures were destroyed. "Sabian's brothers will look after his wife and children until she remarries."

The brothers were already married. Otherwise, one of them would marry the widow.

"All men die," Amir said philosophically. "Though it is better to die in combat with another man than with monsters."

Amir might have been forgiving, but Old Harsis held me personally responsible for Sabian's death. A goddess should have been able to prevent such a thing.

Death in battle was the most common fate for the nomad warriors. It was not just the incessant raids against other bands. There were also disputes with other families, bands, clans, and tribes, as well as personal feuds. All resulted in fights. A public duel was the acceptable and honourable way of settling any serious argument. The women, by contrast, tended to die during or in the weeks after childbirth or from sickness. The constant strain of childbearing and the fact that it was a wife's duty to feed her husband first may have contributed. No matter the cause, their mortality rate was as high as the men's.

Nobody was troubled by leaving Sabian's body with the Spawn. Bodies were not especially sacred. The nomads did not have burial grounds but burned their dead on great pyres of dry grass a few hundred yards from the camp. When the fire burned out, they walked away and did not look back. Sabian's name would be put back in the pot, and in a few months, another boy-child would be given the name. Thus, the nomads ensured continuity through the generations. In a thousand years, another Sabian and another Amir would still be riding together.

"The souls of the dead join the wind," Aruru told me. "They do it quicker if you burn them. If you listen closely to the night winds, you can hear them calling the names of the living after they die."

"I never heard it," Puabi said.

"After a while, they forget our world and became one with the wind," Aruru said. "And the living forget about them and go on living."

The nomads mourned fiercely but briefly. The woman who cried for a lost child every night was the rare exception.

"It's because she doesn't have any living babies," Aruru explained. "Everyone says if some of them live, it's not so bad."

In a month, the band would barely remember Sabian. My father had said it was the same during the war. Men simply moved their places round on the mess table and carried on.

"Will that creature die now?" I asked Amir, hoping for some crumb of consolation. It had not shown much sign of being hurt, but it had lost a lot of what it used for blood. Surely the many spear thrusts had punctured its vital organs.

He shook his head with a bitter laugh. "Of course not. By now, it will have healed." He held up his hand and wriggled his fingers to denote tentacles. "They are easy to cut off, but they come back quickly. Like cutting blades of grass."

"How do you kill them?"

"They do not die." He pointed at his head. "They have a brain, a small brain. If you stick a lance through it, the whole body turns into stinking mud. But they come back together and live again in the time it takes to walk a hundred paces. I have seen it several times."

"What about fire?" I asked.

"They do not fear fire. The Spawn do not fear anything."

I should not have been surprised at this unnatural vitality. The things were drawing on a force from somewhere beyond our world.

Amir's tactics had been limited to harassment, watching the slavers and killing any they caught in the open, and driving game away to cut off their food supply.

"But there was a Time of Monsters before," I said. "How did the People defeat them then?"

"With the help of the Goddess," he said cautiously, as though he thought I might be testing him.

"I'm so sorry," I said. The expedition had been for my benefit. Sabian's death was my fault. I resolved to remember his name at least, to put up a stone for him.

"You had to go there, to see them," he said. "Their numbers are growing. They spread like the bad grass which poisons horses. We cannot fight them without your help."

"But I don't know what I can do to help."

"You are from heaven. You told me about the boats made of metal and bows that shoot fire and thunder. You know names of the stars, why the wind blows, the songs of the birds… you will show us how to fight them. Nergal says so. Old Harsis said so." He touched his chest. "I know it."

"Of course I'll do what I can," I said. "For whatever good it will do. Sabian died fighting for me. And you've been so good—Amir, I will repay you, if I can."

Amir's confidence in me was unshakeable, even though I had nothing to offer. Still, if the Spawn could not die, they could be trapped. They could be lured into deep pits, sealed up inside their caves with boulders, or contained by some other means. These were plans which Amir had considered and rejected; he was a hunter, as well as a warrior. I resolved not to make any suggestions which would reveal the depth of my ignorance and stupidity until I could formulate a substantial plan, one worthy of the goddess I was supposed to be. I needed to learn.

I did have my secret weapon. Back in that other life, I had spent some time at the British Museum, finding out how to fight supernatural forces. I had gained access to carvings taken from a temple of Dagon, which are kept away from the general public. The inscriptions, when transliterated into something I could read, had proven to have a sort of repellent effect. It had not worked against the thing that killed Sabian, but maybe I needed to work on my pronunciation or intonation. It was a horrid thing to have to use, but it was all I had.

The night after Sabian died, I dreamed my dream again. This time it was different; only Daniel was there, scratching symbols into the sand with a stick.

"This is a dream," I said.

In life, Daniel ignored statements of the obvious, and he ignored me now. The image was so real, so lifelike, down to his ink-spotted shirt cuffs. "There are a large number of possible arrangements of sand particles," he said thoughtfully, scratching away. "We can express this number as a factorial."

I tried to make out what he was writing but could not read the ridges and furrows. They looked more like a map than writing.

"One of those arrangements might be useful," he said. "Or might have been, seen from the twentieth century. Our temporal topology is not simple."

"What do you mean?"

"It's good to see you again, Jessica, even in a dream," Daniel said, then his face was burning.

Chapter Four: God and Mammon

The nomads moved camp every few weeks. Sometimes we met up with other bands. The men of the two groups greeted each other formally and stood aloof, but the women rushed to embrace, sisters reunited with sisters, mothers with daughters. Cousins chatted happily together, showing off their new babies and growing children. Sons always stayed within the band, but daughters sometimes married out, strengthening ties between bands. Women were the mortar that held the different bands together into a clan and the clans into a tribe.

At that first meeting of bands, almost the entire population formed a circle, and two men fought a duel with spears. This was the final resolution of a feud between their two families. The men themselves were reluctant, but the crowd goaded them, and they started to attack each other in earnest. When one lay dead and the other bleeding freely from a wound in his thigh, Amir and the leader of the other band stuck both their spears in the ground and declared that the feud ended. The people of the two bands shouted their approval.

After that, the men played a game on horseback, halfway between polo and rugby, with a dead goat as the ball. There was some rough play, and I could only hope that no new feuds would result. In the end, there was a minor tussle, and knives were drawn. The leaders were ready to intervene and break it up. One player from each side was held responsible, and both were punished with a public whipping, which was just another entertainment as far as the crowd was concerned.

"Six lashes only," Amir told me. "A warning to them."

The big event of the evening was a wedding. Sabian's widow was being married off to a man in the other band whose wife had died of a fever. Marriage was a practical affair to the nomads, and the fact that the pair had barely met was of no great importance. The two stood proudly during the brief ceremony, not looking at each other until it was over. Amir placed their hands together, and they both smiled, shipwrecked sailors holding on to each other for support.

We feasted on spit-roasted antelope, rather than the usual boiled or stewed goat. The men of the other band eyed me with interest, but none would talk to me directly. I was with the women and stayed close to Aruru and Puabi. They introduced me offhandedly to their cousins as Yishka-from-Heaven, and everyone ignored me to gabble about who was pregnant, who had married, who had given birth, whose child had died or survived illness, whose brother or husband had killed a wolf or been injured in a raid, or who did not get on with their mother-in-law. The pace of life might ebb slowly, but they had months of news to catch up on and pass on from other bands.

The creatures were becoming more dangerous, venturing farther and farther from the slavers' camp. One evening, Amir told me that while the People were trying to drive antelope away from the place of the Unclean, the monsters had seized the animals.

Things rapidly got worse. I was out walking one morning, not long after dawn. The heat of the previous day had almost dissipated, leaving a mild, pleasant warmth. It would be hot again later and dry enough to burn my throat, but now, it was balmy. Mother Nature had painted the scene with a generous hand, adding gold to her palette. On such mornings, it was easy to be optimistic.

A herd of goats was ahead of me, driven by two boys with sticks. They watched me curiously. The nomads did not understand the idea of "going for a walk," and there was no expression for it in Language. I gave them a royal wave, and they waved back uncertainly.

I walked in a wide arc to steer around the slow-moving herd. I still preferred to avoid walking through fresh goat droppings, a fastidious habit which amused Amir no end. A partridge rose from the grass thirty feet away, flapping frantically, a feathered cannonball skimming low over the grass and out of sight. If I had been paying more attention, I would have stopped to wonder what might have startled it.

A goat bleated and started running, triggering a stampede of fleeing animals and a cloud of dust. For a minute, I thought they were running from me. Then the air seemed to solidify, and a mass of tentacles, as black and shiny as liquorice, appeared behind the herd.

The running goats bleated in alarm and dismay. They had been driven towards a second Spawn, only visible as a dusty glass statue looming over them. When waiting in ambush, the creatures extruded their tentacles out to impossible lengths, like living tripwires. This one was seizing goats in all directions, lassoing them around necks or pulling the legs from under them as they tried to escape. As one of them bleated, I was horrified to see a tentacle tip dive down its open mouth, silencing it. The animal bucked violently then crumpled to the ground.

"Run!" I told the boys and doubled back on my path. The last thing I saw was one of the goats being swallowed whole and the tentacle whipping out to catch a kid by the tail to drag it back, feet skidding in the dirt. The boys might be flogged for failing to protect their charges, but terror had gripped them, and they overtook me on the way back to the encampment.

Amir tugged his beard angrily when I told him. The scouts should have seen the Spawns' trail, and they should never have been allowed to have taken up positions so close. He wanted to take a look; I told him to be careful, but he shook me off, already calling for his men. He did not take dogs. The nomads' dogs fled from the scent of the Spawn and were useless for tracking them.

When he returned, Amir was less annoyed and more thoughtful. "The Spawn are cunning. They followed an old track left two days ago, so they left no new trail. They must have come slowly and kept low."

"They are getting closer," I said.

Amir said nothing, but only looked as though waiting for me to say something more.

The question of how to fight these indestructible alien horrors was increasingly pressing. But we had so little to work with. Amir's band was on congenial terms with its four sister bands that made up the clan. Elan, the clan leader, was sympathetic to Amir but could give little help. Any assistance would have to come from the tribal chief above him, Izzar, who ruled over several clans. But Izzar, I gathered, was hostile. He claimed that Amir's father had allowed the Spawn to come and demanded Amir redeem the situation. Besides, what was the point in sending warriors to fight creatures which could not be killed?

The nomads who called themselves the People in their own language were not the only group in the known world. There were other, more civilised races in the surrounding area, though Amir did not think much of them, and they could not teach him anything in the art of war. Some former nomads had taken up a settled existence, mainly in the east, but there were few hamlets in the nomads' range. These people were objects of pity, not even worth robbing. To the nomads, staying in one place was unhygienic, literally unclean. Settled people lived in their own filth, instead of moving away from it to a fresh, clean site.

"They live like goats," Amir said. "Digging the dirt with their horns."

There were settlements on the coast some ways to the south and what sounded like a town, where the people lived by fishing, an idea which disgusted Amir. Fish were no more appetising to him than earthworms. Real men could not live without meat. Furthermore, the boats were ridiculous and dangerous, especially in storms.

"They must be brave," I said.

"But they do not know any better," Amir said. "They cannot even ride."

Far off to the north beyond the hills, there were cities, and these were even worse. According to Amir, people were crammed into confined spaces and stone buildings, which he made sound like prisons. He called the people there by the word they used for castrated goats, a common insult amongst the warriors to anyone suspected of being less than manly. The city people were mostly slaves, and hardly any of them had horses. I probed, trying to find out what level of civilisation had been reached, but Amir was not interested. Whether it was classical Babylon or metropolitan Birmingham was all the same to him.

"Do they know anything of the Unclean?" I asked.

"No. The Spawn belong to this place." He gave a short laugh. "Others do not even believe they exist, until they see. They call us liars."

The band hosted visitors on a daily basis. Usually, there were three of four men from one of the adjacent bands, more rarely some from another clan. They came to trade news, discuss their movements—and to ask about the Spawn. I always asked to be included in these meetings, boring as they were, because they were my only way of gathering information.

Usually, I sat with the other women. One of two of the nomad leaders wanted to see me and fired questions at me as though trying to trip me up. And a few were reverent, bowing and addressing me as Highness. My favourite was a white-haired old man called Elan, whose hulking sons accompanied him. The sons were silent while the old man, Amir's clan chief, told me stories from the past, about the drought, the Great Dying, epic battles and famous feuds, and the colossal wolf pack which had descended from the hills and almost destroyed their goat herds. He treated me like his favourite niece who had asked about family history.

Aruru and Puabi made eyes at Elan's sons, whose attention was taken up entirely with eating and drinking what passed for beer amongst the nomads.

"Heaven is far away," the old man told Amir. "She will not know what has happened since the last goddess rode the grasslands, in my father's time."

"Exactly so, Lord Elan," I assured him. "This is all most interesting and new to me."

There were other visitors, too, including occasional traders with their pack mules and bodyguards. The traders were amazing figures. The first one I saw was gorgeously arrayed in red and yellow, with a floppy wizard hat and gold rings on every finger. He was obese, with a multitude of chins. His assistant looked like a younger version, only moderately overweight and less adorned with gold. Their guards kept their hands on the pommels of their swords and knives, eyeing the nomads with the suspicion of store detectives waiting for shoplifters to make a move.

I was impressed by the fact that they had swords. To me, the sword was a more sophisticated weapon than a spear, but Amir was dismissive.

"Swords break easily, and they have no reach," he said. "When a man with a spear meets a man with a sword, the one with a sword is a dead man."

The nomads occasionally attacked a caravan if they did not have any arrangement with its master, but for them, the game was rarely worth the candle. There was no honour or glory in it. Who would risk death to hold up a shop selling gaudy knick-knacks? Their miserable packhorses were good only for eating.

The caravans had more to fear from the outlaws and renegades, men who valued silver. The most renowned of them was a brigand who went by the name of Crow. He commanded a band of at least twenty warriors, and even Amir grudgingly admired him.

"His men have good horses," he said. "We have not caught them yet."

While the bandits might have been worthy, Amir laughed at the travelling fat men and their comical guards. Even he could not deny their bulk represented a sort of prosperity. The nomads might feast sometimes, but they knew famine well. That merchants were strangers to starvation was a cause for scorn rather than admiration.

The trader greeted me pleasantly with a crocodile smile. The traders did not speak Language fluently, so deals were conducted in pidgin, with exaggerated facial expressions to convey approval or doubt. But while the traders' manners might make them seem idiotic, they were anything but. The fat trader's eyes were predatory, alighting on everything. I guessed he was trying to tell what people I was from and how he could make a profit from me. He was disappointed that I spoke only the nomad language and nothing more civilised.

"Lady, lady, lady…" He guided me around his wares laid out carefully on blankets for the nomads to inspect. "Metal—see metal! This bronze, this tin, this copper—very good quality! Fine cloth for lady, many colours. Tools and trinkets and jewellery. Very fine. Beautiful thing."

The traders bought goatskins and leatherwork from the nomads, trading for cloth, bronze tools, knives, and spearheads. I examined their goods with fascination. Some of these I had seen in the British Museum: little silver brooches and copper bracelets for a young bride, enamelled hair combs, and rings set with coloured glass.

I had been through my purse and brought money. The coppers were useless, but a silver sixpence was surely worth something, even here. The trader examined the coin curiously, scratched it to check it was solid metal, and weighed it on tiny scales. We agreed on an exchange for a quantity of fine thread and some good metal needles.

I was sure he was cheating me, but I needed to darn my clothing. I kept breaking Aruru's bone needles, and their stringlike thread was hopeless.

Amir was contemptuous of the fat merchants. They never raided or hunted. Therefore, they were not real men. They were only interested in acquiring more and more things. "He kept looking at that coin you gave him." Amir laughed. "As if it were magic."

Given that the coins of the day were crude things, with barely recognisable human faces on them, my perfect twentieth-century machine-made sixpence must have been something extraordinary. It would certainly fox future archaeologists. Amir had no interest in trading, which to him it was an irritating necessity, and had no desire to accumulate wealth.

"We have everything here," he said.

"One man, one horse, one spear," Old Harsis said. "One tent, one cooking pot, one wife." It was a litany and a manifesto, the recipe for the good life. Anything a man could not carry was useless.

"Anything more leads to trouble," Amir agreed.

"You could save for a rainy day," I said. "In those lean seasons where there is no food, you could buy some."

"Hah." As far as Amir was concerned, real men hunted and herded for themselves. Buying food was tantamount to admitting he was not a real man. It was like social welfare to some people in my day: the refuge of scoundrels, scroungers, and layabouts who were not fit to look after themselves. His views might have made him a noble savage, but they ensured that his band would remain forever poor. It was a high price to pay for their pride.

The band's visitors also included a steady stream of wandering holy men or fakirs. Some were mute, solemn pilgrims; others seemed touched in the head and babbled things I could not understand. A third type were mountebanks who told fortunes and sold lucky charms and sacred amulets. One day, Amir announced that two distinguished guests had travelled many days to meet me. He ushered an ancient woman, supported by a youth, into the tent. Both were clad in red-dyed robes, and rows of wooden beads adorned their necks and wrists.

"I am the High Priestess," she told me in an unsteady voice. "I am come to see the descended goddess."

"Pleased to meet you, ma'am," I said, curtseying.

I had not realised the priesthood was still extant. This woman was the last survivor of the old priesthood. Deep lines quilted her face. It was impossible to tell what she had looked like when she was young, to believe she ever was young. There were so few really old people amongst the nomads, her state was incredible.

"You are… tall," the priestess said, herself a wizened four feet six. She spent some time gazing at my glasses.

"Thank you," I said, determined to be polite. I was not going to lie to her, but I did not want her telling Amir I was an imposter.

"They found you near the place of the Unclean," she said.

"That was where I arrived from heaven." I told the white lie, or perhaps the nearest to a truthful explanation that I could provide. Seen from here, London 1927 was very like heaven.

The boy started jabbering excitedly. There was something wrong with his speech, perhaps because of a cleft palate, and I could not understand what he said. He kept pulling at the High Priestess's arm and putting the fingers of his right hand around his left wrist.

"Please," she asked, pointing to my own left wrist.

I was mystified, but she held my arm lightly and bent her head low over my arm, staring at my watch. Her breath tickled my arm.

"It makes a sound," she said at last.

"Yes, it does," I said. "Tick, tick, tick."

"Hmmm…" Fumbling with arthritic fingers, she extracted a leather pouch and passed it to the boy.

He untied the complicated knot of leather cords, and from inside, he produced a round silver object, handling it with infinite care. He passed it to the High Priestess with the reverence of one handling a sacred relic. She held it briefly then gave it to me.

I found I was holding a silver pocket watch. It was half-full of sand, the face was cracked, and it had stopped long ago. Still, I could read the maker's name under the central wheel: Lanco. An old Swiss watch. I was confused, suddenly not knowing whether I was in the past, the future, or the present. Was I wrong after all? Had I not really travelled in time? Maybe this was not the Bronze Age, just some peculiar isolated spot that civilisation had never penetrated. Maybe all I needed to do to get home was walk fixedly in one direction until I started to find the outposts of the civilised world.

"The goddess brought it," the High Priestess said. "Long ago. Long, long ago. Her token."

I was not the only one to have come here from another time. The captives at the place of the Unclean, they too might have come from the future—maybe even from the same twentieth century as me. It had not occurred to me before that they must have fallen into the same trap I had, that they might be kindred spirits.

"Holiness," the High Priestess said. Her voice cracked then returned, much stronger. "Highness, you have truly come to purge the Unclean. We honour you."

"Thank you," I said. I had a hundred questions about this earlier goddess. Where was she from? What was she like? Had she really defeated the monsters, and if so, how? "Please. Please tell me what you can about the goddess. Tell me her story."

"It was all so long ago," she said sadly. "Everything was different. The world was different… the grasslands were different. I was young, once. I had children… all gone now. It all changes—the wind dries the rain, they say."

She stopped, and I was afraid she would say nothing more. But she continued in a stronger voice. "The goddess was a stranger without Language. At first, the People did not honour her, and the goddess was… abused. But she endured. She took shelter with the priests and learned the ways of heaven. As the monsters spread, the People started to listen to her. She brought the incantation that quells them."

The High Priestess paused, then in a low voice, she haltingly pronounced a few words in another language—the same incantation that I had learned in another world. I helped her finish it, and the ghost of a fierce smile crossed her lips.

"She taught the warriors battle dance, fighting on foot, with the new weapons. She taught them to move their camps on curves, so the Spawn could not find them… so many night marches. The goddess knew the only way. She taught rituals and warrior ways. She made an alliance with the desert sorcerers. The bands who did not listen perished one by one. The ones who had abused the goddess were put to death. So many died… The creatures were merciless, and so many, so many of them."

"That incantation—"

"Do not speak it lightly," she warned. "The resolve of the god queen was harder than rock. She rallied her army again and again, and the Spawn were driven back and back and destroyed one by one. In the end, their nest was rooted out and their fount destroyed. It was such a long, hard war. None who started it lived to see the end. Everyone was dead. Now I am surrounded by strangers, and I don't recognise anyone. Some have even forgotten the goddess."

"And how did the goddess destroy the creatures?"

"She was strong, like you," she said. "You have victory in you. I see it. Trust your strength, young goddess. I was strong then too. Now I am so weak. You are so young and strong. You cannot imagine… You cannot imagine what it is to be old… in this terrible place." Her words trailed off in silent, self-pitying sobs.

I wanted to grab her and shake her for information, but it would have been useless. The old priestess was exhausted. For a minute, I thought she might expire on the spot, but she recovered when Aruru plied her with an herbal infusion.

"Amir's people remember," she said, sipping it. "Others have forgotten. It was good that Amir found you. He is a good man. You and he will lead the People to victory again."

While there was a frustrating lack of information forthcoming, the old woman's visit boosted my stock amongst the nomads. It made no difference to Amir, who was already my adoring fan—no film starlet ever had a more ardent supporter—but it mattered to the others, especially the conservative Old Harsis. Despite my failing to save Sabian, the High Priestess had confirmed what Old Harsis had initially suspected. He had been right to save me, so that increased his stock too.

Nergal also looked on me with new appreciation, as though I were a horse which had won a race and repaid the price he had paid for it. This was all jolly good, but it also raised expectations that I would be able to do something miraculous to defeat the monsters. I was feeling less miraculous than ever, but now I had some hints.

"Who are the desert sorcerers?" I asked Amir.

"In the stories, they live in great caves underground in a far-off land and work magic," he said. "They say sometimes they come in the night and take children. Sometimes wanderers claim to be sorcerers, but it is all tricks."

"How can we find them?"

"They are like the night spirits. They appear when they want to and disappear. But only in stories."

A more concrete result from the High Priestess's visit materialised some days later. Amir and two of his men escorted an odd-looking individual to my tent. The man was no taller than the other nomads but was immensely wide and brawny, with great thick biceps. His jacket jingled with tiny bronze trinkets, medallions, and charms.

"This man demanded to see you," Amir said then added in an undertone, "he comes with the blessing of the High Priestess, or we would have thrashed him and sent him away. Do not trust him. He is from an enemy tribe."

The big man looked daggers at the escorts who jostled him, but he broke into a big smile as soon as he saw me. He hobbled forwards, revealing a club foot, and bowed his head in an unusual show of respect. His accent was strange, but with a little difficulty, I could make out his words.

"Great Highness!" he said. "The High Priestess said I must come, so here I am. Turm, maker of weapons, has come to serve you. I will make the weapons for your war against the Unclean."

Turm was not a blacksmith. A blacksmith is one who shoes horses, and the nomads' ponies went unshod. Rather, he was metalworker. A bronze smith or, more generally, a weaponsmith.

"You cannot stay here," Amir told him. "You are not of our clan."

"Very pleased to meet you, Turm, maker of weapons." I was already thinking how useful his services might be. "I am Yishka."

"I am honoured, Highness." Up close, his face and hands were covered with tiny white scars. His look was alarmingly direct, then I realised he was inspecting the workmanship of my spectacle frames with a craftsman's eye. "Others have forgotten heaven, but the smiths never will. Give me a place to work, and I will make whatever you command."

The smith's finely wrought bronze and copper ornaments tinkled as he moved. They were mainly animals and flowers, but one was a metal disc with separate hands and the markings of a clock face.

"There's no work for you here, cripple," Amir said.

"Excuse us, Master Smith," I said and pulled Amir aside for a quiet word.

"We have no need of a smith," Amir said. "We have all the spearheads and knives and arrowheads we need. If we want more, we trade skins with the merchants. We don't want another big mouth to feed every day. He is no warrior—his pony staggers under his weight!"

"He will be useful. I promise you, Amir."

Amir gauged my expression and sighed. "If the goddess says so." He looked sideways at the big man. "I suppose he's harmless. There were no smiths amongst the People before the goddess, so perhaps this is as should be."

Amir turned back to Turm. "Smith! You can stay, but behave yourself. If you betray us or touch our women, I'll have you staked out in the sun like a goatskin."

"I accept your gracious hospitality, Lord Amir," Turm said with another half bow. "It will be my honour to serve the goddess amongst your fine people."

"He speaks loftily for a metal beater," Amir muttered.

I had been thinking how useful it would be to have a metalworker, and it was little short of miraculous that one should have turned up. Even Robinson Crusoe did not have his own smith, and Turm was attentive and eager to be of assistance.

A small crowd watched as he made preparations. With slow, deliberate movements, Turm cut out big squares of turf with a long knife and gathered wood. He covered a pile of wood with turves then set fire to it to burn, a slow and smoky fire that would yield a trove of charcoal. While it was burning, he cut more turves and built a small furnace. Then he went looking for a flat stone he could haul back for an anvil. As a nomad, Turm was accustomed to rebuilding his workshop every time his people moved.

The next day, Turm started work. He briskly repaired broken knives and spearheads, manufactured arrow points, and worked on commissions for me. A pair of tweezers to remove thorns from my still-soft feet were a particular blessing.

After a couple of attempts, we had a pair of robust dental pliers. It was a fallacy that only people who eat sugar have bad teeth, and several of the nomads had complained of toothache in my hearing. It was hard to overstate just how unpleasant that sort of long-term pain could be. Turm acquired a new role: I supervised him while he pulled teeth, checking several times to make sure he had the right one. That won him friends, and there were a few more, albeit gap-toothed, smiles around the camp. Even Amir was pacified when Turm presented him with a new belt of bronze disks, better made than the previous ones. Our main limitation was the supply of metal. We would need to do something to get more ingots of bronze for Turm's small forge.

Sometimes, when everything was too much for me, I went for walks on my own, trailed by loyal Damki at a discreet distance. I would sing

"Jerusalem" and imagine that these were fields of waving corn and there was a village church just around the next bend. I would jingle my pennies in my hand and wonder how much the bus fare would be or whether I would walk and spend the money on an ice cream. In a place like this, even imaginary ice cream was better than nothing, better to think about it melting and running down the cone than thinking about the filth and squalor awaiting me in the camp… and the things that lay ahead of me in the grasslands.

Sometimes I just cried, but I felt better afterwards. I knew one thing, however, which the High Priestess had confirmed. I was not alone. I could not do this on my own, but I could get help.

CHAPTER FIVE: RESCUE MISSION

To DEFEAT THE SPAWN, WE have to rescue those captive women," I told Amir. "To stop the monsters multiplying further."

My real aim was getting the women out. I knew, though, that Amir would only be persuaded by an argument on strategic grounds, not humanitarian ones. The nomads would not rescue women just for the sake of it.

Amir stroked his beard. "Easier to kill the women than to rescue them." He caught the look in my eye. "But if the goddess wills they should be rescued, it will be done."

"Thank you!"

"But… it will be difficult." He had never uttered that phrase before in my hearing.

"The last time we went there, we lost Sabian. Since then, the Spawn have become bolder and more numerous."

"A diversion?" I suggested. "Could you distract them somehow?"

"What a clever idea," he said with light sarcasm. I was, as they say, teaching my grandmother to suck eggs. Amir was a light cavalry commander. Feints, feigned retreats, and other manoeuvres to deceive and divide the opposition were his stock-in-trade. "The woman cages are in the centre of their settlement. Drawing the men away from there will be hard, and there are many of the Spawn in the caves and pools. Others may be patrolling or watching."

"I know," I said. The slavers were deadly with their slingshots, and any nomad who came within striking range of one of the creatures had little chance of escaping alive. Some of his men would be killed or injured, for a purpose of which he was clearly doubtful.

"We may lose many spears, and the rescue may fail. I am not afraid, but I am wary. Is this the best way? How can it be?" Amir opened his hands, begging me to see reason.

"Each woman you rescue is one less monster you will have to fight," I said.

Amir was not a strong debater, but he was the leader. He could turn down my request. I had to use whatever authority I had, to get him to do this one thing. Because, after all my thinking, this was the only plan I had which might give us a chance against the Spawn. Last time around, generations ago, a woman from my era had helped the nomads to defeat the creatures and had been hailed as a goddess. Somebody in those cages must know more than I did. She might be able to give us gunpowder or some other decisive advantage. God knew that I could not do anything on my own.

"The goddess wills it," I said. "Amir, you must do it. You must. Heaven demands you rescue heaven's women."

Maybe I could have wheedled and told him how brave and clever he was. I was not a wheedler, though. And in his perverse way, he liked being set an impossible challenge to prove his worth.

"We will rescue the women." He bowed, and the matter was settled.

Persuading his warriors was difficult; Amir's leadership was not absolute. Old Harsis, ever cautious, wanted to veto the entire plan. I could hear their arguments from the other side of camp. Amir owned most of the band's horses and goats, and he offered many of them to win the support he needed. Captured women were usually lawful prizes, but I had made it clear these women were not to be molested. I hoped Amir had enough control over his men to enforce the order.

"So, you are making your move." Nergal had insinuated himself into my tent. "I thought you might try to conjure up a storm or summon demons to aid us. I did not expect you to coax Amir to a suicide mission."

"You know little of the ways of heaven," I said loftily.

"I know much of the ways of the wandering miracle workers. If they can claim credit for a child getting better or a drought ending, they eat well… Instead, you try to advise Amir on strategy. But what are you trying to gain?" He narrowed his eyes as though trying to make out my thoughts.

"You will understand in time," I said. "If you are as clever as you think."

"If you are as clever as you think, you will want to be my friend," Nergal shot back. "A woman without a man is in a perilous position. I do not know if Amir will support you after this raid—if he survives."

If Amir died, I would be at Nergal's mercy. I would deal with that if it came. I did not want to be any closer to him that I had to be.

"Your brother is honourable and brave," I said. "Also wise. Whereas you are merely cunning."

"I congratulate you on your improved grasp of Language. You express your meaning most clearly." He smiled and departed.

The nomads started training for the raid. They carried small round shields of goatskin, which I had not seen before, shields which were used for warfare.

The nomads were not disciplined, but they had some organisation. Amir issued orders by gesturing with his spear to advance, halt, and open or close formation, chivvying them about with a mix of insults and praise—"Igmil, are you deaf or just stupid?" and "Samu, your father would be so proud to see you today!"—and they gradually took to the battle plan. They practised their tactics for the raid for two days. Galloping around on their ponies, they threw javelins at imaginary enemies and rescued imaginary captives, while signalling to each other with waves and whoops. It was a curiously modern spectacle, like watching soldiers on manoeuvres.

The raid was carried out in late afternoon. The monsters were mainly seen abroad in the night or at twilight and tended to rest deep inside the caves in the heat of the day. I watched Amir ride off with fifty warriors, practically the whole of his force. Even Damki was amongst the party.

I was not allowed to take part, even to observe from a distance. It would be too much of a risk. I was not a good enough rider, and they needed every good horse they could get. The goddess might be a goddess, but she was not allowed to get in the way of military operations.

"So much bravery," Nergal said beside me. He had been given charge of defending the camp in Amir's absence. "Heaven will surely smile on them."

I spent the next few hours pacing around the camp. I could not sit still. I could not concentrate on my vocabulary; I could barely string a sentence together. My eyes were constantly drawn to the horizon, and I strained for the sound of hoofbeats or distant cries.

"I don't know how you stay so calm," I told Aruru.

She was working, scraping a goatskin. They did not tan hides but merely smoked them, which contributed much to the camp's foul smell. The dried goat dung which was the main fuel for their campfires contributed a different and hardly less unpleasant whiff of goat. I noticed it less and less as the days passed, though.

"It is always like this," she said, sounding almost sympathetic. "The men go; the women stay. We do not know who will come back. But whatever happens, we carry on."

"You're very brave," I said.

Aruru did not see herself as brave. Like all the women, she was stoic, accepting what life gave her, knowing no other world.

Nergal was scratching a pattern in the dirt with a stick with the abstracted air of one doodling. Perhaps he was more nervous than he let on.

"Were you not picked to join the raid?" I asked.

"We have a saying about not carrying all your eggs in one basket. It is not my choice."

If Amir died, Nergal would succeed to the leadership of the miserable remnant of the band. He did not want that responsibility, and in his own way, he loved his brother. He had been left back here, as helpless as me to affect matters. He was too distracted even to bother me.

Hours passed. I was forced to take my watch off and hide it under a cushion in my tent. I could not stand to keep looking at it. Then, after an interminable wait, there was shouting and barking from the edge of the camp. I could not see anything, but Nergal told me a smudge on the horizon was the dust of approaching horsemen.

We all gathered to meet them and cheer as they came. The riders sped up to a gallop for the last few furlongs. I could not count their number, but there were others amongst them wearing white or black or other colours—rescued captives. I recognised the figure in the lead by the sun glinting off his polished metal belts long before I could see Amir's face.

He galloped ahead of the others and jumped from the saddle to stand before his people. "Rejoice! We lost only two—Alshu and Ilsha fell in battle. Glory to them! The raid was successful, and we rescued many captives."

A woman started wailing at once. It was Ilsha's wife—his widow.

The action had gone as planned. The main body had ridden through the edge of the slaver's settlement at high speed, spearing at least three of them in the process. As the slavers started to rally and organise themselves, a smaller and much quieter group—led by Amir—had penetrated to the centre of the camp on foot and levered open as many of the cages as they could, only breaking off when monsters started out of their caves.

Some riders had been injured by sling stones. Alshu has been struck in the head and fallen from his horse. Amir had ridden back to save him, but Alshu was already dead. He had been reckoned the best archer in the band, able to hit a flying bird at fifty paces. Amir claimed that Alshu's arrow had killed the man who killed him. Perhaps a shield would have served him better than a bow.

Ilsha, one of the party on foot, had been caught by a monster which had emerged suddenly from a pool. He was dragged under the water before his companions could react. Ilsha was the one with the necklace of wolf teeth, a proud family heirloom for generations. Like Ilsha, the necklace was lost forever.

The mood of the returning riders was more of relief than joy in victory. When they were fighting their traditional opponents—the other tribes—they won glory for every enemy killed, and there was booty. There was no glory in fighting the Spawn. No enemies bested. No booty except what their leader gives them. Amir did his best to jolly them along, praising them all and distributing horses and goats, but the reaction was muted.

The warriors had carried out the raid out of respect and deference to their leader, and because they were bribed. Amir had done it out of respect and deference to me.

"We have rescued ten women," Amir said. "I should at least let the men have one of them."

"What?"

"It is not natural to take women and not even touch them," he said. "They are the only booty we have. When we take the dogs hunting, we let them have the entrails. The men are better than dogs. They deserve something."

"Those women are my handmaidens," I told him. This was a word I had gleaned from Aruru. The wives of great tribal chiefs had attendants. She had never seen one but thought it must be nice to have someone to do her work. "My sisters from heaven. I told you, none of them may be touched. You agreed."

"They are just women," he said. "Women without fathers or brothers or husbands. Like ownerless goats. Who can object to what happens to an ownerless goat?"

In the nomad way, a woman was protected by her father or her brothers, then by her husband. A woman with nobody to protect her was liable to be raped by any man who had the opportunity. Not that Language had a word for rape; the People just did not have the notion of female consent any more than they thought about game consenting to being killed. To Amir, it was the natural way.

I wanted to say that the women were people, living, feeling human beings, but Language did not allow that sort of subtlety. Women were not part of mankind and did not have rights. What Amir was saying was not just a statement of belief—it was a truth embedded in his language.

"You can choose which one to give them," he said.

"No. You must do what I say, or I will never help you. I will leave here. And you will never have your vengeance, Amir."

He tugged angrily at his beard. "It is not natural! Two of my spears died for this."

"You must not let your men molest those women."

I held his gaze and would not look away until he did.

"As the goddess wishes," Amir growled.

I hoped desperately that the raid would be worthwhile. My debt to Amir had multiplied, and I needed to repay it somehow.

Food and drink were laid out in my pavilion. As well as water and milk, and Aruru insisted on making a pot of their herbal infusion. The nomads did not drink it themselves, but it was essential for honouring visitors from heaven. It was not tea, but not unpleasant. A nearby tent was arranged with buckets of water for washing and fresh clothing. In another, I had set up an earth closet. The last thing I wanted was the newcomers wandering off outside the camp for their ablutions.

The women were led in, looking stunned and shell-shocked. Aruru and Puabi tended them, carrying trays as I had shown them, and the women soon began to thaw, gobbling down food and laughing nervously.

I had fervently hoped for someone from my own time and place, who had been taken as I had, someone I could talk to. The confused, broken chatter showed how vain that hope was. The place was a Babel. Everyone was trying to find someone they could talk to, but none of them could understand each other. Or practically none of them—two of the women were conversing in what might have been Arabic, but with questioning looks, showing that their mutual understanding was fragmentary.

I joined in the attempts at conversation. I guessed that many of them were Middle Eastern or Indian from their appearance. The catchment area for R'lyeh's net centred on this place, and there were fewer of us from more distant regions.

My first success was with Marie-Therese, who addressed me forthrightly in French. She was a small woman, lively and ferocious, suspicious of me at the start. I soon found out why: she had been snatched away in the 1850s, when the English were the enemy. Marie-Therese was a virulent Jacobin who had marched in the 1848 uprising. Bad though the English might be, here, we had a common enemy in the Spawn. She was willing to make peace, for the time being.

"*Alors,*" she said, and kissed me on both cheeks.

I told her what little I could of the place in my mediocre but correct French, and she nodded quickly.

"So you are the mistress of this Amir?" she asked. "The leader of the ones who rescued us, with the belt of metal discs on his chest?"

"Not mistress in that sense," I said, blushing to my roots. "He listens to me because he thinks I am a goddess."

"It's the same thing," she said.

"Have you been able to talk to any of the others?"

"Not a word. They are all"—she waved irritably—"barbarians."

As I met each new arrival, I tried out every language I knew in turn. Some talked back to me rapidly in languages I did not recognise, before I could convince them I could not make out a word.

Izabel was more of a surprise, a big-boned, broad-shouldered woman my own height. Her complexion was a warm brown, her hair was short and frizzy, and peculiar tattoos curled around one muscular arm. I assumed she was from some West African tribe, but I was on the wrong continent entirely.

"Do you speak English?" I asked hopefully.

"You are freaking kidding me," she said slowly. Her accent was curious—a mix, it turned out, of American and Portuguese—but I understood perfectly. Then she swore, in a mixture of languages. She was not swearing at me but in sheer disbelief at her situation.

"My name is Jessica," I said, extending a hand. "I'm from England. It's so good to meet you."

"Izabel. Brazil. Likewise."

I did not recognise the names of her home province or her city. Izabel's English was unlike anything I knew, full of strange expressions. Many words had different meanings entirely. Not quite the language of Shakespeare, but we could make ourselves understood with a little effort.

"This is crazy," she said. "You're from 1927? That's more than a hundred years ago."

Izabel was from the future. My future, at least. She had been born in the middle of twenty-first century. I was momentarily stunned, but it made as much sense as anything else. I had travelled thousands of years back in time, so there was no reason why Izabel could not come back an extra century or two. At least I had come to terms with my situation, but Izabel could not accept the reality of it all.

"This is a game," she kept repeating. "It is all a game. It's not real."

Where Izabel came from, a "game" was something like a manufactured, shared dream, one that millions of people took part in. In their games, they conjured fantastical worlds and inhabited them.

Izabel thought that she was trapped in one such dream world. As an explanation, it made as much sense as my version of events. I did not bother to argue with her.

Izabel and Marie-Therese were my two successes. Few of the others shared a language, either, although Izabel had a little Chinese and introduced me to Lu Zhu—a midwife-doctor. Again, I did not recognise the name of Lu Zhu's home city or province. I could only guess that she was from some time before Marco Polo, as she had never heard of Europe or America.

Most introductions were of the "Me Jessica. Who you?" variety, and after a fashion, we started to get to know each other. There was much ooh-ing and ah-ing over each other's clothes, the different fabrics and weaves, not to mention fussing over each other's hairstyles. It was all terribly friendly, if rather too tactile. I was forced to let the others try my glasses, twitching in case my one pair would be broken. They all laughed and passed them around, showing each other how strange my eyes were. Fortunately, the spectacles were returned intact, if somewhat smudged.

I managed to place one other of the women. Timi wore the remnant of a long dress that made me think of Holbein portraits, and she seemed less like a frightened captive than a traveller trying to get her bearings. She understood better than the others the need to use simple words slowly to establish communications. When I tried Latin, she smiled sadly and said haltingly:

"Linguam latine! Sed ego… non loqui… non latine loqui." She had just enough Latin to say that she did not speak Latin. We had the same experience in reverse when she addressed me in recognisable German.

"Nein," I said. I spoke only enough German to say I could not speak it. *"Nein spreche Deutsch."*

"Nein?" Her face fell again. *"Ach du scheisse,"* she said ruefully, and we both laughed.

She touched her chest and said "Ungarn" and "Magyar" several times, and I guessed she was from Hungary, or what would one day be

Hungary. When I said "Budapest" and "Danube" slowly, she beamed and came back with "Buda" and "Duna," making a boxlike house movement to indicate a city for one and snakelike motion to signify a river for the other.

When I said "Englishe," she nodded vigorously and pointed to a sheepskin rug. *"Ja, Englishe—Londun!"*

I smiled and nodded. In her day, England was known for its wool trade. Unfortunately, I could not think of anything to say about Hungary. I smiled more and shrugged, and so did she.

Rachel was from one of the tribes of Israel. I recognised the knotted tassels on her sleeves; Daniel had once explained the topology of the knots and their numerological significance. We could share the names of some of the patriarchs—Noah, Moses, Abraham—and she nodded when I sketched a Shield of David symbol in the ground, but there was no communication.

Without any clues of language to go on, I was forced to judge by dress and physical appearance. None of the others looked modern. One of them, pale-skinned Illi, was wearing only skins, suggesting a society even less advanced than the nomads. I immediately identified Lalit as an Indian princess, which eventually proved to be quite accurate. She would have won the best-dressed award, being clad in gorgeous, if somewhat immodest, silks, with jewelled armbands, rings, and anklets. Most of the others looked Middle Eastern—with the notable exceptions of Lu Zhu, who was apparently Chinese, and Inzalu, who was surely Burmese or Malay.

"What strange names they all have." Aruru laughed with her sister.

Being imprisoned together had given the women something in common. They were working out where they had all been held, in relation to one another and carrying out conversations in mime. Eventually, I decided that it was time to bring things to order. I banged on a pot with a ladle and addressed the assembled group.

I did my best to indicate by gestures that this was a safe place for them. There would be food and water, and they could sleep unmolested, but it was best for them not to go outside. They looked at me in various states of confusion. I might as well have waved my arms about and uttered a ritual blessing, which some of them appeared to think I was doing. Organising them was going to be harder work than I'd thought.

"Please help me," I said to Izabel, and to Marie-Therese, I translated, "*Aidez-moi, je vous prie.*"

They both nodded, and for the first time since my arrival, I felt I was not alone.

CHAPTER SIX: HANDMAIDENS TO THE GODDESS

A WEEK AFTER THE HANDMAIDENS were rescued, I woke to barking dogs. Often, a few of them sounded off when a wildcat, wolf, or some other nocturnal prowler came close to the camp to scavenge bones or scraps, but this was different. Every dog in the camp was barking at the top of its lungs, as though their vocal power alone could drive back danger.

Amir came in a moment later, face grim. "Get up."

I was already on my feet.

"We must go. We must all go, right now. They are raiding us."

"Who are?" I asked, but I knew already.

The other women looked about, confused. With help from Marie-Therese and Izabel, I shooed them out. There was no time to collect our things, and we were herded off with the rest of the women and children while men on foot or horseback whirled around in the dark. There was a sliver of moon aloft, just enough to tell the contours of the ground, but details were drowned in the murk.

"This way! This way!" a mounted man shouted. It was Igmil, I think—and we changed direction to follow him.

"Quickly, quickly!" he urged.

Something appeared out of a depression to our left fifty paces away, and for a moment, I saw it silhouetted against the pale skyline, a writhing shape which was neither horse nor man.

"Go, go!" Young Harsis shouted, riding between us and the Spawn. He approached as close as his horse would allow, flung a javelin, then galloped off.

We hurried on. Far behind us, shouting men were waving torches. We half ran, half walked, trying to keep together. Eventually, we reached a stand of trees, a landmark on the plains, where others were waiting.

More and more people arrived at the rendezvous, family groups coming from all directions. We were missing several people some hours later, but as they sky grew light, the stragglers joined us. Amir was one of the last. He'd stayed at the camp until he was sure everyone was out and safely away, then harried the monsters with some of his men as best he could. If he could not kill them, at least he could get some satisfaction from hurting them.

We returned to the camp after dawn. It looked as though steamrollers had been driven through it. There was little on the way of systematic destruction, but the Spawn had ferreted out every bit of dried meat and even devoured some of the newer goatskins. The damage to tents and other property was incidental.

"They are moving outwards," Amir said. "Their raiding parties are bigger, and they range farther every week. This time, there were twelve in the main group and six more placed to ambush us. I do not have enough men to follow all of them. Heaven must help us." He looked at me expectantly.

"The handmaidens are still learning to speak," I said. "But their wisdom will soon be yours."

Amir tugged his beard. He did not want wisdom. He wanted magic spears of fire to kill the Spawn and recompense for his dead warriors.

"Some of the handmaidens are most beautiful," Nergal said. "If we gave three of them to Izzar, our tribal-chief, he would lend us a good number of warriors. Izzar likes pretty women."

"My sisters are not commodities to be traded." I might as well have said that goats or antelope skins were not commodities for all the sense that the sentence made in Language.

Being able to communicate with them, one in French and one in English, made Marie-Therese and Izabel my closest friends. Aruru and Puabi were helpful, but there were so many things I could not begin to express in Language, and they understood so little. With Izabel and Marie-Therese, sometimes just a word and a facial expression were all that was needed.

It helped that Marie-Therese was the most dynamic person I ever met. She was a compact ball of energy, never hurried, but always active. And nothing stood in her way. Marie-Therese was an organiser, and in spite of her small stature, she was able to command others through sheer force of personality. When she wanted something, she marched up to the nomad warriors and ordered them about; if they did not understand, she pushed them aside to get what she wanted herself.

Izabel was more relaxed, too relaxed for Marie-Therese's liking. The Frenchwoman was always up and about, learning and teaching, organising and beautifying our quarters. Izabel preferred to spend long hours lying in bed. Vana had brought some puppies into our tent—the nomads always kept their dogs outside the camp, but Vana felt safer with dogs around—and they would arrange themselves around Izabel, the one who slept longest. But she was far from lazy. Marie-Therese had speed; Izabel had momentum. Her strength and stamina were considerable. Mainly, I was glad to have friends whom I could confide in and share my worries with.

"I keep thinking that I should be able to show the nomads something amazing," I told Marie-Therese. "So they can defeat the creatures. But in reality, they know so much more about their world and their way of fighting than I do."

The nomads were perfectly adapted to their existence. Though materially poor, they had everything they needed for their lives. Over the next three millennia or so, great civilisations would rise around them—and then fall. Mighty cities would be raised and crumble back into the earth while the nomads endured. In my own time, there were still nomads on the margins of Europe still eking out the same sort of existence as Amir's bands. And when our civilisation destroyed itself with tanks and aeroplanes dropping poison gas, the nomads would doubtless come down from the hills and drive their goats through the ruins once more.

"We can't offer them anything," I finished.

"Of course we can. Look at them. The women are stupid and ugly. Yes, they are—you cannot deny it! They are stupid because they have never been educated. Their brains are empty. They are ugly because nobody has taught them to be beautiful, which is an art." Marie-Therese tucked an errant strand of hair back in place. She might have been in the Bronze Age, but her coiffure was impeccable. "We can teach them to be real women."

"I meant, offer them something to help fight the creatures."

"Fighting is easy," Marie-Therese said. "It is organisation which is difficult."

"They are organised, in their way."

"*Ils ont sauvages,*" Marie-Therese said. *They are savages.* She believed that nineteenth-century France had plenty to teach the nomads. "They are not soldiers. They can't even cook a goat properly."

Perhaps she was right. The previous goddess achieved much of her success through rallying the tribes, not teaching them to build steam engines.

Izabel's reaction was different. "They're good at what they do," she said. "They're adapted to their environment. But they don't know jack about fighting alien monsters."

"I don't know much about it, either," I said.

"You've got ideas," she said. "And between us, we'll have more ideas."

"Also, Izabel—do you know anything about time travel?"

"Me?" She snorted. "I don't know about *anything*."

"In my era, it's just a theory... but what bothers me is this. Can we change the past? There is no record of these creatures ever existing, so does that mean they are fated to die out, and we don't need to worry about them? Or could they spread and conquer the world? And what if we change the past—will we ourselves cease to exist? Or..."

She smiled and shook her head. "Crazy science fiction stuff. I told you—I don't know anything. The way I see it, this is an invasion through time. They are trying to change the past, and if they do... they win. I don't know."

"You don't think it's predestined that they will be defeated?"

"Uh-huh." Izabel shook her head. "We've got to do something."

"But what help can we give?"

"We'll put our heads together and think," she said. "I'm taking it one day at a time until I can get my head around this place."

"Still figuring out how the game works?" I said playfully.

"Something like that."

While I could talk easily enough with Izabel and Marie-Therese, and even carry out three-way conversations as I translated between English and French, communication with the others was frustrating at first. The situation for them was as it had been for me: their need to learn Language was paramount.

At least I knew how the group could learn together. There was a famous story of how a man called Berlitz was forced to employ a French language teacher who knew no English. Berlitz fell ill and left the man in charge of a class to communicate with them as best he could with gestures and mime. After six weeks, Berlitz returned and was astonished to find that the class had learned more French, and spoke it far more fluently, than other classes taught by bilingual teachers. He resolved that all his teachers would use the same technique in the future.

The Berlitz method was still too avant-garde for our schools. I had no alternative, though, and with the aid of Amir's sisters and anyone else we could rope in, I set up the world's first Berlitz language class. Some of the women were already fluent in more than one language. Timi, the Magyar, had acted as translator for her father's business and had picked up several trade languages. She raced ahead of the rest— she was soon correcting my grammar—and acted as a teacher and translator.

The women, bewildered and shy at first, soon began to emerge as personalities. I expected them to be traumatised after their ordeal and finding themselves in this strange, alien world, but they all proved to be resilient. They were young, healthy, and in a place of safety. Within a few days, we were laughing together like a class of fourth-formers. Even Puabi and Aruru, who had been rather stony-faced with me, laughed just as freely as the rest of the group.

In the process, we extended Language considerably. Whatever its strengths in other ways, the nomad speech was impoverished when it came to expressing many things, not the least emotions. Heartache, longing, grief, and many of the other things, we needed to convey. We ended up speaking a hybrid slang with loanwords from other languages. Inevitably, it was far easier communicating amongst ourselves than with the native speakers, but it was such a blessing to speak easily with people whose minds extended beyond grasslands and goat husbandry.

Despite everything we had been through, or perhaps because of it, we formed our own little society, much to the bemusement of the nomads. The band could not afford to have ten more useless mouths to feed, and I was determined that the women should be seen as drones. Everyone must earn their keep, so lessons were conducted while baking, grinding seeds for oil, pounding grains, churning milk, collecting dung, or carrying out other domestic tasks. If we all pulled our weight, then we might escape the resentment of the nomads. We might not be able to give them steam engines, but we could share in the work and perhaps make things better.

I divided the day into a series of one-hour lessons with breaks for meals and recreation. Marie-Therese and Izabel helped me keep the others to timetable, as mystifying as they found it at first. Pre-modern people did not have the same idea of fixed hours, and they never grasped why I checked my wrist before issuing instructions.

Tackling domestic chores was predictably hilarious. Most of the women were already familiar with most of the tasks, with some exceptions. Lalit, our Indian princess, initially held herself aloof, as though she were too good for this sort of thing. An hour after we started making pottery, though, she had quietly joined in, because she did not want to be left out of the fun. For a princess, she was surprisingly capable.

Being from the middle classes in the twentieth century, I had never needed to learn the skills that most of the others had grown up with. It seemed like I was the only one who had never milked a goat or something like it.

Our pots would have been hopeless, in spite of Aruru's halting efforts to demonstrate how it was done, except that Noora, a dark-eyed Moslem, turned out to be something of an expert. Her village was known for its potteries. Working with strong fingers and as if instructing rather slow apprentices, Noora patiently showed us how to roll out clay into a long cylinder and coil it into a pot, layer by layer, making a perfect cylinder. Even Aruru was impressed.

Izabel lacked all domestic talents but made up for it with sheer power and persistence. When it came to digging clay or carrying leathern buckets of water on a yoke, she was indefatigable.

"Muscles not brains, right?" she said in English while she was grinding grain, which was more like grass seed, into flour with two flat stones.

"I didn't say—"

"Joke!" she said, grinning at my confusion. "I'm like you. I've got skills these people couldn't begin to understand. Just nothing that works in the Stone Age."

"I know what you mean," I said.

When others stopped for breaks, Izabel kept on working with a tenacity that verged on frightening. She was pounding the grain as though she hated it.

"Bet you wish you had some muscles now, huh?"

"I'm not that feeble," I said, though in truth, I was less sturdy than the nomad women, hardened by a lifetime of endless physical labour.

Inzalu, the smiling Malay girl, showed us how to weave broad-brimmed straw hats against the sun, though I could never match the speed of her nimble fingers. My hats looked decidedly rustic, but West End shops could have sold hers as ladies' summer wear. The hats were comfortable and absolutely essential for the noon-day heat. The children liked them and enjoyed unravelling the hats to see how they were made, gazing in wonder when they were left with just straw.

I was sure everyone would have some particular skills or knowledge from their own culture. It was impossible to tell what century most of them came from, but they were surely thousands of years ahead of the nomads.

Marie-Therese had grown up on a farm and was determined to show everyone how to do everything properly—the French way. She went to great lengths to make goat-milk butter and goat-milk cheese.

"Butter keeps longer than yoghurt," I told Amir after this achievement. "We can store it for months."

"It tastes strange," Amir said. "I'd rather eat yoghurt when we have it and go without when there is none. As we have always done. We don't need anything we can't carry."

I did not argue. I could see the use of food which lasted longer. I would have preferred guns to butter, but there was no gunsmith's daughter amongst the handmaidens.

The nomads had their own fermented drink, a repulsive cloudy concoction I had only tasted once. It was technically beer, being made of barley, but to me, it was closer to porridge. Izabel was the only one hardy enough to drink it. Vana, whose home was somewhere in North Africa, came from a baking and brewing family. The nomads knew only how to make flatbread, but Vana conjured up proper loaves similar to sourdough. And she steadily improved on the nomads' vile beer. The only problem with Vana was her impish sense of humour.

"Try this," she said, and I swallowed a mouthful of something spiked with vinegar or some other concoction while Vana cackled like a witch at the faces I made.

"How dare you? My palate is sacred!" Marie-Therese told her angrily, spitting out Vana's latest prank, which only made it funnier to Vana.

When Vana produced the real thing, a fine pale ale, I was more than willing to forgive her tricks. It had been a long time since I had enjoyed a proper drink. Beer was hardly my tipple, but it reminded me of home, of motor-trips to country pubs when Sophia and I would scandalise the locals by drinking pints. Those golden days were far, far away now, but the taste was as evocative as any madeleine.

"It's stronger than the nomad beer, isn't it?" I asked.

"Much stronger!" Vana said, laughing heartily. "They make goat's piss. This is real beer."

"Learn to make wine," Marie-Therese grumbled.

Izabel's failure in the domestic arts was one thing, but I was crushed when I found that she had no scientific knowledge of gunpowder, engineering, or anything else.

"What about your education? Don't they teach girls science?"

Izabel shrugged. "Education isn't learning facts. It's about understanding."

"Understanding what?"

"I don't know! I never paid much attention."

What appalled me was that the woman of the future had no better education than me. She did not know anything about chemistry, engineering, or anything practical. In her world, anyone who wanted that sort of information could find it instantly—one had only to ask a question, and a mechanical voice from a loudspeaker provided the answer. The rote-learning of my schooldays had disappeared from her world. Severed from this fount of all knowledge, Izabel was as ignorant and helpless as the pampered aristocratic ladies whose end at the guillotine Marie-Therese gloated over.

Izabel exercised every morning, after bending and stretching. She did high kicks and used stones for weights to maintain her muscles. The nomads viewed the activity as only slightly more eccentric than Noora's bowing to Mecca five times each day. In my era, muscles on women were not in fashion; for clothes to fit properly, the more boyish one looked, the better. But, as our little group showed, standards of beauty changed over the centuries.

Marie-Therese, by contrast, was endlessly practical, as well as impeccably dressed. She was the girl at school whose handwriting was always neater than the others', whose stitching was straighter, and whose work always won the teacher's praise. Her only flaw was that she saw everybody else's way of doing things not just as interestingly different, but in need of correction.

"We must not act superior to the others just because we are white Europeans," I told Marie-Therese. "They have their knowledge too."

"Our skin has nothing to do with it. It is because we are thousands of years more advanced," she said. "And yes, you may be from the twentieth century, but you are *bourgeois*, and you know nothing about real work."

I would have joked about France being the birthplace of chauvinism, but she would not have appreciated it. Marie-Therese tried my patience sometimes, but it was easy to forgive her because she was such a source of useful ideas.

"If only we could write things down," I complained one day. My notebook had long since been overfilled with tiny script, the first dictionary of the nomad language, packed with attempts to record grammar and declensions. "My head is fairly bursting with trying to remember everything."

"You are right," Marie-Therese said. "We should record everything."

"Except that we have no pens, no paper, nor parchment or papyrus—even the traders don't seem to understand! Unless someone here knows how to make paper?" I asked hopefully.

"Why not use clay tablets?" she said. "We have plenty of clay, don't we?"

My jaw actually dropped. I had been here for months, and it had not even occurred to me to use the materials we had to hand. Noora, who could make beautiful vases, mugs, jugs, and plates, could easily produce flat, rectangular tablets.

Our first writing tablets were crude, and it took a while to find how to scratch marks on them that remained legible. The Roman alphabet was not well-suited to this medium, and except for my own personal notes, it would not have made sense to write in English, anyhow. What we needed was a written version of Language and a new alphabet to write it in. We invented a kind of cuneiform, all *V*'s and *N*'s and *W*'s. it was a simplified, abbreviated form of the spoken language, but quick enough to write in clay. I soon developed strong fingers from the exercise of scratching out letters with a wooden stylus.

Amir had seen me writing in my notebook, but clay tablets were less surprising. He said that they had them in the cities far to the north. The cities were called things like Stone, River, and Hill. Amir did not know how many there were or who their rulers were. His only experience with them had been through traders and occasional military expeditions sent out to pacify the tribes.

I was not the only one to be distressed by the nomad's lack of soap, but at least four of the women had recipes to make it. Soap, I discovered, could be made from animal fat and ashes. The results were less than ideal, but infinitely better than no soap at all. In addition, I learned how to brush my teeth with the right sort of twig, which was a great improvement. The nomads thought us highly peculiar, but I was much less self-conscious in a group.

It lightened the mood having happier souls around than the nomad women. Young Inzalu la-la-la-ed through the camp, a flower tucked behind her ear, as if she didn't have a care in the world. Vana's braying laugh could be heard from the far side of the camp, and I had to smile in sympathy. Others, though, were prone to dark moods. Marie-Therese had periodic temper tantrums when someone crossed her, and she was not the only one.

I did my poor best to cheer things along. I had never been the jolly-hockey-sticks, let's-all-get-along sort, but now, I pretended to be one. I was head girl at school again, having to comfort the homesick ones and provide practical advice for bewildered newcomers. And I dealt with the spats and jealousies that cropped up with tedious frequency, even among supposedly grown women.

After the first few weeks, once we could all talk properly to each other, things became trickier. I explained my role as protectress and that our survival relied on all sticking together, but there were lapses.

They expected me to know everything, and I did my best to help. Noora wanted to know where Mecca was for her prayers. Mountains lined the northern horizon, and the coast south of us ran approximately from northwest to southeast.

That narrowed down our location. It might have been the coast of Italy or Dalmatia, but the terrain was wrong. It might also have been on the Black Sea, Western Turkey, or on the coast of what would one day be Persia. I took an average and pointed Noora towards the southwest. The Prophet would not be born for some centuries to come… but given that my own religion came from somewhere in the future, I was not going to argue.

Finding silk thread to fix Lalit's skirt was impossible, but there was always something, even if invisible mending was out of the question.

"We must all just learn to get along," was a phrase I found myself saying repeatedly, until I sounded like a broken record.

Much of the trouble revolved around Lalit, who had an unmatched ability to irritate everyone with endless talk of her cousin, who had a palace by the sea, and her uncle, who had twelve trained elephants, and her other cousin, who had flower gardens which stretched for miles, and many more. Her tendency to order the rest of us around as though we were servants gave us something to laugh at, though not everyone took it well.

Things came to a head when Lalit, reclining on the pile of goatskins she had amassed, called for a jug of water. Inzalu, eager to please, would have complied, but Izabel was there first. She hefted the jug, a dangerous gleam in her eye.

"You want water?"

Lalit held up her hands to shield herself from the anticipated torrent.

"Don't you dare," I said. "Izabel!"

Izabel turned and emptied the jug onto the ground. Lalit was only lightly spattered. Two of Vana's dogs, which had been curled up nearby, leaped up and started barking.

"Hush," Vana said, raising a hand, and the dogs obediently sat down again. I envied her how easily she controlled her charges.

"Jug's empty," Izabel said, dropping it. "You'll have to go to the stream to get some more."

"You're black, and you're ugly," Lalit spat at Izabel.

"Izabel," I said, seeing her balled fist. "Don't rise to it."

Izabel took a deep breath.

"Fine," she said, stalking out.

"The black one has such a bad temper," Lalit said.

"Her people used to be slaves, if you can imagine that," Marie-Therese said. There was something rather pointed about the way she spoke to Lalit. "She does not like to hear you ordering people about."

Lalit turned away but did not answer back. I went after Izabel.

"You should never let her make you feel inferior because of the colour of your skin," I said later.

"Right," Izabel said, and I could hear her teeth grinding. "I'll remember that."

I knew I had offended her awfully in my attempt to smooth things over. I did not understand the nuances of twenty-second-century views of race. Instead of digging myself in further, I tried to make light of the situation. "More importantly, if you kill Lalit, there won't be any pudding for you for a week."

"Oh, I'd better behave then." She smiled though, like a tolerant older sister willing to forgive her junior's ignorance.

Marie-Therese came up with an ever-growing list of items for Turm to make, compiled from suggestions from the handmaidens. They wanted everything from hair clips and shears to heavy-based cooking pots and stirrups, and of course a complete set of medical instruments for Lu Zhu. They would certainly tax Turm's skill, but I sourly noted the lack of actual weapons on the list. I instructed him to make any weapons Amir needed first, but he always seemed to find time to tinker at Marie-Therese's ideas. He was intensely curious about every new thing we suggested. Explanations were tricky, so Marie-Therese made clay models to show Turm what the finished article should look like. He handled these carefully and reverently in his big hands, working long hours to satisfy all our demands.

Marie-Therese was determined to push Turm to his limits. Her uncle had made his own brandy, and she instructed Turm to make copper pipes and distilling vessels so we could make our own spirits. I had allowed him to continue this frustrating challenge, even though tubing was something new to him, partly because he was developing new techniques in the process and partly because I thought alcohol might be useful for cleaning wounds and perhaps as an incendiary weapon.

As the women gained fluency in Language, we were able to discuss how we had come to be here. The elements were arranged differently in each case, but all were fundamentally similar. Each of us had a brush with something supernatural or demonic immediately before falling down that shaft and ending up in the pool.

Izabel's brother had been involved in a religion called Candomblé, Brazilian voodoo. He had invited her to a ceremony, and at the climax, an earthquake had struck and the ground swallowed her. Lu Zhu had been called to a house infested with bad spirits; she went into the cellar, where the floor disappeared beneath her. Marie-Therese had been exploring hill caves where Royalist counter-revolutionaries were supposed to be hiding out. Instead, she had found the underground shrine of a bizarre sect. Rachel, the Jewish girl, was the exception: she would not give details, but like me, she had been involved in a deliberate confrontation with the forces of R'lyeh.

All of their stories involved a place that was supposed to be haunted or cursed, places where outside forces broke through into our world, like the church at Dulwich, which George had said was the site of a pagan temple. Like a cosmic telephone operator, something kept switching from one to another, opening the line briefly before cutting the connection again for another century.

We were the lucky ones. Some women had not survived the fall, and their dead bodies had been carried from the pool and thrown to the growing Spawn as food. Others had been injured and died later. Some had been killed by the slavers while trying to escape. Many had gone mad and either died or killed themselves.

"Breeding stock. That's all we were to them," Marie-Therese said, surveying our companions. "Young healthy females."

"But why women from the future? Why not nomad women?"

"Who can say? Some mad, devilish reason."

The captive women had not been molested, at least not in the normal sense. The slavers had not shown any interest in them except as captive animals to be fed, watered, and mucked out. But if there had been no physical abuse, there was a psychic torment. They had been assaulted in their dreams and had suffered terrible nightmares. I never heard any of them describe the content of these nightmares, except what Marie-Therese told me once.

"*Incube*," she said. "A demon that comes into your bed at night."

Incubus, I thought. The medieval devils that lay with women and begot demonic children.

Later Lu Zhu told me that several of the women had confided in her about their condition. She said they were not with child in the normal way so much as growing a tumour inside their wombs. She had few resources here but was able to identify and gather some of the local herbs with a little assistance from Ili and the nomad midwife who was the authority on herbal lore. After experimenting with several remedies, she found that the tumours were not as tenacious as she'd feared. With the right treatment, they could be dislodged, like aborting a foetus. One by one, the handmaidens were freed from the monstrous things they were carrying.

While I might have preferred a group of English women from my own era, perhaps there were advantages to having the breadth of knowledge that we possessed between us. Each woman carried the seeds of a whole culture. We were a sort of female League of Nations, of all different languages, colours, and religions. My fond hope was that these differences should be enough to smooth out any individual extremes and give us an ensemble with the skills for any challenge.

We shared something about world history. I could tell Marie-Therese that in my time, France was still a great power, still had her colonial possessions, and was a staunch ally of Britain. Izabel was less reassuring about the future of both our countries. She had heard of neither the British Empire nor the French Empire. As far as she was concerned, Europe was one homogenous entity. She had heard of

Paris and London—the Eiffel Tower and London Bridge were still tourist attractions—but knew nothing of history.

"Do women in your country have the vote?" I asked.

"Huh?" she said. "Why bother? Politicians are all the same."

"But do you have female politicians?"

"Sure. Half the congress are women. So's the president. So what? Male, female, black, white, natural, or new—they're all the same. They don't care about us."

The vote that I so prized, that my mother had struggled so hard to win, was useless as far as Izabel was concerned a hundred and fifty years later. She did not know what the major political parties of her time stood for and was equally hazy on world politics.

One night, the camp was disturbed by screams: one of the nomad women was giving birth. This was the third birth since I had been there; a ridiculous proportion of the nomad women were pregnant at any given time. Family planning was non-existent, and the women were expected to just keep having children. This time, she sounded bad, though.

Lu Zhu was agitated and wanted to go to the woman in labour. In the heat of the moment, her grasp of Language failed, and she switched to her native tongue.

"This is her responsibility, her duty," Izabel said, translating for her. "That woman needs her help."

I was not in favour of interference. The last thing I wanted to do was to annoy the nomads or upset a woman in labour by having some strange foreign witch intrude on her. And if the child died, which was all too likely, she would most certainly be blamed for the death. But Lu Zhu was insistent, and the noise was terrible. Also, Lu Zhu radiated the right sort of quiet confidence.

I had Damki fetch Amir and explained the situation. The suffering woman was Ninsa—Young Harsis's wife. The husband was, however, nowhere to be seen. The female members of the family were gathered round, wringing their hands, while the poor expectant mother writhed on goatskin matting. The old woman who was supposed to be the band's midwife instantly made way for Lu Zhu, practically shoving her forwards and scuttling out of the way. Lu Zhu kneeled by the woman, speaking softly in Chinese. The whole family seemed to understand help was at hand.

Whatever era she was from, Lu Zhu was probably much more at home in this place and better able to use the resources at hand than a modern English doctor would have been. Certainly, she knew the business far better than the nomad women.

By the end of the evening, Lu Zhu had delivered two baby boys, both very much alive and kicking. Twins were unusual here, and the midwife seemed astonished that both of them survived. Ninsa herself survived the ordeal, also against expectation. The family was hugely grateful, even Young Harsis, when he showed up. Amir was as pleased as if he had delivered the children himself, and the handmaidens crowded round to lavish halting praise on Lu Zhu.

"Now we are even," Marie-Therese said with satisfaction. "We cost the nomads two lives, and we have given them two."

I doubted Amir would see it that way. They did not value women and children as they valued warriors. But it made me wish I had studied to be a doctor, an engineer, a chemist, or anything that might actually be useful.

Chapter Seven: Memories of the Future

In those six weeks or so while the handmaidens learned to speak Language and to make themselves useful, I made sure there was time for recreation. Picnics, guarded by the faithful Damki at discreet distance, proved very popular. Festive outdoor meals must be universal to all human cultures, and being able to get out into the countryside, away from the encampment and its smells, always felt like a liberation. The women chatted freely and loudly—much of it gossip about our hosts and their strange ways.

Inevitably, they compared notes on which of the warriors was the best looking. The front runners were usually Young Harsis and the dashing Igmil. If Young Harsis was Little John, Igmil was Will Scarlet, perhaps a bit of a show-off, but more gallant than the others and undeniably handsome. When Amir was mentioned, it was usually with a sidelong glance at me.

Izabel rarely joined in this talk. Once, after hearing Vana praising on of the warriors, Izabel abruptly turned on her. "You know what these handsome men do when they find a woman from another tribe?"

Vana shrugged, bewildered.

"They take it in turns to rape her," Izabel said. "When they've finished, they put a spear through her. Ask Aruru. That's how romantic your men are."

"Only women from enemy tribes," Aruru said. "Not our women."

"You mean they only rape women like us," Izabel said.

"No, not Damki," Inzalu said, looking towards our young guard. He had picked the flower she wore behind her ear.

"Maybe not him yet. Maybe next year," Izabel said. "They'll take Damki on a raid, and he can prove what a man he is."

"They are a primitive people," Marie-Therese said. "This is a savage land. Men are strong, so women have to be clever."

Izabel turned her back, muttering to herself. I could sympathise with her, but the others found her strange. Izabel's ideas were too advanced for the time she was living in; at home I was quite the radical, but she made me feel conservative.

There was, of course, a good deal of gossip and talk about our homes. Food and family were two of the commonest topics of conversation, narrowly ahead of passing comments on the nomads. Everyone missed their home comforts, and for some, the diet was very alien. Izabel, a lifelong vegetarian repelled by the thought of eating meat, took some time to be reconciled to a carnivorous diet. Others fretted whether it was in accordance with their dietary rules. The simple effect of having eleven of us, all in the same boat and all forced to each strange food, provided some reassurance.

Boys and men at home formed no small part of the conversation. Some of the others were betrothed. For some reason, I mentioned that I had a fiancé. It was simpler than explaining my actual relationship with William.

"Is he handsome?" Inzalu asked.

"More handsome even than Amir?" Vana asked.

"Very different to Amir," I said. "But just as good-looking. And rather taller."

"Ah," Vana said, smiling knowingly. "Is he bigger than Amir in every way?"

This triggered a burst of giggles and started the women on a rather indecent route of discussion. Afterwards, Inzalu persisted with her questioning. "Is your William more attractive than Amir?"

"He is to me. But the two are very different." Of course Amir was physically brave, and nobody could ride a horse or handle a spear better. But he was still illiterate. His mind travelled well-worn paths of fighting, hunting, eating, and little else. Whereas William lived in an infinite universe and could chat equally easily about Epstein, Einstein, and Gertrude Stein—and more unusually for a man, he listened to what I had to say about them too.

Amir was undoubtedly tougher, and some of the women probably found that attractive. But William knew more of gentleness.

"How you sigh for him," Inzalu said.

"Poor Amir," Vana said. "Maybe I could console him?" She fluttered her eyelids, eliciting more giggles.

Whoever had decided that romantic love was an invention of the European eighteenth century was well wide of the mark. But then I don't suppose he'd spent much time listening to groups of young women.

We learned something about each other's homelands, though some found it easier to describe than others. I had a fairly good notion of Renaissance Buda from Timi, but I struggled to find the vocabulary to tell her about modern London, with its trams, buses, and pea-soupers. Illi also found it difficult to describe her own home.

"It's a lot like this," she said, nodding at the grassland. "But not nearly so hot. We have snow in winter. The sunlight is different. There are far more trees instead of grass. And the animals and birds and plants are not the same as here. But it's like this."

Izabel shocked the others by saying that in her country equal rights were universal. There were no longer men's jobs and women's jobs.

There was no difference between men and women in any sphere of life.

"There is always one big difference," Marie-Therese insisted.

"Not really," Izabel said. She explained that men and women took lovers from either sex. None of the others was convinced that this could possibly be true. "And, you know, people can change from being male to female or female to male, if they want to," she said. "Nobody thinks it's that important."

"Now you're just making fun of us," Inzalu said, laughing.

"I would like to live where women can do men's jobs," Timi said later over needlework.

"The men only hunt and fight," Inzalu said. "I don't want to do that."

"There are plenty of other jobs besides hunting and fighting," Timi said. "Like making things and trading."

"Women always do the important work," Marie-Therese said.

"You couldn't eat without the men," Aruru said, shocked by Marie-Therese's attitude. The nomad women had been brought up from birth to see men as the lordly providers of all things good with women inferior in every way.

"I have been watching the food the men bring back each day and comparing it to the weight of the goats and kids we slaughter," Marie-Therese said. "The men make a lot of noise, but at least two-thirds of what we eat comes from women's work. And if the herds were secure, you could easily keep twice as many goats, and we wouldn't need men at all."

"We'd have a surplus of milk and meat we could sell," Timi added.

"But we still need the men—to keep the goats safe from raiders and from the Spawn," Aruru said, amused by Marie-Therese's simplicity. "It all depends on them, you see. You can't do without men."

"Perhaps," Marie-Therese said.

Some of the women might not have been looking beyond the sort of domestic existence they had known before. But some, like Timi and

Marie-Therese, were thinking of the possibilities of this new world. Timi, the daughter of the house, would never get to play a role in her father's business, even though she knew far more than her brother.

Illi, whose tribe lived like the nomads without permanent buildings, was not skilled but learned quickly. Besides, she was a capable huntress; being able to bring back food was a talent universally valued. She could catch a bird in her bare hands and wring its neck before it even saw her.

Illi showed us how to make snares and would go out after dawn then return with a bounty of hares and partridges. Other times, she would bring back bird eggs, and once, even a dripping honeycomb, achingly sweet after so long without sugar.

"You haven't got one damn sting on you," Izabel said. "I'd get ten stings if I even went near a bee's nest. How do you do that, girl?"

But, as with all her feats, Illi would never say anything. She only smiled and looked away. Her skills were too deeply ingrained, learned in her earliest childhood, for her to be able to explain any of it. She probably thought the rest of us were lumbering clowns because we could not do as she did.

Some of the older nomad girls started following Illi around to find out how she brought back so much game. After a while, a small gang of girl scouts were learning her skills and bringing back extra meat for the family pot.

Another day, Illi presented me with a kind of feathered shawl made from the plumage of game birds strung together. "You should have this," she said, so quietly I had to lean forwards to catch her words. "Leaders wear them."

"It's lovely, but Amir is the leader," I said. "I'm just his advisor."

Illi simply smiled, shaking her head as she slipped away

I could not keep Illi confined. The others could be persuaded, but from the beginning, she would slip out, at any time in the day or night, and be gone for hours. I tried to explain to her how dangerous it was, that some of the nomad men might take advantage of a lone woman and that the creatures, as well as wild animals, could be anywhere. She always smiled and went anyway. Certainly, she had an uncanny knack for sensing danger and moving unseen and unheard. Aruru and Puabi called her "ghost woman" and were scared of Illi. I was always terrified she would come to some misfortune. None of the other women was as bold.

I was not quite last in the domestic stakes, though. That honour went to Izabel. Even Lalit, once she chose to join in, was better. She might have come from the most scientifically advanced era, but she was the sorriest housewife ever. She could not darn a sock or boil an egg.

"If she was cooking water, she would burn it," Timi said. "If she were my maid, I would not let her touch anything. Or clean anything."

"You wouldn't find much use for me either, I expect," I said.

"You can read and write," Timi said. "You would be useful."

In Izabel's time, everything around the house was done by machines. I had wondered if she came from a rich family to be so pampered, but she said she lived in a poor neighbourhood.

"But how do you afford all those machines?" I asked.

"We're not *that* poor," she said. "We only have cheap old machines."

"I suppose you have to work yourself?" I ventured.

This was where language let us down. The English words "work" and "job" did not have currency in Izabel's world, or at least not as I used them. I eventually established that she was paid a certain amount every day for playing games.

"I guess that sounds crazy," she said. Izabel was well aware of how much harder the lives of the others had been, how we were among the few not to have been slaving away for our bread.

"Not really," I said. We had professional athletes even in the twentieth century, but in her day, everyone was paid to play games. It sounded a lot like the old Roman approach of bread and circuses to keep the populace quiet. Only this way the two were combined, entertainment and a subsistence allowance, all provided by machines.

In spite of her lack of skill at almost every practical task, Izabel was never discouraged. She was a game girl, trying her best at everything and, when it turned out badly, leading the laughter at the results. She was also an exceptional sportswoman. She even played football at home. That seemed highly unsuitable, and tennis was impossible, but we could play a version of badminton with woven straw fans for rackets and a woven straw shuttlecock. The games frequently had an audience, kept back at a safe distance by the ever-watchful Damki.

Damki took his role of protector seriously. The other men mocked him for staying at home with the women instead of riding with the men.

"Damki is one of the girls! Pretty Damki!" they would call out and "Haven't you found a husband yet, Damki? Let's pick some flowers for your hair!"

He shrugged off this barracking. Unlike many of his peers, Damki was not in the slightest fiery-tempered, but he occasionally displayed a kind of quiet malevolence. He had a knack of picking his time for a fight with those who mocked him, when his chosen opponent was tired, hungover, or had just lost a bout. His slight build was deceptive, and he was tenacious almost to the point of vindictiveness. Enemies tended to come away from spear sparring with a mass of bruises. Marie-Therese said Damki was much too clever to be a nomad.

"He is a good one to protect us," she said. "They mock him, but they will not risk fighting with him. And they cannot provoke him."

"He's a good kid," Izabel said in English. "And he's herding cats."

Having been "herding cats" myself for some time, I felt some sympathy with this description. Not that I could complain. In any classroom of girls, there was always a joker like Vana, a headstrong individual like Marie-Therese, and a spoiled beauty like Lalit. It was just a matter of degree. Any assortment picked from the history of womankind would probably have been just as diverse and difficult to handle.

Though I tried to keep everyone together, perhaps it was inevitable we would form cliques. Izabel, Marie-Therese, and I were a sort of leadership group from the start. Timi, Rachel, and Lu Zhu were the mature ones, sitting together, talking about religion or philosophy or playing games with a board scratched on a goatskin and pebbles for pieces. The others—Lalit, Noora, Vana, and Inzalu—were the younger set, chattering and laughing noisily or singing and dancing. Quiet Illi did not belong to any clique, but all of us made a place for her when she approached; she talked little but enjoyed everyone's company.

All of us had to adjust to the native diet and the local germs. We all suffered the collywobbles to some degree, but Rachel suffered terribly. She lost weight alarmingly and spent days at a time bedridden. Finding foods she could eat and digest was difficult, given the band's monotonous diet of game and goat meat supplemented with roots and vegetables. I did what I could to nurse her, spending an hour each day at her bedside and keeping her up-to-date on what the others were doing. Lu Zhu was worried about Rachel. And not just for Rachel's own sake.

"If she has an illness which the nomads have not had themselves, it could spread," she said. "It might kill all of them. And not just Amir's band."

After a while, some of the band's children began to join me at Rachel's bedside. To keep them entertained, and because I did not have that much to say, I would tell stories, spinning out my own nursery tales— "Goldilocks and the Three Bears," "The Three Little Pigs," and the works of Hans Christian Andersen and the Brothers Grimm. I could not remember many, but they preferred repetition to new tales anyway.

"You are a good storyteller," Rachel told me.

I told her I could not claim any credit. Lu Zhu decided Rachel's illness was one of the spirit as much as the flesh. The others might have found themselves here by accident, but Rachel believed she was in her own hell because she had failed, that it was a punishment.

Persistence paid off, though. The human spirit recovers, and Rachel's digestive system adapted to the new diet. She gradually started to eat again.

Amir was baffled and not a little irritated by the amount of attention I paid to Rachel's health. The strong lived, the weak died, and there was nothing you could do about it.

"She will recover," I said. "And one day she will amaze you."

"That will be interesting," he said, not sounding convinced.

Midsummer had passed before the rescue, but afternoons were still hot. The nomads were torpid, lying semi-comatose in the shade. We sat cooling ourselves in the shade with straw fans. I dreamed of iced lemonade, ice lollies, and electric fans. Activities were slowed, but at the least we could continue our conversation classes.

I did not let the handmaidens succumb to idleness. One of my pet projects was to improve the sanitation and the water supply at the camp. Florence Nightingale had always been a childhood hero; I might not have her drive and knowledge, but I had ten pairs of hands to help me. And in the process, we could create a better way to cool down.

Camps were always located close to streams, large or small. In the relative cool of the pre-dawn morning, we dammed the small stream with stones. I remembered the technique from a line in a textbook describing some of the earliest human constructions. We started with stones as large as we could roll or carry to build the base, then filled in the gaps with smaller stones of decreasing size.

"This isn't so difficult, is it?" I said, a little too brightly.

Izabel glowered at me as she struggled with a boulder.

We completed the first dam in a morning and an evening and a second the next day. A day later, both pools had filled, giving us a higher pond for collecting drinking water and bathing and a lower pond for washing clothes and watering the animals. We spent more mornings and evenings laying more stones as cobble paving to prevent the banks being trodden into mud when people used the ponds.

The sluggish stream was slow to fill the ponds, but how wonderful it was to come back in the evening and find that the upper pond was deep enough to immerse oneself. I explained to Damki that he would have to do his sentry duty from a distance, while facing in the other direction.

The pool was not big enough for all of us at once, but we could not create a bigger one without a much higher dam or a better stream. We arrayed ourselves like a collection of water nymphs selected to represent different continents. Vana's dogs ran around, happily plunging in and doggy-paddling.

"I want a proper swimming pool," Izabel said, lying full length and splashing languidly. She was the only one of the others who could swim.

"I want a lot of things," Marie-Therese said. "First, a good meal, and then some wine. And a cup of coffee."

Noora did not join us in the water. I suspected she was still trying to hide her condition. Lu Zhu had attempted to corner Noora a number of times about the thing growing inside her. I told the midwife that the best thing was to leave it a few more days until Noora approached her. The last thing we wanted was to force her into anything. Lu Zhu looked mistrustful, but she complied.

We talked about our homes. I usually tried to turn the conversation away from this, but everyone was too fluent by now, and my two supposed helpers were leading the rest towards weepy nostalgia. There would be tears at the end of it, I knew, but it was hot, and I was just enjoying the water. I could not be in charge of everything all the time, and it was nice to finally have a little utter relaxation.

Timi was telling us about Buda, which had tall stone buildings, stone streets, three bridges across the river, and a wonderful market with all sorts of food, which she was struggling to describe—home food was an obsession for all of us—when there was a scream.

"They coming!" Vana shrieked from behind me. I thought she must have caught the alarm gong, though I had heard nothing. "Quick, get up!"

We all bolted, slipping in the mud and splashing water everywhere as we scrambled to get to our clothes. The dogs dashed about, barking excitedly. I was half-dressed before I saw that Vana, rather than screaming, was doubled over with laughter at the panic she had created. There were no Spawn.

Izabel pointed a menacing finger at Vana. "I swear I'm gonna drown you."

"You're so funny!" Vana hooted.

Once I had calmed down, I would explain to Vana about the dangers of crying wolf. Damki ran up, spear in hand, looking for the source of the disturbance. He was probably hoping for a snake he could kill to save us all.

"There is no danger," I told him. "You can go back."

"Yes, yes, my lady," Damki said, eyes fixed on the ground at my feet. I don't know which of us was blushing more. There was a lot of giggling.

Vana's practical joke had at least diverted the conversation, which turned to horrible things the others were going to do to get Vana back, involving creative use of horse dung, prickly plats, and biting or stinging insects.

Chapter Eight: Digging for Victory

Amir's people were not true nomads who were always on the move. They were more like semi-nomadic pastoralists, who moved to a new site and occupied it for a few weeks until the grazing land and game were depleted. Once all the easy firewood had been gathered and the area around the camp thoroughly polluted, they moved on. Now we were moving at ever shorter intervals to keep away from the Spawn. Five days, three days, far shorter than usual.

One day, Amir came back with three extra horses. "An enemy raiding party after our herds," he said. "There were five of them. We were chasing them, and they ran into the Spawn. One of them came back our way, and Igmil killed him with a javelin. The others died quickly, but some of the horses got away."

"You don't seem too happy," I said. Normally, he would have been jubilant over such an easy victory.

"Things have changed. I don't like to see those things killing men, even my enemies."

The handmaidens had been with the band for two months, and the weather was changing. I had noted the shortening of the days, and while it was still stiflingly hot in the afternoon, a strong wind cooled the evenings, and there were thunderstorms in the distant hills.

"The clouds say we must go to winter camp," Old Harsis told me, pointing out a row of clouds scudding along the horizon. "We must slaughter and make harvest. We cannot keep moving in winter."

According to Amir, winter was bitterly cold. Not so cold that they had frost or snow, but the wind was cold, the grass stopped growing, and grazing was sparse.

"The goddess will help us," Amir said, looking to me.

"Heaven must protect us from the Spawn," Old Harsis said. He glowered at me like an Old Testament prophet accusing a king. "Otherwise, we will have to go far away and fight for a new territory away from the Spawn."

"No," Amir said. "We will stay in our own winter camp."

"We can only stay if heaven can protect us," Old Harsis said.

Aruru had explained that in winter, the band slaughtered many of their goats and dried the meat, setting most of the rest of the herd loose. Spare horses were similarly put out to graze where they could. The women harvested grain and fruit to last through the season, and the men traded all the skins they could with merchants for salted meat and other supplies.

In springtime, the animals would be rounded up, and the band would assemble itself as a fully mobile entity. The People were at their most vulnerable in winter camp. Wars were suspended and the tribes did not raid each other in winter. An attack by the creatures could leave them starving and without shelter.

I had been considering for some time how the nomads could defend themselves and their winter camp. It was time to test my plan.

"You watched the creatures when you were prisoner, didn't you?" I asked Illi.

She nodded, never one to waste words.

"Did you ever see them climb up stairs or a steep slope? Walking or slithering?"

Illi thought about that for twelve paces. "Never."

"They always used the ramps," Marie-Therese said. "Only the men used the stone steps, not the Spawn."

The others confirmed what I thought. The creatures avoided all but the shallowest slopes. They were not stable when they were walking, and when crawling, they scrabbled for purchase. They were poorly adapted to movement, like a child's first attempt at making an animal. Perhaps, they were exactly that.

I asked Amir, and his scouts confirmed the conclusion. To them, it was not a significant piece of intelligence. The creatures were not agile climbers, or climbers at all. One scout had escaped them by hiding up a tree until they left.

"If you get on top of a crag, you can be safe from them for a time," Amir said. "But our winter camp is not on a mountain. Nor is there any mountain here, not even a big hill."

"We'll see about that." I was thinking of something in the style of a Roman marching fort, with a defensive ditch, ramparts, and a palisade. I took a stick and sketched it out on in the dirt for Izabel and Marie-Therese.

"It looks big," Izabel said.

"There aren't enough trees for this fence," Marie-Therese said, tapping it with her toe. "And it will take weeks to make the ramparts."

"There are stands of trees half a day's ride from the winter camp," I said, having questioned Amir on this. "If all the men go there and brings back two dozen stakes each"—a number I glibly pulled out of thin air— "and put more on the spare horses, then we'll have our palisade in no time."

"And the walls?"

"We make a ditch and use the spoil to build ramparts. The wooden spikes on top of the ramparts will add height and stop them climbing over. We will cut turves and apply them to build the ramparts up and make them stable."

From memory, I recalled that the ditch should be five feet wide and three feet deep. A Roman legion could build such a fortification big enough to house the whole unit at the end of a days' march, taking just a few hours.

"You have done this yourself?" she asked.

"I know about it," I said. "For centuries, every Roman force built a camp every night when they were on the march. How difficult can it be?"

Marie-Therese blew out her cheeks then seemed to make up her mind. "We will do it. We invented this, you know. The revolutionary committee edict of 1789. Every able-bodied citizen was conscripted against the forces of counter-revolution, every man, woman, and child. That's how we won against the Dutch and the Prussians and the Spanish—and the English. It was the women of France that won that war, because we did everything while the men fought."

"Wonderful," I said. "We should be finished in no time with a Frenchwoman to organise us."

We were forced to divert our route of march several times when the scouts warned us of creatures in our path. While the band continued its slow trudge, I rode ahead with Amir and Old Harsis to survey the site. The rest of the band would not arrive in the middle of the afternoon, far later than I would have liked.

The winter camp was as sorry a sight as I expected, a shanty of dilapidated wigwams of hide and wood. For storage, they had hollows dug into the ground and roofed with reeds, half-cellars for earthenware jars which would be filled with the grain collected by the women. A shallow ditch ran around the camp as a barrier to prevent goats and horses from straying.

"The Spawn will not trouble us on the first night," Amir said. "They move slowly. But in day, or two at most, they will send a raiding party."

That meant we had one good day at least to build our defences, far more time than the Roman legionaries had required. After I arrived, there was still an hour of daylight for surveying and planning. I had acquired a supply of leather cords and tent pegs to mark out the work.

"We will need to get everyone up before dawn," I told Amir. "The men to ride off to collect the wooden stakes, the women to build the ramparts."

"But the day after we get to winter camp is a day of rest," he said. "After that, we slaughter the goats and the women harvest and prepare for the winter. And when that is done, we have a day of feasting."

"The band can do all that once it is secure," I said. "Unless you want us to die in our beds."

Amir could not argue with that. "As the goddess wishes."

The men, naturally enough, would not be helping with the digging. Those who were not patrolling were dispatched to collect the wood for our stake palisade. That left me with a workforce of women, children, and a few old men. I had them all assemble outside the encampment at dawn. They milled around talking animatedly. The first day in winter camp was a day of excitement. The handmaidens, who had been briefed on my plans, were gathered behind me. Damki banged a pot with his spear until the crowd was quiet and every eye was on me. They looked as though I might be about to perform some feat of magic.

"Women of Amir's band!" I said. "Home-makers, keepers of homes, protectors of families. Today, we will work together. All of us. Marie-Therese will organise you into groups; you must stay in these groups, work together, and complete the section assigned to you. The chain is only as strong as its weakest link, and all the links must be strong. Today, we will ensure the protection of the children. Today, we will build a wall between us and evil!"

Izabel led the handmaidens in a ragged cheer which left the crowd unmoved.

"Why do we have to dig dirt?" someone asked.

Aruru stooped down and held up a handful of soil. "The Earth is our mother. She will protect us."

This apparently made more sense to the nomads, who muttered something like assent.

"I didn't know there was a mother goddess," I said to Aruru.

"There's a lot you don't know, Yishka."

Marie-Therese lost no time in organising the women and children into work teams, showing each the stretch of ditch and rampart that they should cover. And so began our longest day's work.

We had commissioned Turm to make shovels, but there had been little time, so we had only four, which went to the four strongest nomad women. Digging sticks, usually employed to grub out roots and tubers, were put to use breaking up the ground. Cooking pots and leather water buckets were pressed into service to carry the spoil. Ladles and stirring spoons doubled as trowels, but many of us just used flat pieces of wood, scooping the earth into pots or buckets or just flinging it as far as we could.

We made an enthusiastic start. Even Vana's dogs helped, kicking up sprays of dirt behind them, to the children's delight. The work was more laborious than I'd expected, not because the soil was harder than anticipated but because it was so sandy. A shallow ditch collapsed immediately, and a shallow rampart was like a pile of sand. Digging deeper, we reached a layer of claggy, clay-rich soil, and that could be used to shore up the collapsing sand.

Turm was in charge of cutting turf blocks, using a big, flat-bladed knife as he did every time he made his forge. But he was only used to working with a few dozen blocks at a time. Now we needed turf on an industrial scale. Timi watched him for a while before taking over, showing two of the nomad women how to cut out long strips of turf rather different to the compact blocks Turm had been carving.

"You should use your muscles," she told Turm. "See how well those shovels work."

Turm looked into the ditch doubtfully. "I am a smith, not a mole. You are the trading woman. What trade are you offering?"

"How does a jug of Vana's best beer to yourself sound?"

After some discussion, Turm clambered awkwardly down into the ditch, shovel in hand, having agreed to take on the undignified task for two jugs of beer.

By mid-morning, our workforce was getting dispirited. The sun was high, and the unaccustomed work was uncomfortably warm. We were about one-tenth of the way though the task, and the pace of work was slowing. The nomad woman did not see the point of it, and they were tired and dirty. I was angered to see one of the shovels had been discarded, its user gone to milk goats. She should at least have handed it over to someone else rather than leaving them to dig with sticks, and how badly did the goats need milking anyway?

"Take this!" Marie-Therese ordered, passing the shovel to a woman who was worrying away at the dirt with a twig. "And use it properly. See her digging over there? Do the same as she is doing. I will be back to check on you."

She took it well. The women were used to being ordered about.

Even the children were flagging and disappearing to lie down in the storage cellars, especially the older boys. Marie-Therese rousted them out, shouting at them that any who did not dig would be eaten by monsters.

I found tellings-off exhausting, but each time she returned from scolding someone, Marie-Therese went back to work with renewed vigour. Shouting at people exhilarated her and charged her with energy.

Turm was doing a good job of digging a section of ditch all by himself, hurling spadesful of sand onto the rampart. Still, the digging progressed with agonising slowness. The most willing and active members of the female workforce were Aruru and Puabi, who also tried to chivvy their sisters and cousins along. Even the handmaidens were not at full strength; Rachel was still too weak to help, and after a while, Noora dropped out.

"I told you," Vana said. She had been dropping hints for weeks that Noora was concealing a pregnancy, and this confirmed it for her. Not that the many pregnant nomad women had stopped work.

"This is not realistic. We need an alternate plan," Marie-Therese said, coming back from a circuit of the ditch. I did not need to go that far to see how far behind we were. "Wait until Turm can make us more shovels, then this will be much easier. We should get the men to help. We're just tiring ourselves out for no reason."

"We dig now," Izabel said. "We keep digging until this mother is dug. Simple as that." She went back to her work.

"Marie-Therese," I said, "if you don't mind, we might as well dig as much as we can. It's not as though we have anything better to do."

Vana organised the cooking of a sort of porridge or gruel in a few pots, flavoured with piquant berries collected by the children. I fretted at the wasted time, but the food helped morale, as much for the novelty as for the nourishment.

Inzalu organised the children into bucket chains to move earth, making it into a game for the them. Some of them were clambering up the ramparts, bringing down avalanches of dirt and undoing our work. Inzalu showed them how they could roll along the slope, helping compact the earth rather than bringing it down.

"That doesn't do any good," Marie-Therese said.

"But it doesn't do any harm," Inzalu said. "Come on, children, let's make some more digging sticks."

They were not the ideal workforce, but the nomad women continued to help. Many of them were loyal to Lu Zhu, who had helped them or their sisters or cousins in childbirth and were repaying their debt. They did not seem to understand the point of the ramparts, though, or the importance of building them as high as possible. To them, the ramparts were a symbolic defence, and they seemed to think we had done enough to gain the magic protection of the Earth-Mother.

"Maybe the ramparts don't need to be all that high," Izabel said doubtfully.

"Maybe they need to be higher," I said. What worked for Roman legions against the Gauls would not necessarily be adequate against alien monsters. "We have to make the defences as strong as we can."

Turm seemed indefatigable, and Izabel was scarcely less powerful. Between the two of them, they seemed to be doing half the work. By common consent, they kept two of the good shovels as they made the best use of them. The rest of us took turns.

"I have never been so muddy in my entire life," Lalit said. She was digging where the camp was lowest, and the dirt there was rich and damp.

"You look better black," Izabel said.

Lalit threw a handful of mud at Izabel, who responded by launching a shovelful back. Lalit nimbly dodged, scooping up more ammunition.

"You two—" I started, and both of them pelted me with mud, laughing.

Two riders came to tell Damki that a dozen creatures had been spotted a horizon away. They had been lured away from the direction of the camp by driving goats past them, but the creatures were still in the area.

I broke off, arms aching, to walk a circuit around the encampment. The ditch had been deepened, and the rampart started around the entire perimeter, but in many places, it was barely knee-high.

My mood was not lifted much in the afternoon when groups of men started to arrive with their loads of wooden stakes. Even at a rough approximation, I could tell there would not be enough for a palisade all the way around, and there was no time for them to go back for another load.

"I don't know what to do," I said.

"This can still work," Marie-Therese said. "We just need to make the spacing between them a little more. And we alternate between full-length stakes and half-length. If we cut the longer ones into two, we can get enough to make up the difference."

She showed Young Harsis what was required. He started chopping up the stakes like kindling.

"In half, you idiot!" Marie-Therese's patience had been wearing thin as the day went on. She tore the axe out of his hands. "Two equal pieces. How stupid you are. Like this!"

Fortunately, she did not injure herself, or Young Harsis, with the hatchet.

"I know, I understand," he said, chastened, taking back the axe. "Like this."

"Yes, yes. Now, quickly, do a hundred of those, and we will see how many more we need."

"Is it finished?" Amir asked, surveying the encampment, the filthy female workers, the scattering of broken tools, the piled-up dirt.

"Not quite," I told him. "But it will be finished much sooner if your men help."

"This is women's work," he said. "Why is there no food ready for the men?"

"Because we have all been working, *espèce d'imbécile*!" Marie-Therese told him. "You can help dig the ditch and the ramparts or make your own *foutou* dinner!"

"I will organise patrols and find where the Spawn are," Amir said, turning away.

"Afterwards, roast some goats," I called after him. Women were in charge of cooking pots, but barbecuing meat was a male privilege. It would give them something to do and ensure that we were fed. "Please."

"As the goddess wishes," Amir called over his shoulder.

Many times that day, I was reminded of my own childhood, building sandcastles on the beach with my brothers, all working diligently with tin bucket and spade. We built huge, fantastic castles in the sand, with towers, concentric walls, and a little flag on the topmost turret. I never imagined I would be doing it for real.

The joy of the game of sandcastles was the fun of seeing the sea come in and batter the walls down. The game always ended the same way—however strong and high we built our surrounding wall, the tide always won in the end. We would always be huddled together as ankle-deep water foamed about us, then we fled, laughing, for dry sand and an ice cream.

As darkness fell, we were still working. Meat had been passed round, and I had stopped long enough to gnaw on some barbecued grouse. The outside was bitter charcoal, the inside was half-raw, but they tasted remarkably good.

The men had eventually finished cutting the stakes and putting them in place, with a certain amount of shouting from Marie-Therese, but in places, the ditches or ramparts had slumped. In other places, they were nothing like the regulation height. That meant a depressing process of taking out the stakes, removing the turves, then rebuilding the lot.

"My arms hurt so much," Inzalu said, rubbing them.

"My everything hurts," Izabel said.

My fingers were bloody and blistered. My arms, as well as my back and thighs, had been hurting for many hours. Other parts were probably hurting, too, but those pains were lost in the red fire of my arms. All of us were hurting. All except apparently Turm, who refused to admit any fatigue, although he had slowed noticeably.

"The arms of a weaponsmith never tire," he said. "Not when there is still work to be done. But tomorrow, I will make proper digging tools. Then I will rest. And drink beer!"

We kept digging, until there was nothing else but the alternation of breaking up dirt with the digging stick and scooping it up and carrying up to deposit on the rampart, ignoring the little avalanches of sand and earth that constantly eroded our work.

More of the women had returned to work. And as it was dark, Damki was working with us, too, determinedly hacking away and shovelling as though making up for lost time, while making sure he was not spotted by any of the men above.

"You should call it a day," I told Izabel. She had been going at the work with great energy for hours, managing a much greater pace than me, and she looked properly exhausted.

"I'll quit when you quit."

We kept digging. The pain swelled and grew until it was all around like a cloud. But somehow, it was detached from me, and I kept digging. I was going slower and slower, but it only really hurt when I stopped and rested.

The job was never quite finished. Every time we thought we were almost there, we would discover another section that was not up to scratch. I must have sat down for a break and something else to eat and fallen asleep. It was full dark when Inzalu gently nudged my shoulder.

"Why didn't you wake me before?" were my first words. I wondered what time it was. It was too dark to see the hands on my watch.

"They are coming," she said.

I made a circuit of the defences. The ramparts were low enough to look through the gaps between the stakes of the palisade. Many of the nomads had climbed on top of the ramparts for a better view, and already, the earthworks were showing signs of collapse in places.

There still had not been enough stakes for the palisade, and Marie-Therese had requisitioned any piece of wood that came to hand, including tent poles, to make up the shortfall. The ramparts were uneven, but the ditch looked sound.

All the animals, the horses, the goats, and even the dogs, were inside the encampment, adding to the noise and the smell. The men milled about, spears and javelins in their hands, ready for action but with nothing to do. Some of the more active started moving piles of rocks to the ramparts.

Inside the camp, we had torches, bundles of resinous twigs that gave off more smoke than light, our only illumination but less effective than a candle. The nomads did not have much use for lights at nighttime. Overhead, a quarter moon spilled its beams over the grassland, enough to create shadows and tell the ground from the horizon but little more.

There were shouts and hoofbeats outside. We had no gate, but there was a gap in the ramparts protected by a triple row of stakes. When they were removed, the horses could easily jump the ditch.

The last patrol, led by Igmil, was returning.

"Over there," he said. "A half-horizon away, about thirty of them, moving this way, but slow-slow. Two other war parties—ten-twelve each—over there and over there. Moving faster, going around to encircle the camp."

"We are surrounded," Amir said. "They will try to flush us out and ambush us as we flee."

"We could leave now," Nergal said. "Before they are in position. Draw some of them away with riders and slip between them."

Old Harsis was stony-faced, arms crossed, saying nothing.

Amir looked at me. "We will stay here, and we will fight."

The wait was interminable. Lu Zhu brewed herbal tea. I usually hated the stuff, but for once, it was welcome. I wished that we could fill the moat with burning pitch. The defences did not look like they would stop a determined goat, but as Marie-Therese said, the creatures were not as agile as goats.

"Nobody has ever seen the Spawn climb anything this high," Marie-Therese told me. "They are as clumsy as oxen."

"They've never needed to climb," Izabel said. She was lying down and sounded utterly drained. She must have kept working after I fell asleep. "They've got a lot of tentacles."

"We will see," I said. Nothing on earth crawled along the ground with tentacles. Octopi were almost helpless on land. Or so I hoped.

We heard the creatures before we saw them, a steady rustling of grass getting ever closer. From the sound, it might have been a herd of cows, except there was something infinitely sinister in that slow advance.

The sounds stopped for a moment. The entire encampment held its breath.

Then the Spawn lit up. The body of each one glowed with a pale, flickering red-orange light, like an enormous lantern. The dark tentacles waved around them like seaweed. They were no more than fifty paces away.

"They do this to frighten prey," Amir said. "We will not run away."

As the line of Spawn advanced, it became almost a wedge, with one farther forwards than the others. It paused at the edge of the ditch, feeling with delicate tentacle tips.

I had made my way forwards and stood at the closest point on the rampart. I shouted the incantation which was supposed to banish evil, the one the High Priestess repeated. This time, I felt something; the words were reflected back to me as though I were shouting at a wall a few inches away. The Spawn ignored me.

Somebody yelled beside me, and a javelin struck the Spawn, then another. An arrow was followed by a shower of fist-sized stones. The men shouted and jeered with every hit. The Spawn paused, hesitating at the edge of the ditch.

Turm stepped forwards, holding a javelin which glowed red at its tip, heated over his forge. He hurled it with a grunt. The javelin struck squarely and hissed as it went in, with a puff of steam.

"Good throw, smith," Amir said.

The creature was untroubled by the smoking wound in its side.

"The men must not damage the palisade." I was worried there were so many of them on the rampart that they might cause it to collapse in their eagerness to get close to the enemy.

Amir shouted orders, but the men were enthusiastic to be at the front.

The creature began a ponderous progress around the circumference of the ditch. The other Spawn spread out to encircle us and were joined by others from other directions. I counted fifty-five of them: one for each warrior in the band.

The creature circumnavigating the camp finally arrived back at its starting point. By now, it had a dozen or more javelins and arrows in it, like a walking pincushion, and it had removed several more.

Even Izabel stepped up with a javelin, and drawing disapproving looks from some of the men, she threw it square into the creature's side. I was surprised she had any strength left, not that it made any difference.

The Spawn paused then seemed to reach a decision. It edged forwards until it half-fell half-slid into the ditch. A murmur went up from the waiting warriors. The Spawn tried to slither up out of the ditch onto the rampart then reached out with its tentacles, wrapping them around the stakes and trying to pull itself up. It was as ungainly as a beetle on its back. I thought the powerful tentacles would tear the palisade apart easily, but the stakes were rooted deeply, and the creature did not have leverage. Each time it tried to get a firm hold, nomads with sharp spears and hatchets moved in to dislodge or sever a tentacle before they could get any purchase.

Whip-like tendrils kept slipping through the palisade and feeling around like adder's tongues, but the men were too wary to be caught. A severed section twisted like a dark cord for a few seconds, then it dissolved. The men cheered again. I wanted to retrieve some of the pulpy material, but it was trampled into the raw dirt too quickly.

Injuries sealed up almost as soon as they were inflicted, and even as it was testing the palisade, the creature was pulling out spears and javelins with its many other limbs. It was a question of who would tire first.

Turm, bracing himself against the palisade with one hand, threw a heavy double-headed hatchet with all his force. It spun end over and buried itself between the base of the eyestalks, opening up a huge gash. The light from the Spawn flickered, and when it returned, it was dimmer than before. Turm growled, angry that the thing was stubbornly refusing to die. I was astonished he had any strength left after the day's digging.

The smaller stones had little effect, but now the warriors were lobbing larger projectiles. Young Harsis hefted a rock bigger than his head and, with the skill of a shot putter, sent it sailing in a high arc over the palisade. The rock struck the Spawn with a sound like wet leather. The huge gash from Turm's axe had not yet healed, and it ruptured open, spilling disgusting alien innards everywhere.

The thing's light guttered like a candle in a breeze and went out. There was just enough illumination to see it slumping into the ditch, disintegrating into a soggy mass in the dark. A foul odour wafted over us. The men cheered and threw more stones, which spattered as if falling into a mud pool.

"Dead! Dead! Dead!" someone cheered.

"Not dead for long," Amir said. He had been coordinating the action rather than fighting, trying to keep his men spaced out and ensuring that some were keeping an eye on the other creatures so they did not slip around and enter from another side. He had called back warriors, who, in their enthusiasm, tried to make gaps in the palisade to clamber through and engage the Spawn face-to-face.

After a minute, wet flopping noises emanated from the ditch, and the creature, whole again with all its tentacles intact, rose again. Arrows, javelins, and stones struck the mark one after the other. It was a game which the warriors were beginning to master.

"Aim for the eye-stalks!" Amir ordered.

The Spawn, though, was no longer interested in attacking. If it was not troubled by pain, perhaps the process of death and reintegration was unpleasant. I hoped so.

It struggled to haul itself back out the way it had come, and it scrabbled at the edge of the ditch with several tentacles at once. It brought down a quantity of earth and could have got out eventually, but two other creatures came up and intertwined tentacles with their comrade to haul it up to the other side.

Arrows and javelins thudded into them. Another big stone from Harsis fell short as the Spawn topped the slope. He must have been hoping to overbalance it so all three fell into the ditch.

"Come back and give Young Harsis another go!" someone yelled, and the men laughed.

I expected the Spawn to advance together in a mass attack. If they focused their efforts, they could easily swarm over the ditch, pull apart the rampart, and bring down the palisade. There were too few men to stop all of them. Even if the nomads killed them over and over, they could keep coming back.

I was seeing it from a point of view of knowing our weakness. As far as the Spawn were concerned, they had probed the defences and not found any way through. They were not to know that they could have overwhelmed us. Rather, the defences were a puzzle, like a cliff which could not be scaled. Perhaps they would find a way to conquer it in time. The Spawn moved to their own steady pace. They were in no hurry, any more than vegetation was in a hurry to overgrow a deserted house.

The creatures on the perimeter started moving, gathering together in groups of four or five. Then they departed in different directions, their lights dimming and going out one by one. The swishing sound of the grass faded as they went.

"They are going," Amir said. He sounded as though he couldn't believe his eyes. "The Spawn are running away! The wall of wooden spears has stopped them."

The nomads went mad. They were whooping and ululating with joy, hitting Amir on the back and shoulders or shaking their spears at the heavens.

"This has never happened before," Amir said, bewildered. He was making history, and he did not know what to say. "Quick, scouts must follow them—Igmil, collect a party to ride out."

"Praise to the goddess!" Old Harsis said, the white gleam in his smile visible in the half-dark. I had not seen him smile before. "Heaven has saved us!"

Old Harsis was proud of me. Of course, he had been the one to first recognise me. He had been the one to bring me back to the band. When I was a success, my glory was his glory.

The cry was taken up by the People and repeated again and again. I would have told them that this was their victory, not mine, that everyone who had dug the earthworks had really won the day. But it was too noisy to make myself heard, and I was suddenly feeling very, very tired.

"Praise to the goddess," Nergal said by my ear.

"*Vive la France*," Izabel said, and Marie-Therese grinned.

PART TWO: LIFE UNDER SIEGE

CHAPTER NINE: WINTER CAMP

We were an island in the sea of grass, a castle under siege with the enemy always at the gates. But the days were peaceful. By the end of the first week, as well as strengthening the defences, we had built a wooden watchtower, where a sentry could see creatures approaching from a mile away. The tower was little more than a pole and two ladders with a platform on top, given some stability with guy-ropes. It still wobbled, but it was a great attraction for the children, who all wanted to go up to enjoy the view and screamed loudly when it swayed in the wind.

An alarm gong was sounded when the Spawn were sighted, and everyone came in behind the ramparts. Alarms were rare in daytime, though. We had visitors from neighbouring bands and clans, all curious to see the strange construction. They listened patiently to Amir's explanation. Few thought the Spawns were as numerous or dangerous as I tried to tell them. To most, they were like the invading packs of wolves that sometimes troubled their goat herds.

Nights were a different matter. We never knew where the creatures were until they lit up, and groups of them were always circling the walls, as though looking for an entrance. They never came in such force again, though, and never attempted to get across the ditch and scale the rampart. Sometimes they would try to get close and extrude a long tendril through the palisade, feeling for an unwary child or dog, but our lookouts were attentive.

"If they cannot get us, they will seek easier prey elsewhere," Amir predicted.

The Spawn were drawn by the concentration of human, horse, and goat flesh inside the camp. I also suspected they wanted the handmaidens back. Much of the time, though, they seemed to be engaged in their own mysterious but purposeful activity. They rarely travelled in straight lines but in long arcs, driven by currents invisible to us. They were efficient hunters, but some of their movements seemed to be surveys or laying down lines of communication, like scurrying ants which seem to be moving at random but always found the shortest route to the spilled jam.

In their own way, they were as organised and methodical as we were, but few could see past their alienness. The other nomads saw them not as horrifying and dangerous carnivores, but as slow-moving animals confined to the range of Amir's band. The men shook their heads and said how strange the Spawn were, but they did not seem to understand the threat from the huge, living lanterns prowling outside. At least we were secure. Turm was as good as his word, and a few proper shovels made a world of difference to our efforts. I did my bit. Once my muscles had recovered, I actually enjoyed digging as a break from other activity. It was healthy physical exercise, and I enjoyed having tangible progress.

By the second week, the ramparts, fortified with a triple row of stakes and a proper turf walkway, were enough to stop any assault by monster or man. We had extended the area protected with enclosures for animals.

Gangs of little boys took to charging to the top of the ramparts and hurling sticks and stones at phantom monsters, cheering wildly at the end of every performance as the imaginary enemy was routed. Now the ramparts were properly covered in turves, there was no danger of collapse, and they could play all they liked. The need to cut turves had an unexpected side effect. I was proud when I showed Marie-Therese the latest product of Turm's forge, a flat semi-circular blade set on a long wooden handle.

"Another new weapon?"

"This is Tom Smith's Patent Turf Cutter," I said. "For cutting and lifting sections of turf."

I had only the vaguest recollection of what a turf cutter looked like, half-remembering seeing them in museum collections of old agricultural instruments. But I had asked the others, and Inzalu, of all people, had described how they cut peat for fuel in her home country. Between the two of us, we had made a clay model of a turf cutter. Turm had duly fashioned a full-size one in bronze the next day. I had been trying it, and it sliced through the turf like a dream.

"What for?" Marie-Therese said. "The ramparts are almost finished. Turm should have made this before we arrived."

"The Romans used turves to build temporary structures, and with this, we can cut far more, more quickly and easily. Ten times quicker than a knife. If we're going to be here for any length of time, tents and holes in the ground are not enough."

"Buildings made of turf blocks?" She raised an eyebrow.

"Roofed with goatskin or woven grass mats or reeds," I said. "Inzalu can show us how to weave them."

"And while the rest of us weave, Izabel will do all the cutting?"

Izabel lacked the manual dexterity to weave two pieces of straw, a feat which Inzalu made look effortless. But she hefted the turf cutter enthusiastically and insisted on going outside the ramparts with us to try it out. Damki trailed along, scanning left and right.

"Cuts cleanly," Izabel said after some experimental slicing in the ground. "Nice. Throw in a free juice squeezer, and you'll sell a million."

"I'll time you and see how many blocks you can cut in ten minutes," I said. "That will give me a starting point for the quantity estimates."

As bad luck would have it, two warriors passed by on their horses halfway through the experiment. They stopped to watch Izabel hacking away and rolling up strips of turf. I ignored them.

"Women stab the dirt," one of them said. His name was Tema, easily identified by a face pockmarked with acne scars. He raised his spear in one hand. "Men prefer to stab into flesh."

They laughed coarsely. Izabel disliked being laughed at by men and turned around angrily. "*Filho de puta*," she spat.

"This is important work," Damki told them. "Stop bothering the woman."

"We don't take orders from girls," Tema said, pretending to look around. "And I only see girls here—at least I think the black one is a girl. Maybe she's a man."

They laughed louder. I wondered where Amir was. He was surely in the camp somewhere close.

Damki was about to speak, but Izabel pushed him aside.

"I'm warning you," she said, and she spun the turf cutter around and held it like a spear, the blunt end pointed towards Tema.

He laughed again, until Izabel jabbed him in the midriff and he fell off his horse. A shocked silence was broken by the other man laughing as Tema, red-faced, leapt to his feet.

"Izabel…" I started.

Tema had his own spear, holding it reversed with the butt forwards as they did when sparring. He lunged and tried to knock her weapon aside, but Izabel blocked the move and jabbed him again, this time in the chest.

The weapons clattered together twice more. Tema, frustrated, swore at Izabel.

"What are you doing?" Old Harsis called from the ramparts. Others were gathering around him, drawn by the commotion.

"I am teaching this stupid woman a lesson," Tema said. He attacked again, pushing forwards, but Izabel parried the thrusts easily, moving smoothly out of the way. Tema renewed his assault; Izabel parried, fell back, then counter-attacked. They went back and forth for half a minute before Tema received a rap across his knuckles that made him drop his spear.

"Idiot!" Old Harsis shouted. "Get her!"

There were people around us and more on the ramparts. Any disturbance in the camp quickly drew attention, and everyone could tell something unusual was happening.

Tema took up his spear again and resumed the contest, more wary. Izabel was taller and considerably stronger. The nomad had a longer weapon, but he had less leverage when the two met. Izabel moved with a fluid elegance I had not seen from her before, slipping out of reach then darting back to jab. She was clearly relishing the combat, but Tema's face was a mask of concentration.

"Go on, Izzy, get him!" Vana shouted, shaking a fist beside me.

Tema kept falling back farther and farther, driven in a wide circle by Izabel's determined assault. He could not seem to land a blow.

"Why can't you beat her, Tema, you weakling?" one of the warriors demanded scornfully.

Tema broke off and turned on his critic, rightly guessing that Izabel would not attack while he was looking away. "You think it's easy—you try fighting her!" He held out his spear for the other to take.

It was a shrewd move. The newcomer, his bluff called, squared his shoulders, looked around the assembled audience, and laughed nervously.

"Come on then," Izabel said, spinning the turf cutter like a drum major twirling a baton, drawing an appreciative laugh from the crowd.

The second warrior started as boldly as Tema had, but his confidence waned as Izabel pressed her attacks home, and he repeatedly failed to strike her. Izabel's self-assurance grew; she held her spear like a quarterstaff, whirled it round in showy moves, and repeatedly hit her opponent seemingly at will.

Not all in the audience were enjoying the combat, especially the men. One of them came up behind Izabel and made as if to grab her weapon from behind.

He was arrested by Amir's hand on his shoulder. "If you want to join in, you wait your turn to fight," Amir said. At that moment, Izabel whacked her opponent across the kneecap, and he shouted in pain. "I don't advise it. She's better than you."

Before long, the second warrior had acquired more bruises. Izabel kept threatening the knee, and when he moved to defend it, he got hit somewhere else. He became angry, and that did nothing to help him. Izabel drew back a little then, with less flashy moves and more careful defence, but she would not give up.

"She's a good fighter," Amir said quietly to me. "Slow on her feet, but she blocks and parries better than most."

The second man eventually threw down his spear in disgust, pushing his way out past the crowd.

"Does anybody else wish to fight the woman?" Amir asked, looking about. None of the men present stepped forwards. The one he had collared earlier was nowhere to be seen.

"How about you?" Izabel asked.

"You are tired, and I am fresh," Amir said. "It would not be fair."

"I'll risk it. If you will."

Amir glanced around his assembled people then threw off his leopard-skin cloak. He bowed to Izabel, picked up the spear, and relaxed into a fighting stance. Izabel adjusted her grip, and they set to.

They shuffled back and forwards, and the murmurs of the crowd mixed with the thock of wood on wood as they thrust and parried. Amir was a better fighter than the others, and Izabel was having a harder time of it. When she pressed an attack, he somehow sidestepped it, and a moment later, the blunt end of his spear was touching her throat.

"Enough," Amir said.

For a minute, I was worried Izabel would want to fight on, but luckily, she called it a day. The handmaidens crowded round to congratulate her.

"I'm sweating like a pig," she said, but she was grinning.

"Bravo," Marie-Therese said.

"I suppose you think that was clever," I said. "We're trying to make friends with these people, not brawl with them."

"Sorry, Chief," she said. "I lost my temper. I'd just had enough of those men… laughing at us."

"Better laughing at us than hating us," I said.

Old Harsis pushed his way through to confront Izabel. "It is taboo for a woman to hold a spear!"

"That's not a spear," I said, indicating the turf cutter. "See? It's a tool for cutting turves."

The others laughed. Old Harsis saw he would not be able to exert authority here and turned on his heel.

"I know Iz shouldn't have done it," Vana said. "But I thought she was great!"

Izabel flashed a smile at her, and the others all chimed in with noises of approval. All of us had felt like hitting the nomad men at times, especially when they just loitered around, watching us work. Izabel had struck a blow for all of us, even if it might have been a disaster in terms of diplomacy.

"What's done is done," I said. "We have to live with it. But, Izabel—no more fighting without approval from Amir and me. Even if—especially if—one of the men challenges you. Because after this, believe me, they will."

"Okay," Izabel said. She was chastened, but only slightly. I envied Amir the power to have people flogged for disobedience. Not that I would have actually done it, but it gave him iron authority instead of having to wheedle and reason with his men.

"Besides," I said. "You didn't tell me you could fight like that."

"A lot of the games I used to play were fighting with swords and spears and things. It's realistic but... I didn't know if I could do it for real."

My brothers used to fight each other with sticks for swords or anything else that came to hand. The "games" in Izabel's era were something more like military training.

"You can," Inzalu said. "You're better than any of them! I wish you'd broken Tema's nose. He's a pig."

"Well, at least you had the sense not to beat Amir," I said.

"I'm not that stupid," Izabel said.

When I talked about the incident afterwards with Amir, he was philosophical about the taboo being broken. "Izabel is a handmaiden, not like our women," he said. "Maybe the rule does not apply to her. Anyone can see she is a born fighter."

"Old Harsis says that success in combat is proof of right, and she bested two men," Nergal said. "He can challenge her if he wants."

"I'd like to see that," Amir said, laughing. "Izabel can be a warrior-maiden as far as I am concerned."

"A sort of honorary man?" I asked.

"Hah! Don't say that in front of Old Harsis."

The event boosted my confidence in Izabel as a military advisor for the fight against the Spawn. Earthworks would stop them, but killing them, or even doing permanent damage, was the problem. The creatures could survive anything.

"The tentacles just grow back," Izabel said. "Like Hercules and the Lernean Hydra. It's got several heads. Every time you cut one off, it grows back."

"Where did you learn about classical mythology?" I asked.

"In a game."

Maybe the similarity was more than coincidence. Maybe the thing really was the actual Lernean Hydra from the original myth. It came from the water, and it resembled a many-headed snake which could not be killed however many heads were cut off. I also thought of Scylla, the many-headed monster that snatched sailors off ships. Maybe those were tentacles too. Scylla was a mortal woman cursed by the gods. She had my sympathy.

"And how do you kill the hydra in the game?" I asked.

"You can kill all the heads permanently with fire, except the boss one. It's stronger than the others, and you've got to bury it under a big rock."

"If we can catch one in a pit, we can leave it there to rot," Marie-Therese said. "To starve."

"Starving is just another way of killing it," I said. "But when they die, they come back. Might be worth trying."

"Fill the pit in, bury it alive under rocks," Izabel said.

"Except that the Spawn are clever enough to rescue each other," I said, remembering how two of them had come to the aid of the third. It might take them a long time to dig another out, but they would do it eventually. "And if it dies and turns into ooze, it'll probably just come up to the surface."

Perhaps I was being pessimistic. But something in me knew that such things could not be stopped so easily. Without a way of killing them permanently, any attempts to lure the creatures into pits would be futile, as well as dangerous. Amir, though, was expecting me to show him how the Spawn could be destroyed. Heaven had supplied a miracle to defend his band. Now it would show them how to attack.

In the meantime, there was plenty of other work. The handmaidens helped with the autumn harvest, the slaughter of goats, and drying of meat. Some of them had their own ideas to contribute about food preservation. Marie-Therese had Turm forge long curved sickles to cut the grain twice as quickly as the short blades the nomad women used. A thousand years of progress in a day.

The question of Noora's condition would not go away. Lu Zhu had questioned the women closely about what they knew of other captives and the birthing process. Nobody had ever seen a woman alive after she had been taken away to give birth. Noora would not survive if we allowed matters to run their course. The danger was not imminent. But Lu Zhu was becoming anxious. The longer Noora left it, the riskier it would be.

We did our best to find out more about the cities. In the past, they had sent ambassadors with gifts or threats. Occasionally, they wanted the nomads to supply horsemen for a war somewhere or simply to stop raiding caravans. The nomads took the gifts—all valueless, nothing but children's toys and decorations for women, according to Amir—and ignored the threats. They did much as they pleased, depending on how the mood took them. Sometimes, when the raiding became too much, the cities sent armies to destroy any nomads they could catch, but that had not happened for generations.

"The cities seem much more civilised," I said to Izabel and Marie-Therese. "And safer. Perhaps we should send the handmaidens to the north."

"You wouldn't go," Izabel said.

"No," I said. "I've got to get home. Even if some of the others are happy to stay here."

Some of the women had mixed feelings about going or staying. Illi the huntress was impressed with how much game there was here, and she had no family ties to go back to. Others had been facing forced marriages or uncertain futures.

"This place is not so bad," Marie-Therese said. "We can make something here, if we work together."

"The air is so clean here," Izabel said.

"You must be joking," I said. "It stinks of goat dung."

"But it's *clean* dung," Izabel said. I knew what she meant.

"You want to go back to that shaft," Marie-Therese said. "But you know, everyone who comes here comes from the future. We all fall down to get here, even Illi. I do not think we can go up the other way."

"I intend to try."

"We know." She had always been sceptical of the possibility of return. "You think there will be a signpost for a turning—'Paris, 1852' or 'London, 1937'? You could end up anywhere. For myself, I think we are trapped here."

"But you haven't gone off to the city," I said.

"They'll spread," Izabel said, and Marie-Therese nodded. "At least we're safe here."

"All that we need to do," I said, "is find a way to defeat the creatures."

Chapter Ten: Debut Night

MARIE-THERESE SUGGESTED WE HOLD a victory feast. The food would be cooked and served by the handmaidens, to honour the warriors who had rescued them. I could foresee any number of ways in which the event could go terribly wrong. Marie-Therese waved away my objections and said that Amir had already agreed to it. Old Harsis had tried to argue, with little effect. He was far from happy with this parcel of foreign women who had been dropped into his camp. The miracle of being protected from the Spawn had already lost its lustre. Some people could never be satisfied.

I was beginning to appreciate that Marie-Therese overcame obstacles as an avalanche sweeps away trees. She still saw the nomads as poor savages who needed to be introduced to the wonders of good French cooking, and she had persuaded the others that a meal would be the best way of expressing gratitude.

It would be the official coming-out for the handmaidens. They were all fluent enough to talk to the nomads, and keeping them sequestered was becoming troublesome. We could get much more done if we did not always have to stick together in a group. Also, I had had enough of clucking over them like a mother hen, with Damki assisting in keeping them corralled into a group. I could not face living permanently in purdah with all ten. The feast would formally introduce the women to their rescuers.

Amir understood that his men were not to take any liberties with the women, who were still handmaidens of the goddess even though they appeared in the guise of serving wenches, and he undertook to make this very clear to them. I wondered how well they would remember once they were drunk and outside of his immediate supervision.

Marie-Therese ignored my suggestions, so I asked the others to make sure the dishes were not too strange and alien for the nomads' palates. When the colonisers were backed up with Maxim guns and gunboats, the natives might take an interest in copying their ways. When they were refugees, and female refugees at that, they might be less curious, and I was not sure what sort of reception to expect.

I was helping mix batter in our open-air kitchen when Old Harsis came and pushed my shoulder to get my attention. Manners were not his forte. "We cannot eat your food," he told me. "One of your women is in her time of bleeding—she is unclean."

Marie-Therese swooped across the room, a sparrow hawk defending its nest from a crow. "Don't be ridiculous, and get out of my kitchen."

"We will not eat unclean food. A woman may not touch food when she—" He spoke slowly and deliberately, and that made him easy to interrupt.

"Now you look here, Mr. Harsis," I said, respectfully but firmly. "I have the greatest respect for your knowledge when it comes to traditional lore. I also happen to be a representative from heaven."

"You are a woman—"

"From heaven, yes. And while your knowledge was perfectly accurate at the time, the situation has changed. We are all fighting monsters—they are unclean, and while the fight lasts, we are purged of uncleanliness."

"That is not the tradition. We—"

143

"I'm telling you the tradition has changed," I said. "By the authority of heaven."

"Now get out of my kitchen, you old fool," Marie-Therese said, brandishing a spoon at him.

Fortunately, Old Harsis complied before matters between him and the Frenchwoman could deteriorate. I excused myself to go and talk to Amir before Old Harsis could completely wreck our plans.

Amir was doubtful. As far he was concerned, Old Harsis was the oracle in matters of custom.

Nergal insinuated himself into the conversation to speak in my favour. "Yishka is the messenger of the gods. She may not know how to put up a tent or stitch a goatskin, but surely in such matters, she speaks with authority."

"Thank you," I said.

"All Harsis knows is what he heard from his father and his father's father a hundred years ago. Yishka gives us a more recent report from heaven. Do you trust the scout who reports something third-hand from a hundred years ago, or the one who saw it or last week for himself?"

"I suppose so," Amir said, stroking his beard.

"And, brother," Nergal continued, "unless we do something, Old Harsis will always push us around with his old sayings. He can always find one that fits what he wants to do. The goddess will break his power."

"Why should I care who cooks the food?" Amir said. "So long as it is good."

"The feast will be wonderful," I said.

"Good," Nergal said. "We will let it be known that Old Harsis is a doddering fool, and women can cook the whole month long with no taboo."

I felt I had won a small victory for the rights of women. Old Harsis and a few of his cronies might boycott the feast, but it was their loss.

My worries proved to be unfounded. Everything ran beautifully. I wore my feather shawl, but in a new dress she had stitched herself, with slippers to match, Marie-Therese outshone me. She wore her hair up in what I would have called Empire style, and she even borrowed my lipstick. There would be nobody as *chic* for another thousand years at least.

The nomads' idea of a feast was as much roast meat as they could eat. Taste was secondary. This was something different, though. Consommé, goat-liver pate on squares of toast, and *omelette aux fines herbes* were wolfed down in short order, and that was just the beginning. The nomads looked as though they were enjoying the food of the gods and gobbled the many courses with obvious appreciation—even the little bowls of stew generously seasoned with rosemary.

The beer undoubtedly helped. Vana had surpassed herself, and the nomads were highly appreciative of her latest brew. Jug after jug was passed through and drained.

"Stop wringing your hands," Vana told me. "I haven't given them the really strong stuff. Though that would be funny, wouldn't it, getting them all drunk?"

"No," I said.

The food and drink were eclipsed by the entertainment. Lalit, our Indian princess, was a musician. She had carved herself a little flute and played strange, wailing melodies. The tunes had a certain wistful charm, and though they were not to my taste, Lalit was clearly an accomplished flautist. I was worried how the audience would take it. Rather than being irritated by the strange wailing sound, they were all utterly entranced, some of them stopping with food halfway to their mouths.

There was a long silence after Lalit's performance, then the room erupted into conversation as the men all talked about this strange new thing they had heard.

"She sounded like a bird singing, a bird with a beautiful song," Amir said later. "When she played, I saw rivers rushing down deep valleys and high waterfalls and vast lakes and other things I have never seen."

The nomads had no musical instruments of their own, perhaps had never even heard anything other than horns, drums, and cymbals.

There were more dishes. Marie-Therese prepared an endless succession of delicacies, as though she wished to impress them with sheer diversity. The nomads might have preferred a few fat roasted antelopes, but they tried each new dish with undiminished appetite. The honey cakes went down well. And of course, there was more of Vana's good beer.

Satisfied at last that all was going well, I stepped outside to get some fresh air. Inside might be a strange barbarian banquet, but the stars were still my familiar friends. I turned to see the shadow of a man beside me.

"Yishka, I believe you owe me something," Nergal said, suddenly taking my wrist. "Without my help, Old Harsis would have ruined it all." His breath smelled of beer and garlic.

"I will repay you at a suitable time," I said, trying to remove his hand without starting a struggle.

"Amir will marry you," he said. "And when he dies, I will marry you, and you will be mine. But I want to taste you now."

"No," I said.

Nergal moved to kiss me then froze. There was a blade across his windpipe.

"Let her go," Illi said in a low voice.

Nergal let me go.

Illi spoke lower still, almost a whisper into Nergal's ear. A second later, he was gone, disappearing back into the noise and bustle of the feast.

"What did you say?" I asked.

"I told him," she said, still quiet, "that if he ever tried anything, I would slit the side of his tent in the night and castrate him like a goat. And the same for any other man who bothered any of us."

"Thank you, Illi."

"Men are brave until you threaten their balls." She contemplated the edge of the blade then wiped it on the ground before putting it away. "I told him to tell the others."

I was not sure that Nergal would share such am embarrassing incident. But then, he would need some excuse for failing to force himself on me, and the men were already half-afraid of Illi.

"Izabel and Marie-Therese's idea," she said.

Then Illi was gone, too, leaving me to wonder if all of them were in on this little plan.

Afterwards, Izabel and I were recovering in the tent I called the common room. Tomorrow, we would be able to rearrange our tents so we were not living in each other's pockets.

Marie-Therese came in, eating from a bowl.

"You finishing the snails?" Izabel asked. "No, you keep them. The party was fantastic."

The snails were one of the few dishes which had not been polished off. Vana had derived some innocent amusement going around handing them out and afterward telling the recipient what they had just eaten.

"*Un grand success*," Marie-Therese said, throwing herself down on a heap of cushions. "Now we have our debut, we are free. Yishka cannot keep us in the harem any longer."

"That was only for protection," I said.

"*Pfft*. You are too scared of the men. Nergal will have told them what will happen if they bother us. I don't think there is anything to be afraid of. Not if we are careful."

"They aren't that bad," Izabel said. She had changed her tune, given how adamant she had been that the men were all rapists. "They have a sort of code."

147

"I can't stop you doing anything." This was another one of my overused sayings; maybe I would not need to use them so often now.

"Maybe you need a lover," Marie-Therese said. "He would calm your nerves."

I wondered if Marie-Therese was not a little drunk, or more than a little. While she had been rude about Vana's ale, she drank plenty.

"I have a fiancé back in England," I reminded her. "That's not how we do things. Were you planning on taking a lover yourself?"

"You think I haven't already got one?" She tossed her head. "I should marry Amir and become queen."

"Feel free," I said.

"I think he's only got eyes for one person," Izabel said.

"He's not interested in Yishka," Marie-Therese told Izabel. "Not like that. It is like the Dauphin and Jean D'Arc."

"Who?"

"Joan of Arc," I said. "A French religious fanatic who fought against the English in the Middle Ages. She persuaded the French military commander to put her in charge. The English burned her as a witch—"

"I know Joan of Arc," Izabel said. "Hundred Years War. Played the game."

"Amir is an orphan," Marie-Therese said. "He needs a mother, someone he can look up to who tells him what to do. Yishka is his mother now. A mother sent from heaven for a little boy."

I had not heard this theory before, and Marie-Therese seemed pleased by my shocked silence.

"Doesn't mean he's interested in you," Izabel told her.

"We all have our secrets."

"I don't think that's quite true," I said.

"Of course it is! So many secrets. All of us pretending to be something we are not. We reinvent ourselves as we want. I could tell you things…"

Illi, who had been sitting silently in a corner, cracked open a nut. I had not noticed her there before. Marie-Therese flicked a gaze at her and went on.

"Lalit saying she was a princess," Marie-Therese went on. "She was never a princess! She was something low, a slave. I think she was given up as a human sacrifice, with all those jewels." She looked at me sideways. "She will not deny it if you ask her."

"I wouldn't dream of asking."

"And Noora, you know she was one of the enemy? She pretends so hard to be a good Muslim. Really, she worshipped at Tulu's altar. That's why she's so scared of the thing in her belly. I don't know for sure if she's even on our side now."

"How could you say that?"

"I'm not scared of the truth. Even when it makes you uncomfortable." She speared a snail with her fork—an anachronism in cutlery, centuries ahead of its time, forged by Turm—and bit into it.

"Lu Zhu," she went on, "is not from the middle ages. She is from some later time. She thinks we are evil colonialists, you and I. But she knows to keep quiet."

"Obviously, we all try to present ourselves in the best light," I said. "We show our best side. Lu Zhu just wants to help people, and that's wonderful. Where she came from, what she was before doesn't matter—"

"Oh, you make me sick. You are always so happy-happy," she said. "But we are not all so nice. None of us are."

"Nobody ever accused me of being nice before," Izabel said.

"We are not 'nice,' not the way Yishka wants us. Even your favourite, little Inzalu. You know her people are cannibals?"

"As if that would make any difference," I said, keeping my voice calm. "Even if it were true."

"Don't spoil a great evening," Izabel said. "You did good. That was a fantastic meal. Everyone loved it. Don't make Yishka slap you."

"All I am saying is, you don't have to be always nice to me. I am not your friend, Yishka."

Her words fell like stones. I sensed the others waiting for me to snap back at her as being an ungrateful, drunken Frenchwoman. I was not about to undo all my work with a careless word.

"If you say so," I said. "But you will always be my sister. And I will still look after you and get you home safe. You are the closest family I have, even if you're not my friend."

Marie-Therese chewed another snail and said nothing.

"That's sweet," Izabel said, patting my knee. "You're going to choke me up. And don't worry about Mamzelle. She's just jealous that you're the one who gets to play the white saviour." Her voice dropped to mock-whisper. "Plus, Amir thinks she's scary."

"Well, enough secrets for one night," I said. "No more revelations."

"There's one thing you ought to know before tomorrow," Izabel said. "As you probably didn't notice them sneaking off at the time."

I looked from her to Izabel and waited for them to enlighten me. Both of them looked to Illi, who did not return their gaze.

"Not Damki and Inzalu?" I asked.

"Inzalu is too young," Izabel said. If she were a nomad, she might have been married with a baby by now. "We explained to Damki."

"Then…?"

"Vana and Young Harsis," Marie-Therese said. She and Izabel burst out laughing.

"She practically dragged him outside," Marie-Therese said, appalled by Vana's lack of subtlety.

"Illi followed them," Izabel said.

Illi would not comment, but Marie-Therese described in some anatomical detail what Illi had reported seeing. Izabel laughed until she choked. I had never thought of myself as prudish, but there were limits.

"You wouldn't want Vana getting pregnant," Izabel said.

"But she mustn't"—I stumbled for words, rejecting various new terms I had learned—"you know. And Young Harsis is a married man!"

"It's only a fling," Marie-Therese said. "I don't think she's serious about him."

"Isn't… adultery as taboo for Vana's people as it is for the nomads?"

Vana was from North Africa, from some time between the Romans and the Arab conquest. I did not know much about her people, but I could not believe they approved of licentious behaviour.

"Back home maybe," Izabel said. "But Vana is off the leash here. The way the nomads see it, she's the property of her father, and he's not here to object. So she's enjoying herself."

"We can't have this sort of thing."

Izabel might have argued, but Marie-Therese nodded agreement.

"*Elle est trop indescete,*" Marie-Therese said. *She is too indiscreet.* "I will talk to Vana. We must avoid scandal."

Chapter Eleven: Trading

People talked about the victory feast for weeks afterward. Old Harsis was even more curmudgeonly than usual, but if he was trying to tell the nomads we had bewitched them, nobody was listening. Vana's indiscretion did not cause any difficulties; Young Harsis might have the brains of an ox, but he was smart enough not to boast of the encounter.

I was resigned to the other women now being free agents, not permanently confined to quarters. It made less difference than I'd expected. We were all so used to being together and had nowhere else to go that life continued more or less as it had before. Damki still kept an eye on the women, though I suspected Illi's presence—or suspected presence—provided more protection.

Our band was safe, but others were not. The Spawn were hunting down the scattered groups who lived in the grasslands, the misfits and exiles. If ambush failed, the creatures would simply plod after their prey for days on end, as relentless as walking doom, until the victim was finally overcome by fatigue. Several had taken shelter with us. In theory, these refugees were only supposed to stay a few days, but nobody could say where else they might go. Ultimately everyone who survived would come here, simply because we offered the only possible refuge.

The first we knew of the slaughter was when some of Amir's scouts brought back a little boy from another clan, one that was not an ally. He was about six. If he were a few years older, the nomads might have killed him or violated him—Izabel said they did that to boys—and left him to die. But as he was so young and had a story to tell, they brought him back.

The scout, who wore a bracelet of buzzard claws, threw the boy down in front of me like a dead goat. "Amir said you would want to talk to this."

"Where did you find him?" I asked.

"Poor little thing," Inzalu said, stooping to the bewildered child. "Come here! Come to auntie, little one."

He burst into tears but let himself be hugged and comforted.

"Over by Black Bird Stream," Buzzard Claws said. "He is of the band of Pazar, of the clan of Tanoman. Their winter camp is five or six horizons off, so he must have strayed. We looked; we did not find any others."

"Thank you," I said. "You did well. Please leave us now."

The little boy was terrified of the warriors. He calmed down a little after they left, but still clung to Inzalu sobbing. When I left her, she had wiped his face and got some milk and bread for him. As she showed him how to crack and eat almonds, Noora talked to him in low murmurs.

I busied myself with planning, working on a revised street layout, and had almost forgotten about the boy when Inzalu brushed my elbow an hour later. The boy was curled up, sleeping on a straw mattress, a puppy in his arms.

"His band moved to their winter camp two days ago," she said in a low voice, even though the boy was on the other side of the tent and sound asleep. "The monsters attacked them. The people tried to run away, but they kept running into more monsters. His mummy told him to run and keep running. He doesn't know what happened, but there was a lot of shouting. He hasn't seen anyone else; he just kept going in the direction she showed him."

"There must be others," I said. "We should send out search parties."

By nightfall, Amir's men had found the remains of the encampment and a trickle of survivors, mainly women and children. Most of the men had perished defending the families. There were also flocks of goats and horses which had escaped. The Spawn had not made a clean sweep, but they had been efficient in their destruction.

"We followed the trails in the grass," Amir said. "There were at least forty of them spread out in four groups, concentrated across the paths and streambeds."

"Clever," I said.

"It was a good attack. It is the way I would have done it."

"But we warned them!" I said, my voice suddenly breaking. "We told all of them. Why…?"

"They did not believe us. Maybe they thought it was a ruse to gain more range land."

"But some of them have been here and seen the earthworks."

"Not everyone believes in you as easily as I do, Yishka," he said sadly.

A small band of miserable refugees was gathered in the middle of the encampment. Handmaidens were providing soup and tea, but the survivors were physically and emotionally exhausted. Their band had been shattered, their menfolk largely wiped out.

The children were least affected. The little boy who had been brought in first was already playing at fighting monsters with the boys and girls of Amir's band.

"We will take them in, of course," I said.

Amir shook his head. "A few, I can accept as guests, but strangers may not stay in our camp. These people can disperse to their sister bands, where they have family."

"It is forbidden to take in strangers from other clans," Old Harsis said. "Strangers bring the Great Dying. Those who took in strangers accepted their curse from the gods. These must be sent away."

"We will take them in," I said.

"So many more mouths to feed from our winter stores," Amir said.

"More hands to work," I said.

"It is forbidden," Old Harsis insisted, as though I had not heard him the first time.

"We have been through this," I told him. "I am the one who interprets what the gods do or do not wish. And Amir is the leader. You must follow his will."

"We will take them in, but we will keep them separate," Amir said at last.

"Who could possibly argue with that?"

"Who indeed?" Amir said.

There was no precedent for harbouring warriors from another clan with no allegiance to Amir. But his status as a slayer—the first ever—and the promise of revenge on the Spawn that had killed their brothers and fathers would be enough to bind them to him. Or so Nergal had advised me.

"We will extend the camp," I said. "They can have a new section all to themselves if you don't want them mixing."

"The goddess's will be done," he said. "And you will be thinking of sheltering bandits next?"

We had received a messenger from the bandit chief Crow, making a polite enquiry about finding sanctuary behind our earthworks and asking what terms might interest us.

"They offer to bring more spears for you," I said. "I hear Crow is a man of his word."

"One camp, one leader," Amir said.

"So if he acknowledges your leadership, you will not object to him?"

"Old Harsis will," Amir said. "But if Crow will kneel and swear loyalty to me, his men can join our band and share our meat. They are good horsemen."

Marie-Therese was pleased with the prospect of more fighting men, but she was less happy with accommodating refugees.

"As if we did not have enough problems," she said.

"They're people who need rescuing," I said. "Like you were a few months ago, remember?"

"How you English like *fair play*," she said, as though helping others was an eccentric quirk. "And just where will we put them all?"

"We are expanding the settlement," I said. "We need proper pens for the animals and a civic centre. Accommodation for a few dozen extra people will not add much. Now we have more shovels, making more earthworks is a doddle. We built this whole place in one day with digging sticks and pots, remember?"

"Oh, it will be easy then." She rolled her eyes, but she could not argue.

The Spawn increasingly ranged through the surrounding lands. The merchant caravan still arrived, though, with the chubby character in yellow and red who exchanged winter supplies for skins. Most of his pack mules were laden with strips of dried meat—and dried fish from the coast, which the nomads would not touch—but he also laid out bolts of cloth, metal ingots, and shiny new knives and spearheads in fans, and copper cooking pots and utensils. The handmaidens crowded round the wares on display.

The merchant's guards and his assistant stared at the gaggle of strange young women of all races. Some of the men grinned; others just ogled. Most of the girls pretended not to notice, except Izabel, who met their looks with a venomous glare, and Vana, who winked at two of them.

"We should charge them a *sou* each for looking," Marie-Therese said. "Then we could buy something."

"Timi thinks she can trade," I said.

Lalit had some impressive jewellery, though she had kept most of it hidden. I had seen one huge ruby which would have been the star of any jeweller's shop window in Bond Street. She had not been able to bribe the slavers, for whom the gems were just pebbles, and the nomads had no use for gemstones, but the merchants were another matter. Timi had persuaded Lalit to give up one of her jewelled rings for trading purposes, and now she insisted she should be the one to haggle.

"But it's my ring," Lalit said.

Timi placed a finger on Lalit's lips. "Lalit, the goats know more about trading than you do. Be quiet and watch. You will learn something."

Lalit was so astonished that she offered no resistance.

The trader touched his palm. "What you trade?"

Timi held up the ring in front of her eye and looked at him through it. The gold gleamed, and the blue sapphire glinted in the sun. "Best quality," she said with conviction and placed it in his palm. "Most valuable."

He examined the ring without interest, sucked his teeth, and smiled ingratiatingly. "Ring metal good," he admitted, making a circle with his thumb and forefinger. "Stone not good." He picked up three different rolls of patterned cloth, some of the best on display. "Make good trade."

Timi wandered over to the neatly stacked metal ingots and nudged one with her foot. "How many?"

"Beautiful lady!" he protested, unfurling a roll of cloth to better display the pattern. "Good cloth. Lady not want war metal."

Timi picked up an ingot. "Ten metal for ring."

He laughed and shook his head. "Seven and two of this cloth, two of that cloth."

"Seven metal and three cloth—and twelve spearheads."

The conversation went on for some time. Timi was keen to find the trading value of everything in different commodities and how the price changed with the amount. Rather than being bored by so much questioning, the merchant enjoyed the game of adjusting his offers each time. After a while, they retired to the shade, and the dealing got more complicated as Timi worked out an exchange involving skins, tools, the ring, and the growing collection of household wares and fabrics that the handmaidens were selecting. Illi, I noted, added only a simple but highly practical knife.

Once everything we wanted to purchase was piled up, Timi took out the ring again, and they prepared to complete the deal.

"Ring good," she said, "Stone not good?"

He nodded complacently. "Metal good, stone bad."

His expression changed quickly when Timi produced a blade and started to prise the stone out of its setting.

"Ring good," she repeated, and he took the ring stripped of its gem. To my surprise, he did not try to back out of the deal. The gold alone must have been worth more than what he was trading.

Timi held the sapphire on her palm and exchanged a look with the merchant.

"Clever lady," he said, and this time his smile was genuine. "Now we make deal for stone?"

"Yes, let's make deal for the stone, you fat thieving bastard," she said.

The merchant gurgled with pleasure. "Hahaha! Yes, yes. We make good deal for stone now!"

They launched into a second round of negotiation with every sign of enjoyment on both sides. Timi succeeded in adding several more ingots and more cloth than we could possibly use, along with other seemingly random items. I would have protested at her odd selection, but I was beginning to feel that Timi probably knew what she was doing.

"Another ring, please," she asked Lalit, who pouted. "You see that roll of pink silk? All yours if you give me another ring to trade. And I'll throw in those shiny buckles."

Lalit had been admiring some silver buckles to ornament slippers. She acquiesced, and Timi purchased a supply of dried meat and dried fish, along with half of the merchant's stock of trinkets.

Timi still thought we were being robbed, but she was satisfied that we would not be able to get any more for the jewellery. And she had shown the trader that, unlike the nomads, she could not always be cheated so easily.

"You and he were getting on well by the end," I said.

"He wants me to join the business and marry his brainless nephew," she said.

"Are you tempted?"

Timi wagged a finger at me. "Yishka-from-Heaven, you have to learn never to take the first offer! He said he has a couple of other nephews, maybe I'll have a look at them. More important, now we have a stock of trade goods so we can start dealing with the other nomads."

"They don't trade with each other," I said, recalling times when the two bands had met.

"Yes, they do. Every time they meet, they always exchange gifts. They just don't understand commerce," she said. This was true; even the word *commerce* was borrowed, as Language had no word for it. "Now we need to find some other merchants, or we are at the mercy of Fat Face here. His monopoly is not good for us. And I want to go to one of the cities so we can turn the rest of Lalit's rings into goods and really get into business."

Lalit might have had other ideas, but I was sure that Timi would be able to bargain with her and buy her off with gaudy, cheap trinkets.

"This is your calling, isn't it?"

"My mother and I kept the books and did the stocktaking," she said. "My father and my brother did the trading. I was never allowed to—even though I'm better with numbers than either of them. Here, I can do everything."

"Don't get over-confident," I said. Timi might have been enthusiastic, but she was still a girl. She would be dealing with experienced traders, dealing in a foreign language, with commodities she had no experience with, and with so many unknowns.

"Be quiet," she said, placing a finger on my lips. "And watch."

Timi was not the only one who had her own ideas.

"I am going to the Place of Monsters," Illi told me one evening.

Illi had never previously told me where she was going or where she had been. But the Place of Monsters was different. The Spawn were more active and numerous than ever, and Amir's scouts gave the centre of their activity a wide berth. I had wondered whether there were any more captives there, but a second rescue mission would have been suicidal. Even getting close was a risk too far.

"You mustn't," I said. "It's too dangerous."

"I want to see," she said.

"Why do you want to see? What is it you know?"

"Nothing," she said, shaking her head. "I'll say when I get back."

"Don't go," I said.

She shook her head. While apparently revering me, Illi never felt obliged to take orders. "I wanted to tell you, so, if I didn't come back, you would know I had not run away. It might take a few days."

"Is there anything we can do? Should I get some of Amir's men to go with you?"

"No! But maybe if some of them can ride around after dusk and make some noise to the north of the camp."

"As a distraction?"

Illi nodded.

"I'll talk to Amir," I said. "Please don't do anything until we've arranged it."

"She'll be fine," Izabel assured me later. "Illi just disappears when she wants to. The girl's a ninja."

"I hope so," I said. Whatever a ninja was.

"She told me the creatures can't sense her when she thinks green thoughts."

"What?"

Izabel shrugged her big shoulders. "I don't know. But she knows what she's doing."

"Did you talk to her about this scouting expedition?" I asked.

"It was her idea," Izabel said, suddenly defensive. "She has a hunch she wants to follow. But there's some things I asked about. And I told her to be careful."

I was expecting Illi's disappearance, but Noora vanished, as well, the day before Lu Zhu was supposed to examine her. But while nobody could track Illi, Amir said following Noora would be easy. Her escape attempt was not sophisticated. She had run away through the grassland on foot, without even a waterskin or a bag of dried meat.

"Don't worry," Amir told me. "A woman on foot—a pregnant woman—is easy hunting."

The pack of dogs was barking madly. They sensed when a hunt was imminent.

"Don't hurt Noora," I said. "Please."

"As the goddess commands," Amir said. For him, it was just another sporting challenge, and catching Noora without injuring her only made it more interesting. He took three men, and Marie-Therese rode with them, supposedly to talk to Noora and reassure her if needed. I could not tell if she wanted to ensure that Noora was unharmed or that she did not get away.

Less than an hour later, they returned, with Noora holding on to the spare horse Marie-Therese had insisted on taking. The warriors looked cheerful enough. Marie-Therese wore a grim expression.

"I am sorry," Noora told me, her face streaked with tears. "I was so afraid. I don't know what to do. They told me I would be blessed, reborn as the child of Tulu. They told me I would be cursed if it was harmed… but now I'm so confused. And it moves inside me!"

Noora was scared, terrified of what would happen to her if she did not let the thing in her womb keep growing but equally scared of the alternative. She knew she had been told lies, but she did not quite believe us, either.

Marie-Therese did not want to give Noora any choice. She just wanted to kill the thing growing inside her as soon as possible. I insisted that we had to work by persuasion, not coercion.

"If you do not let Lu Zhu act soon, the thing will kill her," Marie-Therese snapped angrily. "And we will have another monster."

"Quite," I said. "So it should not be a very difficult matter to convince Noora. We just have to make sure she knows that we will protect her from the wrath of… you know."

"Of Tulu," Marie-Therese said. "Yes, well, we all need protecting from that. But your walls seem to be working."

"Our walls," I said.

We all sat down with Noora, and the others shared their experiences. There were tears, but it was easier than I had expected. Noora wanted to be convinced. She wanted absolution.

Lu Zhu examined Noora. Her condition was grave. I had suspected that the unnatural gestation would develop rapidly, but she was considerably more advanced than even Lu Zhu had thought. The ancient Romans knew about Caesarean sections, and so did the Chinese of Lu Zhu's era—whenever that was. It was a technique reserved for emergencies, and this was one.

"Cutting it out is the only way," Lu Zhu said. "But she may die."

I involuntarily crossed my arms across my own stomach. "How dangerous?"

"I will do everything I can," Lu Zhu said. "I told you we should have acted sooner."

Amir's people knew a little of the virtues of the poppy. Lu Zhu knew far more. Everyone wanted to help, and we gathered plenty of seed heads and learned how to cut them and collect the milky sap.

Lu Zhu carried out the operation the next afternoon in my tent, with new instruments fresh from Turm's forge. I had been banished outside; I was too fidgety and distracted her. The old midwife who was now Lu Zhu's nurse assisted her, along with Puabi, who was now an apprentice midwife.

After waiting outside for a while, I took a walk around the camp, then another and another. I repeatedly thought my watch had stopped because time dragged on so slowly. Eventually, it was over, and I anxiously awaited my chance to talk to the surgeon.

"Noora is sleeping," Lu Zhu said. "It was not easy, but not so bad. She has lost blood, but if she is strong, she will recover. That is, if the wound does not go bad."

This was an important qualification. Lu Zhu, though, had much the same idea of the importance of antiseptic operating conditions as modern doctors, which had surprised me. Though perhaps that was less surprising if she came from a more recent era.

Lu Zhu passed me a large earthenware jar stoppered with a round stone and bound with straw. Something wet moved and flopped inside it. "You wanted this." Her words were almost, but not quite, an accusation.

"Thank you," I said.

I knew that Lu Zhu would not help me with what had to be done next. I summoned Izabel and Marie-Therese. Both had the character and the determination it would take to carry this through. I had wondered about asking Amir, but he would not be suitable for all sorts of reasons.

It was already dark when the three of us gathered in my tent, squatting on the ground with the jar between us. As soon as they sat the jar, they knew what it was. Lanterns hung in all four corners. I wanted as much light as possible. A brazier was ready on one side, its heat uncomfortable in the warm evening air.

"It is alive," I said. "And we need to find out how to kill it."

"Amir says they cannot be killed," Izabel said, and Marie-Therese nodded. "So does everyone else."

"There must be a way," I said. "The previous goddess destroyed them." I had gathered all the tools I could get my hands on: blades, hammers, saws, tongs, hatchets, and spikes. The brazier was stoked up to red heat. The tent looked like a medieval torture chamber.

Damki was on call outside. I did not think he would be needed. Izabel stood by with a javelin and Marie-Therese with a knife as I unstoppered the bottle. The thing slithered out on to the ground, rearing up and extruding tentacles. It was a perfect miniature of the creature we had encountered in the place of monsters, half-octopus and half-slug.

Izabel swore and impaled it with the javelin. It bled green ichor but showed no real sign of distress.

As Izabel held it up in front of her, like a skewered piece of meat for roasting, the creature wrapped its tentacles around the spear. With a series of muscular efforts, the thing pushed itself off the end and flopped back onto the ground. The wound in its side seethed like swarming ants then settled. A moment later, there was no sign of the injury.

Pain, as Lu Zhu had told me, was the body's way of warning against damage. It stopped a person from walking on a broken ankle and making it worse or from leaving a hand on a hot pan. But these Spawn could not be damaged in any real sense, so they had no sensation corresponding to pain.

"Watch out," I said as Marie-Therese stepped closer to get a look, but it had already fastened on to her shoe.

"Ai!" Marie-Therese shouted.

Izabel kicked the thing across the tent then speared it again before it could move.

"I'm not hurt," Marie-Therese said, looking down at her shoe. The leather had been torn through, but there was no blood. "It was just surprise."

"Thing is tough," Izabel said. She had pinned it to the ground, but it was crawling up the shaft of the javelin, leaving a slimy trail.

Piercing it with several sharp objects then smashing it with a hammer eventually did the job, and the thing subsided into a mess of jelly. Maybe the brain had to be destroyed, as Amir had suggested, or maybe it was just a matter of damaging enough vital organs.

"It's dead now," Izabel breathed.

"For how long?" I asked.

"What are those in it?" Marie-Therese asked, pointing at the pulpy mess from a safe distance. Two dozen tiny jagged objects were left in the pool of liquid. They were its teeth, the only truly solid part.

We watched expectantly. Sure enough, the remains bubbled like a witch's cauldron. After a minute, they writhed into worms and flowed together, gathering in the teeth. Then the thing knitted itself back into its original form. The hairs on the back of my neck prickled. This was truly uncanny. After two minutes by my watch, the creature was intact and unharmed. We had to pin it down to stop it from escaping or attacking one of us.

The process was not like healing. It was more like the shattered ice on a pond reforming or iron filings lining up under the influence of a magnet. Some force caused it to always settle back into its original form.

"It's magic," Marie-Therese said, crossing herself. She had told me she was an atheist, but sometimes she forgot. "It's impossible."

We killed it again and again. The actual killing was never quick and clean. Afterwards, we tried everything we had to make it stay dead. We tried fire, red-hot blades, and scalding hot oil. It could not be drowned, and even boiling it in water was only a temporary inconvenience. Nothing stopped it from regenerating. When we hooked the teeth away, it reformed without them.

At first, I was troubled that splitting it into two would make two copies, but it only had one mind, or one will, and always coalesced into a single individual.

"Bury it under a rock," Izabel said.

"Maybe acid," Marie-Therese said hopefully, knowing that we had none, and none of us knew how to make it.

Tired and dispirited by our failures, Izabel maneuvered the thing back onto the earthenware jar with a pair of tongs. But either the jar had been weakened or the thing had become stronger or more cunning: after a minute, cracks spiderwebbed the surface, then the jar popped apart into fragments.

Izabel swore and pinned the thing to the ground with a javelin before it could move, then added another to be sure. "Any ideas?"

The Bible specifically prohibited the use of sorcerous powers, even if they are used against the demons themselves. I had tried the words before on the first creature I had seen, the one that had killed Sabian, with no effect, and on the one that had tried to cross the ramparts. I recited again the words etched on my memory. They had not the slightest effect.

"What is that?" Izabel asked.

"Failed attempt at magic," I said.

"I have heard it—something like it, very like it—before," Marie-Therese said.

"Yes, I tried it during the night attack."

"That's not what she means," Izabel said. "I've heard it too. At the ceremony, before I fell here. The same rhythm and words, but different."

"In those dreams," Marie-Therese said. "Those dreams… I had forgotten."

"Then too," Izabel said. "When we were prisoners. At night. But it's like you're saying it backwards."

It suddenly struck me that the phrase was the reversed form of the chant used to evoke the thing. I had been chanting it when I fell into the abyss, and for the first time, I wondered if that had been what opened up the channel to come here. I had been trying to expel that thing, but it was stronger, and like someone pushing against a brick wall, I had been expelled instead.

The evocation could be used forwards or backwards, to attract or repel. Why would they have heard it then? Unless it related to the way the Spawn implanted themselves in human bodies. Unless it was a way of summoning the thing into its housing on earth. This was the same magic that gave Cthulhu's Spawn their foothold in our world. The Word made Flesh. Magic that could be reversed. Then the idea came to me fully formed.

"Let's kill it again," I said briskly.

It was no easier than before, but soon, the thing was reduced to a vile mulch. This time, I spoke the chant with more conviction. Something tightened in my chest, like the resistance a cyclist encounters while tackling a steep hill. Something was happening.

I repeated the words again and again, and it was easier each time. The green mess started to steam. Then something gave way, and it disintegrated entirely, melting into smoke. The smoke faded even as it formed, then the last dozen wisps spiralled up into nothingness.

Marie-Therese swore. Izabel just looked dumbstruck.

Unnatural forces bound the thing's soul or animating force to its body. As long as that bond existed, it could never be truly destroyed. But if we could break that bond, it was gone like melting snow. It was gone completely, leaving just those triangular teeth like a scattering of black corn kernels.

"How did you do that?" Izabel asked.

I felt slightly dizzy, as though I had just downed a large glass of brandy.

"Dispelled," I said. "Literally, dis-spelled. Unspelled it. Spelled backwards. Back where it came from."

"Are you okay?"

"I will be in a minute," I said. "'To them will be given the power to bind and loose.'"

"Sit down," Marie-Therese ordered, and I did.

167

"That was incredible," Izabel said. "Woman, you're a witch."

"Don't joke about it," Marie-Therese said.

Izabel was right. It was magic—the devil's magic—and I had performed an act of witchcraft. The same incantation reversed could be used to summon the seeds of the Spawn, as the slavers had done.

I picked up one of the teeth. It might have been a tiny obsidian arrowhead, etched with complex grooves. Everything else had gone. This was just mineral residue, hard earth-stuff taken up to give the soft Spawn a sharp edge, the stones in a chicken's gizzard.

"Now we can destroy them," Izabel said. "Spear those things, kill them into slime, and—whoosh!—say those words to vanish them."

"Maybe," Marie-Therese said. "If they don't kill us first."

Chapter Twelve: Lord Izzar's Council

The morning mingled celebration and sorrow. Noora was still alive after her ordeal, and Lu Zhu was more confident than ever that she would make a full recovery. Illi had returned, alive and well, from her reconnaissance mission. Even her talents as a scout were not enough this time, though. It had been impossible to get close to the creatures' camp.

"There is a rampart all around it," she said, gesturing towards the earthworks. "They copy us, build, like wasps."

"What do you mean?"

"The Spawn eat dirt. Like wasps. They vomit it back up, and they build with it, layer on layer, this high." Illi indicated a height above the level of her head.

"So you couldn't get to the cave with the pool," Izabel said.

"I'm sorry."

"Does that matter?" I asked.

"I dropped something there when I fell," Izabel said. "Something that might have been useful to us. I guess it will have to wait."

"What about the slavers?" I asked.

"Many Spawn, no people," Illi said. "None. No sound, no smell, no tracks, no traces."

Illi's hunting skills were second to none. If she said there were no men, I believed her. I hoped the creatures had eaten them. Slowly.

"Can you tell me what you had a hunch about?" I asked.

"I thought they had changed. I wanted to see how," Illi said. "They don't need the men now. Now they build their hive."

The two handmaidens I had been worried about had both made it through. The sorrow came from another quarter. Our Indian princess had disappeared. Lalit was another runaway like Noora, but better organised. She and the handsome Igmil had taken two horses. Inzalu said Lalit had spoken about going back to her homeland, sounding the others out on whether they could go with her. She had not believed, or had not fully understood, my explanation that the only way to get back would be via the cloaca through which we had arrived. Finding out that her jewels had real value had given her the spur she needed. Lalit hoped to get to the coast and buy passage back to her home country.

"Idiot woman!" Timi said. She seemed as annoyed by the loss of valuable jewels as by losing one of our sisters. "It won't work."

"And we are poor again," Marie-Therese said, also taking a calculating view.

"Not necessarily," Timi said. "But it will take longer to get rich."

"How can we get rich if we have nothing to trade with?"

"I hope Lalit is safe," Inzalu said, squinting at the horizon as though she might see the furtive pair.

"It's simple," Timi said. "Suppose you have a band which has plenty of goats but they need a horse. They'll trade you forty goats for one horse. You make the trade. Then you find another band which has lots of horses but needs more goats. They'll give you a horse for just twenty goats. So you trade some of the goats and end up with a horse again and twenty goats, as well. You just keep doing that with different commodities and different bands. The more you can trade, the more you can make."

"We should find out where the other bands are and what they need," Marie-Therese said.

"I'm more worried about Lalit," I said.

"It was her choice," Izabel told me. "You always said you couldn't force us to do anything. What happens to her isn't your responsibility." Izabel still was not on good terms with Lalit.

Amir was irritated but not greatly concerned. He did not think the pair were in any immediate danger. They were young and fit and had good ponies, and Igmil was an experienced warrior, skilled with spear, bow, and javelin. There were hostile tribes, but the two should be able to outrun most danger. Snakes, scorpions, wolves, quicksand, and other hazards lay in their path, though, which became more hazardous as they moved away from familiar territory.

"She was a songbird," Amir said, recalling Lalit's fluting. "And like a songbird, she has flown away. But mainly, I could wish she did not take one of my best men when she went."

That made two women I had misjudged. Others might go, as well, and I could hardly blame them. This was a miserable place, and there was no reason for them to stay. I had to remain, though. It was my responsibility to fight the Spawn, and I wanted more than anything to get back to my world.

Knowing that the creatures could be destroyed was one thing. Actually killing a full-sized one was another matter entirely. They were dangerous, and we lacked the means to kill them from a safe distance.

Turm, Izabel, and some of the others spent two whole days digging a pit trap half a mile from the camp. However well it was camouflaged, and however temptingly we baited it, the Spawn could not be enticed to come close. Perhaps the ground vibrations told them of the shape of the terrain ahead, or they could see waves invisible to us. However they did it, my dreams of trapping them one by one like flies in honey then smashing them with boulders before dispelling them were destined to come to nothing.

I would dearly have loved to conjure up some gunpowder. I was sure Turm could have cast us a bronze cannon, given enough metal, or at least a musket able to do far more damage than an arrow or a javelin and kill one of the things with a single shot. But gunpowder or any of those modern explosives I knew only by name—gun cotton, cordite—were beyond any of our knowledge.

I sketched engines of war, medieval tanks that Leonardo da Vinci might have built and armoured carriages with many whirling blades like lethal threshing machines, but the nomads did not even have carts. I imagined man-powered aeroplanes dropping giant spears, but those were even less practical. I could talk about and dream about rockets, steam-tractors, Greek fire, and giant spear throwers, but I was perfectly useless when it came to actually building any of those things.

Izabel was the most warlike of the handmaidens, with an extensive, if somewhat superficial, knowledge of warfare from ancient times to her own era, when they presumably fought with death-rays and rocket ships, garnered from a lifetime of playing war games. When it came to practicalities though, she was as ignorant as me.

"If I had my…" She made a gesture towards her ear. "There isn't a word for it. A magic charm full of knowledge. If I had that back, in five minutes I could get all the plans for weapons you'd ever want."

"You dropped it in the cave pool when you arrived," I said, putting two and two together.

"Yup. I wish—"

"If wishes were horses," I said, "beggars would ride. We will have to work with what we have. Do you know how a crossbow works?"

"A light crossbow is just like a bow," she said. "The heavy ones, you crank up with a handle and get more power."

I tried to picture it but only had vague images of medieval woodcuts. "I suppose the trick is the leverage and having a strong enough bowstave."

The nomad's bows were compact, but feeble compared to the English longbows I knew from history. Their bows were used for hunting rather than warfare, with arrows more suited to killing pheasants than men. Javelins, which could be hurled when riding at a gallop, were their weapons of war. But javelins were pinpricks to the Spawn.

Longbows needed to be made of yew rather than ordinary wood, but I didn't know what a crossbow should be made from.

"Heavy crossbows are made of high-tensile steel," Izabel said knowledgeably. "It's like a giant spring-storing energy. It's so strong, you need a mechanism to pull it back."

"Ah yes," I said. "Steel. That's another thing it would be nice to have. Even if we had iron, I don't think we'll get decent steel until the Renaissance."

"Not with me making it," Izabel said.

Crow, the bandit chief, appeared in person to parlay with Amir. Visiting an enemy camp took some courage, especially for an outsider who could not even rely on the nomad's rules of hospitality. I wanted to join the discussion, but it was over before I even reached them.

"Crow's men join us in the fight," Amir announced. "It is settled."

"My Lady Yishka," Crow said. He was wearing black, a short sword at his belt. A twist to his lips gave the impression that Crow was always about to smile, that life amused him. "A woman from heaven. The plains echo with your name, and with your feat of conjuring the fortifications in a single night." He had an accent, but spoke fluently and more elegantly than some of the native speakers.

"They also echo with your name," I said. "And I am pleased you chose not to attack our caravans."

"Ah," he said. "The Lady Timi had made it known that we would be hunted down and killed slowly if we did. It did not seem a worthwhile risk." His eyes laughed. It was all a game to Crow.

"Better you fight with Amir's men than against them," I said. "We all have a common enemy now."

"The Spawn," Crow said. "When you watch, they stumble around slowly, but there are always some ahead of you. We have lost men to them. We could not keep riding away from them forever."

"Crow has brought me four good horses," Amir said, clapping a hand over Crow's shoulder. "I have given him and his men my protection."

Amir was proud to have the only refuge from the monsters, like a senior boy sharing his umbrella with a junior. Crow acknowledged his new leader with a small nod, showing the appropriate level of respect for a nomad chief.

"They say you will fight the Spawn and rid the plains of them," Crow said, looking directly at me.

"With the aid of heaven," I said. "As happened in the olden days."

"You can count on me." He gave another nod.

"You must meet my warriors," Amir said. "We can share stories, and you will drink our good beer!"

The two went off with every sign of friendship, but, as I told Izabel, Crow looked like he might be a handful if he decided he wanted to be in charge.

"He can't challenge Amir for the leadership," Izabel said. "He's smart, though."

"Not bad looking, either," Vana said.

The extra men that Crow brought were a boost, but bad news arrived soon afterwards in the form of two riders, their lances adorned with green pennants. These were messengers from Izzar, the tribal leader. Amir's band was one of five which comprised Elan's clan; along with four other clans, it made up the tribe. He was summoned to answer to the chief of all of them.

"What does he want?" I asked.

"I don't know," Amir said evasively.

From what Aruru and Puabi had told me, there was no love lost between Izzar and their late father. Certainly, there had been no help yet from Izzar in the struggle against the creatures.

"What might it be?" I asked.

"He may blame us for the Spawn. They are spreading. The other bands ignore our warnings."

"So what if he does blame us?"

Amir sighed. "Izzar has the power to take away our range land, break up the band. Or order my death. He is the overlord."

"But he could also offer help, couldn't he?" I asked. "Nergal said he could send men."

"Izzar never liked my father, or me. Even Nergal could not talk his way around him."

"Maybe we just need to explain the situation. Tell him we're going to kill the creatures, and we could use some help."

"Izzar does not listen to reason," Amir said. "He only listens to his advisors, and they are schemers, not warriors. They want plunder without fighting. They will take advantage of our weakness."

"You are as cynical about your leadership as Izabel," I said. "I'd better come with you."

"Impossible," Amir said. "I will take Nergal; he is a good talker. But you are a woman."

"I am a goddess," I said. "And I will come with you."

Izzar's envoys demanded that Amir accompany them back as soon as they had eaten and watered their horses. There was barely time for me to talk to the others and let them know what was happening.

"You think they'll replace Amir?" Marie-Therese asked, coming straight to the point. "Put Nergal in charge?"

"That sounds grim," Izabel said.

"I will get the handmaidens ready to leave," Marie-Therese said. "We can go to the cities in the north."

"It shouldn't come to that," I said. "I'm still hoping to talk some sense into them."

"Take these gifts," Timi said, passing me a cloth-wrapped bundle. "Just some knife blades and arrowheads, but good ones. Turm's best. They love that sort of thing."

"I don't know—"

"Trust me," Timi insisted. "They like shiny, pointy things."

We rode fast, the two envoys in the lead, followed by Amir, Nergal, and me. After several hours with only one short break, we reached a goatshair tent standing all on its own in a sea of grass. A dozen horses were tethered nearby, and warriors sat about, their spears planted near them, eyeing us sullenly as we passed.

The conference took place in the semi-dark interior crowded with tribal totems. These were wooden staves with carved semi-human figures adorned with fur and feathers, weathered remnants of centuries of nomadic existence. They represented forgotten gods whose authority was the source of the leader's power. They radiated a certain heathen magnificence; a historian or anthropologist would no doubt have been fascinated, and Picasso would have stolen them on sight. I had other things on my mind.

Izzar and his cronies intimidated Amir. He saw them as imposing figures, vested with the power of tradition. I saw only three shabby, smelly, illiterate old men sitting cross-legged on the ground. Being brought up as an Englishwoman had given me one advantage: I always felt equal to—if not superior to—anyone else. A sense of unshakeable superiority might be just what was required.

It reminded me of university, all those old men who did not think women should be admitted. They just made me angry.

Izzar was a big man, and muscular, for all that his hair was greying. The day he could not fight in the front rank of his warriors would be the day he ceased to be leader. He sat cross-legged on the floor with two others. The nomads had not yet learned how to intimidate their inferiors by the use of platforms and tall thrones, so we looked down on them until we were seated.

"Why have you brought her?" Izzar demanded of Amir.

"He did not bring me. I brought myself," I told him. "I ride a horse; by that alone you know I am a goddess."

In another culture, they might have laughed at me and said any woman could ride. Not here. Izzar scowled, and I gazed coolly back, hoping I looked queenly.

"Women are not permitted here," Izzar said, still addressing Amir.

"Heaven is above your rules," I said.

Amir looked at the ground; Nergal struggled to contain a smirk. I was checking their headmaster.

"Nevertheless," I said, unwrapping the items that Timi had supplied. "We have brought gifts."

"It is not customary," Izzar grumbled, but he took the proffered metal, while his cohorts were unashamedly pleased with their presents. Timi had a shrewd grasp of their values. One of them, the swarthy one whom Amir had identified as Anbu, even made a small bow of thanks.

After a minute, Izzar started again. "The band of Elan was destroyed. My scouts found out yesterday. The survivors are scattered and few."

I recalled the kindly, white-haired old man who had recounted his stories of hunts and wars, feuds and reconciliations. The clan chief had probably died with his sons, defending his people.

Amir struck the floor with his hand. "We warned them! The Spawn range farther every day… Elan should have camped farther away."

"Their winter camp is where it is," Izzar said. "They have no other."

"Your Spawn killed them all," the man at Izzar's right hand said. This must be Sessec, with one arm reduced to a stump. Nergal had warned me about this one. His deep-set eyes flicked from face to face as though hoping to catch us out. "The Unclean brought forth by your father."

"My father did not bring them—he fought them and those who brought them." Amir's voice was quiet, but anger was not far below the surface.

"Now your band has fallen into alien practices," Izzar said, looking at me. "Harbouring strangers and strange women. Taking on foreign ways."

"Heaven has shown us how to withstand the attacks of the Spawn," Nergal said. "Our earthworks and our wall of wooden spears keep them out."

"Your people have turned into moles," Sessec said.

This was a real insult. The mole was the most despised creature on the plains, worse than a snake or a scorpion, because of the number of nomads killed or injured when their horses stumbled on molehills. Dangerous animals like leopards were admired, moles were blind, evil underground crawlers.

"Earthworks!" Izzar snorted. "Hiding in ditches! I always knew you were a coward, Nergal. Your brother is stupid, but he is brave."

"Neither of them is fit to lead," Sessec said. "Like their father, who—"

"You will not insult our father!" Amir said.

"Sessec One-Arm," I said, raising my voice in turn, "they tell me you are wise. Please tell this woman which is better: for a band to remain secure behind earthen walls or to be annihilated like Elan's people because they could not defend themselves?"

"Earthworks!" Izzar said again.

"Well?" I asked.

"Cowards may stay alive by avoiding fighting," Sessec said. "It is not honourable."

"Not honourable." Anbu, the third man, spoke for the first time. "But sometimes wiser."

"We do not avoid fighting," I said. "We are gathering our strength to kill the creatures."

"Liar," Sessec said, looking from me to Amir to Izzar. "The Spawn cannot be killed."

"The Spawn cannot be killed," Izzar affirmed. "They always come back. Everyone knows that. Amir, are you letting this woman lead you by the nose?"

"Or by something else?" Sessec added.

They all had a good laugh at that. As their mirth subsided, I spoke up, in my best speech-making voice, projecting to the corners of the tent. "A goddess came before to destroy creatures."

"Fairy tales and myths," Izzar said. "Big talk. The priests take credit for everything. They called her 'goddess' and said she drove out the Spawn. But the Great Dying came, and after a time, it went. The drought came and went. The great wolf pack came and went. The monsters came, and they went. Everything goes in the end, goddess or no."

"The wind dries the rain," Sessec said, as though imparting unassailable wisdom.

"Yet I can destroy the creatures," I said. "Heaven has sent this gift. Once warriors kill them, I can send their spirits back to hell so that they never return to this world."

"I have heard liars boast they fought a leopard barehanded," Izzar said. "But I have never heard such an empty boast as yours."

"It is not a boast," I said. "I swear by heaven. We will kill the creatures, as Amir's people did before, in olden times."

"Can you bring down the moon with a javelin too?" Sessec asked.

"It's easily tested," I said. "Come back with us and you can watch us kill one." I had not discussed this with Amir or Nergal. "Amir's warriors are brave and strong. They will kill the Spawn one by one, and we will destroy them all. But we will need more warriors for the hunt."

"Then will you hit the moon with a javelin?" Sessec persisted. "That would be easier."

"I have never heard anything like this," Izzar said.

"*We* are not afraid of the Spawn," Amir said, with a subtle emphasis on the first word. "My father never ran from them. Nor do I and my brother. We will kill them."

"Try the woman's claim," Anbu said, leaning close to his chief. "What she says is easy to prove, if she can. I would like to see one of these Spawn killed! Try her, and if she fails—then we can deal with Amir's band as we discussed."

"I'll lend her a javelin," Sessec said. "Then—"

"Shut up, Sessec," Izzar said. "You, so-called woman from heaven, Anbu will go and watch you kill a creature, if you can."

"I will bear witness for my leader," Anbu said solemnly.

"Agreed," Amir said.

"And when we do, will you send men to aid the fight?" I said. "Can you find warriors brave enough to face the spawn of Tulu?"

"You could be whipped for insolence," Sessec told me then looked to Izzar. If it was an attempt to curry favour, it failed. The tribal leader was stroking his beard thoughtfully.

"Maybe I will send men. If you can produce a miracle, who can say?" He turned to Amir. "I give you six days. This woman's boasting gets you six days. But after that, if you fail—"

"As you shall," Sessec said.

"—then I will take the strange women, all of them." He favoured me with a smile. "Because I see the strange women are fair, though they need taming. And then we will discuss how your band are disposed."

"As my leader wishes," Amir said quickly, and Nergal mumbled the same. I would have continued the discussion to settle the details, but it was time to leave.

Chapter Thirteen: Hunted to Hunters

ANBU AND THE TWO ENVOYS came back with us. While they rode some distance ahead, I talked again with Amir about how to kill the creatures. The nomads' experience of hunting and fighting did not go beyond spears and javelins and light bows. Amir's preferred approach was to throw javelins to slow a creature down then charge at it with lances until one of the riders killed it.

"What else can we do?" he demanded. "Those are all the war weapons we have. Should we use stones or knives. Or our bare hands?"

My brothers played with toy soldiers, and I knew all about artillery, battleships, and aerial torpedoes, none of which was the slightest use, either. I tormented myself with thoughts of steam-powered cannons or compressed air guns, things we might even build, given enough years. We had only six days. Even if we had the wood and carpentry skills to build a stone-throwing medieval siege engine, we would never be able to get it close enough to one of the creatures.

We arrived back late that night. Marie-Therese and Izabel were waiting for me. The other handmaidens were packed and ready to go, but I sent them all to bed. My two closest advisors remained.

"We stayed up this long," Izabel said. "You may as well tell us the story."

She added handfuls of twigs to the fire and put a pot of water on to boil. Even Izabel was acquiring domestic habits. I gave them a brief summary, and they perked up on hearing Izzar's terms.

"So all we have to do is kill one?" Izabel said.

"All?" I said.

"Illi has some great ideas. Her people kill big game."

"Illi can kill anything," Marie-Therese agreed.

My reply was cut off by a scream from a nearby tent, followed by another. I froze.

"That sounds like Vana," Marie-Therese said, grinning delightedly.

"What have you done?" I asked, looking from one to the other.

"Oh, we put some spiders in Vana's bed roll," Marie-Therese said. "I don't think she likes spiders very much."

The battle of practical jokes that Vana had set off by scaring us at the bathing pool was still going strong. Marie-Therese was determined to have the last laugh.

"You did what?"

"Don't worry," Izabel said. "They're not poisonous. Here, have a look."

She tossed something spindly into my lap. I jumped up backwards, brushing the thing off with both hands, much to their amusement.

"I told you she wouldn't scream," Marie-Therese said. "The goddess is brave."

I eyed the spider, which remained where it landed, motionless. It was made of woven straw. "Very clever. Inzalu's handiwork, I presume?"

"Please, we can't all be serious all the time," Marie-Therese said. "We can laugh sometimes. Sit down, and Izabel will make you a cup of tea. And tomorrow, we will go and talk to Turm about making weapons."

I slept badly, in spite of fatigue. I kept thinking of things I should have said in the meeting. It was perhaps the best outcome possible, but our situation was still desperate. I would have been less worried if only my fate hung in the balance, but they kept raising the stakes. It was not just my chances of getting home, but Amir's life and the future of all the handmaidens.

The other women would not be kindly treated if they fell into Izzar's hands. Of that, I was sure. They would probably be passed out to his lieutenants as extra wives. Those with useful skills, like Lu Zhu and Vana, might expect to be put to using them. Some of them might be able to bend to that, but I could not see Izabel or some of the others faking a smile and bowing to their new lord and master.

I uttered a brief prayer, which was less consolation than it might have been. As Marie-Therese had mentioned more than once, our Saviour would not be born for another thousand years at least. If the land of Israel was overrun by monsters, what was the chance that he would even be born?

Why does this responsibility always fall on my shoulders? Why couldn't I be as carefree as Inzalu, dancing through life with a flower in my hair and no sense of the seriousness of the situation?

We found Turm pottering about in front of his furnace, feeding it with charcoal as though tossing tidbits to a tame dragon. He must have had some idea that he would have a commission, because he was getting ready for a day's work, with flat bronze ingots laid out and ready to be forged.

"Highness, and my lady." He rubbed his big hands together as he saw us, like a tradesman greeting customers, hopeful of a big order. "Turm the weaponsmith is at your service."

"We want you to make these," Marie-Therese said. She had created little clay models of the weapons we wanted him to forge.

Turm leaned over to inspect them, an elephant next to a gazelle, the charms stitched to his jacket tinkling. His frown of concentration gradually cleared as she pointed out the details and explained their function.

"Like a hunting arrowhead," he said. "So it sticks in and doesn't come out. Clever! Like several arrowheads together. And with a ring for this cord…"

"Can you make it?" I asked.

"The barbs make the work complicated," he said. "I need to make it in several pieces and braze them together. And it fits onto a spear-haft. That end is easy enough. Different, though. I have never made anything like it before—nobody ever has!—but I am Turm the weaponsmith. Nothing made of metal is beyond me." He beamed, challenging us to contradict him. Turm was his own promoter, publicist and salesman, a one-man business. And a skilled craftsman.

"What about the other one?"

"You really want an axe this big?" he asked, holding his hands a foot apart.

"As big as you can make it without being too heavy to wield," I said.

"I can forge one big enough for a giant! But it will take so much metal." He ran his fingers over the clay gently as if he might break it. "Hmm. I can make it so just this curved edge is weapon-metal and the rest is low-grade copper, but—it's still a lot of bronze. I can make three of these, and three of the others, and I will have no bronze left. I could have made twenty fine spears and twenty knives with that much metal. More." It pained Turm to use more of his scarce stock than he had to.

"We can't kill the Spawn with twenty spears. We need these."

"As the goddess wishes," Turm said, a twinkle in his eye.

It was going to cost all his bronze, but Turm was about to make something that had never been made before: a weapon for heroes, to slay unkillable monsters, on the order of a goddess. Turm was not just working bronze. He was forging legends.

"Thank you," I said.

Turm was already at his bellows, the fire starting to crackle.

For his part, Amir, to give him credit, listened patiently to what I had to say. It was difficult for a seasoned warrior to have a girl, one who had never raised a weapon in anger, telling him what he ought to do. I showed him Turm's first prototype as soon as it was ready.

"Illi says the hunters in her land use a similar weapon to hunt the great fish there from their canoes," I told him.

"Fish," Amir said, with a small laugh. He had never seen a fish more than a foot long.

"We have a similar weapon in my country," I said. "We can immobilise a creature so it cannot get away. We can kill them without getting close."

"But it's much too big and heavy to throw properly," he said, examining the three rows of barbs. "There's a reason why a javelin is half the size of a spear."

"I can throw it," Izabel said. "And hit a target too."

Amir said nothing, but his look spoke of disbelief.

Izabel hefted the harpoon, took three steps, and hurled it like an Olympic javelin thrower. It flew sixty feet and stuck firmly into the ground, making an angle with its shadow like a sundial. "See?"

"You have a strong arm." Amir's eyes flicked over to me. "But Young Harsis is a man, and he can throw better."

"Him? He couldn't hit a horse at ten paces. He's strong, but you never know where his javelin will land."

"Hah! You have watched him at practice." Amir could not help laughing. "I worry one day he will kill someone by accident. But you cannot throw from horseback. We can."

That was true. Izabel could barely stay on a moving horse.

"I can dismount. It's not going to run away."

"Izabel really is rather good at casting, as you can see," I said. "I'd very much like her to be in the hunting party. If you possibly could allow it. Heaven's weapon, heaven's handmaiden."

Amir looked from one of us to the other. "Old Harsis will oppose it."

"Old Harsis can come and fight me," Izabel said. "I'll show him where I can stick a harpoon."

"It's not quite so simple," Amir said, stroking his beard. I was prepared for a lengthy debate, despite Izabel's obvious talent. Customs were not easily changed. But Amir surprised me. "Your fate is at stake too, Izabel. And I do not think you would wish to be Sessec's third wife. So you may join the hunting party—if you can follow orders like a warrior."

"It would be my honour," Izabel mumbled.

"And once we kill this thing, Yishka-from-Heaven will stop it from rising again," Amir said.

"Absolutely," I said, fingers crossed for luck.

"We will practise with these new weapons," he said. "Then the men will be ready, and we can go hunting."

Two days later, we rode out, thirty strong. The pick of Amir's warriors included Young Harsis, though Old Harsis had been excluded from the group. Izabel, Marie-Therese, and I joined them, as well as Izzar's observer Anbu and his two escorts. I was so sick with worry, I had left breakfast untouched. Amir was not troubled, though.

"Women always worry too much," he said. "It is the place of a woman to worry. You are very good at it. My men are good at what they do too."

"I see you are serious about this killing," Anbu said, riding alongside me. He had been quiet for the past few days, accepting Amir's best hospitality, saying little. "Izzar will be surprised to hear this tale, however it ends."

I would have preferred to engage the Spawn somewhere closer to our defences, but Amir's scouts had some idea of their regular movements. Our best chance of encountering a small group was a couple of hours ride away. The creatures went out in hunting parties, often six or seven of them. The majority would spread out and lie invisibly in ambush while one or two circled slowly around to drive game towards them. Now the hunters would become the hunted.

We were met by two of Amir's scouts, and after a shouted conversation established that there was a hunting group of the Spawn nearby and that they had split up, Amir dispatched a party to keep track of the other creature so we could go about our business undisturbed. We rode on, and a minute later, I saw a lone creature bulldozing through the grass. It looked bigger than I remembered, bigger than the shadowy forms that circled the camp. As we approached, it turned to face us, and its skin rippled into dull shades of brown, khaki, and olive. It extended tentacles like a man drawing six swords at once.

"That is a true monster," Anbu said, appalled. He had never seen one before, and I had forgotten how strong the reaction could be at first sight. "It's more hideous than... than anything."

Some of the nomads rode a wide circle around the creature, making sure of the terrain. Amir waved his spear over his head and addressed the thing in a commanding voice.

"Unclean spawn of hell," he said. "I am Amir, son of Tena, leader of my proud band. This is Yishka-from-Heaven. We have come to destroy you. We will have vengeance!"

One of the riders threw a javelin, which landed several yards away from the creature.

Izabel had dismounted, leaving Damki to hold her horse, and approached the Spawn on foot, the big harpoon balanced in her hand. From my angle, she seemed to walk right up to it, though Izabel well knew how far the danger extended. She paused while the Spawn shuffled closer then threw her harpoon with a grunt of exertion, the line playing out behind it. The weapon struck right into the centre of the target.

"Good throw," I said under my breath. I tried to keep the hope fluttering in my chest under control.

The barbed head sank deep into the fleshy body. Tentacles started feeling at the shaft, attempting to get a grip on it. The Spawn tugged ineffectually until the wooden haft broke away, as it was meant to. While the creature was still working out what to do, Amir galloped past, hurling his own harpoon at a downward angle so it struck through the creature's blubbery foot.

Before Amir was clear, his horse stumbled, throwing up a cloud of dust, caught around its back legs by a tentacle that shot out like a frog's tongue catching a fly. Amir somersaulted clear, hit the ground, and rolled. The creature was fully engaged with Amir's unfortunate horse, two tentacles wrapping around its neck and cutting off its terrified screams while Amir scrambled to safety. While the Spawn was still wrapping itself around the horse, Young Harsis went by on the other side, and a third harpoon found its mark.

Amir was shouting as he returned. The lines from the harpoons went taut as men hauled them in three directions. The stout leather cords were the longest and strongest that had ever been woven, according to Aruru. We had tested them playing tug-of-war, and Amir said they were strong enough to hold a horse.

The Spawn flailed about, wrapping tentacles around the restraining lines and the harpoon heads. Young Harsis dismounted, and Izabel handed him a new weapon, while Amir took up his. The creature tried to move, straining first one way and then another, but it was held in place.

"We have it!" shouted Amir exultantly. Too soon, I thought. Much too soon. "Pull it to the left there!"

Men hauled on two of the lines, and the Spawn toppled. It started swimming on the ground with its tentacles. Before it could right itself, Amir moved in.

In addition to the harpoons, Turm had fashioned poleaxes, big razor-sharp axe-heads mounted on hafts longer than spears. They were cumbersome, but they gave a good amount of reach. Swung downwards, the poleaxe cut with tremendous force. On Amir's first practice attempt, he had cut a dead goat clean in half. The boneless Spawn presented much less resistance.

Axes rose and fell as the three of them chopped away at the tentacles, staying well back. Gelatinous flesh spattered the ground.

Young Harsis had the poleaxe wrenched out of his hands. Amir made a series of short slashes, more to distract than to damage. This allowed Izabel to step closer and deliver a blow that half-severed the limb holding Young Harsis's poleaxe. A moment later, she had fully severed it before using her own poleaxe as a rake to claw back the dropped weapon.

I watched, fingernails digging into my palms, catching my breath with every sweep of the tentacles.

"More coming!" someone shouted. Behind them was a line of creatures, six or seven of them, wading towards us through the long grass, all standing out in bright green. We had just a few minutes.

"Faster!" Amir ordered.

A young warrior called Kuwar rushed in to stab with his spear. Maybe he wanted the glory of killing it. More likely, he was just careless. The thing must still have been able to judge distances exactly, because it struck like a snake. A thick tentacle wrapped around his head and crushed it in an instant, as easily as crushing an egg.

One of the harpoon heads popped loose as a poleaxe carved away a chunk of flesh holding it, but the Spawn was no longer in a state to fight or to flee. More warriors crowded around it, thrusting with spears. Young Harsis, looking as though he were chopping wood, delivered blow after blow with maniacal speed.

It was clumsy, brutal work. We still had no real knowledge of the anatomy of the things and how to kill them, but after what seemed like an age, it collapsed into green-grey sludge. A wave of acrid gas hit me.

Amir stepped back, spattered with gore but unharmed, gesturing me forwards. "Now! Destroy it!"

The warriors drew back in a circle. Parts of the creature were still moving. Anbu watched intently, his arms folded across his chest.

I raised my hands and started to speak the chant in a low voice. Immediately, I felt a constricting pressure around my chest as though I were deep underwater. I had to physically force the words out one by one. It was so much more difficult than before, but everyone's eyes were on me, and I could not let Kuwar's death be in vain.

As I spoke, the shattered flesh around me stopped twitching and started to disintegrate. It changed from mush to a thick jelly, which melted into viscous liquid studded with black triangles: the thing's many teeth. I spoke the words again. The liquid did not boil but seemed to relax and thin out, changing into a fog that spread over the ground in a widening spiral. As I spoke the words again and again, more easily each time, the fog rose into to a dust devil and dissolved at last into pure air.

Everything was silent. My vision was still blurred; it was like being underwater. I took off my glasses. It did not make any difference.

"We have killed it!" Amir yelled.

"The wind spirits have taken it," Anbu said.

Shouts and ululations filled the air.

"Get her on to the horse," Marie-Therese said.

"I'm fine," I said, but when I looked around, more Spawn seemed to be almost on top of us, green tentacles reaching out. Strong hands took hold of me, and the next I knew, I was jouncing along on the back of a horse. My vision recovered a few minutes later, but I found I had difficulty forming sentences for some hours, as though something inside my head had been jumbled up.

A party of warriors went back a few hours later to collect the teeth. There were about six dozen of them, black triangles up to two inches across. The mature version was weirdly complex, with edges built of many spiral points like the turrets of a miniature castle, layers of serration upon serration. They reminded me of seashells. Everyone in the camp marvelled at them and touched them, feeling their weight.

"I have seen impossible things," Anbu said gravely. He had been strangely serious and respectful since the killing. "I have seen brave warriors die, but never had I seen unclean things of hell and the work of heaven. The work of the goddess. My testimony will be like a fable."

"You are a sworn witness," Amir said. "Izzar cannot doubt your word. Your men saw too."

"And you will take back this proof." I held up a garland of teeth strung on a leather thong.

"Nobody has ever destroyed a monster," Anbu said, taking it with something like reverence. "Not in living memory. And nobody has seen such a trophy as this."

"Will Izzar send us more men now, do you think?" I asked.

"I will pass on the goddess's wishes," Anbu said. "I will talk to Izzar. And, Lady, Anbu honours you."

"I never thought he was religious," Amir said, as Anbu and his men rode off with their prize.

Amir was still buoyed by the kill. After more than two years, he finally had his first taste of revenge, and it was intoxicating. His decision to shelter me and to rescue the others had been vindicated. Everything was proceeding according to the dictates of heaven, and Amir was heaven's chosen warrior. He was not superstitious as Anbu was, but he was beginning to believe in his destiny. I was less convinced by destiny, but painfully aware that we had lost another warrior.

The nomads had no permanent graves or markers and did not remember their dead. But it would be wrong to forget the fallen in this struggle, and I was determined their names would live on. The next day, Izabel went out and found a suitable stone, one which we could drag back to the camp on a goatskin and stand up to remember the fallen. We ended up getting four stones: one each for Sabian, Alsu, Ilsha, and Kuwar. When Amir asked about others who had died before, I said they would be remembered too.

There were enough teeth for a second garland, and we draped it over the stone carved with Sabian's name. Every dead warrior would be avenged, and more than avenged. Amir swore it with renewed confidence.

We now had fifty-nine effective men, according to Marie-Therese's census, plus Izabel, who now counted as part of the fighting force.

Crow's brigands, whom I did not entirely rely on, added another fifteen. There were at least a hundred full-grown creatures, according to the most optimistic estimate. Many small Spawn had been seen in the area immediately around their lair, prowling for small prey. We could not begin to guess how many.

King Pyrrhus of Epirus beat the Romans at the battle of Heraclea. Or rather, he would beat them in some centuries' time. But at Heraclea, his victory lost Pyrrhus so many men that his name became synonymous with victories bought at too high a price. Amir was so joyous at killing this one Spawn that he had not wondered whether we could afford this war.

I hoped Izzar would send plenty of good warriors.

CHAPTER FOURTEEN: THE PRODIGALS

THE BAND, OR RATHER THE settlement, continued to receive as many visitors as ever, despite the increased danger outside. Riders from other clans arrived on a daily basis, eager for news. Some of them hoped to join in Amir's creature hunts and get teeth as trophies. Others just wanted to find the truth behind the strange stories they had heard about the goddesses, the settlement, the Spawn, and the slaughter of entire bands.

Merchants also continued to visit. If the danger from the creatures had grown, the number of nomads and bandits preying on the traders had plummeted. Strangely, though, the population of wandering madmen and holy fools in the grasslands had grown. Some of them were outcast survivors from the destroyed bands, while others seemed to be drawn to the area like moths to a flame. The creatures never seemed to attack these people. Most of them were beggars in rags, obviously simple-minded. Others exhibited more elaborate mental conditions. Some were confidence tricksters, claiming to convey messages from the ghosts of the dead or the wind spirits, warnings, blessings, or whatever else would win them a few days of food and shelter. Others seemed to be genuine visionaries, oppressed by hallucinations which they could not properly express.

One gaunt bearded wanderer, a starving John the Baptist filled with holy zeal, ambled into the settlement and started preaching to anyone who would listen about the coming end of all things. He said we should eat all our winter supplies and drink all our beer, spit in the faces of our enemies, and run wild through the camp, whatever we wanted, because there would be no tomorrow. He had seen the future, and the spawn of Tulu would destroy everything from here to the end of the world.

"It is the end of all things! They come numberless as the grains of sand, like raindrops! Like water from a spring, a torrent, a flood, from the fount-of-monsters! The end of all things is upon you! Live while you can!"

End-of-All-Things might have been an entertaining lunatic for the nomads, but I was concerned about morale. Fortunately, giving him food and drink shut him up. I insisted that any more religious maniacs should be brought before the handmaidens to check that they were fit to let into the camp. This meant that Inzalu interviewed them while Lu Zhu gave them a medical, with Damki on hand in case they became violent. I'd picked Inzalu because she was a good listener.

Most of what Inzalu reported back was nonsense, but a few sounded like genuine seers. One told her that he could keep the Spawn away by imagining scorpions. He knew the dream-scorpions were not real, but if he became sane, the creatures would eat him.

Another said he had talked to the Spawn. They were men in another shape, he said, and they had come to replant the world and make it better. They had asked him to join them, and he was still considering the offer.

A third said that the Spawn were harmless and that the real enemy lay to the east. That was where the evil ones dwelled, the ones who brought plagues of serpents, poisonous rain, and whirling dust-devils that ate men alive. The Spawn would save us from the evil ones.

These visitors, whether pathetic or alarming, added little to our intelligence. But there were more welcome arrivals.

"Yishka, come quickly—she's back!"

There was a hubbub in the camp. Inzalu pulled me into the centre of the disturbance where Amir was angrily facing off with another warrior who looked oddly familiar—it was Igmil who stood protectively in front of Lalit. The runaways had returned and brought with three horses loaded with goods.

"Oh, Yishka!" Lalit cried when she saw me, literally throwing herself into my arms, sobbing, and begging for forgiveness.

"Oh, do let go," I said, examining her for signs of injury. Both of them seemed somewhat the worse for wear. Igmil's leg was awkwardly bandaged, but his return brought our fighting force up to fifty-six.

The handmaidens fluttered around Lalit like anxious pigeons, ecstatic to see her. You would think she was a childhood friend, not a rather obnoxious woman they had known less than a year. There were shrieks, tears, laughter, and a great deal of hugging. Not everyone was overjoyed, though. Izabel's greeting was brief, and after Timi assured herself that Lalit was in one piece, she drifted over to check the pack horses.

"You are a traitor," Amir told Igmil. "You will be punished."

"But he has come back," I said. "And brought Lalit back safely too. We can defer judgment until we have heard the whole story."

Amir shot me an angry look. "We will hear the story, then there will be punishment."

There was no such thing as privacy for the nomads, and there would be eavesdroppers whatever we did. So we sat down in a circle, with Lalit and Igmil—holding hands, I could not help but notice—in the middle. With many interruptions and digressions, we extracted their story.

As we thought, Lalit had beguiled Igmil and learned everything she could about the coastal settlements. When he told her there were merchants there with whom she could exchange jewellery for services—such as a passage on one of the many boats which worked the coastal trade—she had formed her plan. Igmil had done all the practical work of acquiring horses and supplies.

They'd made a hard three-day ride across the plains and along the coastal salt desert, and they had survived some close shaves, losing a horse along the way when they almost ran into one of the creatures. The city was no city, Lalit said. It was hardly even a town, and a sprawling, crumbling slum at that. Igmil's description had implied something far grander, in her mind at least. The place stank of fish, which were drying on poles everywhere, and echoed with the raucous cries of gulls attracted by the fish guts. There was no harbour full of fine merchant ships. At the ramshackle quay, a collection of fishing boats were tied up, along with a few small vessels that plied the coastal route.

Lalit had assumed getting a ship back to her home country would be an easy feat. She did eventually find captains who recognised some of the place-names she gave them and even met sailors from her home province. But their language was not the same, and they shook their heads when she described her home city and the tall, many-masted ships. They told her also that the ruler of the province was a king called Yudhishthira—to Lalit, a figure from the mythical past.

Lalit had not been too discreet about her wealth. Robbers had followed them and attacked them at night in their tent. Igmil had been alert, though; although injured, he had killed, or nearly killed, one of their assailants and rescued Lalit. That was when they lost their horses and most of their gear.

The pair had escaped, and since Lalit still had her jewels, they were able to buy more horses and supplies. Lalit had agonised over where to go after she finally accepted that she could not get back to her own country. Rather than setting out for someplace strange to both of them, they decided to return to the only place where they could be sure of friends. They had been warier on the journey back, avoiding other riders and constantly alert for Spawn.

And, absurdly enough, the two had become intimate. I had no doubt that Lalit had been stringing Igmil along at first, but loneliness, shared peril, and his obvious determination to look after her had made an impression. Somewhere along the way, they had decided to get married, and Lalit solemnly requested my permission. The whole thing was altogether too mushy for words. I was strangely grateful to see Lalit back again, though, and I assured her that they could be married in due course.

Seeing the women reunited again, a close knot around Lalit, chattering nineteen to the dozen, I started to realise how close we had become. And I had to admire the silly girl. It had taken a great deal of pluck to undertake that journey then come back to face the music.

"You know what we will have now?" Marie-Therese asked. "Six weeks of hearing nothing but the adventures of Lalit. And then six weeks of her wedding preparation—I bet you."

To add to her credit, though, Lalit started unloading the horses and distributing goods. Like any woman who lived in the country, she could not resist a shopping spree when she visited town, and she had bought gifts for everyone. There were some pretty fabrics, nicer than the ones the many-chinned merchant had been trading, along with a few utensils and practical tools.

Amir still insisted that the pair had to be punished. "Igmil disobeyed his leader. He went away without permission. He was seduced by this woman."

"Punishment must always follow disobedience," Old Harsis said.

Desertion was a crime in any military unit. Amir was Igmil's rightful overlord as well as his superior officer, and he would not see his authority undermined.

"What is the punishment?" I asked.

"Sixty lashes with the whip," Amir said.

Igmil sat up uncomfortably. Sixty lashes was not necessarily a death sentence, but it would leave him incapacitated for days or weeks. That seemed a pointless waste when we needed all the men we could get.

And if the wound became infected, which was not uncommon, then he really would die. And we would be back down to fifty-five.

"So many?"

"If he is a man, he will survive. If he is not a man, he does not deserve to survive," Old Harsis said.

Amir seemed to be enjoying my discomfort. He was asserting his control.

"I beg you to show Igmil mercy," I said. "Heaven has favoured these two. They will be the first union between the people of Amir's band and the women of heaven. Igmil has showed his loyalty by returning to you."

"Igmil left, but he came back," Nergal said. "He is foolish, but he is loyal. And he brought back the woman who is a songbird. And valuable gifts besides."

Igmil had given his leader a knife with an elaborate silver scabbard, such as would only be carried by a chief. Others had received knives, only slightly less showy.

"Even the best warrior runs away sometimes," Old Harsis said.

"I will fight always beside my leader," Igmil said, bowing to Amir, and there were murmurs of approval from the crowd.

Amir made a show of reluctance. This was a challenge to his authority, but he could afford to be generous. "Twelve lashes then. But only because the goddess pleaded for mercy."

"Punishment always follows disobedience," Old Harsis added. "The leader has spoken."

"And Yishka, you must punish the woman Lalit yourself," Amir added.

I was not about to order a whipping, but Timi was well ahead of me. "A fine," she said. "Lalit will pay for her disobedience with a fine in jewels."

Lalit looked about her. "I accept the punishment."

As easily as that, she was taken back into the sisterhood. Not that she had actually changed. But while Lalit was excited over the prospect of her marriage, Izabel was not so pleased.

She cornered me in my tent later that day. "You've got to do something."

"How do you mean?" I asked.

"Yishka, you know how nomad men treat their women. We've talked about this."

It was true. I was one of the few people who would listen to Izabel's rants on sexual equality and how terrible things were for women in this century. I broadly agreed with her, but she did go on.

"They're young, and they're in love. Why do you care anyway? You hate Lalit."

"Because it's a principle! And because she's one of us."

"Lalit is old enough to make her own choices."

"She's clueless," Izabel said. "She'll be property. The men treat their horses better than their wives. 'Horse first, wife second.'"

"They don't actually say that."

"They don't actually need to."

"You think I don't have enough on my plate that I need to start getting involved in marriage counselling?"

Izabel made an angry gesture. She expected me to do something.

I took off my glasses to polish them. I had recently become aware at how I tended to do this at moments of stress, but now I had to be careful. Any carelessness that left traces of dust or sand could mean scratched lenses, and there was no prospect of ever getting them replaced. These days, I cleaned them very carefully, and that was not something to do in an emotional state.

I put my glasses back on. "What do you want me to do?"

"We've got to change the marriage laws, so he's not allowed to rape her or hit her or anything. He's got to show respect."

The nomads did not have a legal code beyond Old Harsis's trite sayings about what was and was not permissible. There was no marriage law to change, just immemorial custom which could not be altered.

"The nomads understand swearing oaths," I said. "Why don't you and Lalit and the others get together and draw up some vows for them both to make. Make sure you write them down. On grounds that Lalit is a goddess, of sorts."

"Goddess of being a pain in the rear end. Bringing back all that fancy cloth and no weapon bronze."

Lalit had not thought to bring back any supplies of metal, but now we knew what could be bought at the coastal town, and Timi was eager to trade with them using our newly restored capital. At the same time, Lu Zhu was being called on to visit at least three of the neighbouring bands, and it was a question of whether we could send out one party or two.

The episode had at least established one thing: our location. Following the coast southeast would lead to India. Hence, I was positive that we were in what would one day become Persia, somewhere towards its southern coast. Following the coast northwest would lead to Mesopotamia and beyond that, the Holy Land. If we sailed south across the sea, we would reach Arabia, the land beyond the sea. Marching north, over the plains and the mountains, we could get to Central Asia, at which point, my geography became hazy.

It seemed that we were just beyond the fringes of the region where all the great civilisations rose and fell and merged into each other—the original Akkadian Empire, Assyria, and Sumeria and the Hittite Empire, Babylon, and the Hurrian Empire. The cities to the north, if they were cities, must be the forebears or remains of one of those. I wished I had studied more of the history of the region. It felt good though to be able to sketch a crude map of the world, though, and put an X on our location.

As for timing, it was hard to tell. I estimated somewhere between one and two thousand years before Christ. Lalit had proven, if any more proof was needed, that the only way back home was the way we had come.

Chapter Fifteen: The Desert Sorceress

A GROWING NUMBER OF HUNTS had concluded successfully, with Spawn separated from their groups and dispatched. We had experienced no casualties on our side, or at least no more deaths. The teeth were prized as trophies. A garland of teeth went to honour the dead, and the rest were handed out as rewards to the warriors who had taken part in the killing. Some wore them around their necks as amulets. Others traded them; the first merchant to visit offered to pay for any teeth we could spare with their weight in silver. Timi soon bargained him up from there.

Our offensive operations were expanding. Amir would send out a score of scouts to locate the creatures then lead a body to cut one out from its mates and kill it, with me in tow to carry out the ritual to prevent it from regenerating. The process left me addled and stupefied each time. Some days were harder than others. On one occasion, I stumbled over the words, and my brain seemed to unravel, like bicycle pedals going the wrong way, until I mastered myself and pushed the chant to its conclusion. One day, it was easy, and I thought I was getting better. The next, though, it was harder, and on the third, it was an uphill struggle.

Every night, there were excited discussions of the day's hunting, of narrow escapes, and of lessons learned. I was making bigger plans. I had put my surveying skills to use, marking out the ramparts with pegs and cords, and the building progressed at a respectable pace. I was so pleased that my course had included bricklaying. One of my architecture professors had been adamant that his students needed to know the materials, and the only way to do that was to work with them. So all of his students, including the women, had been sent to do a week's building work. Even wearing gloves, my hands had blistered. I'd learned about the perversity of inanimate objects and the difficulty of building a perfectly straight wall. Bricklaying had been a ridiculous exercise, but it was one of the most valuable parts of my long education.

"We can start building with turf, like the Roman legions did," I said. "Then we can use clay bricks."

"Building what?" Marie-Therese asked.

"A cook house and mess hall so a few women can cook for the entire band. And you know we need a permanent hospital. A permanent smithy for Turm with a decent-sized forge and a proper bakery for Vanu and a pottery for Noora. A buttery for making and storing butter and cheese. A laundry! Storehouses to keep all the supplies. And a meeting-place out of the wind and the sun and the rain—which can also be a school. A nursery for the little ones. And a military headquarters for us to plan operations."

"Is that all?" Izabel asked.

"The other important thing is proper sanitation—we can make clay pipes instead of using the gutters."

There was a terrible risk of disease with so many people confined into such an area, especially when so many of them were barely house-trained. Lu Zhu was a stickler for hygiene, and hand-washing was beginning to catch on amongst the women, but the men were another matter. Given a regular water supply, though, I had high hopes that there would be no recurrence of the outbreaks of "winter disease," which struck when they were camped in the same place for months at a time.

I showed Marie-Therese sketches of my ideas scratched out on tablets.

"So… colonialism on the French style," she said.

"What do you mean?"

"You English, when you make a colony, you have your own little enclave, and you leave the natives to their own ways. Whereas we make everywhere a piece of France, and we turn the people into good French citizens."

"If you like," I said. We had argued about our respective empires before; I did not want to argue now. "We will give them a European settlement."

"Whether they like it not," Izabel said.

"What do you mean?" I asked.

Izabel looked from me to Marie-Therese and back. "You don't get it, do you? You don't have any problem playing god."

"Not at all," Marie-Therese said. "Especially when you look at their other gods."

"You shouldn't treat human beings like clay bricks," Izabel said. "I may not know a whole lot of history, but I can tell you the whole white-Europeans-bringing-civilisation thing did not turn out great."

"But you say the nomads should treat their women better," Marie-Therese said. "You want to change them too."

"That's different."

Marie-Therese puffed out her cheeks to protest what she saw as hair-splitting. I could not see the discussion ending well.

"I register your protest," I said. "And if things were different, we could win the nomads over gradually."

"And listen to what they have to say."

"And listen to what they have to say." I ticked off points on my fingers. "But we don't have the luxury of time. We are fighting a war.

There are elements here who want to undermine us. And it is not a democracy anyway. We cannot just hand power to the people."

"Registered likewise," Izabel said. "But I wanted you to know what you were getting into."

"In any case, there is so much here," Marie-Therese said, who was looking over my plans. "Too much for us to build."

"We built the ramparts in a day," I reminded her. "And building with turves doesn't take long—"

"I know, the Romans. And then we make it all again with clay bricks, *facile comme bonjour*," she said, as easy as that.

"Bricks are just clay and straw," I said. "It's in the Bible. It can't be so very difficult. Clay and straw, and let them dry in the sun. The land is made of clay if you dig deep enough, and it's covered in grass for straw. We can fire the bricks in an oven if they need to be really hard."

"You talked to Vana about baking bricks?" Izabel asked

"And pipes. And maybe tiles for the roofs." I wanted to tell them about my other secret weapon: a wheelbarrow. It was only a prototype, constructed with help from Turm, and it would be invaluable for helping the women shift building materials about. But I wanted to wait until the thing was robust enough before unveiling it. A carpenter—or proper carpentry tools—would have been a great help.

"It is all a good idea," Marie-Therese said. "You make everything central, instead of having it all done separately in little places. That way, we can make better use of the women."

"Exactly," I said

"They are people," Izabel said. "You don't just 'make use' of them."

"This way, their contribution will be recognised," Marie-Therese said. "This will be a step towards equality."

"Sure," Izabel said.

I hoped I could win Izabel round, show her how a little organisation might reduce the drudgery and wasted effort which were such a feature of the women's lives. And while the women of Amir's band might be less than enthusiastic about changing anything, I was counting on the gratitude of the refugees and the support of the handmaidens to gather momentum for change.

One of the first jobs was the rebuilding of Turm's forge. The plan was to enlarge the structure so a second smith could work alongside him. The new smith, older than Turm but just as muscular, had shown up and pledged his allegiance to me, much as Turm had done months before. Turm was as suspicious as a house dog finding a stray usurping its place in front of the fire.

"Let him work somewhere else," Turm said. "I don't want him in my way."

"He will be your assistant," I said. "You can show him how to make the new weapons."

"I don't want an assistant."

"He will be obedient and make himself useful," I said. "Or I will have him thrown out of the camp. And you will not just be the smith— you will be the master of smiths."

"I suppose I'll find something for him to do." Chronically overworked, Turm should have been pleased at the prospect of help, but he still wanted to do it all himself.

"Wonderful," I said. "So, finally, can we agree the dimensions of the building?"

Turm looked up and down. "We'll need to change the layout for two men working," he said, as though I had only just suggested the idea.

A little girl, a messenger, was tugging at my skirt. "To meet you in the meeting tent," she lisped then ducked away.

"Some riders came in from the north a few minutes ago," Izabel said. "While you were arguing with Turm."

Seven riding horses were gathered at the water trough in the open space at the centre of the camp, while their riders splashed water over themselves in the shade. Some of the men wore armour, and all were armed. They looked like warriors from one of the northern cities, not soldiers, more like mercenary bodyguards. There was something wolfish about them, far more dangerous than the timorous sheep who pretended to guard the merchant caravans. Four pack horses stood apart, loaded with ambiguous bundles.

Three nomad warriors were leaning on their spears, watching them from a safe distance. Amongst them was Damki. He nodded towards the tent used for receiving visitors. "There's another waiting for you."

"Who are they?"

"Strangers. They do not seem hostile, but we're gathering all the men we have in camp."

The newcomers were talking quietly amongst themselves, shooting glances at the nomads. They must have recognised the sound of armed men assembling, but they seemed at ease, confident, while the nomads were skittish and uncertain. Something had spooked them, but Damki did not want to speak about it. I would have to find out for myself.

Timi and Marie-Therese were waiting outside the tent.

"You go in, you go in," hissed Marie-Therese. "We'll listen out here." Marie-Therese knew how to use my seniority against me when there was a job she did not want. Both of them looked terrified.

The visitors' leader was waiting in the audience room alone, completely draped in black. I looked not at a face but a black wooden mask. I could see only the suggestion of eyes behind layers of dark mesh. The customary food and drink lay untouched

"Welcome to our settlement," I said, forcing myself to sound confident. "You speak Language?"

The figure rose, and for a minute, I had the sensation of being stared at. My visitor was smaller and slighter than I had expected, especially in comparison with the burly guards.

I repeated the question, and the figure abruptly removed its mask and outer headgear and started unwinding cloth. It was like seeing a mummy unwrapping, and for a moment, I wondered if I would be faced with some ancient, desiccated creature.

Then she shook her auburn hair loose, and I was looking into the hazel eyes of the most beautiful woman I had ever seen. This place aged people, the sun, wind, and dust eroding skin before its time. This woman had preserved a youthful freshness and might have just stepped out of a wooded glade rather than a trek across the plains. She slipped off her kidskin gloves. Gold gleamed on her hand: a signet ring stamped with a curious geometric symbol.

"Yes, I speak Language," she said.

"Do you speak English?" I asked impulsively, overcome by the feeling that she was another modern woman displaced in time and space.

"I do not understand that," she said in Language.

"I am Yishka-from-Heaven," I said. I had long since given up on trying to convey the alien consonants and strange vowels of "Jessica." "The People call me a goddess."

This succinct summary was usually enough. The distinctions of angels, goddesses, and my exact origins mattered only to the few. I preferred to get down to business.

"I know. And the people say I am a sorceress," she said matter-of-factly. In Language, the word indicated a superior and not necessarily benign witch. She did not offer a name. "We did not expect to find a fortified settlement here. Do your walls really keep the out the Spawn of Cthulhu?"

Her manner was casual. She asked as though enquiring about a neighbour's lawn. I had almost forgotten what it was like to be condescended to by another woman.

"Very effectively, thank you," I said. "And we're extending them, as well as building fortified outposts and watchtowers."

"The Spawn will multiply. Your settlement is doomed."

The Sorceress was cool and untroubled. Her words did not seem like either a warning or a threat, just a bland statement of what was going to happen.

"If you bothered to look, you'd have seen the garlands of monster teeth over the stones of the dead in the main square," I said. "We aim to exterminate them."

Her expression did not change, but I could hear my watch ticking as she stopped to consider this. When she was not speaking, she looked like the statue of some ancient goddess: perfect, beautiful, but inhuman. She glanced at my wrist involuntarily. Slightly louder than before, she asked, "Who are you?"

"I think I have explained that," I said. "And, as this is my camp, I think I should ask who you are."

She seemed to notice the water cup beside her for the first time and took a sip. "So another goddess really has appeared to fight the Spawn. One goddess or more than one?"

"I have my sisters." Every nomad for miles around knew our story and how the others had been rescued, so there was no point in being coy.

"We were your allies once," she said. "We have been fighting the Spawn for many ages."

"And exactly who are you?"

"There is no good word for us in Language." She experimented with the limited vocabulary available. "They call us sorcerers. A group of friends, a war party, a secret council of elders. People acting with common purpose. People from many tribes. Keepers of knowledge and power not shared by others. Wielders of… magic. We oppose Cthulhu and all its kin."

It sounded like one of the ancient secret societies or mystery cults that my friend George had been so enthusiastic about, one of those groups which tried to wield power from the shadows.

"We are always pleased to find new allies," I said.

"You are doing well," she said. "We had expected this place to be overrun by now."

"We are holding our own."

"The Spawn cannot be stopped by swords and spears."

"I think we can hold on," I said. "But we'd be very grateful of any assistance—especially if you're offering more powerful weapons. Or troops. Or gold."

Marie-Therese had been compiling assessments of how many creatures there were, against how many warriors we could muster. It made grim reading, but our capability was steadily improving.

The Sorceress gave a small, superior smile. She was beautiful, and also, I sensed, dangerous. As though the danger and the beauty were intimately linked. "We have many powerful weapons. We will plant the seeds of devastation. The air will turn to fire, the rain will eat the earth, and the plains will toss like a stormy ocean until everything is buried."

It sounded like Sodom and Gomorrah, or worse. It was like Noah's Flood, destroying every living thing on the face of the Earth, except called down by mortals rather than at the whim of the Almighty. But she might have been talking about killing slugs in her garden.

"And what will this do to the People and their animals?" I asked.

"It will be a burning wasteland for a hundred horizons. An ashpit. Take your nomads far away from here as best you can." The way she said 'your nomads' was dismissive, but it suggested that while they were mere animals, I was their shepherdess.

"Why not use force more moderately? Just destroy a horizon or two around the creature's stronghold?"

"Once invoked, these forces run their own course," she said. Again, with a small, superior smile of one who knows better.

"It sounds to me that the cure may be worse than the disease. Especially if you can't control these forces."

"There is no other way," she said. "The Unclean bring certain destruction. Any risk is worth taking."

"There is another way. The previous goddess—your ally—beat them. They were defeated before, and they will be defeated again, without resorting to hellfire."

She took a languid sip of water.

"It is not your choice to make," she said.

"I rather think it is. Sorceress though you are, you are not flying on a broomstick. You still ride a horse, and you have human bodyguards.

I believe that at this moment, I can muster more fighting men than you, and if I have to use force to stop you destroying the land, I will."

I guessed that whatever magic she wished to work would require the Sorceress or one of her colleagues to be physically present, and close to the place of the Unclean. Since we controlled the area, we could physically prevent them, if we had to.

The temperature in the tent seemed to drop ten degrees. "Try to harm me, and everyone in this camp will die," she said. "Slowly."

Behind the threat lurked her vulnerability. The Sorceress did not laugh at me or ignore me. That meant we did count for something, and she could not just sweep the nomads away like ants.

"I'm simply trying to make you aware that there is another way," I said. "The goddess won before. We can win again—and without turning this place into a poisoned desert. I am not a sorceress, but I do know things, things I cannot properly express in Language. This is a war for all of humanity against something utterly implacable. We must work together."

She may not have fully understood me. I was speaking in the bastardised dialect of the handmaidens rather than true Language. I think I conveyed my message well enough, though.

"We do not need to be enemies, you and I," she said, as though it were her idea. "But we understand something of the geometries that the Spawn follow. They are free of our limits, but they have limits of their own. As you know, they cannot be permanently killed by any natural thing. And their strength waxes and wanes like waves."

"They appeared at a certain alignment of the stars," I said, to show I was keeping up.

"The Spawn live and die by the stars," she said. "We draw charts of when they are strong and when they are weak. I must warn you they are approaching a time of strength."

"Fine," I said. "We will sit behind our defences and wait. And when they are weak, we will come out and hunt them down again, one by one."

She thought about this for some time. I knew I must sound young, foolish, and overconfident. But these are not always bad qualities when fighting a war.

"The goddess before did not build earth walls," she said. "She showed the nomads how to keep moving their camp to avoid the Spawn, and how to fight on foot with long spears. She united the bands. With our guidance, she always chose the best days to fight and to run… and in the end, she prevailed."

"Of course," I said. "As we will again."

"Other stories of new goddesses have been lies," she said. "But you are not like them. You are more like her. She was… different."

"What happened to her afterwards?"

"Afterwards?" She cocked her head as though trying to remember. "I believe she renounced her divinity and married one of the nomad chiefs. Before her band was obliterated by the Great Dying."

That was not what I had hoped to hear.

"She still serves heaven, I believe," the Sorceress said. "She became High Priestess."

I was dumbfounded. The High Priestess had never said a word, never tried to speak to me in any modern language. Never revealed herself.

"We can give you something better than gold or spears," she said. "Knowledge. We can tell you when the Spawn are at their weakest and strongest. And other information. And you will lead the nomads in the fight against the Unclean."

"Absolutely," I said. "I can promise you I will do everything I can to destroy them. The chief here, Amir, is already won over the cause."

She nodded slowly, approvingly. "You have questions."

Finally, I had a chance to quiz someone who might know something. Questions crowded my head, forming a logjam. "Can the creatures be starved?"

She shook her head. "The Spawn eat to grow. They do not eat to live."

I had suspected as much. That scuppered a raft of potential plans. "Can they be poisoned?"

"No more than a fire can be poisoned."

"Who are the men who help them?"

"A corrupted race," she said, her nostrils flaring fractionally. "With twisted minds. Kill them on sight, or you will regret it."

"Do the creatures think as we think? Sometimes, they seem like animals. Sometimes, they seem to think like men."

"You ask interesting questions. All I can say is that they are not like us, not in any way. Their thoughts are as unlike ours as snow to stone."

"How do the creatures multiply? Can they only breed by using women, or do they lay eggs or something?"

Despite the number we had killed, their population increased. I did not believe that the creatures could be keeping scores of women in cages, not without the assistance of human jailers to feed and look after the captives and to perform the necessary magics. I wondered whether they were breeding amongst themselves, or perhaps if they had a queen producing brood after brood.

"There are different ways," she said.

"Ways which you won't tell me? Or you don't actually know?"

"Enough questions, Yishka-from-Heaven," the Sorceress said. "I have shown goodwill. I think you will be a good ally for us. There is no need for us to invoke hell, not yet. We will aid your struggle, and if you heed the tides of power, perhaps your nomads will prevail. We will be watching."

"Then we have an agreement," I said. "Why don't you stay and eat and drink with us this evening?"

I had not warmed to her in the slightest, but she appeared to be a fount of information. But she was winding the scarf around her face again. The Sorceress left without saying another word.

"Is she an enemy?" Marie-Therese asked afterwards.

"Not necessarily," I said. "Our enemy's enemy, I think. She'll sacrifice us if necessary."

"That was just her opening offer," Timi said. "To get you to agree to help."

I was not so sure. I had seen the look in the Sorceress's eyes. She did not strike me as a woman who bluffed.

"Does she come from another time also?" Marie-Therese asked. "She did not look like the people here."

"I don't know where she's from. I'm not sure she's even quite human." Perhaps I had been amongst the nomads too long, but the Sorceress's too-perfect complexion was more like a doll than a living woman. And her expressions, her emotions, all seemed somehow off.

"Do we need to send a patrol to follow them, stop them from doing magic?"

"Do that just in case," I said. "But I think for the time being, she has decided that we will be a better weapon to fight the Spawn for her than magic."

CHAPTER SIXTEEN: CRUSADERS AND EXORCISTS

AMIR WAS CHAMPING AT THE bit for more hunts. His whole band of warriors shared his enthusiasm. Those who had not been involved in the earlier hunts demanded to be blooded; others who had been along wanted to be able to claim the killing blow for themselves. Some still stuck to their spears and bows, but more of them were taking up the new harpoons and poleaxes.

A merchant had arrived with a message for me. He did not say who it was from, and he did not need to. It was a goatskin, inked with rows of symbols, circles and crescents and semi-circles, each surrounded by stars. Marie-Therese, Izabel, and I studied it. Three sets of symbols were arranged in blocks of twenty-eight. The number immediately suggested what it might be.

"It's a lunar calendar," I said. "Full moon, waning, new moon, waxing."

"I would have got that," Izabel said. "Eventually."

"And the markings, those stars, next to them show how strong the Spawn are."

Some of the moons had two or three stars. Some had five or six. Sometimes, the stars were larger and heavily emphasised with double black lines. I did not believe in astrology, but the charts compiled by the Sorceress did seem to correspond with the creatures' level of activity. On some days, the Spawn were active, alert, and difficult to destroy. On other days, they were sluggish and dull, and the job was easier. Some of the nomads claimed that the creatures grew bigger or shrank from day to day, but I put that down to the power of suggestion.

Whatever the forces that governed them, whatever accidental correlation the Sorceress and her ilk had discovered, it was a useful approximation of how dangerous the Spawn would be at any given time. Perhaps they were like the priests on the Nile, who had discovered that the movements of the stars told them when the river was about to flood and spread its fertility. Of course, the stars had no real connection with the flooding, but they were an excellent clock. The calendar warned us which days we were likely to be ambushed and which days were good for hunting.

Amir now had eighty spears to command. Our ranks had swelled with refugees and the men that chief Izzar sent to us. These were a mixture of criminals sent as a penance for shedding blood, young warriors hungry for glory, and a few who believed that heaven required their services. One or two more turned up every few days.

Caution had to be the watchword, though, and by now even Amir was aware of the need not to take too many risks. There were at least a hundred of the adult Spawn to destroy. We could not afford any casualties. That meant only taking on a Spawn when we could separate it a safe distance from its fellows.

"We fight like cowards," Amir told me, riding back after a frustrating day's work when we had encountered groups of four, five, and seven Spawn. They had tried without success to harpoon one and drag it away.

"This is hunting, not fighting," I said. "It is not cowardice if you do not jump off your horse and fight hand-to-hand with a leopard."

"You are clever with words," he said. "I cannot argue. But my heart does not agree. Who are these people?"

We were approaching the camp, and a body of perhaps twenty horsemen were arrayed outside the main gate. Nergal, holding a javelin, had rallied the warriors on the ramparts, and they looked ready to repel an attack. The newcomers were nomads from some other tribe, their shaved heads and florid moustaches distinguishing them at once from Amir's people. Some of them wheeled around to face us, spears at the ready.

A figure in a long dress moved away from the horsemen; it was Timi. The merchants advertised their prosperity with physical bulk. Rather than imitating them, Timi displayed floor-sweeping outfits with layers of gorgeous material. She seemed quite casual about mixing with the band of armed men, who made way and let her through without demur. Then they resumed jeering at the men on the ramparts who gestured back.

"Yishka! Tell Amir to make his men behave themselves," she said when she was close enough.

"What's happening?"

"These men are friends," Timi said. "They have come to fight the Spawn with us. But your stupid brother is throwing javelins at them."

"I know this tribe," Amir said, eyeing them with dislike. "They are old enemies."

"They are holy warriors," Timi said. "The High Priestess told them we needed more spears, and they have come."

"How do you know this? Can you talk to them?"

"They speak the same language as you!" Timi said, practically shouting. "It's just a different accent and some dialect words. Why is it always so difficult for men to listen to each other?"

She was more diplomatic than Marie-Therese, but not much.

"That's wonderful news." I rode up to the newcomers, slowly raising one arm. "Welcome, in the name of heaven."

I hardly thought I looked like a goddess, especially after a day of riding, but I supposed all they needed was fair skin and light-coloured hair to persuade them that I was some otherworldly creature. After exchanging a few words amongst themselves, they dismounted and formed up in two rows, like guards for inspection.

They were all rather young but enthusiastic, naïve monster-killers with no idea what they really faced. Their leader was some chief's son on a grand adventure.

"What did he say?" I asked Timi.

"He says they want you to teach them the old ways," she said. "The ways of their grandfathers when they stood together on foot against the Spawn."

That chimed with what the High Priestess had said. Perhaps my predecessor had taught them to fight in close formation, like a Roman tortoise or a Greek phalanx. Well, maybe we could resurrect that technique too.

"If the High Priestess sent them, they will be reliable," I told Amir. "And they can stay with the people from other bands. I know Old Harsis won't like it, but…"

"Twenty more spears," Amir said, forgetting he had called them enemies a minute before. "Inexperienced, but that will change. We'll see how cocky these boys are when they meet the Spawn at a spear's length!"

Timi was already amongst the newcomers, talking earnestly to their leader, who kept glancing up at Amir. He seemed bemused at talking to a female ambassador instead of a warrior, but pleased by having met heaven's representatives. We must have seemed like an unlikely myth indeed. I caught the occasional word here and there, but my ear was not as well tuned as Timi's, and I could not have carried on a conversation.

"Amir is agreeable," I said. "But we'd better keep them apart from the others, at least to start with."

"Obviously. If there is a fight, they will all murder each other."

We made yet more changes to the encampment, enlarging it again. The crusaders would pitch their tents in what was now designated the foreigners' quarter, separated from the rest of the camp by part of the original rampart with a single entrance point. This outside area was for anyone not considered one of Amir's band. This helped persuade Old Harsis that the foreigners could be kept at bay easily if necessary. Amir's men frequently loitered around there, ensuring that the strangers stayed in their own section. The only fights were sparring matches with spear-butts, which relieved some of the friction between them and helped the newcomers show their mettle.

Izabel was a local legend. Every week, some unsuspecting warrior stepped into the ring with her for a contest. The more confident he was, the worse the newcomer fared. The crowd laughed and hooted at the bewilderment of this week's victim as Izabel struck them again and again without being touched. Izabel was happy to play along, and the fighting stayed within limits. I also gathered she rode out with Amir for sparring bouts away from the public gaze. She said she was keeping score but would never reveal who was winning.

When I saw the animation with which she discussed weapons and tactics with the warriors, I realised that Izabel had found her people. She had never been as comfortable making pots or grinding grain, but with a spear or a javelin, she was in her element. She spent more time with the warriors than with the women.

Timi, meanwhile, was building her little trading empire. The other merchant caravans had been ambushed by the creatures. They lacked our network of scouts and watch posts keeping track of the creatures' movements and did not know the signs to watch out for. Most prudently, they had decided to keep a wide berth. Timi had set about buying up their pack horses and hiring their guards, and she was setting up regular routes to trade with the coast and the other nomad groups. She had introduced novelties like credit and interest, as well as paying for goods with mercenary service, which had significantly augmented our forces.

One afternoon, while I was supervising work in what I called, with only light irony, our great hall, Timi returned from her latest expedition.

"You didn't lose anyone," I said, seeing her expression, which was pleased, mischievous even, suggesting good news. My great fear was losing more warriors on these trips.

"No," she said. "Just the opposite, in fact."

"Here," I said, pouring a cup of ersatz coffee. "We've improved the formula."

She sniffed at it suspiciously and surveyed the room.

"So, now we have tiles?"

"Aren't they pretty?" Inzalu said, who was helping put the tiles up. They were an attractive shade of blue, thanks to Noora's efforts to find the right minerals. They would certainly brighten the place up.

Timi asked, "That's a bit frivolous, isn't it, Yishka?"

"We needed to make tiles for the water system anyway, and—oh, you're being funny, are you?"

"The trading went very well," Timi said. "We made a good profit. I've got you some dried figs and dates you'll like. And…" She paused for effect. "I bought us a wife."

I noticed for the first time that the woman behind Timi was a newcomer. She was looking around the hall, obviously puzzled.

"What? You bought a woman?"

"This woman here—say hello to Dota. You know the bands trade women, just like horses and goats. When they have surplus daughters, they sell them as wives." She glanced at Inzalu. "I thought maybe Damki would want her. He's still single."

Inzalu stuck her tongue out at Timi.

"Timi, we are not getting involved in the slave trade," I said.

"I'm joking! Dota needed rescuing—like us. I thought I'd take her on. I need an assistant, and the other handmaidens are all so busy now."

"Dota," I addressed the bewildered woman. "I am Yishka. Has Timi explained what is happening to you?"

Dota frowned, struggling with my accent and the strange question. "I was sold as a bride," she said. "I thought my husband would be here."

"She doesn't really understand things," Timi said. "I thought coming here would be the best way of explaining it."

"We could find her a husband," Inzalu said. "What about Turm the smith?"

"Turm says that when he wants a wife, he will make one out of bronze and gold," I said. "When he works out how to make the mechanism."

Turm had pestered me to see my watch. After cautioning him not to touch, I had opened the back and shown him the inner workings. He had stared raptly at the wheels and cogs in motion, mouth open, as awed by the workmanship of the intricate mechanism as a man gazing upon the face of God. Moving parts, self-powered machinery working of its own accord, was something outside his experience: this was more like an animal than the work of a smith. He had started talking of all kinds of new things he would build when he had the opportunity, not least a clockwork wife. Turm was nothing if not ambitious.

Dota looked even more confused.

"Dota can help me, or she can help Lu Zhu as a midwife or work in the pottery or dig turves, whatever she prefers," Timi said. "She can find a husband here, if that's what she wants."

Timi was not so keen on the idea of a husband herself, at least not for the time being. I suspected her plan was to achieve sufficient wealth and power so any marriage would be very much on her terms.

"I don't understand anything," Dota said, appealing to me. "Where must I go? What must I do?"

"You don't have to do anything," I said. "You are a free woman. Although I would expect you to pull your weight in the war against the creatures."

"Please, what is a 'free woman'?"

Timi looked at me expectantly. It was a fair question. In the nomad language, the two words did not fit together. There were free men, free horses, and free dogs, but women were unclaimed rather than free.

"You see the problem," Timi said. "She's like Amir. There are some things he can never understand because he doesn't have the vocabulary. And he can't pick up the vocabulary, because he doesn't have the concepts. Like me with your *economic science*. Or Lalit about anything that isn't Lalit."

Timi was right in that the nomad women shied away from any change in their traditional role. They had little interest in "liberation," which was meaningless. A few of them had cottoned on to new ideas, though. Puabi had quietly become a career girl, clinging to her role as honorary handmaiden and a trainee midwife under Lu Zhu's tutelage. She'd even turned down an offer of marriage from a visiting band chief.

We could certainly use more women as scribes, medics, teachers— and especially workers—but most women were still too busy with their domestic duties, and husbands and fathers were reluctant to let them go. Perhaps buying them as slaves, appalling as it seemed to me, was the best approach. No worse, really, than those missionaries who bought slaves in the West Indies in order to free them. And if we expected them to work hard, it was better than domestic drudgery.

"You'd better warn her about the spiders," Inzalu said.

Wide-eyed, Dota asked, "Spiders?"

"Straw ones," I said.

Fake spiders still appeared in unexpected places, and new arrivals were attractive victims. They might find a fake arachnid inside a cooking pot or a sandal one morning. The more artful jokers placed them underneath an object, so their natural springiness made them jump as they were uncovered.

Dota would also have to adapt to the settled life. There were plenty of grumblings about the new quarters, especially from the older nomads, arguments about living spaces and disputes with neighbours.

Amir was kept busy going from one to another, shouting and threatening floggings and trying to assert his authority. In general, though, the nomads were pleased with their new accommodation as a mark of status. None of the other bands around had permanent lodging and brick wall and tiled roofs, with wells, pipes, and sanitary arrangements.

There were few of the decorations and homely touches I might have hoped for. The settled existence was new to these people. They did not have much idea of possessions which could not be carried on the back of a horse, no chairs, tables, or beds.

Dota was our first female recruit. Timi bought more as part of her ever-expanding trading operation, but we soon started getting them for free. Once it was known that we had a use for excess women, we soon acquired more at bargain rates. These were the female equivalents of the men who were swelling the ranks of the fighters, troublemakers and ne'er-do-wells sent off to the wars to mend their ways.

After a few months, we started getting wanderers and runaways, women and girls who thought that there might be something better for them here. Our streets might not be paved with gold—most of them were not even cobbled yet—but we received them with open arms. We needed clerks, medics, labourers—and those with other talents.

I brought Marie-Therese along on a hunt. By now, Amir's men had their tactics down pat. Several men on foot had approached a group of the Spawn and lured them into splitting up. They rode their horses in a wide circle around the creature. Amir believed that this disoriented and confused the thing. I was starting to think he was right. The creatures did not rely on sight as much as we did, but they responded to vibrations in the ground and used other senses. As soon as the riders started circling, the Spawn stopped moving and hunched over, like a man listening for something. It rippled into fleshy and floral shades of pink, like a cooked lobster.

The hunters harassed it with a few javelins and arrows then stayed back so the harpooners could get a clear run. One of the tricks was avoiding getting tangled in the line from previous harpoons.

"Don't get too close!" I shouted, though I had not meant to. Izabel knew what she was doing.

She swore when her first cast overshot, but she quickly hauled the harpoon back for a second try, which struck home.

The killing was conducted with less haste, but almost the same ferocity, as six men with poleaxes moved in from all directions on Amir's signal. The Spawn made no move to escape but kept making quick lunges after the men surrounding it. My heart was in my mouth every time it snapped forwards, but the men moved back out of its grasp or beat off its attacks, whooping with savage joy.

"*Quel carnage*," Marie-Therese said.

"They're improving," I said. It was just two minutes by my watch before the flashing blades sliced deep enough into the soft flesh to cut the rubbery integument that encased the thing's brain, and it convulsed and disintegrated.

Holding a handkerchief to my nose, I led Marie-Therese into the circle of slaughter, an odiferous spatter painting of noxious green-black vomit studded with black triangles.

"Go on," I said.

She spoke the first two words then stopped, choking. Marie-Therese looked at me, gagging on the words, unable to breathe. I took up the chant myself. I felt that same pressure crushing me, but I was able to continue, slowly. I heard Marie-Therese gasping for breath beside me, but I was too focused to look around.

When it was over and the Spawn was dispersed, there was no trace of blood, of moisture even, no scrap of gore. The only things that remained were the black teeth, which two of the nomads were busily collecting like boys gathering seashells.

"Victory to the goddess!" shouted Amir amongst the cheering.

"I couldn't do it," Marie-Therese said. "It was like being drowned."

"It's difficult the first time," I said. "And it's a two-star day on the chart. Maybe you should try again when—"

She shook her head violently. "I won't do it. It's too difficult."

We needed someone else for the job. Amir was adamant that none of the men could do it. Dispelling Spawn was not work for them. They were fighters, and they would not have any part of evil magic and Unclean forces.

"Me neither," Izabel said. "I do the harpoon thing. Muscles not brains, right? Look, I don't want to hear those words, ever."

"You have brains—"

"End of." She turned away.

I did not expect any of the handmaidens to volunteer for monster-destroying duty. It meant riding out with the warriors, which was much more uncomfortable and dangerous than staying in the camp. No one else had the peculiar talent required for reciting the phrase without freezing up. Marie-Therese had as much sheer determination as anyone I'd ever met, but she was never able to do it.

Rachel, despite still being weak from her long sickness, volunteered without being asked. "I will be able to do it," she said with certainty.

I gathered that Rachel had some experience of dealing with evil spirits, and that was how she had come into conflict with Cthulhu. I tried to explain that this was a completely different order to prayers and rituals, that it was not simply a matter of memory but of stamina, and she nodded impatiently. She obviously wanted to help, but I worried her strength would not be enough. But Marie-Therese backed her, and I let her come with us on the next hunt.

Rachel proved highly effective. Maybe her pronunciation was better than mine, and she uttered the chant with such ease and fluency that the thing effervesced like sparking water, vaporising more rapidly than I had ever managed.

"There," Rachel said, breathing heavily as the last foul wisps of steam spiralled away into infinity. "We can create, and we can destroy."

"How are you?" I asked, remembering how scrambled my brains had felt after the first time.

"My body is weak, but my mind is strong," she said.

"Good work," said Amir, patting her on the shoulder as he would a favoured horse. "Yishka said one day you would amaze me, and she was right."

"You did good, Rachel," Izabel said, fitting the head of her harpoon back on its haft. "With two of you, we can really go to work on exterminating them."

"We should have a third," Rachel said. "Let me ask Noora."

"But she…" I was wary of involving a former follower of Cthulhu, just as I would be careful about letting a former alcoholic have even a whiff of a strong drink. What if she changed sides again and turned on us in the middle of a fight?

"Izabel can kill her if she tries to betray us," Rachel added.

"Yeah, sure," Izabel said, raising her eyebrows. Rachel might seem weak, but she was ruthless.

Noora accepted the offer with alacrity. She had all the zeal of a new convert and was eager to prove herself. I did not go along for her first hunt, but Rachel and Izabel agreed that Noora showed great aptitude as an exorcist and a burning desire to destroy more of the Spawn. I agreed to hand over dispelling duty to Noora and Rachel, so long as Noora trained someone to take over running her pottery.

The nomads regarded both women with awe. Destroying monsters was a disturbing power and an undeniable proof of the presence of heaven. Increasingly, the men retreated to a distance, and the more pious crusaders put their hands over their ears, lest their souls be eroded by the force of the incantation.

Rachel and Noora were both insistent that only women could be exorcists.

"This is for women," Rachel told me. She was usually so docile, but on this point, it was like finding a layer of hard rock concealed in soft sand.

"You mean men can't, or just that you don't want them to?" I asked. "We need as many exorcists as we can get. Men—"

"You don't understand," Noora told me. "You were never a captive. Only women can do this."

It was true—I did not understand. But it was clear that I had to work with Rachel and Noora or lose the only other two people capable of carrying out the rite.

"Very well," I said. "I will leave you two in charge of training and organising the corps of exorcists. Recruit whoever you can."

"We will," Noora said.

None of the women of Amir's band would take the role, but some of the new arrivals were more adventurous. Soon, there was a small coterie of them, and we could send out multiple hunting parties and have others in reserve. Increasingly, the exorcists kept apart from the rest of the encampment, becoming a separate community, almost like a religious sect.

Amir was not seen often in the camp, but every evening, he and a lieutenant or two would come and look at the square, where every stone now had several garlands of teeth draped over it. Satisfied, they departed to their tents outside the ramparts. Despite numerous growing pains, the settlement was looking increasingly stable, with no outbreak of winter fever. The food supply was adequate for the time being, and if Timi's optimistic reports were to be believed, the prospects for future trade were bright.

This did not mean things were going well on the strategic front. Marie-Therese frequently reminded me that the Spawn were multiplying.

"Do you still think we can win?" she asked me confidentially one evening.

"Of course we can," I said.

"But these numbers…" Marie-Therese had completed her census, logged every new arrival, birth, and death in the camp and every sighting of the creatures. The task would have been difficult without our system of numbers. Doing arithmetic even with Roman numerals was painfully complicated, and they were centuries ahead of this era. Arabic numerals and base ten made everything so much easier. Maybe that was one of Timi's advantages over the other traders.

"We have not got enough men. Yesterday, there were at least three groups of monsters twenty strong seen at the same time, and forty more in smaller groups. There are more in their hive. The total number must be—"

"Irrelevant. Plenty of wars have been won against superior numbers," I said.

"*On dit que Dieu est toujours pour les gros bataillons,*" she quoted. *God is always on the side of the big battalions.*

"Not in my day," I said. Modern firepower counted for more than numbers. Conquistadores' cannon defeated Incas, Maxim guns mowed down armies of tribesmen. "God is on the side of the heavy artillery. Three thousand years of scientific advancement will give us weapons to annihilate the Spawn."

She smiled and shook her head. "You are a very stubborn woman, Yishka."

"Excuse me! We have a saying about the pot calling the kettle black."

She gave me a patronising smile. "You and Amir are such idealists—like your crusaders. You will fight your war if you have only a toothpick against an army of monsters. You are so romantic."

"You think we cannot win because the creatures are multiplying faster than we can kill them?"

"It is true!" Timi said. "We all cheer and celebrate every time they bring back more teeth, but I collect all the reports from the scouting parties. I record everything in my tablets. And you know what the tablets say? In the time it takes to kill ten Spawn, they breed twelve more."

Perhaps I could have questioned her methodology and criticised the lack of consistency from week to week. The overall trends, though, were depressingly obvious. The number of our enemies was slowly but unquestionably growing larger. "We are only just starting. We will get better, when we get organised. We can easily double the number of hunting parties per week and get more exorcists, and with better co-ordination, they could go from only killing one Spawn each hunt to two. That would quadruple the rate of killing at a stroke. Our forces are still growing."

"So romantic," she said. "Just like Amir."

"If you give up when things are going against you, you will never win a war," I said. "You have to look ahead. Have faith."

"Now you are playing the goddess—but I am an atheist, Yishka. I do not have faith."

"In that case, you can tell me just what you propose to do instead," I said. "Ask the desert sorcerers to blast this area to ashes and hope that works?"

"No," she said. "We are surviving, but we are not winning. There will be more and more of them until we cannot leave the camp. Then we will starve, and they will spread over the world."

"We will win so long as we do not give up," I said.

"I keep my bags packed to travel."

PART THREE: THINGS FALL APART

WINTER TOWN: THE THIRD YEAR OF THE WAR

CHAPTER SEVENTEEN: THE AMBASSADOR'S VISIT

THINGS HAD NOT GONE AS badly as Marie-Therese had predicted, nor as well as I had hoped. She believed we were slowly losing, and technically, that may have been true. But my plan was always to hold on until we could find some way of delivering a knockout blow. Finally, my plan seemed to be reaching its fruition.

We could win if we could just gain the aid of the city of Stone. However, it was the visit of their ambassador, which brought things to a head and sent them spiralling out of control.

The ambassador's name was Baaz, but his name was never used. He was always addressed as Ambassador, which made him an important man. Hierarchy mattered in the city we called Stone, which its inhabitants called *Susiana,* the nearest outpost of civilisation. I did not recognise the name; my best guess was that they were an outlying part of what historians of my day called the Hittite Empire. Stone was tremendously important as a potential ally, as well as being our most significant trading partner. The real heart of civilisation lay some hundreds of miles farther north.

Timi, who had been there several times, said Stone was a vast sprawling slum, an extended shantytown whose only distinguishing features were its ugly pyramid temples.

"You would not want to go there," Timi told me when I quizzed her about it. "It's such a dirty place. Even the temples smell of goat blood, and they're always crawling with flies. More than here, even."

Unlike our own settlement, there was no urban plan, and the city of Stone was choked by its own growth. The abattoirs, brickworks, and tanneries were mixed in with the residential districts. The wealthy lived well away from the urban centre, which was filthy and riddled with disease. They preferred their own walled compounds over villa complexes.

"They could teach Amir's people something about brutality when it came to keeping their slaves under control," Timi added.

However, Stone could muster an army of many thousand foot soldiers, and if necessary, they could call on their allies for far more. That would be a truly irresistible force. If we could secure their assistance, we could finally win the war. The niceties of Stone's civil code were less important to me than gaining their support.

Timi was convinced that Stone would deal with us. "In Stone, the merchants have no power. There is no law, not like the modern world. If they get too rich, the nobles tax them or just confiscate their property or have them killed," she said. "If the merchants have a haven where they can store their wealth safely, Stone will lose half its taxes. They must negotiate with us, or their traders will hide their wealth here."

Discussions had taken longer than I had expected. The Ambassador was charm personified and regularly apologised for how slowly we were progressing, but there were procedures to be followed before any alliance could be concluded. He smelled of rose water, and his dark beard was arranged in perfect curls like an Assyrian vase painting.

The people of Stone had their own gods, which were human in form: a sun god, a god of the underworld, and others which reminded me of the Greek pantheon. The Ambassador clearly did not view me as a goddess, but he was too polite to say so.

I had hosted feasts, with Nergal at my side. Amir was not the man for diplomatic events, and Nergal could at least be relied upon to behave himself in public. Marie-Therese and Timi joined us, Timi having the advantage of being able to speak the language of Stone, though the Ambassador and several of his entourage were passably fluent in Language. Lalit occasionally condescended to give a flute recital.

The Ambassador was not content to simply talk. He wanted to see everything for himself, to inspect everything.

"This is a place of wonders," he told me. "This Wintertown has so many unlikely stories swirling about it, that I must see things for myself before I report them as true. And taste them for myself." He raised a cup of spirit to me. We had maintained a monopoly by keeping the distilling process a state secret. The merchants of Stone would have liked to duplicate our distillery and cut us out of the trade.

"It is a place beset by war," I said. "We would be happy to exchange a little military assistance for commercial benefits."

"Ah, this strange war of yours," he said, as though it was a curious custom in these parts. "This war without battles, without victories. You may be surprised to know it is discussed even in the council-chambers of Stone, where we have many learned men and philosophers from all corners of the world."

It would be like the court of a medieval English king discussing an outbreak of dragons in the highlands of Scotland. A mixture of distrust of travellers' tales mingled with pleasure that it was somebody else getting eaten.

He seemed more interested in Amir. "He is feared by all the other nomads," the Ambassador said. "They call him the King of the Plains."

"Raiding was a sport for them," I said. "Amir showed them that this was no time for sport."

When a hostile band moved in and sent raiding parties after our livestock, Amir had assembled a force of two hundred horsemen and ridden down the entire group, killing all of them. He spared the women and children, if only to humour me.

"The war against the Spawn is more important," I said. "Ultimately, the conflict might threaten Stone."

"There are some who say that this conflict simply feeds on itself," he said. "That the Spawn are like weeds—the more you cut them down, they grow back all the more."

"Who says that?" I asked, too sharply.

"Wise men who have travelled," he said negligently. "Perhaps different to the wise men who advise your own councils. Others say this war is more like a game: how can you continue for years without a decisive battle? Surely, you are just toying with these creatures?"

"You will be able to learn otherwise when you have seen for yourself," Marie-Therese said.

"These wise men," I said. "Do they revere or revile the being called Cthulhu?"

"Ah, the name is mentioned," he said. "The strange dead god who dreams. The dreams are stronger here, aren't they?"

"I have never experienced them," I said.

"Some of my entourage have those dreams," he said.

The dreams came at the high points of the cycle, when the force that motivated the Spawn was strongest. They were commonest amongst the crusaders and the exorcists; mercifully, I was exempt.

"Dreams are not good guides," Marie-Therese said. "And here, you will be able to learn the facts."

"I look forward to being educated, my lady," he said, possibly with a hint of flirtation.

The Ambassador showed little interest in the war, but he was most attentive when it came to trade and in particular our unique export: the teeth of monsters, our city's currency. Some were sold as trophies, like elephant tusks or narwhal horns, or worn singly as charms or jewellery, but most were ground down for medicine. Lu Zhu assured me that they had no more medicinal effect than ground pebbles, but we did nothing to discourage the belief. The trade was extremely profitable, and the steady stream of gold flowing from Stone towards us had been noted.

Timi was working on a complex array of potential trade deals, like a merchant offering bolts of cloth and shiny buttons. The Ambassador had been no more than lukewarm. I increasingly mistrusted his intentions. He looked around our territory like a man planning on buying an estate, and buying it as cheaply as he could.

The first signs of trouble emerged several weeks into the Ambassador's stay. My secretary, Dota, and I crossed the main square, arms full of new-made blank tablets, keeping to the shade. The tail of a crowd of workers was disappearing down the street, sturdy women in straw hats with tools slung over their shoulders returning from the pre-dawn shift. A few had babies strapped to their backs. The rest would have left their children in the nursery, where they would have been eating bread-and-butter with milk, playing with toys, and learning songs and rhymes. The workers were mainly widows who needed the food and pay we offered, but married women were encouraged to work too.

A light breeze eddied round the plaza, stirring the sun-baked dust. The horizon was smudged with brown. Out in No Man's Land, they were burning grass. It was all part of the endless, deadly game of hide-and-go-seek between men and monsters. They came up in the night and set their ambushes, and in the daytime, the men went out and tried to kill them. The tactics on both sides were evolving constantly.

The Spawn had learned how to catch men and use them as bait, breaking their legs and lying in wait for rescuers to come. We used pits and barriers to channel them; they lay in ambush along our approach paths. Vana's dogs had become adept at sniffing out ambushes, and I had encouraged her to train as many more as possible.

We had learned how to use soot-bombs, thin pottery shells filled with charcoal powder, to mark the creatures and prevent them from using their chameleon-like powers to disappear. These proved far more effective than Molotov cocktails using distilled spirits, which the Spawn barely noticed.

We used every method we could think of in our total war: "Every man fights; every woman works," was Marie-Therese's slogan.

The Spawn never appeared methodical, but they were relentless, roots seeking and probing through rocky ground. Always turned back, they were always advancing, wearing down resistance, infinitely patient. Their forces seemed to be disposed at random, but found our weakest spots in our defences.

Dota followed obediently three paces behind me, quiet and diligent. I was hoping not to spoil her, but the girl needed to speak up more for herself. We were both burdened with wooden racks of fresh writing tablets, still warm.

"Dota, can you remind me where the Ambassador is today?"

"Lord Amir has taken him to the coastal town."

That was the place the nomads called Fish Port. The old settlements had all been wiped out. A large force of Spawn had swept down the coast, killing everything. Only those who took to their boats had escaped. Our men had followed the creatures, though, picking off stragglers until all were destroyed.

Fish Port was on the site of a former fishing village, chosen because it gave us our nearest access to the sea. It was now a busy harbour for fishing and trading. The coastal trade of dried fish bound inland was stronger than ever.

"Of course. They're due back this evening, aren't they?"

"Yes, Highness."

The Ambassador may have gone, but most of his considerable entourage would still be around, a troop of guards, servants, grooms, advisers, translators, and friends, along with a good many hangers-on and others of indeterminate status. The lowest of them were slaves; Amir was not wrong to call Stone an unfree society. They occupied four of our larger houses, which were styled on Roman villas. The Ambassador sent off groups of two or three to convey messages on a regular basis, and more always seemed to come back than he sent. His people always seemed to be loitering about or poking into things, more like spies than curious travellers.

On market day, the square would be crowded with stalls, selling produce, handicrafts, food, and drink, and the gendarmes would be busy keeping order. Today, it was all but deserted. Three dogs lay comatose, each in its own shady doorway, all wearing the collars of hunting hounds. A pair of old men in goatskin tunics played draughts under a sagging awning. The game had caught on in the last year, and now it seemed everyone was playing. Some children played at stalking monsters, with reeds for harpoons, on the other side of the square. Two of the Ambassador's entourage were watching the draughts players from a polite distance. They bowed conspicuously as we passed.

"That one in the yellow cape smiles too much," I said when we were safely out of earshot. "Don't you think?"

"Yes, Highness."

"You can't just agree with me," I said. "Tell me what you think of him."

We walked on several more steps.

"He has nice clothes, but he smiles like a merchant who is trying to cheat you," Dota said.

"Exactly," I said.

A warrior was waiting outside my office, standing respectfully at attention.

"How was the hunt?" I asked, wishing I could remember his name… something like Ozan.

"We found all four of the Unclean and killed three," he said. "None of the men were killed."

"Was it a hard fight?" By the calendar, it was not an auspicious day, but sometimes, we had to fight them, come what may.

"Our exorcist was strong to destroy three souls. Some hunters came, and we left them on the trail of the fourth. It will not get away, and another exorcist will come for them soon."

"How is your exorcist?" I was starting to worry about the effect the job was having on them. Some of our exorcists had been reduced to nervous wrecks by overwork. The mental toll was severe.

"She is a strong woman," he said. "She is in the House of Prayer."

"Well done," I said, already thinking of the other two groups of Spawn that had broken through the lines and were currently on the loose. I was expecting news of them later today. More importantly, I wanted to hear the confirmation that the gap in the lines had been fixed and that a full survey had been carried out. "Please give your report to headquarters."

Everything had to be recorded and cross-indexed by Marie-Therese's scribes. Organising our limited resources was everything.

There was an argument outside, and I recognised Marie-Therese's raised voice. At first, I assumed it was a continuation of her previous day's acrimonious discussion with Timi. The two were at loggerheads over the profits Timi's latest caravan to Stone had generated. Marie-Therese insisted they were needed to pay for soldiers, engineers, and Wintertown's other expenses. Timi was equally adamant that it should be reinvested in the business to reap bigger profits with the next caravan.

"We double the money each time," Timi said. "It doubles and doubles. After a few trips, we will have enough money for everything you want."

"But we can't wait that long," Marie-Therese said. "I need money now."

"Well, you can't have it. I need it to trade. You manage your treasury. I'll manage the trading."

"You will give me the money!"

"Don't you shout at me! I can shout back just as loud!"

The two had been increasingly coming into conflict over money. Usually, it was just a matter of aggressively inspecting each other's accounts, looking for errors, and ferreting out concealed or mis-spent funds. This time, it sounded like they might come to blows.

"Girls!" I said in my headmistressy voice. "Let's work this out calmly. Perhaps over a cup of tea."

I oversaw the rest of the discussion, which was conducted in more measured tones. Afterwards, I wondered if both of them shouted as a negotiating ploy, like a trader offering an unrealistic price at first. If I could see these things from the start, I would be a real administrator.

However, this time, it was not Timi arguing with Marie-Therese, but Marie-Therese with a woman I did not recognise.

"Highness! Please, Highness!" said the woman.

A soldier held the unfamiliar woman by one arm, and Marie-Therese was there, her face sharpened by anger.

"What is it?" I asked.

"*Cela ne devrait pas vous concerner*," Marie-Therese said, in French, using the formal *vous*. *This should not concern you.*

"What is it about?"

"*Alors*, you will have to know at some point," she said, switching to Language. "This stupid woman wishes to petition you."

"Highness…" She was a woman of middle years. One of Damki's aunts, I believed. "I seek justice. Your gendarmes beat me. And tried to rob me."

I caught a look from Dota, stylus poised, wanting to know if this should be part of the official record. Judging from Marie-Therese's expression, I thought not.

"Would you like to explain, briefly," I asked Marie-Therese.

"This woman is trying to set herself up as a *madame*." There were no words relating to the oldest profession in the local language, so Marie-Therese used the French term. "Without asking for permission or a licence."

Our legal rules were more like the Ten Commandments than a proper civil code. There were so many grey areas, so many things that fell into the region between custom and crime, and nobody had spent much time drafting laws. Disputes were handled by the governor, based mainly on nomad tradition combined with our sketchy legal framework. His rulings then became case law.

"Surely that's one for Nergal," I said. As governor, Nergal settled legal questions. Technically, the responsibility role should have been Amir's, but delegating these tasks to his brother freed him for his role as military commander. Nergal was shrewd, and he understood the nomad traditional law and custom and what was acceptable. Disputes over everything from alleged theft of clothes to drunken brawling, events which had been rare in the band's nomadic existence, were increasingly common. The combination of material wealth, a higher population, and plentiful alcohol meant we needed a police force.

Amir's situation was complicated. He was not exactly a supreme commander, but the destruction or decimation of other bands and the mass flight of others to the east had effectively made him tribal chief, though some of the others viewed him only as first amongst equals. Holy warriors had continued to arrive. The High Priestess was on an endless pilgrimage to preach crusade, and some of them were from tribes of which Amir was only dimly aware. These men would not pledge loyalty to Amir, but came to kneel embarrassingly at my feet. I regularly had to order them to listen to Amir. There was also a large group of freelancers—the hunters—who came and went as they pleased and were only under the loosest control, exercised by the former bandit Crow.

Then there was the town gendarmerie, which also provided caravan guards, effectively a mercenary force paid for by Timi's little trading empire. They were under Nergal's control, with Damki as their commander in day-to-day matters. Damki had proven a shrewd and efficient commissioner of police.

"It was Nergal who sent her to you," Marie-Therese said. I sensed wheels within wheels and waited for her to elaborate.

"Why should we be denied when others are allowed?" the woman asked, holding out her hands. "Why can we not profit from our daughters as others do?"

"What others?" This was certainly news to me. I was not aware that prostitution even existed here. One of the jobs of the gendarmes or military police was to ensure that the soldiers were kept away from nomad women.

"You know the taverns," Marie-Therese said. We had designated an area for the entertainment of off-duty soldiers, selling beer and spirit. It was the most heavily policed spot in the town. Incidents were rare. "There are girls working there, in rooms at the back."

I raised an eyebrow. "With official permission?"

"Of course. Every garrison has its brothel, even in England, and the army always regulates them—you can't deny it! It is clean. But an unlicensed, unregulated brothel, we cannot allow this."

I took a deep breath then another before replying. "I don't think you mentioned this establishment to me."

"I didn't mention when we set up the *patisserie*, but you didn't object to that."

I bit my tongue in an effort not to say something I would later regret. I could not afford a rift with Marie-Therese. Setting up a brothel under my nose—and under the banner of my authority—was shocking.

"*Je m'excuse,*" she said in apology. "There are so many things to do, you know. I did not want to get into long arguments about this and that. Please do not let us argue."

I could quite understand why she had not wanted to raise it with me; this was one of those questions of morales on which we never would see eye-to-eye. And, in the greater context of fighting the war, it should not be allowed to become a distraction.

"The gendarmes should not have been rough with you," I told the petitioner. "They believed you were trying to break the law… the law is not clear on this. We will make some arrangement."

She looked at me expectantly. Not for the first time, I wished for a few books on civil governance. Fortunately, Marie-Therese took my cue.

"Don't worry," Marie-Therese said, taking the woman by the arm. "I will talk to you, and we can work out an arrangement between the town and you, and your girls."

"That would be best," I said.

The petitioner looked suspicious, as well she might. But she allowed Marie-Therese to lead her away. It was the second such argument with Marie-Therese in three days. The previous one had been about the opium trade and only exporting it for medical purposes. I'd also found out what was going on via a circuitous route, a mercenary captain offering his services and asking for payment in opium, "like the others." A mercenary from Stone, I realised.

"Finally," I said as they left. "Dota, can you get the notes about the southern embankments we started yesterday?"

Before we were halfway through reviewing the previous day's work, a distant clamour started up. Both of us stopped to listen. It was not a returning hunt, an arriving caravan, or any of the other familiar patterns of commotion.

"I will go and look," Dota said, putting down her tablet and stylus.

A herd of bleating goats passed outside. They would be on their way to the daily slaughter. Our forces required a certain number of goats per diem. Maintaining that supply and ensuring that between our own flocks and what we could procure, we could keep it going had become one of my obsessions over the last two years. My dread was that one day, we would be turning away volunteers because we could not feed them. It had not happened yet, but there were times when we were badly stretched.

She returned a minute later, looking serious. "It is between the gendarmes and the hunters. They said the gendarmes have arrested Crow. I don't think there will be any fighting, but the men are very angry."

The hunters were a heterogenous bunch, men from tribal and non-tribal groups who had banded together into groups to hunt and bring down the Spawn. Their motive was purely monetary, driven by the trade in teeth.

Many of the hunters were former outlaws like Crow, who had preyed on the caravans, forced into a new occupation. Others were exiles from the cities, driven out here to live by their wits. They were as colourful as any pirate crew, an eclectic mix of races and styles of clothing and with a wild assortment of weaponry. Some were simply treasure hunters. Every few weeks, a new gang would get the brilliant idea of killing a Spawn without an exorcist present to avoid paying our tax, fishing out the valuable teeth from the stinking, seething slime even as it reformed. The practice had claimed many lives.

The majority were law-abiding enough, and we'd had little trouble with them. Crow was the hunters' unofficial leader and probably the richest individual in town. I gathered that Marie-Therese was a close friend, if not more than a friend. That must have been quite an advantage.

I had only met him a few times; he was always extravagantly polite, and his manners suggested one who had been brought up somewhere far from nomad campfires. He had the biggest private house in Wintertown. He was a shrewd businessman and had many contacts amongst the merchants, despite, or perhaps because of, his history as a bandit.

"What does Damki want to arrest him for?" I asked.

"I don't know," Dota said. "Should we send a messenger to find out?"

"I think you'd better go in person," I said, looking at my watch. "Try to be back in twenty minutes. Don't let them leave you hanging around. Insist on getting an answer. Use my name."

"Yes, Highness," she said, sounding a little doubtful. Dota was not good at demanding things, but she was learning.

I found Izabel in the stables. She would never be a great horsewoman, but she had succeeded in making friends with her horse, a big chestnut mare she was grooming between patrols.

I threw myself down on a bale of hay. "They've arrested Crow."

"I heard," she said, speaking English as she always did when we were alone. "They say he murdered a hunter called Shimun last night."

"But why?"

"Argument over money, they say," she said. "Hunters are always falling out over money. This guy Shimun was paid off with his share. Later on, he was drinking. He starts saying he's been short-changed and he's going to get what he's owed. The next thing, Shimun's dead."

"That doesn't sound like Crow."

"There were witnesses. There're also people saying Mister Big Ambassador from Stone has something against Crow and has been looking at ways to take him down."

"You don't like the Stone delegation, do you?"

Izabel shook her head. "I know too many runaway slaves from Stone. They're worried what happens to them if you make a deal, if you're going to sell them out."

"I won't," I said. "But the other thing I heard—Crow couldn't have been plotting anything, could he? Against Nergal?"

"Well… you know about Crow and Mamzelle, right?" I nodded. I did not know the details of their relationship, but it was a business, as well as a romantic, one. "He wouldn't make a move without her." She gave a humourless little laugh. "She is going to go crazy."

There had been other killings, and we had a judicial system slightly more sophisticated than the nomads' traditional spear-duel between accuser and accused. It would be down to Nergal to weigh up evidence and give judgment. Given that there was enough evidence to have Crow arrested, the outcome seemed fairly predictable.

"So I thought. I had a little run-in with Marie-Therese earlier, as it happens."

"What's the little scamp done now?"

"Set up a house of ill-repute, right under my nose."

"Didn't think you'd like that."

Everybody in the settlement must have known about the place. Everybody but me. "I thought Marie-Therese had some values. I thought she wanted to free women, not make them into whores."

"Hey, don't tell me," Izabel said. "But like she says, it was going to happen anyway. This way, it's controlled, and the girls are protected."

Money probably came into it. Marie-Therese was always complaining about the state of our town finances. The tavern already recovered a large proportion of the soldiers' pay; her additional venture must have taken up a good proportion of the rest.

I had not even asked who the women working there were. Refugees from the coastal settlements, perhaps. Surely, we were not importing harlots from Stone. "Well," I said at last. "I can't say I like it. But I suppose I'll let it stand for the sake of peace."

Izabel let her horse nuzzle grain from her palm, then she wiped her hands on her breeches and sat next to me.

A distant clang announced the hour. By reflex, I checked my watch; the hour-signal was only about three minutes slow today. The sand clocks were working well. Even if my watch broke—heaven forbid—we would be able to get noon from the height of the sun and mark out the hours with sand clocks. Good timekeeping kept everything properly regulated, though to most of the population, it was more like ritual observance.

"We found four and killed three this morning," she said.

"Ozan told me."

"Ozar. There are hunters tracking the last one. It won't get away." The brave tone did not hide her disappointment.

"Three on the trot is hard work for one exorcist on a four-star day," I said. "And to think, I once imagined I'd be doing all of them myself."

"Even Rachel is slowing down. But she's not stopping."

I had not spoken to Rachel for weeks; in fact, I could not remember the last time I had seen her. The gatherings of the handmaidens were less frequent now, and there were so many absences, with Timi always away on trading missions and Lu Zhu visiting other nomad bands like a district midwife on her rounds. Illi disappeared for days on end, scouting. Lalit was a mother for the second time and looking after her baby.

"How is Rachel?" I asked.

"She's okay. I guess. Spending a little time in the House of Prayer. Doesn't talk much." That was where the exorcists went to recover, resting in darkened rooms, lulled with incense and quiet, soothed with opium. I had visited there a few times and found Rachel lying in a darkened room exhausted after a day in which she had ridden from hunt to hunt and destroyed seven of the things. She held my hand and smiled wanly but could only burble incoherently when she tried to form words. She had recovered, but I had not heard her speak since then.

Some of the exorcists took longer to recover than others. Some of them moved on to other roles. I made a mental note to check on how many we currently had rostered for active service. Despite our growing population, exorcists were becoming more difficult to recruit.

"This war takes it out of all of us," I said. "Though I've had it the easiest of anyone."

"Yeah, there's you, living in your palace and drinking tea and wearing fancy slippers," she said, with another laugh.

The palace was not exactly a palace, and the tea was not exactly tea. I had not thought to change my shoes, and the indoor slippers worked with silver thread, imported from the cities, were highly unsuitable for a stable.

"They are rather fine," I said, lifting my feet. "Shall I get Dota to bring you a pair?"

"No! Slippers are for goddesses. I like my riding boots."

"But you're right. I do get all the benefits and none of the danger."

"You keep those benefits and all the bureaucracy and meetings and ya-ya-ya-ya." She made a talking-mouth sign with her hand. "I'd rather be where the action is."

We'd had this conversation before. At first, I had urged Izabel to help us on the organising side. She was literate and numerate and had a far better grasp of administration than any of the Bronze Age people we were trying to work with. But Izabel just wanted to be a harpooner. In fact, she was far more than that: she was a tactician, one who figured out how to approach a situation, and Amir's trusted adviser. Some of the men would have accepted her as a leader, but Izabel was not having it.

"I'm just trying to be a good foot soldier," she said. "I don't need any more responsibility than that."

More importantly for her, Izabel had found her vocation. Riding the grasslands with a band of nomads, hunting monsters, this was her Valhalla. She had found herself in the freedom of the plains, with the winds sending waves rippling through the tall grasses and the clouds sailing above. For a healthy outdoors sort who liked the thrill of the hunt—and the constant excitement of danger—then I supposed it was the good life.

"I meant to ask, could you manage the trench-plough teams for a few days? None of the men can read a map properly." The trench-plough was a heavy device drawn by six horses. It tore up a wide patch of earth, which a team of labourers could quickly convert into a ditch and rampart just high enough to stop the Spawn.

"More? How many trenches do we need?" Now it was my turn to laugh. Izabel had not even seen the plans I had drawn up with Marie-

Therese for even more elaborate lines of defence than the current layout, a labyrinth which forced the Spawn into killing grounds whichever route they took.

"Plenty more," I said.

"Nothing is ever enough, is it?" Izabel could never understand the need to get things done properly.

"Nobody ever said that fighting a war against alien invaders with Bronze Age weapons would be easy." I stood up. "Please be careful, Izzy. I can't afford to lose you."

"I'm not going anywhere."

"You are my Queequeg," I said. "My best, my most faithful harpoonist."

"That would make you Captain Ahab, right?" she shot back.

I raised an eyebrow.

"Obviously, I learned about it from the game, not the book, just in case you were thinking I'd actually read something."

"Sorry." Maybe I had remarked on her lack of reading once too often.

"Don't worry about it, Chief. I'll keep on harpooning. You keep goddessing."

I returned to my office. Maybe I really was Captain Ahab, single-mindedly obsessed with my mission of getting home, killing as many Spawn as I needed to get there. On my way, I passed the Ambassador's men again, loitering outside the stables, watching dirty straw being shovelled into a wheelbarrow. Yellow Cape bowed again and smiled ingratiatingly.

Damki came as soon as he received my message. He looked rather dashing and grown-up in the uniform Marie-Therese had designed. "We have witnesses. Two hunters heard the fight and went to have a look—they say they heard Crow's voice and saw him in the torchlight. He fled when he saw them, but three from the Stone delegation also saw a man wearing black running away from the scene. They described a man like Crow."

"The witnesses could be lying," I said. "The Ambassador could have set it up."

"He could," Damki admitted. "He is a clever man, and he hates Crow. Maybe all the witnesses are lying—but what can we do, if Nergal decides to believe them? Nergal who is a friend of the Ambassador, and who has his own reasons."

"What reasons?"

"Nothing exact." Damki understood the differences between my way of thinking and the nomads. "But they say Crow was something important in Stone, then he was outlawed. He became a bandit, then a chief of bandits. When the Spawn ended that business, he became a hunter and then a chief of hunters. And one with an influential woman-friend… They say he wants to return to Stone and reclaim his name, but he can only do that if he gains enough power and wealth here. Nergal has good reason to look over his shoulder for hoofbeats behind him."

Nergal was the law. Our legal system had no appeal process.

"Amir outranks Nergal. Could he issue a pardon?"

"She asked the same. I told her—you always say how laws have to be obeyed, not broken when it suits us," Damki said. He could have said, "This is the way you imposed on us," but he would never be so impolitic.

"It is a curious case," I said.

"There was one other witness," Damki said. "He told a different story. A caravan-guard from River says he saw one of the men from Stone—the one you call Yellow Cape—washing blood off his hands in a water trough. He thought it was worth telling me, but he would not go before Nergal, and I have not seen him since."

Damki could tell well enough that there was skulduggery under way, but he had no weapons to fight it. "I've been busy with another case," he said haltingly. "Nothing is proved, nothing definite. A man heard it from another, who heard it from another—you know. Trying to hire men for an assassination."

"Who were they planning to kill?" I asked, but the answer was obvious. An assassin would not be a masked man crawling over the rooftop at night. It would be one of the ordinary traders, workmen, or soldiers who passed through our gates every day, made bold by money or other promises.

"The story was they were looking for an archer," he said. "My men asking questions should be enough to stop the plot, if there is one, but perhaps you should beware of windows which are overlooked at night."

"But you don't think there is a plot?"

"I thought it was just their way of putting pressure on you," Damki said. "So I did not tell you. Now though—if they dare to attack Crow, they will dare anything."

"Do you think there will be an execution tomorrow morning?" Dota asked.

"I suppose so," I said. "Unless I intervene."

CHAPTER EIGHTEEN: AN AUDIENCE WITH THE GOVERNOR

SETTING FOOT IN NERGAL'S PALACE was an act of aggression, and things were likely to get heated. I did not trust either Marie-Therese or Izabel to keep their tempers, and there was little point in bringing a secretary. If Damki came with me, then blood might be shed. I had sent messengers and even Dota, only to be told that he was not available. It seemed altogether easier for me simply to turn up in person and have things out with Nergal face to face.

I had intended our grandest building to be a town hall, a seat of administration. Although single-storey, its ceilings were double height, and it towered over the adjacent buildings. Now it had become Nergal's personal palace, with more and more of it taken over by his people, who pushed the administration into whatever odd corners, halls, and corridors were left.

The doorman was an elderly man, doubtless one of Nergal's relations. He hesitated briefly and waved to indicate that I should not go through, but I gave him what my mother would call "an old-fashioned look" of stern disapproval, and I walked through the beaded doorway without opposition.

Nergal had taken the largest meeting room as his audience chamber. I was pleased with the way the spacious chamber had turned out, well-lit by wide windows, and less pleased to see it turned into a private lounge. It was decorated with barbaric splendour. A fan of spears interspersed with animal skulls decorated one wall. The hide of a camel stretched out across the floor, and an enormous garland of monster-teeth draped over the back of his chair. Other trappings, like the huge tapestry from Stone dominating one wall and the throne-like wooden chair on which Nergal lounged, suggested an ambition to be a provincial governor rather than a nomad war chief.

A low side table held bowls of dates and apricots, the latest imported delicacies, and a litter of used opium pipes. It was distressing to see how the habit of smoking the stuff was spreading.

Curtained alcoves ran down one wall. According to rumour, Nergal's bodyguards waited in one of them, ready to tackle any assailant. And behind another one was a couch where he would engage with one of his mistresses or with female petitioners, if men were wise enough to send their wives or daughters.

He was speaking with artisans I did not recognise. Technically, Nergal taxed and regulated them, even if he had little actual involvement, but he was learning governance step by step. And I had heard he was learning how to take bribes in exchange for monopoly rights and handing out preferred sites for workshops. He dismissed them with a lordly flick of the wrist when he caught sight of me. His scribe was similarly shooed out.

"My lady," Nergal said. "I believe you said you would visit, and I am pleased to admit you." He gestured to a chair somewhat lower and less well-cushioned than his own. A copper band encircled his brow, a style copied from the noblemen to the north. Nergal looked chubbier than I remembered him. Every day, he looked more like a merchant than a nomad. On another day, I might have been amused to see the changes, but not today.

"I am concerned about the execution of the man called Crow," I said.

"What a silly name," he said. "And those silly clothes. And I hear a certain lady is fond of this Crow—but the law is the law." He allowed himself a smirk.

"I was more concerned that you should have ordered it on so little evidence."

"I know more about that Crow than you think. I talk to many people." He picked up a copper trinket in the form of a lizard and started admiring it, as though Crow's guilt or innocence meant little to him.

"People like that lying Ambassador?"

"Yishka, you have so little understanding of how justice works here," he said in a pitying tone. "You have seen so little, you don't know how things really are with us. With a spear fight, justice is on the side of the strongest—do you want to go back to that?"

"Why did you convict Crow?"

"It was not a difficult case. He never tried to deny it."

"Because he knew you'd fall in with this little charade arranged by the Ambassador? Or maybe you were part of it?"

Nergal put down the lizard, his expression sharper. Crow's life meant nothing, but Nergal's authority was another matter. "I am lord here," he said. "The evidence was enough, and more than enough to have him executed three times over. But even if it had not been—I am lord and governor, and I have the power to make judgment. That is all there is to it."

"Did you know the two hunters who claim they saw Crow doing it have disappeared. I hear they were headed towards Stone, richer than they arrived."

"Yishka, you are so beautiful, but you do not understand justice," he said. "Leave these things to men. Crow's death will benefit all of us."

At this point, both Marie-Therese and Izabel would have become angry. I would have been standing between them and Nergal, and we would not have been able to make any further progress. I kept my temper in check.

"Nergal, you must understand that the Ambassador has undermined our justice system. These people are subtle. You need to keep your wits about you, or they will trick you."

"Nobody tricks me," he said negligently.

"You must postpone the execution."

"The law must be obeyed, and the law has spoken. Crow dies tomorrow."

I gave myself a slow count of three, already wondering how I could stop the execution.

"Was that all?" he asked.

"As a matter of fact, no. As I'm here, I might ask why you sent that woman to me—the one who wanted to run a brothel."

"I thought you might want to know," he said. "You have opinions on matters affecting women."

"I warn you not to try to stir things up between me and Marie-Therese." I said this louder than I intended.

"If we are giving warnings, then I should warn you of something. The houses in the new quarter will not be available for your people."

I had sent routine instructions about how some of the space in our latest extension were to be allocated. There were artisans clamouring for space, and we needed to move some officers into better quarters. I had worked everything out, and my orders had never been disobeyed.

"You run like an untamed horse, Yishka," he said, picking up a horse trinket from the side table and moving it in a mock gallop. "You give orders, and things happen. That has always impressed me. But now it is so complicated. So many people now, so many families and different demands."

"Are you giving the good houses to your friends? Or just to anyone who bribes you?"

"You always said that Amir has no understanding of politics. I tread more carefully. I nurture bonds with others. I respect rank. I will not offend this man by giving that man, who is his inferior, a better house before him. And I am lord of this place."

I folded my arms. "I gave you this post so you could help me, Nergal. Do not obstruct me."

"Yishka, I would never obstruct you." He smiled, almost apologetic. "I am trying to do things properly."

"Don't play with me!" I had not meant to shout.

"I respect you totally, Yishka, but I am governor, and you are just a woman. A goddess, perhaps, but still a woman. Everything that is done here is done in my name, not yours. Your requests will be dealt with in due course."

"Due course!" I took a step forwards, but Nergal rang a little bell, and two armed men sprang out from the alcoves to stand between us.

I did not recognise the guards. They were northerners, their faces blank and menacing, hands on their sword-hilts.

"Things have changed," Nergal went on calmly. "I no longer sleep in a tent which can be cut open by your strange friend with her little knife." He clearly enjoyed having me at a disadvantage. He had been waiting for this moment. He gestured at the guards, and they stepped back to flank him, still eyeing me suspiciously.

"We are fighting a war, and this town must be run efficiently," I said. "Not for your personal benefit."

"Ah yes, the war. Well, things may change, Yishka. You and Amir are so passionate that we must always be fighting, but it is not necessarily so."

"What do you mean by that exactly?"

Nergal relished the effects of his words. It was no different to my brothers taunting me by saying "I know a secret that you don't" when we were children, and it was still just as aggravating.

"The Spawn are hungry for meat, and they attack us because they cannot get it," he said. "Like any other animals, or men, for that matter.

254

If they get meat and are sated, they will not trouble us. Why should they? All it will take are a few goats and some old horses each month, and we can placate them. They will not trouble us."

"That's ridiculous," I said. "Who told you that?"

"But of course, without your war, we have less need of you. You are the goddess of the war."

"Fortunately, Nergal, you are not in charge of the war effort." My words were clipped and abrupt. "Fortunately, your brother is the ruler. And you are required to obey him."

"I do not have any argument with my brother."

"Nergal… we had an agreement. You swore an oath."

"As if promises to *women* ever mean anything. You are not in your country now. Nomads know how to treat their womenfolk."

"How dare you—" I stopped. Nergal was nothing if not calculating, and he had calculated I could do nothing.

"This is my palace," he said. "My brother commands the army outside. Inside the walls, I am master." He moved closer.

I did not back away. I never backed away.

Nergal reached out and removed my spectacles. "I always wondered what you looked like without them."

"Give those back at once," I said.

He contemplated the glasses a second, squinted through them, then finally passed them back. "Of course, as you ask so nicely."

"Thank you."

"You know I have always admired you." That would not have been how I put it. But perhaps he did see himself as an admirer.

"If you were the wife of the ruler, then you would have your place," he said.

"What?"

"Everything is changing. This is a city now. A marriage would secure your position. You would be a wife and not just a woman."

I was about to tell him that Amir did not want to marry me when I realised that was not his intention. Nergal seriously thought I might marry him, but his smile faded a little when he saw my expression.

"You haven't heard the last of this," I told him.

It was a weak exit line. Nergal was laughing with his bodyguards as I went out. I stomped back to the headquarters, steaming with fury. The Ambassador had found a way to settle his grudge against Crow, upset Marie-Therese, disrupt the hunters, and weaken us. How many birds could that man kill with one stone?

The courtier in a yellow cape, chatting to his friend as I passed, bowed deeply.

Chapter Nineteen: The Execution of the Man called Crow

"It was an accident," Amir said guiltily as soon as I saw him. His right arm was bound up in a sling. His behaviour continued to support the theory I was a mother-figure to him.

"It is just a sprain?" I asked.

"I don't know what *you* call it," he said. Our medical vocabulary was borrowed mainly from Chinese. As far as Amir was concerned, it was just a hurt arm, with no distinction between tendons, ligaments, and bones. "I did this once when I was young. It will get better in a few weeks."

"Has Lu Zhu seen it?"

"Would it be bound up otherwise? She sends her regards."

I had not seen our doctor for some time. She always seemed to find excuses to be somewhere else. Lu Zhu was as busy as I was. Except that her war, she told me, was against disease, malnutrition, and ignorance. She was not much interested in mine.

"And you're sure it was an accident," I said.

"What else would it be?"

Amir got on well enough with the Ambassador, or more accurately, the Ambassador was diplomatic enough to not be offended by anything Amir said or did. But there was a certain jostling for status. Amir claimed never to feel envy for his weak city-bred guest who never even carried a weapon, but the Ambassador's wealth and sophistication were beginning to have an effect. Riding was one thing they had in common. The Ambassador had brought a stable of fine horses with him, and there was an unspoken competition between them. I suspected Amir's fall had been the result of showing off, trying to outdo the Ambassador in some feat. I hoped he had at least learned a lesson, unlikely as it seemed.

"Not that it makes any difference," he added morosely. "I don't need to hold a spear. I am the leader who never fights."

"Not this again."

"Now I just raise my hand and give orders. To take part in a kill, I have to push my way through ten hunters rushing in ahead of me." This was a ridiculous exaggeration, but Amir's feelings were to be respected. If he was feeling sorry for himself, I had to comfort him.

"You are becoming a different type of leader. Like the generals of Stone, who win battles with brains, not brute force. You are still just as brave, just as daring as ever."

"It may not be true," he said, flashing a smile, "but it is good to hear you say it."

"You heard about Crow," I said.

"It's a pity," he said.

The two were rivals rather than friends. There were no official scores for who had killed more Spawn, but both Amir's supporters and Crow's were willing to have drunken arguments about it.

"There doesn't seem to be much evidence, and executing him is going to stir things up with the hunters. He's the one who keeps them under control—he practically controls the trade in teeth."

"Nergal never liked him," Amir said.

"Can you get Nergal to delay until we can be sure?"

"If Crow killed a man, he will die," Amir said, with a shrug of his good shoulder. "If he is innocent, he will live. I do not interfere with Nergal's affairs, or he with mine."

"But if there are problems with the hunters, it affects everyone," I said. The hunters were not the most numerous fighting force, but they accounted for a great many of the kills. Marie-Therese had the numbers to prove it.

"You want laws and justice instead of spear-duels," Amir said, repeating what everyone else had told me.

The next morning, we assembled to see the execution on the edge of No Man's Land. Quite a crowd had made the two-hour trek from Wintertown, gathered on a low rise which gave a view of the killing ground below. People loved any excuse for a holiday, and executions were always festive occasions. I could hardly complain, given that the last public execution in London was in living memory. Humanity had three thousand years of similar entertainments to look forwards to.

As expected, hundreds of hunters turned up for the event, and Amir had ensured that at least an equal number of nomad warriors were on hand in case of trouble. The hunters were armed and ready for action; from here, they would set out to their assigned places for the day's hunting. They carried pikes, double-axes, or a halberd, depending on their background and experience. There were newer weapons too—baroque polearms with porcupines of blades for fending off tentacles, or multi-headed scythes with double edges—as Turm experimented and refined new designs. Some wore cage-like helmets or armoured masks and carried spiked shields.

Warlike as they looked, the hunter contingent seemed resigned to watch from the sidelines rather than trying to rescue their leader.

Four guards preceded the Ambassador. Tall men with round helmets and armour of bronze scales covering their torsos, they towered over the nomads. They did not need to physically shove people away, but cleared a space simply by gesturing with their spears.

The quartet stood in a square, like the corner posts of a boxing ring, keeping the space clear with the implied threat of their presence.

Servants arrived next, assembled a portable table, and spread it with a tablecloth. The servants went back and forth, setting the table with bowls of aromatic herbs, an ewer of water, a finger bowl, and other diplomatic essentials. Finally, three chairs were set around the table. They had brought all this out from the city.

The man himself strolled in, deep in conversation with Yellow Cape and another crony. The language was impenetrable, but their manner suggested they were talking of matters of state.

"Your Highness," the Ambassador said, with a small bow, which his associates imitated. He gave Izabel a nod of acknowledgement, the bare minimum politeness. Like any gentleman, the Ambassador would never give offense unintentionally.

"Ambassador," I said, "I am pleased to see that you have returned safely. I trust your expedition with Lord Amir to the coast was as instructive as you hoped."

"Yes, quite so," he said, taking the larger of the three seats. "I hope Amir's arm does not trouble him too badly."

Yellow Cape whispered in his ear.

"I have travelled this country in previous years," the Ambassador said. "It is sadly changed by the current unpleasantness."

"We are suffering a terrible affliction," I said, nodding towards No Man's Land and the creatures' territory.

"And those who are supposed to relieve that affliction"—he nodded to where the captive was to die—"are themselves murderers bringing further despondency to this unhappy place."

Crow was in the custody of six nomad warriors. They stood around without physically restraining him. In their attitudes, they looked more like comrades than captors. Crow was attired in his customary black, down to black kid gloves and short black boots, his long dark hair drawn back in a ponytail. He looked neither terrified nor resigned at his imminent death.

"I understand this Crow is an exile from your own city," I said. "From a noble family."

"Outlaws always lie about their past." He removed his cap and wiped his brow with a cloth, which he tossed aside. A servant hastened to pick it up. "He was a criminal there before he became a murderer here. You harbour criminals and runaways, you must expect this to happen."

"I hear he was on the wrong side of politics there," Izabel said.

"He was a troublemaker, and good governance cannot tolerate rebellion," the Ambassador said. "Your own Lord Nergal is similarly strict. I understand your exiles are branded on the hand before being expelled."

We had no prison and could not afford one. The only punishments were floggings, execution, and exile. We attracted criminals from far and wide; if they were caught, branding was the easiest way of ensuring they could not easily get back in once they were thrown out.

"It is our way," I said.

"Like today's performance," the Ambassador said. "So much more picturesque than similar events in my own country, where a simple executioner's blade finishes the matter cleanly. A more fitting end, though, for a hunter, wouldn't you say?"

"Our method of execution was chosen so that nobody had to shed the blood of the condemned," I said. "With the nomads, that leads to feuds."

"An ingenious solution," he said. "I wonder if it was suggested by the desert sorcerers?"

"Why do you say such a thing?"

"I gather you take advice from them. No doubt you are aware of their evil reputation for intercourse with demons… they were recently outlawed from our territories."

"I didn't know that." I had not heard from the Sorceress for some weeks.

"The hunters don't believe Crow is the murderer," Izabel said. "There's talk about false witnesses."

If she was trying to rattle the Ambassador, she'd failed. He was merely amused.

"Perhaps Lord Nergal will suffer a rebellion, if he judged a case badly," he said. "That has happened in other places."

Yellow Cape, sitting at the Ambassador's elbow, chuckled at that, and they exchanged a few words in their own language.

"I hate it when they do that," Izabel said in English. "And you know he had something to do with this."

"Obviously," I said. "Where's Marie-Therese got to?"

"Oh, she's coming," Izabel said.

A quarter of a mile away, riders were approaching at walking pace through the long grass, with frequent looks over their shoulders. The group divided, then divided again, until just one was headed towards the ramparts and the group with Crow at it centre.

"Only one," the Ambassador said.

I was surprised myself. Usually two or three of the Spawn were permitted to come close to the ramparts. Luring a single one was more difficult. The party who had led the creatures back must have been unusually skilled—and acting under orders.

Behind the horseman, something was parting the grasses, following doggedly at an infinitely steady pace. Slow but as indefatigable as the tramp of doom, the Spawn approached the condemned man.

The nomads surrounding Crow withdrew. They mounted up and rode off fifty paces before halting, bows at the ready. If Crow tried to flee, as most victims did, they would bring him down, aiming at his legs so he would be reduced to crawling speed. In the race that followed, the victim could stay ahead of the pursuer for some time, crawling away in their trail of blood, only prolonging the agony.

About a quarter of the victims were paralysed by fear and allowed themselves to fall under the advancing juggernaut. Braver victims ran straight at the creature and were usually rewarded with a swift death.

A few tried to fight, but it was like trying to fight several opponents at once. Once the creature was close enough to strike, its target was a dead man. The nomads and hunters had proven that lesson time and again.

Crow tossed some objects to his right, left, and forwards. Rags wrapped around stones, soaked in goats' urine. The hunters used them to confuse their prey's sense of smell. Then he took up the sword and hatchet which had been left for him, one in each hand. He was going to make a fight of it.

The choice of weapons was his own. Unarmoured and shieldless, Crow looked more like a dandy than a hunter, as debonair as a pirate captain. He took one long gaze at the crowd behind him and was greeted with cheering from the hunters. When he saw the Ambassador, he cocked back his arm as though to throw the hatchet. The Ambassador, to his credit, did not flinch.

"Good morning," Marie-Therese said, arriving behind me in a hurry. I was going to ask where she had been, but when I looked up, I saw she was dressed as I had never seen her before: all in black. I was momentarily dumbstruck. It was not mourning, but a statement of support.

The Ambassador and his entourage did not appear to notice Marie-Therese or her choice of dress. The Spawn broke into the open, looking like a shimmering cloud against the grasses. Then it seemed to notice Crow and suddenly flicked to matte black, its outline stark and alien.

"Looks like a medium type two," Izabel told her.

"Pardon me?" the Ambassador asked.

"It is how the hunters classify the Spawn," I said. "This one is moderate-sized and will extend six to eight fighting tentacles at a time."

"What are the ribbons?" Two ribbons, one green and one red, fluttered on one side of the creature, improbably gay decorations.

"Marker arrows," I said. "Barbed arrowheads trailing coloured streamers. It helps us keep track and keep count of the creatures when they are seen and not killed."

"Amir mentioned them," the Ambassador said. "But he did not explain what they are for."

"The process is complex." It had taken long enough to explain how statistical sampling worked to Marie-Therese. Amir, whose grasp of mathematics barely included fractions, had never been very interested.

"The creature looks dangerous," the Ambassador said, a cool assessment rather than mere horror. They affected some people worse than others.

"Crow will kill it," Marie-Therese said. She had moved closer and was standing next to me.

"Has that ever happened?" the Ambassador asked. "That a condemned man has escaped death?"

Nobody replied. He repeated the question.

"Never," I said.

"Not yet," Izabel said.

The Ambassador's entourage exchanged words amongst themselves.

"The sword is an unusual choice," the Ambassador said.

I could not argue with that. It was a substantial blade, the type more often used two-handed. It would not be much use for sword fighting—bronze swords break much too easily—but was perfect for fighting the Spawn. The edge reflected diamond point of morning light: it had been sharpened to the highest pitch that the metal would bear. Such sharpness made no difference against armour, but it would cut soft flesh very cleanly indeed.

Marie-Therese was practically vibrating with tension as Crow swished the sword experimentally and the Spawn laboured towards him, cutting down the distance yard by yard. Then Crow broke into a run, and I sensed a bow raised at the edge of my vision, ready to bring him. But Crow was running towards the creature then swerving around it. The creature stopped, and tentacles lashed out, but they grappled only empty air. Crow ran all the way around, literally running rings around it, severing the end of one tentacle with one clean back-handed blow as he passed, then backed away.

The severed limb twitched briefly, a monstrous, bleeding worm, before dissolving. Crow stamped on the ground twice, then as the creature lumbered towards him, he took off again, this time circumnavigating it the other way. A whiplike tendril caught on the haft of the hatchet—or perhaps the other way around—and Crow deftly sliced through it with his sword without pausing, whirling like a dervish and backing away.

He stamped on the ground again, a matador drawing the bull's attention towards him—or rather, to the place which he was about to vacate. The crowd was buzzing. Crow was putting up as good as fight as they had hoped.

Crow's technique of using the hatchet to fend off attacks and the sword to strike back worked so long as he kept moving. If the creature had more than second, it would strike from several directions at once and he would be seized, overwhelmed, and crushed. His survival depended on not giving it that chance.

The hunter was shrewd and varied his tactics. Sometimes, he would feint one way and go another. Other times, he would dart in close and deliver a quick slicing blow to the creature's front. He seemed to be made of thistledown, dancing around every blow, keeping his distance.

Then a tentacle caught him, and Crow was knocked head over heels. Crow rolled to his feet, seemingly unharmed, but his tunic had been ripped, and one shoulder was exposed. In seconds it went from white to red as blood oozed up.

"Just scratches," Izabel said. The suckered tentacles often inflicted bloody but superficial injuries.

The ground was littered with the puddled remnants of severed tentacles. Crow was fighting a war of attrition, but it was a difficult war for one man to win on his own. He was getting slower, or the Spawn was getting better at anticipating. It tripped him by grabbing him around an ankle, but even as he fell, Crow was slashing at the restraint that held him. He rolled away and recovered his feet quickly.

"Is he winning?" I asked Izabel, sotto voce.

"He is doing okay," she said. "If he can keep momentum."

"He has lost his axe," the Ambassador observed after Crow made another circuit.

Marie-Therese groaned.

Backing off and stamping again, Crow drew a long dagger from his belt. Not as good as a hatchet, it was still better than nothing. Crow looked up then, his gaze directed at Marie-Therese.

Crow closed with the creature, then backed away quickly as tentacles flailed out. Swiping at one with his sword, he failed to connect. He repeated the same move again then, backing away, discarded his dagger. Holding his sword two-handed and whirling it in a figure-of-eight, he ran at it a third time.

Marie-Therese cried out, and Izabel swore, as Crow disappeared under a mass of tentacles.

"Now, he dies," the Ambassador said.

Yellow Cape moved his head, shaking it ever so slightly.

With skill and the strength brought of mortal desperation, Crow struggled to find the vital spot before the tentacles could get a full grip and extinguish his life. Marie-Therese made choking noises as though she were the one being smothered. The Spawn collapsed into a stinking, slimy mess.

I learned later that Crow had thrown himself down to slide forwards on his back and thrust upwards at the monster, aiming at the wound he inflicted with the last blow of the hatchet. Crow knew the anatomy of his prey as well as any hunter, but his victory was still unique.

Almost before the crowd had burst into cheers, the waiting nomads rode forwards. Without dismounting, two of them hauled Crow's body from the carnage. I could not tell if he was dead, dying, or alive.

At the same time, a woman in blue stepped down from the rampart and raised her arms, chanting the incantation to destroy the Spawn before it could reform. Somebody must have primed Rachel. Somebody must have ordered the nomads to be ready to retrieve Crow, who was already being manhandled over the ramparts to where Lu Zhu was waiting with an apprentice. A group of hunters closed around them, looking ready to defend Crow if Nergal's men came to take him again.

"This is most unusual," I said.

Marie-Therese had torn away from me to run to Crow. Amir and Nergal were arguing. Rachel completed the incantation, and the creature's remains boiled off into noxious steam that disintegrated in the morning air like a swarm of evil locusts dispersing.

Crow clambered shakily to his feet, held up by one of his hunters. One of the nomads was trying to give him his sword back, but Crow did not seem able to take it.

Amir was shouting, trying to make himself heard, but his words were lost in the hubbub of the crowd. All of the hunters, including Izabel, seemed to be converging on Crow, yelling with triumph, forming a great scrum around him.

"Presumably the execution of the murderer will resume tomorrow morning," the Ambassador said.

"That would be the decision of the proper authority," I said. "But I'm sure all aspects of the case will receive due attention."

"It is always instructive seeing the workings of justice in other places," he said languidly.

The Ambassador stood. The entertainment had finished, and he was off to find amusement elsewhere. His lofty guards were watching, and by his third pace, they were marching in formation around him. A moment later, the servants were clearing the table and folding up the chairs, leaving me quite alone in the cheering, shouting crowd.

"Most unusual," I said to nobody in particular.

Yellow Cape looked back over his shoulder at me and smiled. Things were starting to slip out of my grasp.

CHAPTER TWENTY: THE CHALLENGE

THEY GET EVERYWHERE," MARIE-THERESE said, looking over the roof edge. "But I don't think the Ambassador's spies are listening right now. And I can't see any assassins."

It was evening, and I was sitting out on the flat roof with her and Izabel, enjoying a well-earned beer under the stars. We had persuaded Marie-Therese that direct action against the Ambassador would not be helpful; Crow apparently agreed and had decamped with some of his men until the delegation from Stone had gone. The Ambassador was simply doing his job, and more than anything, we still needed to conclude an alliance with Stone. Killing him would achieve nothing.

"You think they even want an alliance?" Marie-Therese asked.

"Timi says they need some sort of agreement with us," I said. "With the nomads more or less unified, we control their trade routes south. And we have monopolies on spirit, opium, and teeth."

"They want an agreement," Izabel said. "They just want it on their terms. They'll shake us up so we'll take whatever they offer."

"I wish we would hear back from the Sorceress," I said. There was no fixed means of communication. We passed on verbal messages by merchants. The sorcerers, or their representatives, would appear at night in their camps sometimes, with messages to pass on. It took days to find out whether a message had been transmitted, and they never responded directly.

"You think she would help?" Marie-Therese asked.

"I want to know what's happening in Stone," I said. "It sounds like Cthulhu's supporters are in the ascendant. When is Timi's caravan due?"

"I'm more worried about who runs this place," Izabel said.

"Nergal cannot do anything," Marie-Therese said. "Maybe we should remind him."

"He's still Amir's brother," Izabel said. "If you send the gendarmes after him, he'll have an army on his side."

"And the hunters against him."

"Even if we could overthrow Nergal," I said, "he is the duly appointed ruler. Revolutions are dangerous. You must know that, Marie-Therese. We must have legitimate rule."

"Crow doesn't want to be governor anyway," she said.

"Nergal is not the real problem," I said. "We just need to keep the Ambassador in check."

"You know he tried to seduce me," Marie-Therese said conversationally.

"The Ambassador?"

"How did he do?" Izabel asked.

"He'd heard I like wine, so he brought some of their best, and we drank it and looked at the stars." She made a disgusted face. "He is not so sophisticated as he pretends, and their wine is, as Vana says, goat piss."

"His men tried with some of the other sisters too," Izabel said. "What? You didn't hear about Vana?"

"What about Vana?" I had never asked about anyone's romantic affairs, even Damki and Inzalu's innocent-seeming courtship. In the case of Vana's frequents trysts, I was sure I would rather not know.

"They've been trying to steal her recipes," Izabel said. "And sneaking around the distillery. Then that pretty guy, with the fancy beard, he got friendly with Vana."

I did not like where this was going.

"She got him to go into her room and told him to take his clothes off while she got a jug of something special. So he strips off and lies there, all expectant."

Marie-Therese smiled. She already knew the punch line.

"When she came back in, Vana chucked a bucket of cold slops over him and set her dogs on him," Izabel said. "He ran back naked to the Ambassador's house with Vana's dogs chasing after him the whole way."

I laughed in spite of myself. It could have caused a diplomatic incident, but it was still funny.

"They sent him back to Stone with the messengers the next day," Marie-Therese said. "Everybody was laughing about it."

The distillery was a sensitive commercial secret. Alcohol was also a key ingredient of laudanum, another valuable trade commodity. We could not afford to share the secret with competitors. Beer was arguably just as valuable. The nomads received a beer ration, and the soldiers spent much of their wages on beer. Vana had been right to be protective.

"This is all wrong," I said. "We should be the ones using our womanly wiles and getting information out of the Ambassador's men, not the other way around."

"I have gathered a little information," Marie-Therese said, flicking away her hair.

"Obviously," Izabel said.

"The Ambassador thinks we could do very well as a vassal-state of Stone," she said. "He thought I would make a good queen and that we could work together."

"And me?"

271

"He didn't think you could be persuaded. You are too dogmatic. So he was talking to me."

I was not entirely surprised. The Ambassador had dropped more than a few hints that, if we were to put ourselves under the control of Stone, they would extend as much protection as necessary. He had never used the term *vassal-state*, but it made sense. If we were desperate enough, they could gain control of the town and all the territories and people which depended on it in a bloodless conquest.

"He's right," I said. "I could never trust them to fight this war. What's his game?"

As if in answer, heavy footsteps ascended the stairs to the rooftop. "Yishka!" Amir called out. "Are you there?" The nomad warlord appeared, his right wrist in a splint, and headed at once for the beer jug. He poured and drained a mug, then looked at the three of us. Lamplight played on his face, his expression unreadable.

"Young Harsis," he said then belched. "Young Harsis has challenged me for the leadership. A spear duel to the death, of course. He was waiting for this." He held up his damaged wrist. "He's stupid, but he can see when he has the advantage."

"Old Harsis," Marie-Therese said. "That old fool is behind this. And the Ambassador behind him, I bet."

"Definitely," Izabel said.

"This is insane." I took off my glasses and rubbed my temples. "Have they gone mad?"

We were in the middle of a war for our survival, a war for the survival of mankind against a malevolent alien force. Yet everybody was at each other's throats or trying to profit from the situation. Why was I the only one who could see we all needed to work together?

"It is a legitimate challenge," Amir said.

Of course it was. Old Harsis was the chief authority on the code of honour, of what was allowed and what was not. And we had not yet stamped out this ridiculous custom of spear duels.

"Old Harsis doesn't like all these foreigners," Marie-Therese said. "He doesn't like these new ways."

"He wants to go back to the old way of fighting," Izabel said. "Spears and javelins on horseback. You should hear him."

"Spears are no use against the Spawn—" I said, but I was not arguing against anybody present.

Old Harsis had never stopped complaining to me, though I had stopped listening to his whining months ago. The war was going well. Our forces were far more powerful and efficient than two years before, and we were killing the creatures in droves. Meanwhile, the nomads' standard of living bore no comparison with their previous pitiful state. They were better fed, better clothed, and better off than any of them could remember. I had taken it for granted that Old Harsis's grumblings would subside and he would be just be another old man dreaming about days gone by. Evidently, ignoring him had been a mistake.

"Amir, your men are loyal to you, not Old Harsis, aren't they?"

"It is a legitimate challenge," Amir said again, pouring himself another mug.

"You can't have Young Harsis arrested," Izabel said, reading my mind. "This is serious, blood and honour stuff. The guys will die for this sort of thing. We can't interfere."

"But—"

"If Crow can beat a Spawn on his own, then I can beat Young Harsis with one hand," Amir said. "Or else die like a warrior."

"You'd kill Young Harsis easily with two hands," Izabel said. She had a shrewd idea of each warrior's skill. "He's slow. But with you one-handed…"

Nobody said anything for a while. Amir glugged beer.

"Young Harsis," Marie-Therese said. "I remember when Lu Zhu delivered his son. He was grateful enough to us then."

I did not need to point out that such gratitude was shallow. They left such concerns to other women. Hunting, raiding, blood, and honour were what counted.

"Maybe Lu Zhu could help me." Amir flexed his damaged wrist. "My hand works—but by heaven, it hurts. If she could give me something to numb the pain, so I had two hands, just long enough to fight."

Lu Zhu was skilful, but I doubted that even modern medicine could have done anything. Still, I was heartened that Amir was thinking actively about how to win, rather than resigning himself to his fate.

"When is the duel?" I asked.

"In two days," he said. "Long enough for the clan leaders to gather."

"Enough time to string up the Ambassador from the watchtower," Marie-Therese said. "Him and all his *vermine*."

"No," I said. "We need him. And, Amir, if you insist on fighting, I don't know how, but we need you to win this duel."

"As the goddess wishes," he said, with a ghost of a smile.

Chapter Twenty-One: Breakout and Pursuit

The ditch was full of water," Illi said. "The rampart was already part-mud, and some stakes were loose. They made a way through before we got there."

Izabel swore.

The stars were against us. I had been expecting a difficult day, but being outmanoeuvred was unexpected. At least Illi and her ghost scouts had been alert.

"Can you show us exactly where this is on the map?" Marie-Therese asked, knowing that Illi would not. She could describe the spot exactly, but Illi did not use maps.

"How many?" I asked.

Illi flicked the fingers of both hands up three times.

"Thirty," Marie-Therese said. "And not too long ago."

"I signalled, and I ran straight here," Illi said.

"What types?" Izabel asked. "Fast walkers or ordinary?"

"I don't know." Illi had not adopted Izabel's scientific system of classifying the Spawn by size, shape, and gait. "Just ordinary ones, I think."

"Only the one group. There couldn't be more behind them?"

Illi shook her head.

"We will need to throw everything we can muster at them." I was fearful of what sort of mischief a force that size could do if left unchecked. There were undefended settlements and horse paddocks they might raid. Or they might be intent on taking down signal towers. They had tried that before. Some of the towers were protected by earthworks, but the others would be pulled apart like straw dolls.

"They are all together," Illi said.

If the Spawn stayed in a group, they would be easy to track, but they could not be attacked effectively until they split up into smaller units. We would need at least fifty horsemen to locate and track the group in case they suddenly split up, as well as a dozen more to ride messages. Then we would need to muster as many killing parties as we could. Ten-to-one was a good rule of thumb when fighting the creatures, so it was a question of how long it would take to get three hundred men to the fight.

More importantly, we would need to send a work party out to repair the damage, with more warriors to escort them, and a survey party to find out where the water had come from and find what stream needed to be diverted.

"Every time you move a stream, it causes problems somewhere else," Izabel said.

What we needed was a hydraulic engineer so we could divert water underneath or through the defences without damaging them. Perhaps something could be done with pipes, but that would have to wait for the future.

"I will signal all the parties that are in the area and call them back," Marie-Therese said.

"The hunters will be pleased," I said. "This way, they get to hunt on the open plains with no danger of ambushes. Thirty kills to share between them."

"But always, they are attacking, and we are defending," Marie-Therese said gloomily.

"We'll take them all down before nightfall," Izabel said. "Don't worry, Chief—today isn't That Day."

That Day was the one I dreaded, when an unstoppable wave of the Spawn burst out from No Man's Land and swept away our forces and our settlements. We could only speculate just how many of them were behind their wall. We might even have overestimated their numbers. Their citadel could be just an empty shell, and the ones we saw outside were all there were. "If hopes were dupes, fears might be liars"—but there was no way of telling.

On my pessimistic days, I thought about those rumours which said they were numberless, and that their wall would burst open like an overripe seed pod, spilling an endless horde of monsters across the steppes.

"Thank you," I said to Illi, who had slipped back into a corner when others started talking. "You will always be our best scout."

Illi smiled shyly. "The girls are learning quickly. Some are almost as good as me."

The prohibition on women carrying spears still held, but scouts with knives were another matter. There was no shortage of volunteers for the ghost scouts, and Illi was selective about who was accepted.

"I very much doubt that," I said.

"I will go back," she said. "I need to show the riders where to go."

"Is that a stone knife Illi is carrying?" I asked Izabel. "Has she given up on the Bronze Age altogether?"

"She says the Spawn can sense metal."

"That's interesting. Maybe we can—"

"We're already testing that theory," Marie-Therese said. "But we have more important matters. Maybe we can make sure Young Harsis is in the lead when they fight today."

That seemed unlikely. Young Harsis was a veteran now, one of the few survivors from the original band. He must have killed as many of them as anyone. He was not going to do anything so convenient as getting killed now.

"So long as Amir doesn't do anything stupid," I said.

It took five minutes to sketch out our order of battle and start issuing orders. Everyone knew their jobs, and headquarters ran like a well-oiled machine. The signaller was already semaphoring on the watchtower as I went out to see the Ambassador.

I found him in the main square, leaning on a memorial stele with a couple of his cronies and the usual four guards. The stones, row upon row of them, were crowded together as the spaces between them were taken up. My eye automatically ran down them, noting the larger stone we had set up to commemorate Amir's father.

The men from Stone were looking up, watching the signaller with her flags. I doubted they could have decoded much of our signalling system yet.

"My lady," he said. "There is so much activity—all these nomads and messengers rushing around, soldiers coming and going—we wondered what was happening."

For a mad moment, I wondered whether he could have been behind the creatures' breakout, but that was impossible. I was looking for his influence everywhere.

"Nothing out of the ordinary, Ambassador," I said. "We're just fighting a war, that's all."

"So the town is not in any danger?"

"No," I said. "Sometimes, the Spawn are on the offensive. Sometimes, we are. And we get much closer to their citadel walls than they do to ours."

This was technically true. These days, the Spawn rarely made it through the rows of defences to within sight of Wintertown. On several occasions, our scouts had climbed their wall and survived, though none of them had been able to give a good account of what lay beyond that perimeter.

"Like buildings" was Illi's succinct description. "But not like your buildings."

Assaulting their stronghold was a remote prospect. We simply did not have the numbers for that sort of operation. We were keeping them contained effectively enough, and with reinforcements, from Stone for example, we would be in a strong position to push the attack.

"Some of your people seem so... agitated," the Ambassador said.

The statement was impertinent. He wanted to see me worried. Still, I could pay him back in the same coin.

"Don't worry, Ambassador, you and your people are not in the slightest danger here," I said soothingly. "We'll tell you in good time if you need to retreat."

"Thank you," he said.

My chances of being offered a romantic dinner with wine were poorer than ever, but I was not going to stand any of his cheek.

"And I should remind you that these stones are sacred to the memory of warriors who have fallen in the struggle."

The Ambassador looked at the stele he was leaning against with its inscription, incomprehensible to him. "A quaint custom. I would honour my good horses sooner than the gutter trash and criminals that man our legions, especially those stupid enough to get themselves killed. And you dare to leave garlands of teeth on their graves, in a place where teeth are currency."

"The crusaders deal rather harshly with anyone who dares take them," I said.

Yellow Cape nodded fractionally towards an angle of shade from where three of the crusaders were watching, as silent as tree stumps.

"Of course I mean no disrespect to your dead," the Ambassador said, patting the stele. "And we would not wish to anger your fanatics."

The Ambassador thought the crusaders were wild men. I supposed he was right. While the hunters may have been motivated entirely by money, it was the piercing horror of the Spawn that drove the crusaders. They feasted on it, like men relishing the burn of raw liquor or the exhilaration of bathing in cold water. They were ascetics, their gazes fixed permanently on the horizon, necklaces of teeth around their necks, arms and faces scarred by bloody night-time rituals of initiation and dedication every time they killed.

"I'm sure," I said.

"I am more interested in your generals than your foot soldiers," the Ambassador said. "I would very much like to see how you conduct military operations."

Since his arrival, he had been angling for a look inside our headquarters, as well as trying to find out how many men we had under arms, how many horses, how many engineers, and every other scrap of information about our military strength. I had been firm in keeping his people at a distance, but perhaps I should try a new tack.

"Perhaps when it's a little quieter," I said. "In a day or two."

"I do hope you are still in a position to show us around then," the Ambassador said. "We heard about the challenge to your leader from your… dissident elements."

"Don't worry about that, either," I told him. "It's all under control."

"Quite so, my lady, quite so." The Ambassador turned to leave.

Yellow Cape paused a moment to look at me. I gave him a pout copied from the Hollywood screen goddesses. If we were to descend to face-making, I could give as good as I got.

I did not feel like going back to watch the progress of operations. Once the die was cast, I felt too much like a helpless observer, even when everything went well.

"If anyone needs me, I'm going to the building site in the new south quarter," I told Dota.

Bricklaying was still my preferred form of relaxation. I could still lay a course straighter than most of the labourers, and my simply being there tended to speed things along. The physical effort erased the knots of tension in my shoulders, and building things was always so reassuring. Building things was preferable to seeing them collapse around me.

CHAPTER TWENTY-TWO: NEGOTIATIONS

IZABEL AND MARIE-THERESE CAME with me to the tent settlement outside the walls. I had turned down Damki's offer of an escort of gendarmes. We could have housed everyone comfortably within the city, more or less, but many of the nomads preferred to live in their traditional dwellings alongside their horses. So we had a shanty town on our doorstep.

The crusaders' encampment was located on the far side of the settlement from here, as if to emphasise the separation. Anbu had left Izzar, shaved his head, and come here to join the holy war. He was the de facto commander of the crusaders, who led a spartan existence dedicated to the extermination of the Unclean monsters. Their tents were in rows, ranked according to the length of their services. The men mustered each day at dawn to dedicate themselves to the cause, one of the many rituals they had evolved.

The shanty town was a different matter. I had hardly visited the place before. It was less tidy than the usual nomad encampment, with tents of different shapes and sizes clustered in groups, reflecting the different tribal origins. They were interspersed with semi-permanent wigwams, like conical piles of firewood.

Izabel knew it well enough, but Marie-Therese curled a lip at the heaps of horse manure and the tattered state of many of the tents. Bits of charred bone and burned skin, the remains of a roast left on the fire too long, were scattered over a wide area. Two nomad warriors, sitting on a log and passing a jug between them, eyed us as though we were a hallucination. One of them had a bloody rag wrapped around his leg.

"Welcome to Boys' Town," Izabel said.

A group of women squatted around a cooking pot, shelling beans and tossing them in, but they were the only females we saw. There were few women or children here; the families were inside the city walls. Only the truly conservative insisted their families stay with them in the old way. The warriors lived here like men at a hunting camp. It was a place for bachelors or men who wished to live like bachelors, away from the chains of civilisation.

We practically had to step over a naked man lying unconscious in the path.

"But why do they live here?" Marie-Therese asked.

"This is nomad paradise," Izabel said. "Nothing to do but sleep, drink, and hunt. No nagging wives and screaming kids."

"Are we giving them too much alcohol?" I asked.

Izabel guided us to the large black house of hair, the meeting-place for Old Harsis's faction.

Old Harsis and his cronies, Samug and Ilshu, as well as Young Harsis, were waiting for us cross-legged on the ground. Samug and Ilshu were both of the old guard, grizzled figures with faces chiselled out by years of sun and wind, like disapproving Easter Island statues. The three older men surrounded Young Harsis as though supporting him. Young Harsis had an impressive physique, but he looked sheepish. The dark tent smelled of goat. I had forgotten how dim and smelly those tents were.

"We should not talk to women," Old Harsis grumbled. "Amir should have sent a man."

I suffered an awful sense of déjà vu back to my meeting with Izzar and his sidekicks two years earlier. Now I had descended to arguing with my neighbours. "I don't think your argument is with Amir," I said, sitting down on a cushion to face him. "I think it's with us."

"I taught him everything he knows, but he forgets," Old Harsis said. "He does not listen to his heart, but to others. A leader should not listen to anyone else—especially not women, not his wife or his mother or his sister. He should be strong in his own decisions. Amir has become the tool of witches."

I sensed Izabel quietly seething. Oddly, that calmed me. I spoke, directing my words to each of them in turn.

"Amir is your leader," I reminded them. "He has led you to more victories than anyone in the history of your band. He is not just leader of your band but has ascended to tribal lord. The Spawn are defeated day after day. Amir's name echoes from the sea to the mountains. He deserves your loyalty."

I was focusing on Young Harsis, but it was Old Harsis who spoke.

"Amir is insane for revenge. He wants to kill all the Spawn—they cannot all be killed. Like the grass, they keep coming back, however many you kill. The men from Stone laugh at us for wasting our time fighting the Spawn. We are no longer feared raiders. We trade like the fat merchants. And our camp is full of outlanders and run by women." He spat for emphasis. "Amir will destroy us."

"Your war," Samug said, speaking to the three of us at once. "Your war killed all my sons. Now I have only daughters, and one of them refuses to marry."

"And you profit!" Ilshu said. "You want the teeth so you can get silver, build your houses, and bring more outlanders."

"Amir saved your band," I said. "Without him, the creatures would have destroyed you. As they killed his father."

"We should have moved away," Old Harsis said. "We are nomads. We always move. Only Amir's pride—and listening to women—has forced us into living here in our own shit, stuck in one place. Chew the root too long, and it grows bitter."

"What do you want?" Marie-Therese asked.

Old Harsis looked from Marie-Therese to me and back. Having one woman speak was bad enough; having to talk to two of us was practically intolerable.

"One man, one horse, one spear, one tent," he said. "We should never have abandoned the nomad way."

"And how will you defeat the creatures?"

"We cannot defeat them!" His voice was an angry rasp, and the others muttered agreement. "Try to defeat the wind, the rain, the drought! If we kill a hundred, a hundred more spring up. Your magic does not destroy them. There are more of them every month."

"Nonsense," I said.

"They are a curse from heaven. We can go anywhere, take whatever land we want. Leave this place. Come back when they have gone. Be real men again—not stuck in our own filth, growing weak on vegetables and drunk on strong beer. Men ruled by women."

The others murmured a chorus of assent. The old days had been so much better. It was as practical as a child's desire to pack up some bread and cheese in a handkerchief and leave home. Old Harsis was a stone wall, though; nothing would convince him that a return to the old ways was not the only choice.

"You can lead your life just as you please," I said. "You are nomads. Amir will release any of you from your obligations if you wish to go. If your conscience allows you to desert the leader who needs you, then go."

There was a risk that the nomads would all desert en masse, but I did not think Old Harsis would have too many takers.

"No!" he said, angry at my even having made such a suggestion. "The band stands together! Nobody ever leaves—only exiles. The whole band must leave here and return to the proper ways. And we will, when Amir is no longer leader."

Old Harsis spat on the ground between us again. It was his way of saying that he felt he had made a clinching argument. Further discussion with him seemed pointless. But he was not the only player.

"And you, Young Harsis," I said. "You have not said anything. You have always been Amir's most loyal follower. You really want to fight him to the death now, spill his life's blood with your spear?"

"We must go back to the old ways," Young Harsis said, not looking at me. His arms were bare, showing formidable biceps. He was not the best fighter, nor the cleverest, but he was still one of the strongest men in the city.

"If Amir throws down his spear and submits, he can live," Ilshu said. "He can admit defeat, and we will let him go into exile."

"He will not submit," Young Harsis said. "He will fight."

"It is honourable to fight," Old Harsis said. "Only a woman would wish him to run away."

"You're all such morons," Izabel said, her anger spilling out at last. "Young Harsis, if you kill Amir, then I swear, the next day, I will challenge you. You think you can beat me?"

The men laughed nervously, loud and quick.

"That is not possible," Old Harsis said. "You are a woman, not a warrior. Even if you were a man, you do not have the bloodline to challenge."

"You know I can beat you," she told Young Harsis, who would not meet her gaze. "Easily."

"This is a stupid joke," Old Harsis said. "You cannot challenge a man; you are a woman!"

"Harm Amir, and I'll kill you."

"Out!" Old Harsis ordered. "Get out my tent now! Tell Amir that he is an honourable man, and Young Harsis will fight him for the leadership tomorrow."

"Well, that went better than I expected," Marie-Therese said as the three of us walked the well-worn track back to the town. "The only ones with him are Ilshu and Samug. The worst of the old farts."

"And Young Harsis in the middle," Izabel said. "But you can't blame him."

"I can!" Marie-Therese said.

"Can't you see they're right about destroying their way of life?" Izabel said. She was still angry, but her anger had shifted to us. "We might as well have brought smallpox."

"I can't believe you're taking their side."

"I understand both sides," I said quickly, before they could get too heated.

Progress was always difficult. Robinson's Crusoe's achievements might not have looked so marvellous from the point of view of the natives. And when Mark Twain's Connecticut Yankee had finished with Arthurian England, thousand had perished in the name of progress. We were fighting a war; it was so difficult to take the time to explain everything and bring everyone around, especially die-hards like Old Harsis, for whom all change was poison.

"I've tried to smooth the way—but you've hidden things from me, all of you. I've been too busy, too preoccupied to see the scale of the alcohol and opium and prostitution and what we were doing to them."

"You thought you were bringing civilisation and enlightenment?" Izabel said. She swung her spear like a walking stick at each step. "Why would it be different this time?"

"They are barbarians. We have to force them to change," Marie-Therese said.

I sighed. "It was naïve of me to think we could build Jerusalem here."

"We were never building Jerusalem," Marie-Therese said. "We were building a war machine."

"Out of the bodies of the nomads," Izabel said. "And you're surprised when they complain."

"Oh, you can be the virtuous one," Marie-Therese said. "You are just a soldier. Yishka and I are the evil manipulators. But we sell opium and brandy and useless ground teeth, because it's all we have in this desert. We need something to pay for the food you eat and the horse you ride and the bronze for your harpoon." She looked up to heaven, spreading her hands. "What do you want us to do, eh?"

Izabel did not reply.

"We have to win this war," I said. "But… I didn't want it to be like this. Ends cannot justify means."

"You figured that out by 1927 then? Better explain to Miss 1870 here."

"We have emancipated the women," Marie-Therese said.

"To work for you."

"They are doing necessary work," I said. "And once the war is over, the women will be truly free."

"Only if we can deal with Old Harsis and his cronies," Izabel said.

The town ahead of us looked like a child's model, the buildings lopsided and the ramparts uneven, but it was something we had built. And it was a living thing: smoke rose from the bakery and the kilns, metal hammered on metal in the forge, children played on the ramparts, and the signaller was semaphoring messages from the wooden tower. And now it was all being taken away.

"Can't the others stop Young Harsis, if they all support Amir?" I asked.

"Not when it's a fair challenge," Izabel said.

"Their stupid code," Marie-Therese said. "It's not very sporting, not *fair play*, doing it when Amir has a broken wrist, but it's allowed."

I kicked at the dust, turning over thoughts.

"You rigged the fight for Crow," Izabel said. "Can't we rig this one?"

"It is more difficult," Marie-Therese said.

"Amir's not going to win with a bad wrist," Izabel said. "He could throw his spear at the start, and if he got really lucky… but Young Harsis isn't that stupid."

"We must be ready to leave if Young Harsis wins," Marie-Therese said, looking at me. "If Nergal ends up in charge, things will not go well for us."

"We should give the other sisters a choice," Izabel said. "Some of them might want to stay."

"If Amir loses and Young Harsis leads the nomads away, that's half our forces gone. And without us to co-ordinate them, the rest of the army falls apart in one week. There is nowhere to stay."

"Another thing," I said, "when the Sorceress finds out the fight is lost, she will unleash hell on this place. Fire, brimstone, and heaven knows what else."

Whatever the outcome, this place, our sandcastle city, would be swept away by the tide in a matter of weeks, perhaps days, if Amir lost.

"Where can we go?" I asked, hardly expecting an answer.

"We can get sanctuary, not in Stone, in one of the other cities," Marie-Therese said. "People with money can go anywhere. If we don't need our treasury for the war, it can come with us. We will take some good horses and all the gold, silver, and opium we can carry."

The gateway, the only archway in the town, loomed ahead, made of blocks of cut stone. Twenty feet tall and wide in proportion, it was our own Triumphal Arch. Its imperfection still bothered me, that slight asymmetry. It had been a ridiculous amount of effort to get the thing to stay up, and I was not going to spend any more time on it. The arch was unique; nobody else would have one for another thousand years or so. Part of the function of architecture was to impress. We did not have a cathedral or temple, but we had an arch. Maybe nobody but me appreciated it, but I was proud of that archway. I stopped for a moment to admire it.

Two women pushing handcarts emerged from the city, faces invisible under their broad-brimmed hats. They would be carrying night soil; the use of human waste as fertiliser helped our fields and kept the place more hygienic. The earthy realities juxtaposed with my soaring ambition seemed symbolic.

"Right now, I feel like throwing myself off the signal tower," I said conversationally. "So much effort. We could win this war yet, if we keep at it. And these stupid people want to ruin it all. Why are we always fighting amongst ourselves?"

"Don't worry," Marie-Therese said. "We will find a way."

"We will survive," Izabel said.

Chapter Twenty-Three: To the Death

THE LAST OF THE SPAWN in the mass breakout had been accounted for, and we had only lost four men. Three of them were in a party of overconfident novice hunters who thought they could make their fortune and took on more creatures than they could handle. One of many such small tragedies, they would be remembered, along with every other warrior who had died for the cause.

Once, when Marie-Therese and I had stood on the ramparts to watch a hunting party depart, she joked that we were sirens, luring men in to fight our war, and that we would do better if I arranged my hair in a more attractive style and wore a shorter skirt. I did not find the suggestion very amusing.

"It is a joke, but it is true in a way," she said.

"It's not about personal attraction. It's about exterminating the Spawn."

"Amir may have his obsession. But for most of those young men, they need something more personal. They are not idealists, you know. And a beautiful woman is a good figurehead."

I could not be bothered to argue, partly because I suspected she might be right. But whatever our personal magnetism, it would be nothing without Amir's leadership.

Duels were conducted on the parade ground, the *Champ de Mars* or Field of Mars as Marie-Therese had named it, a bare patch of dirt as large as two football pitches. The sky was an unbroken expanse of peaceful blue. Even though the sun was barely clear of the horizon, the pre-dawn chill had dissipated, and people were taking off scarves and outer garments.

Pretty much the entire population had turned out to watch. If Crow's failed execution had been a Saturday-afternoon football match, this was cup final day, and nobody wanted to miss it. Apart from those who were out on duty, patrolling or scouting, everyone had come. Man, woman, and child, nomad and newcomer, merchants, artisans and hangers-on, all were here to watch. Even the old men and women and the toddlers were here.

The crowd had come to see history being made—not just an epic sporting contest, like a championship boxing match, but the stuff of actual epics. Achilles versus Hector before the walls of Troy. Either this would be the last glorious fight of Amir before being defeated by the new leader, or it would be Amir's miraculous victory by which he held on to power.

Nergal's men had set up a throne-like wooden seat for him on a low wooden dais, and he was surrounded by bodyguards and soldiers from the city's gendarmerie. Old Harsis despised him and his new-fangled ways. The hatred was not necessarily enough for bloodshed, but if the nomads were to revert to their traditional activities of looting and raping, then the foreigners' quarter would be their first target. Amir's influence would keep them in check while he was leader, but there was no telling what Young Harsis or his puppet masters would do.

The Ambassador and his retinue were also seated for the spectacle, looking more relaxed. Whatever arrangements they had made, whatever surreptitious deals, they seemed confident they were in no danger. As with Crow's execution, any outcome would suit them. They just wanted to see nomad fighting nomad.

I felt no desire to join either the Ambassador or Nergal. I stood with my people. It was strange to have so many of the handmaidens gathered together in one place again. I could not remember the last time we had all met. If things turned out well, I vowed we would have more regular, and more festive, meetings.

Izabel had a spear, as well as a hatchet at her belt, but looked ill at ease.

Illi was as calm as ever, but watchful, like a deer sniffing the air for a wolf she knows is nearby. "Don't worry."

"Why must everyone keep telling me that?"

Illi backed away. The others looked anxious, and Inzalu was actually sobbing. Lu Zhu had an arm around her.

"The handmaidens don't have to see this," I said. "They could get the horses and get a head start."

"We're here to support you," Marie-Therese said. "And to support Amir. Don't be so pessimistic."

"Do we have grounds for optimism?"

She shrugged. Marie-Therese has been plotting, talking to people, involving Crow and others. The nomad's sense of honour was absolute, though. Any attempt to assassinate Young Harsis could only be carried out by outsiders, and it was not practical for anybody, even Illi, to get close enough.

Amir's broken wrist was splinted and strapped, bound with layers of leather. There was no flexibility, but he could use his hand to support a spear. He joked with his men, laughing freely. He showed no nerves beneath the bravado. He was as cheerful as though a day's good hunting lay before him. Amir lived for such an event as a singer lives for a royal-command performance. This was his opportunity to show off his skill—even though severely handicapped—to all his people.

Amir's belief in himself was total. He had been in a great many fights, some of them against bad odds, and had never lost one yet. He trusted heaven. He did not seem to realise that every warrior loses in the end. Young Harsis could never have challenged Amir when his leader was fit, but he was a daunting opponent for a man with only one good arm.

"Where are the challengers?" Timi asked. Her garb was simpler today than her usual quasi-medieval outfits. Leather belt pouches bulged with coin; between her and Marie-Therese, they had as much portable wealth as they could extract from the treasury.

I checked my watch, pointlessly. The duel would start when the sun was clear of the horizon, not according to time determined by machines. Or rather, it would start whenever Old Harsis wanted to start it.

"They are over there," Illi said, pointing with her chin.

The conspirators, as I thought of them, were a gratifyingly small group, set apart from the rest. There were at least four times as many men clustered around Amir as there were with Old Harsis. The hulking figure of Young Harsis was not amongst them. I hoped he had suffered an attack of cold feet and run off rather than face his leader.

"I don't like this," Lu Zhu said, holding a first-aid satchel in front of herself. She had bandages and compresses, ready to treat the stabbing and slashing wounds from razor-edged, nine-foot spears. First aid would make little difference. Every fight I had seen ended with the loser being killed on the spot, either slowly after being run through or by a flurry of vicious stabs to the chest, neck, and abdomen after falling.

Three horsemen approached the nomad encampment.

"Young Harsis!"

The name ran through the crowd, and every head turned. The big man was easily recognisable, Ilshu and Samug flanking him. The crowd parted as he rode up to Old Harsis and dismounted, stumbling as he did so.

Lu Zhu said something in Chinese. It sounded like swearing.

"Is he drunk?" Timi asked.

Young Harsis took two steps forwards, supporting himself with his spear, but his knees gave way suddenly. He toppled. Murmurs ran through the crowd, until Old Harsis stepped forwards and addressed the assembly in a hoarse herald's bellow.

"Our man has been poisoned! He cannot carry out his challenge, because he has been struck down by a cowardly act. "

"*Eh bien*," Marie-Therese said, with a small smile. "Ninsa was on our side after all."

Ninsa was Young Harsis's wife, the one Lu Zhu had saved, along with her twin sons. Young Harsis might not acknowledge the debt, but Ninsa did.

"Shame on those who did this!" Old Harsis continued, looking straight at Amir.

Amir strode towards him, spear in hand.

"Is there a challenger?" Amir demanded, speaking as loudly as Old Harsis had.

"Not today," Old Harsis said. "But the day will come. Foul play will not save you then!"

"I am leader," Amir said. "Nobody can insult me—or make false accusations. Apologise, old man. Or we will have a public flogging instead of a duel."

Some of the men—Amir's supporters—laughed. Old Harsis was livid. Instead of facing imminent death, Amir was laughing at him in front of everyone. A more cunning man, like Nergal or the Ambassador, would have eaten humble pie and bided his time until the next opportunity. Old Harsis was a warrior of the old school.

"Yes, I challenge!" he bellowed.

Amir nodded once, as though this was what he expected, and walked to his position, casually spinning his spear in his good hand like a drum major.

Old Harsis's group huddled around him. I could not tell whether they were showering him with encouragement or telling him he was an idiot. Nobody stopped him, though, and seconds later, he followed Amir, holding his spear with both hands.

"Can Amir beat him?" I asked Izabel. Old Harsis was a smaller and slighter version of Young Harsis, a good thirty years older, and a much less formidable opponent. But I knew nothing about spear fighting.

"I never saw Old Harsis fight," she said. "They say he was quite the warrior in the old days… I don't know."

"Now!" Old Harsis said, who was apparently still master of ceremonies as well as a participant. "Now we fight for the leadership!"

A hush fell over the crowd. We hardly dared to breathe as the two men lowered their spears. There was no cheering, no shouts of encouragement. There was no right or wrong. It was in the hands of heaven, and they would only know which man was right when he was victorious.

Old Harsis moved forwards with quick, confident steps. He may have been past his prime, but he was a seasoned warrior. Amir backed off, giving ground. Their spears clashed once, twice.

"Your hands are unsteady, old man," Amir said, loudly enough for the crowd. He was backing in a wide circle.

Old Harsis lunged. Amir parried and backed away at the same time. Holding the spear one-handed and resting it on the other, he could not make any of the fancy moves he showed off while sparring. Amir's defence was weak too; one hand lacked the leverage to push the other man's spear aside properly, but he could deflect it enough to protect himself—barely. Amir was quicker on his feet and more agile than his opponent.

"You have ruined our band!" Old Harsis said. "You deserve your death."

He feinted then lunged again. Amir almost tripped over in his haste to retreat. Old Harsis's spearpoint glided to within a few inches of Amir's chest before he could bat it away.

"Is disloyalty one of the old virtues?" Amir asked, unruffled. "Do you have any proverbs about traitors?"

"I know that—"

Amir lunged, his spear looping around the other man's parry and avoiding it, grazing Old Harsis's bicep before the two sprang apart. Bright red dripped from Old Harsis's arm.

"He's wounded!" someone in the crowd shouted.

"It is not the first blood which matters, but the last," Old Harsis said with a fierce smile. He beat his spear against Amir's, then again, harder. If Amir's wrist weakened, he would be dead. He backed away, and the two went back and forwards in silence, neither venturing an attack for what seemed like an age.

At one point, Amir drew back his arm as if to throw his spear, but then he seemed to think better of it.

"Don't wait until your arm's tired," Izabel muttered. "Just do it."

"Yield, and I will let you live," Amir said. "Go into honourable exile."

"Hah! Yield, and I'll spear you like a pig," Old Harsis said.

They clashed again, both spearpoints going wide. Old Harsis had used his superior leverage to force Amir's spear down, where he held it with one foot. Amir knew this trick, though, and even one-handed, he could jerk his spear back then lunge at Old Harsis's heart.

Old Harsis parried with a resounding thwack of wood on wood and chased Amir back several paces. The younger man almost lost his balance. Perhaps he was feigning clumsiness and daring Old Harsis to overreach himself, but it looked all too real to me. They faced each other, breathing heavily.

"Die, traitor!" Amir said and attacked.

I could not follow the sequence of moves. The spearpoints were a blur of metal. It ended with both men thrusting simultaneously. For a moment, I thought Amir had been impaled. In fact, he had turned sideways, and the spear had scraped across his chest and past him, piercing only his tunic.

At the same instant, Amir's spearpoint cleanly entered Old Harsis's left eye, stopping only when the broad part of the blade stuck in the eye socket. The old man fell backwards, kicked once, and lay still.

The fatal wound was clean, with just a single trail from Old Harsis's eye like the track of a red tear. Amir raised his spear then thrust it into the ground next to Old Harsis's corpse.

"I am your leader!" he said with savage pride. "The traitor is dead!"

The crowd erupted into cheering and ululating. I wondered if they might have yelled just as loud if Old Harsis had won.

Amir shrugged his way through the crowd of admirers congratulating him to get to us, and he raised his good hand to me in salute.

Izabel rushed forwards and hugged him fiercely. "I knew you could do it."

"You actually wanted to fight Old Harsis," I said. My relief that he had won barely outweighed my exasperation over his forcing Old Harsis to challenge him when fighting was not necessary.

"It was the only way," Amir said. "Old Harsis would have made more trouble, even if I killed Young Harsis. I have cut off the head of the snake."

"It was well done," Marie-Therese said.

"My father was a good man, but he was not a patient teacher," Amir said to me. "He put me on a horse and said 'ride.' He put a spear in my hand and said 'fight.' It was my Uncle Harsis who taught me how to ride like a man and how to fight like a man. But he was a traitor, so I had to kill him."

"I'm sorry," I said.

Amir strode out, arms raised as nomad warriors crowded around him. They were dragging Old Harsis's body away. It would be burned that afternoon. There would be no memorial stone for him.

"The wind dries the rain," Amir said.

CHAPTER TWENTY-FOUR: THE GOVERNOR'S RECKONING

As I HAD PROMISED, A FEW days before his scheduled departure, we arranged for the Ambassador to have the guided tour of headquarters he had been after for so long. Sometimes you have to play your cards close to your chest, and sometimes it is useful to let your opponent know what you have. Marie-Therese was a better card player than I was, and she had come to the view that his seeing how we worked would be to our advantage.

We permitted the Ambassador to bring just one associate with him. He was accompanied by Yellow Cape—dressed in buff-coloured robes—and I could sense their excitement while waiting in the anterooms, as clerks and messengers passed us, coming and going. Marie-Therese was by my side, and Dota hovered in the background, ready to take orders.

"Wars are not fought in towns but on the battlefield," I said. "I don't know why our clerical block counting boots and tents should be of more interest than watching Amir's riders practice their tactics. Or Turm's forges."

"Those things are also of the greatest interest," the Ambassador said. "And we have admired both the skill of your horsemen and that of your weaponsmiths. But you are overly modest about the importance of this place."

"Even for a war that does not need to be fought?"

"I never said that," he corrected. "I merely observed that some wise men have suggested that it might be so."

"Wise men who are on the side of Tulu," Marie-Therese said. "The sort we execute for treason here."

"The politics of Wintertown is not the politics of Stone," the Ambassador said. He spoke formally to Marie-Therese, with no hint that they had ever been intimate.

I turned to lead them through the beaded doorway ahead but paused. "Do you believe in magic, Ambassador? Are you expecting to see witchcraft?"

"Since arriving in this place, I have seen wonders of both light and shade," he said. "I leave labels such as 'natural' and 'supernatural' and 'magic' to the learned."

The headquarters was a single large room with a multitude of smaller cubbyholes around the outside. It had as many high windows and skylights I could provide, making it the lightest indoor space in the city. It was still gloomier than I would have liked, but once one's eyes adjusted, there was sufficient light. And it was sheltered; in the heat of the noonday sun or in the worst downpour, everything inside was perfectly insulated.

I did not explain what was happening at once but allowed the Ambassador to work it out for himself. Some of our visitors had indeed been convinced that it was some sort of magic. Others with more imagination had grasped it at once.

The centre of the room was dominated by an enormous table. Clay figures resembling elaborate chess pieces were arranged over its surface, along with wooden cubes and spires. Clerks were seated on benches around the edge of the room, moving piles of counters between etching letters on tablets. The Ambassador walked over, peering down at the table. He politely greeted the women as he passed them and walked around, fascinated.

"It is the world," the Ambassador said. "You have remade the world in miniature. This is your city here, with its citadel and its walls—and this is the road we came in by, and that is the tower in the distance. You have made the world."

"Well, a small section of it."

"And this—'*No Man's Land*' with the defences all around it, and this the field where Amir fought Harsis yesterday. And here is your enemy citadel at its centre."

I said nothing, allowing him to wonder at it. We had not needed to build ramparts around the entire circumference of No Man's Land. The natural gullies which ran north-to-south had provided effective natural obstacles to the east and west of the creatures' hive, requiring only a little work to fortify the areas where the banks were too low. To the north, a line of steep slopes and rocky outcrops had been enhanced and made more impassable. It was only to the south of the hive that we had to build a continuous embankment stretching for miles. It was hardly the Great Wall of China, or even Hadrian's Wall. The setup was more like a miniature Offa's Dyke, the ancient earthwork separating England from Wales.

I had often wondered what future archaeologists might make of our works—assuming we won and there ever were archaeologists in this world. They had never worked out what Offa's Dyke was built for, either.

"Their hive—like the nipple on a breast, no?" Marie-Therese said, with a look at the Ambassador.

"And the moveable figures," he said. "Those signify your forces, in the places where they are?"

"We only track the larger groups." As we watched, one of the clerks moved a mounted figure across No Man's Land. "We can't follow every patrol, but it's where the main bodies are."

"Our generals make sand maps to plan battles, but nothing so elegant, so all-encompassing. But, if I may ask, how can you possibly know where all your men are? Your tower here is tall, but you cannot see the whole of the plains."

"We have our ways," I said.

The Ambassador or his cronies must already have worked out that the watchtowers relayed signals to each other by semaphore, even if they had not cracked the code well enough to tell movement orders from sighting reports.

"Most interesting," he said.

One of the clerks, having transcribed the report brought by a runner, moved three pieces on the table with a croupier's rake. The runner, an eager ten-year-old, accepted a honey-cake before hurrying back to her place at the watchtower.

"A formation of about twelve of the faster Spawn is heading for the place where they made a gap in our lines before," I said. "They'll find they cannot get through. In less than an hour, they will be intercepted and destroyed by warriors and hunters coming from three directions. Others will be in their line of retreat if any escape."

"They have sent another group to cover it," Marie-Therese said. "But we will evade them."

"Is that Amir's force there?"

"No, he's over in the west. Much as he would like to be in the fray, he cannot be everywhere at once."

Yellow Cape had walked around the entire table, counting the pieces of each type. He murmured something to the Ambassador.

"You have a powerful army."

"Those are only the units currently on active operations," I said. "We have others. Keeping them all fed, watered, armed, equipped, horsed, and trained is a monumental effort. Hence all this."

"And you manage it with all these scribes and messengers and tablets," he said. "You count every goat and every bushel of grain, every brick and every nail, and each one goes where it is needed. Like the pieces on your table."

The Ambassador had been observing our town for some time. He would know how Marie-Therese's scribes recorded activity, how the forge and the bakery were supplied with raw materials all duly ticked-off lists. He had seen how their products were already destined for certain people and places before they even existed.

Amir, and even Nergal, had never appreciated the function of the headquarters. In their type of warfare, nomads rode around until they found the enemy, then they fought. Nobody ever estimated how much food the warriors needed or worked out how to supply it. Either there was enough, or there was not. Bureaucracy was as pointless as counting one's teeth. No one could not increase their number. Everyone had to live with what they had.

The Ambassador, though, looked like a man who had experienced a revelation. That everything could be numbered was obvious. That even the blades of grass on the plains could be counted, added, and subtracted was not surprising. Stone had its own system of taxation, and nobody escaped its count. But the idea that so many things could be numbered, accounted for, and therefore controlled to such a degree—and to see it happening—was little short of miraculous. And it was, therefore, worth stealing.

Of course, that task would be difficult without our arithmetic. The people of Stone reckoned in base sixty, which did not make things any easier for them. They lacked the use of zero and our techniques for handling fractions. These were things I would have known at age ten, but this world had yet to discover them.

The Ambassador wore the same expression as Turm after he had seen my watch. He had glimpsed the potential of these new ideas, like a rich undiscovered island, but was struggling to grasp their full extent in every direction. "I would very much like you to come to Stone one day."

"Perhaps once the war is over," I said. "With the help of your armies, we could crush the creatures for good and all, break into their stronghold, and obliterate the source of the plague, all in a few months."

The Ambassador spread his hands and looked coyly at Marie-Therese as if expecting her to speak. She said nothing.

"It is the way of politics that rulers want something for something," he said. "I am just an ambassador. I will report what you say. If yours was a vassal-state under our protection, then cohorts would be marched at the double. Chariots would thunder to your assistance. Sad to say, though, that the troubles of a distant neighbour are not greatly interesting in themselves."

This was not the first time we'd had this conversation. I restated our position. "As you say, we have a powerful army ourselves. If our situation becomes hopeless, where will all these men go? Where will the united nomad bands flee? Where will all the hunters and bandits and mercenaries take themselves?"

Marie-Therese had pulled a tablet from a nearby shelf and was pretending to consult it.

"I hear the lands around Stone are rich and fertile," Marie-Therese said. "We have good maps of your territory."

It would be a misfortune if your peaceful lands were invaded by bands of brigands and nomad raiders because of diplomatic carelessness," I said.

"As you know, we have fought off many barbarian incursions in the past," he said blithely, as though he had personally commanded armies.

"Nothing like this," Marie-Therese said, indicating the map table behind her. "Nothing organised."

"As we are being frank with one another, it is because your army has grown so powerful that some suggest we should aid your enemies," the Ambassador said.

When attacked, do not defend, shift to the offensive. This signalled that we had struck a nerve.

"Of course if we lose, you would have to fight the Spawn yourselves," I said, shifting my own tack. "They will keep multiplying, they will come north, and your armies have no experience of fighting them. Nor the means to prevent them from reforming if you kill them."

"Perhaps we should herd a few dozen towards Stone so your soldiers can try them first-hand, if they don't believe you," Marie-Therese said, raising an eyebrow.

"You are joking, of course," the Ambassador said, with a forced chuckle. "But I appreciate your intent. But I must also report other views."

"I think you'll find Amir agrees with me in diplomatic matters," I said.

"Quite so," the Ambassador said. "Lord Amir has no interest in policy, and he makes himself very plain. I understand that he delegates such subtleties to you. He, however, only rules outside these walls. Inside these walls—"

"We rule," Marie-Therese said. She stood up and looked at me expectantly.

"I understand that Lord Nergal is, technically, the ruler of the town." The Ambassador allowed himself a small smile. "And he has views very much of his own."

I glanced at my watch. Marie-Therese clearly thought it was past time. "Shall we pay our governor a visit and see how Lord Nergal's rule is getting along today?"

Bemused, the Ambassador and Yellow Cape followed us, with Dota bringing up the rear. As soon as we were out of the building, the Ambassador's four guards fell into step around us.

"I don't think arms are necessary," I said. "Lord Nergal may be feeling a little jumpy this morning."

The Ambassador spoke a word, and his men turned into statues to wait for his return.

Damki stood in the shade around the corner from the town hall. A dozen gendarmes were lounging around him, staves propped up against a wall. They were brown-skinned, weather-beaten types, ex-fishermen from the coast, with biceps toned from hauling nets and rowing. At Damki's command, they sprang to their feet.

"Any trouble, Captain?"

"No, Highness," Damki said, using the formal title as others were present. "A little noise, but no trouble. We'll be ready outside if you need us."

"Thank you." What I liked about Damki was that I did not need to explain things to him twice.

Nergal's palace, or more properly the town hall, was quiet. The old doorman looked pleased to see us. "So glad you've come to sort everything out, Highness. None of the women have arrived for work, and nothing is happening. We send messengers out, and they don't come back."

"No clerks," the Ambassador said. Unlike the doorman, he realised the significance of the words chalked on the door even though he could not read them.

"Lord Nergal is in a bad temper," the doorman said in a lower voice. "Even his secretary isn't here."

"How strange," I said, walking past him.

The doorman trailed behind us as we approached Nergal's reception chamber. Men looked out of doorways but ducked back out of the way as though expecting trouble. The Lord Governor was seated on his wooden throne, brooding over a silver cup. It was early in the day to be drinking brandy. His bodyguards stood by him, looking like subordinates who had been subjected to a protracted rant.

"You!" His eyes fastened on me as soon as I entered, and his bodyguards grasped their sword-hilts as though I were a threat to his life. "I recognise your *practical joke.*" He spat out the foreign phrase. "Or was it yours, little woman?"

"I see your clerks have not turned up for work," Marie-Therese said.

"What are you doing here?" Nergal demanded of the Ambassador. "Have you betrayed me?"

The Ambassador raised his hands, palms upwards in the universal gesture of innocent ignorance. "I was invited to come with Her Highness. I know as little as you, Lord Nergal."

"Well, then you'll see some punishments meted out, Ambassador. Every one of those women who is absent is going to be flogged in public by tonight. And whoever is behind this will be flogged double, whoever they are." His eyes travelled around all of us. "We have a saying: 'The puppy should not bite the dog's tail, even in play.' I'll show you what that means."

"Do you have a list of the women's names?" Marie-Therese asked. "Ah, I am forgetting, Lord Nergal does not know how to read."

"Twelve lashes for you," Nergal said. "For insulting your ruler. Maybe I'll give them myself. I'll teach you."

"You won't teach me anything, you ignorant savage!"

Nergal's bodyguards half-drew their swords at the vehemence of Marie-Therese's attack, even though she did not brandish anything deadlier than an accusing forefinger.

"You know nothing! You understand nothing!" She pulled a clay tablet from her belt and waved it in his face. "This is how we run the town, and you cannot read one word or one number."

"I don't need tablets to give a flogging," Nergal said.

Marie-Therese crossed her arms and raised her chin, daring him to go on.

"Lord Nergal," I said. "We hoped this morning would be a gentle demonstration to you of how much you depend on your clerks and scribes and messengers. We have a saying in my country that the stylus is mightier than the spear."

"I depend on a goat for milk, but I can still kill her if she dries up," he said. "And get another."

306

"Don't make me send the town gendarmerie to drag you out," I said.

"The gendarmes answer to me," he said. "Damki is my kinsman, not yours."

"The gendarmes answer to us," Marie-Therese said. "We pay them. We pay everyone. Where does the money come from, Nergal? From Timi's trading caravans, from Vana's brewery, from taxing the hunters. Women collect it. Women administer it. Women pay it. *Our* women. You don't even *see* the money."

The Ambassador and Yellow Cape watched like keen spectators at a tennis match.

"I give the orders," he said, sounding less certain. Doubts were taking root. People had always followed orders given by the governor. Now, perhaps for the first time, he was beginning to realise that his rule was not a fixed law of nature.

"We let you have your silly law court because you are Amir's brother," Marie-Therese said. "And you give your pathetic orders, and we let you have your little corruptions. But nothing happens without us. You are just another official, and you can be replaced. Your doorman could do the job as well as you do."

The doorman shrank back as though he did not want to be involved.

"Amir is my brother," Nergal said. "And he rules the army. You do not."

"You can't threaten us with Amir," I said. "He would not use force against you, but he would not use it against us, either. But I do think the crusaders would take my side, and I think Marie-Therese might be able to rally a few hunters, especially after your attempt at executing their leader."

"And we have the gendarmerie on our side," Marie-Therese reminded him. "Nobody is loyal to you outside your guards. Assuming the Ambassador hasn't bought them, too."

"But that's not the point," I said. "This is not going to be settled by force. We need to work together, and that means working for the common good. You can't rule without your scribes and clerks and messengers. They are loyal to the town, to their people—not to you personally."

"We'll see who's loyal to who," Nergal said, drawing a knife. He glanced at the nearest bodyguard. "Hold her arms."

"Ah, but Lord Nergal," the doorman said. "The gendarmes are outside."

The bodyguards did not move.

"You are pathetic," Marie-Therese said.

Nergal snarled and came forwards. I thought he really meant to hurt Marie-Therese, who was determined to stand there and provoke him until he stabbed her. Yellow Cape was faster, though, moving like a shadow between them. He caught Nergal's wrist in both hands, twisted, and slammed it down on his knee. The blade clattered to the floor. Yellow Cape stepped back, drawing a concealed short sword from under his cape and facing the bodyguards. They hesitated. Maybe they suspected Yellow Cape would kill them both easily if they tried to draw their weapons.

"Lord Nergal," the Ambassador said. "I think the ladies have made their point very well, don't you? Let's not make fools of ourselves over it."

"You haven't heard the last of this," Nergal said, holding his wrist. I recognised my own words from a few days ago. Like most inexperienced amateurs, he borrowed his lines.

"Yes, we have heard the last of this," Marie-Therese said. "Otherwise, we will convict you of treason, and you'll be the one out there fighting a creature, with the crowd cheering. And it doesn't matter whose brother you are."

"You can't convict me—"

"As I say," the Ambassador said, "the point is well made and well taken on all sides. Good morning, Lord Nergal."

He turned on his heel and departed. Yellow Cape waited a second before sheathing his sword and following. Marie-Therese and Nergal continued staring at each other with murderous hatred.

"Enough," I said to Nergal. It was half a question, half an order.

"Yes, enough, enough," he agreed, looking away.

"Enough," Marie-Therese said.

He was not broken, but Nergal was certainly re-evaluating his options. He did not look at her as Marie-Therese followed the Ambassador out.

"I gave the clerks a half-holiday. They'll be back this afternoon. Just carry on as though nothing had happened."

"As the goddess wishes," Nergal said, with something of his usual self.

"Marie-Therese hasn't quite forgiven you for that business with Crow. Please, keep a low profile and behave yourself, and I'm sure it'll all be fine."

"You know," he said, "that I would never harm you."

"Of course not," I said.

Outside, Marie-Therese told Damki to dismiss the gendarmes. He seemed disappointed not to have any part to play. Arresting Nergal would have been the most exciting thing he had done for months.

"Well, Ambassador," I said. "I think that concludes business for the morning, and I hope you now have a better understanding of how our little community operates."

"I understand entirely, Highness," the Ambassador said. I hoped he did.

We saw them off the next day. At Marie-Therese's insistence, the Ambassador's entire party departed, leaving nobody behind. No doubt Stone would send spies amongst the merchants, artisans, and mercenaries who arrived at our gates, but there was no need to make things easy for them.

A strong escort of nomads had formed up. They would see the embassy safely to the grasslands' edge. I did not think that Crow would attempt to settle his score with the Ambassador now, but it was as well to be sure.

"When we meet again, I hope that it will be to conclude an alliance, Lord Ambassador," I said.

"My words are a featherweight in the scales of the councils of the powerful," he said. He sounded tired. "If only you knew! They might have me beheaded for not bringing better news. If they can be bothered to interrupt their orgies long enough to listen to me, instead of some toady who knows nothing but feeds them rumours and lies."

"I have faith in your ability," I said.

"Thank you, Highness."

"A parting gift for you," Marie-Therese said to Yellow Cape.

He gave a start when he saw what she put into his hand, then he smiled.

"A spider?" the Ambassador said.

"A straw spider," I said. "To remind him that what looks dangerous may be harmless, and what looks harmless may be dangerous."

Yellow Cape weighed it in his hand, saying nothing.

"And because you like playing tricks," Marie-Therese said.

"I wish you a safe journey home, Lord Ambassador." I even curtseyed.

After he had given a long, formal departing address, we watched the party ride out with mingled relief, hope, and fear.

I felt drained. I had spent all my time and energy for several weeks fending off the Ambassador's moves. He had been working away at the fault lines, and there were fractures everywhere. The rifts between Nergal and Crow, between Amir and the conservative nomads, and even between Marie-Therese and me would remain. At least I had escaped assassination. Or had that just been a ploy, a way of putting pressure on me?

"Surely they will offer us a deal," I said.

"Of course they will. It is just the exact terms we are still working out. It's a pity you want help so badly. That put us in a weak bargaining position," Timi said, as if it were my fault. "The trade balance means Stone will have to conquer us or negotiate with us," she added, as if to pacify me.

"They cannot conquer us," Marie-Therese said. "They have seen enough of our forces to know that."

"Also, my caravan arrived from Stone last night," Timi said. "The news is that some of Tulu's followers have been murdered by masked men or had their houses burned down."

In my haste to get everything arranged for the Ambassador's departure, I had not had a chance to ask about the latest news. Or perhaps Timi had her own reasons for not telling us until now.

"The Ambassador will be surprised," Marie-Therese said.

"All this trouble," I said. "If Stone could only send us a few thousand troops, this war would be over by the winter solstice. Just a few thousand."

Timi looked doubtful. "Yishka, the people of Stone don't want us to win. We are nothing but a problem. They want Wintertown to sink back into the grassland. They'll do as little as they can just to keep us alive."

"Well, if Stone doesn't send enough men, the war might be over by solstice anyway," Marie-Therese said. "My travelling bag is still packed."

PART FOUR:

WINTER TOWN: THE FIFTH YEAR OF THE WAR

CHAPTER TWENTY-FIVE: THE PENULTIMATE BATTLE

I THOUGHT THAT DAY, OUR day of reckoning, had come. We knew the stars were against us, and larger bodies than usual of the Spawn had been roaming about, testing our defences. Now it peaked, and the power that motivated the creatures reached high tide. Higher than ever before.

At times like this, the standing orders were to draw our forces back as far as possible and wait them out behind our defences, but this time was different. This time, it was not just a few of them spilling through odd gaps in the earthworks.

A huge force of Spawn moved against the ramparts to the south of No Man's Land in the night—to the exact spot where the earthworks were weakest. According to witnesses, they poured into the ditch, filling it with their bodies, while more came forwards over them, until they started coming over the top of the palisade.

The defenders withdrew, and a skirmish line of scouts watched as the Spawn awkwardly clambered and dropped over the palisade. There, they assembled themselves into a compact mass of bodies and started moving off. By dawn, we knew they were headed directly for Wintertown. There might be two, three, or even five hundred of them.

Back at the headquarters with the General, we received a steady stream of messages reporting on their position. In practical matters, though not officially, the General was the commanding officer. He leaned forward on the sand table, inspecting every change in position.

I spoke the language of Stone passably well now, but he always addressed me in Language. Like the Ambassador, the General had a name—his childhood friends called him Hano—but he was identified exclusively by his rank.

Marie-Therese liked to describe the soldiers from Stone simply as mercenaries. The arrangement was not quite so simple, and a tangle of trade and other agreements bound us to Stone, and them to us. We were not, however, a vassal state: Stone could not interfere in our politics.

The cohorts from Stone were rotated every year, but the General and some of his officers would be here for the duration. Without their army, we would have crumbled long ago, but just as Timi had foretold, they would never commit enough to turn the tide, however much the General petitioned his superiors.

Technically, I outranked him, and Amir was emphatic that I was in overall charge rather than the foreigner. Fortunately, as usual, the General's conclusions and mine were the same: fighting from the walls would restrict us and prevent us from manoeuvring, when mobility had been our biggest advantage.

"The walls are the last line of defence," the General said. "We should not start with the last line. We should meet them as far forwards as we are able."

"What would you suggest?" I asked.

"Go out and dig like hell," Izabel said, before the General could reply. "Put a defensive line in their way so they have to attack it."

"Our forces should be sufficient to hold back this number of Spawn, if used wisely," the General agreed, looking at the figures massed on the sand table. "But as you know, this cannot be the totality of their army."

"If anything else comes out, we are watching out for it," Marie-Therese said. "They don't catch us that easily."

The idea was to move our foot soldiers out into the plain. We would impede the Spawn with defences that would break them up into small groups, which we could surround and exterminate one by one. I would accompany the General's own cohort.

The cavalry was deployed to slow the creatures' advance. The Spawn had no strategy or formation, but just edged forwards like a swarm of giant ants, shuffling towards anything that looked like food. Keeping together in a group prevented us from splitting off any individuals to kill them, but it slowed them down to an even more laboured crawl than usual.

A cluster of the ones we called fastwalkers split off and moved around the central body, trying to outflank any of our men who got too close. The fastwalkers had four stumpy legs and scuttled about like monstrous crabs. Horsemen could evade them easily, but not men on foot.

Amir's cavalry showered the fastwalkers with barbed arrows and with javelins trailing hooked anchors to catch on the ground and slow them down. The horsemen circled about, riding close, trying to lure the Spawn away from their line of march. The mass continued to move slowly but steadily towards Wintertown.

We marched out so many thousand paces, and it was like the first night at the encampment all over again, racing franticly to get a ditch and earthworks in place. This time, we had trench ploughs, though, new ones drawn by eight horses. Everything was calculated, finely engineered. Packhorses laden with short, double-ended stakes, with fire-hardened points were led to the front line. The stakes were stuck in at a forty-five-degree angle to catch the belly of any creature trying to get over it. The General's men had been trained and equipped to make earthworks, as well as to fight. Unlike the nomads, they did not stand on their dignity. If the General ordered them to dig, they dug.

We even had portable defences: *cheveaux-de-frize*, long wooden poles with two-foot spikes pointing out in all directions. The General positioned these well in front of us with gaps between them.

"A human commander would see this line and outflank it," the General said, inspecting the works.

"Lucky they are stupid in some ways," I said.

"They are not stupid," he said. "I do not understand their reasons, but they are never stupid. Sometimes it looks as though they are borne along by on invisible river, which both guides and limits their movement."

"We can extend the earthworks sideways," I said, putting down my entrenching tool and gauging the state of the defences.

Riders appeared in the distance, swarming around the still-unseen enemy like bluebottles over a corpse.

"I doubt that will be necessary," the General said, eyes fixed on the horizon.

"Get them to start on a second line two hundred paces back." Izabel looked about. "I'm needed with the cavalry. Good luck. This isn't going to be easy."

The riders came closer, and as they parted, the Spawn became visible beyond the horses. A slow, remorseless tide, an incoming tide. I thought I was used to the Spawn, but seen in a solid mass, they were breathtaking. The line of them shimmered and wavered like heat haze coming through the grass. Ripples of dark and light kept running through them in ever-changing shapes. The chaotic movement made me feel sick.

We could hear them coming, a slow steady rumbling like an oncoming storm. As expected, they made no effort to avoid the defences but ploughed onwards. They came closer and closer, then they broke against the ramparts like a slow wave. Along the whole length of it, tentacles flicked over and around the stakes, and their flabby, inflated bodies came into view. A wave ran through them as they shifted colour together.

At first, I could not understand what I was seeing. It looked so much like a stormy sea, before I grasped that the Spawn were not moving so much as the patterns were flowing across them, like dark water crested white foam, endlessly rolling and swirling. It was difficult to make out the individuals, and some of the soldiers watched slack-jawed, like rabbits hypnotised by a snake.

They slithered into our ditches like breaking waves then slouched into the lines of pointed stakes. Feeling no pain was not always an advantage; many advanced with such force that they impaled themselves and were stuck there until the end of the battle. There was little response from our side, no hail of missiles. The General's men were well-disciplined enough not to waste ammunition when there was no prospect of killing.

We had left a gap in the defences forty yards wide. The Spawn opposite the gap paused and seemed to mark time. Then, like liquid seeping through a hole, they rolled forwards to meet us, breaking away from the stalled advance on either side of them.

The pikemen were ready with their long spears. The nomads' spears, usually eight or nine feet long, put the wielder in danger because of the creature's elastic reach. Now most of our foot soldiers had pikes, each nineteen feet long with a slender two-foot bronze point. When used with skill and determination, enough pikes could inflict mortal damage without the pikemen getting in striking range of the creature. Getting a supply of wood for them had been a saga in itself. Thank goodness we had Timi.

The drums started up, and the pikemen marched to meet the Spawn, several stabbing each attacker. The pikemen were interspersed with halberdiers, who bore nine-foot polearms with axe-heads, each with a long spike and a hook on the end. These were brutally efficient at chopping off tentacles and keeping the creatures at bay. If they worked properly together, the pike and halberd formations were lethal in attack and invulnerable in defence.

That open space was our killing ground. The Spawn would come in a few at a time, and we would kill them a few at a time. They pushed forwards, like infantry battalions throwing themselves onto barbed wire, and one by one, they were stabbed, disintegrating like punctured balloons. I steeled myself to perform the exorcism. Gasping out the words, I felt my chest pounding. Today, it was hard work, like slogging uphill while carrying bags of wet sand, and black clouds seemed to close in on me. Maybe I was stupid to do it on my own. Elsewhere, the exorcists were working in choruses of two or three, a technique that Rachel had recently spent days perfecting when some of her girls were not strong enough to carry out the rite on their own. I was supposedly the strongest exorcist of all. As with the General's politeness about my godhood, my supposed power was more of a nod to my status. I began to wish I had not been so adamant that I could cope singlehanded.

Destroying the first one left me half-blind; a clotted darkness obscured my central field of vision. I had consoled myself with the calculation that we needed to dispel only a few of the Spawn each, over the course of some hours.

"Exorcist, another, here!" someone shouted at me.

I had to push them away, and after a few minutes, my vision cleared again. Two Spawn that had been killed were rearing up again. There were discarded pikes and halberds around them and, to my dismay, a mangled human body. The soldier had been wrung out like a dishcloth full of blood. It was the first corpse I had seen for months, and it sent a shock through me. It was as though in the rush to get to battle, I had forgotten that men would die.

I steeled myself and managed another exorcism before two women in blue arrived to relieve me. I joined the General, who was grouped behind the front lines with his officers. It was like being stuck in the middle of a crowd, impossible to see any distance or tell what was happening. Riders were still galloping about beyond the rows of foot soldiers, and the cavalry were keeping busy.

Amir's men focused on the scrum of fastwalkers. While the mass of the Spawn stuck together in a single unit that the infantry could deal with, this group threatened to get around them. The nomads knew their tactics; they would get several harpoons into one then drag it away from the pack where it could be hacked apart. The work was difficult and dangerous when done hurriedly, and Amir lost some of his best.

Young Harsis was at the heart of the action, wielding a harpoon from horseback. His horse stumbled, dumping him practically at the feet of two of the Spawn, which seized him at once. They had long since learned to go for the rider rather that the horse. If any man could have pulled free, it was Young Harsis, but instead, he was pulled apart.

Igmil, still Amir's most trusted lieutenant, was helping finish one off when it grabbed the haft of a halberd held by the man next to him. As he struggled to free the weapon, it came backwards, and the axe-head embedded itself in Igmil's shoulder. He bled to death before they could staunch the wound. Lalit was left to raise their three children alone.

At such cost was the enemy's mobile unit destroyed. The main body of Spawn pushed forwards and through, seething and squirming like an ocean. Finally, they overran our hasty defences, forcing gaps in the stakes and scrabbling until the ditches and ramparts were worn down into shallow pits they could negotiate. At first, the defenders were able to kill those that came over. Not all could be exorcised. Pikes and other weapons were thrust into them as they reformed, sometimes pinning them to the ground or hobbling them.

Their advance was too strong, though, and the casualties did nothing to deter them. They kept coming forwards. The General wanted to move the unit that was facing the killing ground with fresh troops, but the fighting never let up.

Then, slowly, they started to break through the defences. Their front rank was a different type, with long tusks or horns to dig away at the earth. They were inefficient, but in time, they could hack through. I wondered for the first time whether the city defences were strong enough.

The creatures had come through in too many places. The General gave an order, and drums sounded a different rhythm—three beats, pause, three beats, pause, three beats. Then we started to retreat.

Whole phalanxes of men walked slowly backwards, increasing the distance between our men and the enemy. It was taking them a long time to force their bodies through the gaps they had created, and they would not advance until the whole body was ready.

As we retreated, I could see the litter left behind: helmets, pikes, and mangled corpses. At least a hundred, I estimated. The men scrambled back through the second line of defence, breaking formation, then hastily assembled the stake wall on the rampart.

The General was trying to make sense of the reports he was getting of how many Spawn there were and how our forces stood. The horde was still heading for the city. We could withdraw all the way behind the walls, but that would be a temporary solution. As the General had noted, if they came spilling over the walls, then we would have to fight them in the cramped confines of the streets.

If they got into the city, we would need to have a mass evacuation. And we would leave everything for the Spawn to devour or destroy… and that would never do. We needed to stop the horde.

The men waited warily behind the second line.

"Can we halt them?" I asked.

"We have destroyed a good number, and many are stuck in place," the General said. "It all depends on you exorcists."

He was right. I was exhausted after dispelling two and was still nerving myself for a third. I had seen several women in blue escorted back through the ranks, and desperate cries of "Exorcist!" told me there were not nearly enough to go around. We had a chance to wipe out a sizeable number of the creatures at a stroke. If only the exorcists were strong enough, we would win the day.

They came on again, under their camouflage of waves and sea-foam. The men seemed ready, but the second line of defence was more hastily dug than the first. The Spawn started to break through almost at once.

When the armies met again, it turned into a confused melee. Our men were doing well in the section closest to me, killing efficiently and maintaining their formation. Four exorcists worked together, chanting slowly and destroying what they could.

Then something happened over to my left. Men were screaming and shouting, and Spawn were rearing over them, killing and maiming in all directions, like blood-soaked carnival wheels. Finally, they were brought down by weight of numbers.

I later found there had been gaps in our lines. One of the phalanxes had been withdrawn, and the replacement had not moved to the right place. Elsewhere, the wrong troops were in the front line—men without polearms, who by bravado, stupidity, or confused orders ended up in a hopeless fight.

"Yishka!"

I turned at my name. Damki was beckoning me forwards. "The exorcists there are down. They need you!"

Pikemen were holding back several Spawn while another was starting to reform. I was not ready, but I tried anyway. Every word was a stone I had to force out of my throat. I was being pushed down. I was drowning. My vision blurred. I had to go on… The creature's remains bubbled and roiled like exploding lava, before dispersing in a hot black smoke that burned my skin.

"She's dead," Damki said, looking up from the body of the exorcist. "The others ran away."

The cause of death was heart failure, one of many that day. Many others would never be able to pronounce the chant again; some could not even say their own names.

I could not see, but Damki guided a waterskin to my hands. I splashed myself to soothe the stinging and glugged greedy mouthfuls.

"Some of the soldiers are running away," Damki said. My brain was still fuzzy, and it took some time to understand what he was saying. "The General is trying to move the army."

We backed away on a diagonal, units becoming hopelessly confused with each other, hunters mixing with soldiers from Stone and mercenaries. The creatures seemed to be milling around and not following us. Discarded weapons, armour, and body parts littered the ground around them.

The sergeants did their best to shape the formation into a straight line and bring the pikemen to the fore, shouting and lashing out with their whips. In the distance, beyond the Spawn, another line of soldiers faced us. Our army had split in two, with the Spawn in between us and their way to the city clear. They seemed to head off first in one way then another, like an amoeba pulling in different directions. If they tried to pass, we would attack in their flanks—if the General dared.

A small force of cavalry still stood in the creatures' path, with others rallying to them from all points of the compass. I recognised crusaders.

"Can you count the Spawn?" I asked Damki. My vision had cleared, but my glasses were covered with filth, and cleaning only smeared them. "How many left?"

"A hundred," he said a minute later. "Maybe a few more."

The Spawn gathered. A few stragglers tore themselves free or were hauled out of ditches to join the remaining force, which started their relentless roll forwards. The General hesitated, but the crusaders knew no fear. Anbu had assembled his cavalry and brought them forwards at the gallop, hurtling across the grassland. Lances lowered and pennants streaming, men on horses raced into collision with the monsters.

As the riders crashed into the enemy force, the crusaders dismounted acrobatically, hurling themselves onto the Spawn with battle-axes and cleavers. I could not see many blue robes still amongst them; their exorcists must have already been exhausted. Without help, the crusaders would not survive long. The infantry still had exorcists able to function.

"Forwards!" I shouted. "Attack!"

"Forwards!" the General echoed.

The drums sounded, and the men charged. It was too late to think whether our formation would be effective. Courage and ferocity would have to take the place of precision and organisation. I was not sure I could manage another exorcism, but I would go on until I dropped.

What happened next surprised me: the Spawn broke ranks. Instead of staying to fight, they attempted to flee, dispersing in all directions. The melee was brutal but brief. The crusaders had done most of the work, and it was a matter for exorcism or pinning the creatures in place.

I tried—I really did try—to finish another one. But the words stuck in my throat and left me floundering like an actor in the spotlight who had forgotten the lines. I signalled the soldier to get back out of the way.

"Find the General and tell him we can't destroy any more," I told Damki.

The battle ended with soldiers, some on foot and some on horseback, following the Spawn at a distance, spreading out over a wide area. A few hours later, some of the exorcists had recovered enough to go around and help destroy those that were still trapped. By then, the chant was easier: the stars had shifted in their courses, and whatever alignment was against us had broken up.

The battle was the biggest and bloodiest we had ever fought. Amir, angry over his losses, wanted to have the soldiers from Stone who had run away flogged, or worse. Personally, I was sympathetic with them, and besides, my immediate concern was preventing any further escape from No Man's Land. I pushed out of my mind the question of what would happen if the enemy came in larger numbers and with greater determination.

"How many men did we lose?" I asked Marie-Therese in our headquarters that night. She was supervising the clerks tallying the day's casualties, organising for the dead to be burned, the wounded to be treated, and the missing to be accounted for. Each clerk worked in a circle of lamps, recording and compiling lists of names.

"Not so many," she said. "Not many at all, really. Just a few hundred."

"Any how many wounded?"

"More," Marie-Therese said with a shrug. "Yishka, we can afford to lose soldiers. And the crusaders want to martyr themselves. But we cannot afford to lose the city."

"We won," Izabel said. She was holding what looked like a black rhino horn: spoils from the new type of Spawn that dug at our earthworks. She did not sound triumphant. She had been with Amir's men in the battle and had seen Igmil and Young Harsis die. "We took out a critical number of those tuskers, and they knew they didn't have a chance of threatening the city."

We had destroyed their expeditionary force. But we also had killed many, many of the Spawn in the preceding years, without making any dent in their numbers. Pessimists compared the creatures to ants. Every year, hundreds of winged ants left the nest, seeking to build new nests elsewhere. Even if you kill all of them, the nest remains, and more ants will keep issuing forth. They only send out those they can spare, and their loss does not affect the nest.

"It doesn't feel like victory," I said. "And dispelling was awfully hard work today. I must be getting old."

"No," Izabel said. "We knew it would be hard today. The chart said so. We were ready."

"It was a victory," Marie-Therese said. "If you had not stopped them... what then? The town would have been overrun; the soldiers would have fled. We would lose our herds and everything... disaster."

"It wasn't a disaster," I conceded. "But there was so much... so much..." I saw again the broken bodies of young men scattered over the grass like the aftermath of a terrible railway accident. I tried to finish the sentence, but I was crying. I turned my face away into the shadows, so none of the clerks would see. Commanders were not supposed to weep like children just because some of their troops had been killed.

"We're still here," Marie-Therese said.

"Highness," Dota said. "A messenger to see you. I think she's from"—her voice dropped to a whisper—"from the Sorceress."

The Sorceress invariably communicated with us indirectly, passing on messages via merchants. I had not seen her since that first day. We had never even had a direct messenger.

The messenger was waiting in an anteroom. She was a small, dark-skinned woman in black who indicated by gestures that Dota must leave and that she would see me alone. The woman was not a nomad, a northerner, or any of the other races I was familiar with. I could only guess that she must have come from somewhere deep in the Arabian Peninsula.

"The guards don't know how she got here. She doesn't talk. She just makes signs," Dota whispered then left.

The lower half of her face was covered by a wooden mask. When Dota had gone, the woman removed it. She took a black stone the size of a duck's egg from a leather pouch and placed it in her mouth. It should have obstructed her speech, but she spoke clearly enough, with the same clear accent as the Sorceress. "You are Yishka, of Wintertown."

"That is correct," I said when I finally understood she was awaiting confirmation.

"Messengers were sent," she said. "To warn you of a dangerous conjunction. They may not have arrived."

"We have had nothing since your last chart some weeks ago," I said. "It was enough to prepare us for today's action, although it was worse than we expected."

They should have warned us. Not that we could have done anything differently.

"The conjunction was higher than first thought. New stars have risen. More conjunctions will follow." She drew a rolled-up goatskin from her sleeve. "Higher tides than ever. You must study this very closely."

I took the scroll, weighing it in my hand. I did not bother unrolling it. "What are you saying? Are you telling me we're doomed?"

"There is a high tide—this now passing—and an even higher one to come. There will be a lower tide than ever, too, between the highs. In two months, the stars will be in your favour for one day, like a strip of blue sky between dark clouds. That will be your one chance. After that, they will grow strong—very strong. You have one chance." It was as polite an ultimatum as I had ever heard.

"I understand," I said.

The messenger made a small bow, signalling that her job was done.

"You must have had a hard journey," I said. "There will be food and drink and a bed—"

"I go." She leaned forward, let the stone drop from her mouth into her cupped hands, and replaced it in its pouch. She gave me a last look before donning her mask. She stood up abruptly and slipped out of the tent like a shy animal, one that would stay nearby for a minute but bolt at a distant sound.

The guards said later she'd just disappeared into the night, but they may have been scared to follow her too closely.

Ten minutes later, Marie-Therese was placing goblets on the four corners of the goatskin to keep it flat and a lantern on either side. She ran a finger over the symbols. "Two months… In two months, we can destroy them. Perfect."

"Perfect because of the treasury?" I asked.

"Because we need to end this war before you all go mad," she said. "But also because of the treasury."

"Not this again," Izabel said.

"This again. Now, while we still have some money, we will spend everything we can. We will get every nomad, every man in the grasslands, every mercenary. Just for one battle, we can do it."

Marie-Therese had been warning me about our imminent economic collapse for months. I had always Micawberishly believed that something would turn up. Now it had, but not quite in the way I had expected.

The battle that day had made a chilling kind of sense. It was pre-emptive: the Spawn had done all they could to meet us in battle and cause as many casualties as possible before we had our opportunity to attack them. They had certainly wounded us, but not mortally, and if it was just a matter of one more battle, we could gather a much larger force. There was no telling, though, exactly what we might be facing on the other side.

"So it all ends in two months?" Izabel asked.

"One way or the other," Marie-Therese said.

Chapter Twenty-Six: The Gathering of the

Great Army

WE SHOULD DRINK A TOAST," Marie-Therese said. "To the final victory!"

The army of Stone had been with us for three years. This was the first time we had talked of victory, and even now, the word sounded brittle.

Inzalu passed me a goblet. There was quite a gathering of us in Marie-Therese's drawing room, with Vana, Timi, Izabel, Lalit, and even Lu Zhu, more of the handmaidens than had been in one room for some time. Illi was with her scouts, Rachel and Noora with the exorcists. Lalit, though, was quiet, holding her youngest child and talking more to the baby than to us.

Marie-Therese's villa had been extended since my last visit. Her drawing room boasted a wooden floor and matching furniture, with *objets d'art* arranged on low tables. Though they were the talk of Wintertown, I had not been to one of her gatherings in some time. Her house was quite a contrast to my own spartan spinster's apartment.

A small knot of secretaries waited discreetly in the corner, ready to take orders. Outside, the streets rang with the sound of hooves, shouted orders, and the clatter of weapons.

"Golly," I said at the sharp fizzing on my tongue. For a moment, the taste transported me back to Dulwich Park, a picnic in the sun, sitting decorously on a tartan rug, watching the boys play cricket. "Sparkling wine! Wherever did you find champagne?"

"It's nothing like champagne," Marie-Therese said. "It's not even Mousseaux. But I finally managed to get Vana to make wine with bubbles in it."

Fascinated, Inzalu asked, "How do you make it?"

"Secondary fermentation," Marie-Therese said. "A trick from my home country."

"It's a lot of work, getting sultanas and everything, but it's not bad," Vana said, taking a swig. There were dark rings around her eyes after the big party on the eve of battle. The woman who ran the brewery was a well-known figure, and Vana had many farewells to make.

"Not bad," Timi agreed.

"If nothing else, I've given this place decent beer, and spirit, and shown them how to raise dogs," Vana said. She sounded still a little drunk from the previous night. "What did the rest of you do?"

"I helped pay some of the men who shared your bed," said Timi. "Izabel kills Spawn, Lu Zhu heals the sick, Inzalu runs the nurseries, and Yishka mainly lays bricks. I don't know what Marie-Therese does."

"Me neither," Marie-Therese said. "But it takes a lot of time."

Champagne really should have been reserved for victory, but Marie-Therese, pessimist as ever, did not assume I would survive the action. We were throwing everything we could muster into this last, desperate assault, and I had to be part of it. We were short of exorcists anyway, and that was still one skill I could offer. Besides, I could hardly send so many others to their deaths without taking any risk myself. Things were different with Marie-Therese. She had always watched from the battlements and counted the dead on both sides.

"Crow is looking forward to the outcome," she said. "Though I tried to tell him about the risk of flooding the market with too many teeth."

Though she never had married the hunter, their relationship was an established fact, even if it now seemed more like a political alliance than a romance. People had started calling him Lord Crow, at first as a joke, but the title had stuck. Under Marie-Therese's influence, his men had become steadily more organised. They were still a gang of misfits, chancers, and escaped convicts, but they were more of a disciplined force.

"We will stockpile teeth," Timi said. Today, she was clad in a full-length affair with layers of rich green material, but she looked almost as exhausted as Vana. "The price will drop at first, but when we wipe out the source of supply, there won't be any more, and the price will just go up and up after that."

"That's clever," Inzalu said.

"Yishka has taken all my money, and now she's destroying the basis of our fortune," Timi said. "But you wait—we'll be rich again. We'll give you a better wedding than Lalit."

Lalit though, whose wedding to Igmil was still the benchmark for lavish celebrations, did not notice the gibe, being too absorbed in letting her baby grasp her finger in his little fist.

We had been learning economics the hard way, and I now understood why the Venetian and Florentine bankers had so much power in the mediaeval world. Financing a war meant borrowing large amounts of money, and there were no banking facilities to speak of. Our borrowings were in the form of debts, promises made, and earnest assurances to Stone and various nomad chiefs that we would repay them. If any of them started trying to collect on those debts or even if enough of our mercenaries demanded their back-pay, we would be in serious trouble.

DAVID HAMBLING

"We used up all our trade goods to pay for this battle," Timi said. "The warehouses are empty. We cleared them out. If there was the smell of a mouse left in there, I would have sold it."

"Easy for you," Vana said. "I've been making beer and bread from ground goat bones and floor sweepings for the last week to feed all these new people."

"We do what we have to." Timi clinked goblets with Vana. "For the war effort."

I felt a pang as I noticed the secretaries, servants in all but name, with eyes studiously downcast as we enjoyed our sparkling wine. In all the hurry and bustle of everyday life, it was not easy to think of everyone. There were so many things that needed to be changed after the war, after this final battle.

"This isn't too bad," I said, putting down the empty goblet. "But I should go and check on things."

"Don't you go out fussing," Marie-Therese said. "At least try to keep some of your mystique."

"And don't touch your hair," Inzalu said. "It looks nice like that."

"I don't see why I needed to have my hair done to fight a battle."

"Why not?" Vana asked.

It was not just the hair. I had a brand-new outfit, rustled up by Marie-Therese's own couturier, all in deep-blue cloth with silver braid. It was just the right side of practical, and the colour marked me as an exorcist.

"You are the goddess, leading her army. You must be *formidable* in every way."

I had looked at myself in my hand mirror for the first time in ages to check my appearance. What I saw shocked me. Not just the ageing; that was to be expected. But seeing the stern features of Yishka the God Queen took me back. I was sure I never used to have that penetrating look.

My reflection looked so pale, so different to all the faces I saw around me. And there was something else too. Beneath it all, I could still see the ghost of Jessica Merton from London, that bright young thing from the twentieth century, with her future all before her. Seeing myself had been a sobering experience. The hair and the dress looked good enough, though.

"You should have at least some gold epaulettes," Marie-Therese told Izabel, touching her shoulder.

"People know who I am," Izabel said, shrugging her off. "I'm not letting you dress me up."

"As you like, you with your rough masculine clothes," Marie-Therese said then mischievously added, "You have proved us all wrong—you really have become a man after all."

We were interrupted before Izabel could respond.

"Highness," Turm boomed from across the room. He had entered quietly and limped towards me, bowing and offering me the hilt of a sword.

"My own sword. How sweet." I was lost for words. Turm had not slept for days, the forges had been working day and night in a last-ditch effort to supply enough arms and armour for our final battle, and still, he had found time to craft this special sword. The pommel was shaped into a clockface, a motif repeated along the blade. It was smaller and lighter than the broadswords Crow's men favoured, the right weight for one not used to holding a weapon. "Not that I know how to use it. Thank you."

"It looks well for a leader to have a sword," Turm mumbled. "I know you probably won't use it, but… it would be a pity not to have a blade if you needed one."

If I ever needed a sword, then things would have gone terribly wrong. Turm's gift was not an optimistic one.

"Turm, you are the best and most skilled of weapon-makers, first amongst the many artisans of the city. I'm afraid after this day, you will not have much to do."

"There's plenty I'll be turning my hand to, Highness. Many things I shall be making besides weapons. I'm glad you like the sword. Mind out, that blade is sharp. Here's the scabbard and belt. Good. I'd best get back to overseeing the arsenal."

"The belt does not match your outfit," Marie-Therese complained, but I strapped it on anyway. The sword slapped awkwardly against my leg when I moved.

I chatted with the handmaidens some more, but I was distracted. I wanted to see the order of battle, to count the numbers. Eventually, Marie-Therese allowed us to go outside, and we stood on the platform by the main gates where we could watch the army form up on the Field of Mars. They may not have been military, but this was by far was the largest force we had ever fielded. It made me think of ailing plants which suddenly put all their energy into one final flush of flowers before dying.

The ramparts were lined with women who had massed to watch the army depart—wives, mothers, and children. Labourers and scribes, clerks and artisans, the women of the city waved their men off to battle.

"Never enough men to win decisively," I said, repeating the old refrain.

"Yishka," Marie-Therese said, "you should be proud. You are the architect of our republic! Look at all of this—this army we built up from nothing. None of them would be here except for us. We will be victorious!"

"I hope you're right." It was the most encouraging thing I could think of, but I could not disguise the fact that my heart was in my boots. The long war of attrition had failed. Now we were staking everything on one throw of the dice. The only thing that was certain was that we would take heavy losses. Many of the men assembled here would never return.

The buzz of excitement from the gathering army was palpable. There was unnecessary galloping about and whooping, and good clothing, boots, and polished metal on display as the different units sought to outdo each other.

"It's like watching stags showing off," I said.

"Just as well," Marie-Therese said. "Otherwise, they wouldn't be so willing to go out there and die to defend us."

"If I don't see you again, Yishka, I wanted to thank you," Inzalu said. "For everything you've done. I'm just sorry I'm so useless."

I wanted to tell her that her contribution had been invaluable and that I wished there had been more helpful women like her. Inzalu's constant good cheer and friendly presence had held the group together at times when it could easily have fractured. I struggled to frame some line about needing mortar to hold bricks together, or perhaps that they also serve who only stand and wait. But that would have sounded patronising, even to me.

"You have never been useless," I said.

"I wish I could be confident like you."

"It's all show. Marie-Therese could teach you confidence."

"Me?" Marie-Therese said. "You are joking. I'm the biggest coward here. I'm not going into battle."

"I'm only going myself because we need all the exorcists we can muster," I said.

"Damki will look after you," Inzalu said.

I was not so sure. Damki had seen relatively little action against the monsters, but like every other able-bodied man in Wintertown, he was in the vanguard. I had even seen Nergal on horseback with a spear in his hand for the first time in years. He looked determined rather than warlike.

Marie-Therese kissed me on both cheeks and wished me good luck. "Go tweak the devil's nipple."

"She never tried to upstage you," Timi said as we parted. "Things must be serious, but I'm sure you'll win."

Illi had gone on ahead with her scouts. I did not usually worry about her these days. Illi always knew how to look after herself and how to avoid trouble. But she was at the tip of the spear today, at the most hazardous place, going into unknown territory full of unguessed-at dangers. She would need luck... just like the rest of us.

The changing of the guard at Buckingham Palace was a piece of nonsense for the provincial tourists. But having been through all the vicissitudes of raising, training, equipping, and organising an army, I was now a great admirer of anyone who could get soldiers to dress properly, keep their equipment in good order, and march in straight lines on command. No wonder the Roman legions conquered the world.

I stood by the triumphal arch as, unit by unit, our army passed by on their way to form up. The differences between our other forces were more apparent than ever. The only thing they had in common was that all of them were dotted with blue—blue cloaks or tunics—the uniforms of the exorcists. We aimed to provide one per twenty men. In practice, it was more like one in fifty.

I could see Amir's leopard cloak from here, followed by his personal banner. Banners were easier to rally around than individuals in the dust of the battle, another of our innovations. Amir's cavalry looked much as they must have done for the last thousand years or so, and probably just as Attila the Hun's men would look in a thousand years' time and Genghis Khan a thousand years after that. They were grouped into squadrons according to their tribal loyalties. They were the scouts, our eyes and ears, skirmishers par excellence to delay and pin down the enemy.

Next came the crusaders, quiet and solemn rather than excited, with less of the flashing metal and colourful horse blankets of the other nomads. A few blue-robed exorcists rode with them: that would be where Rachel and Noora were, with the men who most revered them. Most crusaders had the cavalry version of the poleaxe, a weapon which required great courage and split-second timing. Their preferred attack was one furious charge of brothers then death or glory in the ensuing melee. From where I stood, they looked dark-skinned, but that was just from the charcoal they'd blackened themselves with. Their rituals were a mystery to me. Sometimes at night, they could be heard singing around their campfires, unsettling psalms that invoked my name and praised blood and sacrifice.

The cohorts from Stone at least looked like real soldiers. They were all in the same grey-and-brown uniforms, with curved swords at their sides, and they could form up and march in straight lines. I could hear the sergeants shouting at them and lashing out, applying the discipline of slave-drivers to their reluctant charges. Today, there were over a thousand of them, double the usual number. The annual rotation had been due to take place, but we had persuaded the Lords of Stone to keep the departing unit on for a few more weeks—for a hefty premium on our tribute.

Our own infantry, largely made up of foreign mercenaries, was less regulated, but they had the air of men marching willingly to battle. They were not the sort of men one would wish to pass on a dark street though. Today they included many actual criminals with branded hands: an amnesty had been declared for any who had been exiled if they would fight for us. They were predators. Like Vana's dogs, they were temporarily under control, but they would revert to type if allowed to.

The hunters had become ever more baroque. Some of the wealthier hunters were mounted, but like the troops from Stone, they were mainly a force of infantry. Some were armoured down only one arm, like Roman gladiators; spiked armour was de rigueur for many of them of them, as well as elaborate cage-helmets and shields covered in spikes like metal porcupines. Some wore oversized shields over their backs, and others had spiked staves projecting over their shoulders, so that any tentacle attempting to seize them would be injured. They looked like living metal sculptures or attendees of a medieval-industrial fancy dress party.

The hunters were equipped with a bizarre ironmongery of weapons: flails and pickaxes, chains and polearms with heads like Chinese ideograms, and butchers' cleavers or rapiers on their belts as sidearms. Each type of weapon and armour had its own function within the hunting party, with different groups favouring various tactics, all constantly evolving.

"Highness!" The General was calling me. Today, he was an elegant figure in green and grey, beard elaborately curled, his bronze breastplate freshly polished. The General was the closest we had, perhaps, to a knight in shining armour. A mounted drummer-boy rode beside him, and behind them his officers.

"Lord General," I said. "Your troops are a wonderful sight."

"Your Highness is too kind," he said. "For my part, I can overlook the fact that they march like castrated goats, because today, they will fight like lions."

Amir was never so dismissive of his own men. Our General of Stone had an almost English modesty about his troops. Like the Duke of Wellington, he saw them as an armed rabble who needed strict regulation but were capable of heroism.

We were interrupted by a horseman riding up at speed. The crusaders face was covered with black smears of war paint, bare arms laced with scars. Beneath the paint and scars was a boy as young as Damki when I'd first met him.

"Highness, please, Highness." He did not look me in the eye but held up a small amber figure, one of the little idols they all wore around their necks, now rattling against their trophy teeth, with filigree spectacles around the eyes. Trying to stamp out the heathen practice was futile and would only cause upset. I just tolerated it. I kissed my likeness and passed it back to him.

"Highness! We are javelins in your hand!" The boy-crusader rode off, not daring to wait for a word from me.

"That man should be flogged," the General said, who deplored the nomads' lack of proper military discipline. "He'd probably enjoy it though. And he must be brave to approach the goddess."

Like the Ambassador, the General granted me divine status as a courtesy without showing any sign of belief. He was a tough old solider, with a distinguished record. Rumour had it that he had been too familiar with another man's wife—or several of them—and had been sent here as a punishment disguised as a promotion. In this distant backwater, there was little glory and every prospect of having his throat cut by nomads or being killed by monsters.

"It is good to see so many of your soldiers, Lord General."

By whatever means, the General had delayed sending last years' cohorts back when the fresh troops arrived. For this brief span, we would have double the usual number, and almost two thousand of them marched before us.

"Every part of the army seems to have expanded," he said, surveying the field. "Quite a rabble. Enough to put fear into even the hearts of monsters."

"Enough to win victory," I said.

"If it can be done by man, we will do it, Highness." He bowed solemnly and spurred his horse, galloping with his officers to join the cohorts arranging themselves behind Amir's cavalry.

"The General would never have agreed to this battle if he thought we were going to lose," Marie-Therese said.

The General was not as reckless as Amir. There were plenty of men who had believed in swift, daring assaults commemorated by stones in the town square. The more cautious ones were the survivors in the ranks forming up. I had faith in the steady slog, of keeping back, and only attacking when we had decisive advantage and could slaughter a group of Spawn without any loss. Still, it was this very strategy which had brought us to this pass. Maybe it was time to try the other way.

"Highness," Damki said, guiding his horse alongside mine and Izabel's. He paused to take in my appearance, and I felt suddenly self-conscious. He had filled out and now sported a wispy beard but was still recognisably the same boy who I had met five years ago. Like all the nomads, today, he could hardly keep the smile off his face. They loved a battle, and this would be the biggest and most glorious battle ever fought.

We rode to the head of the army, where Amir was waiting with his captains. He looked royal with a belt of gold discs across his chest; any melancholy had dropped away.

"Your army is ready," he said, grinning. "Now, draw your sword and hold it high above your head so it catches the sun."

He raised his spear as I did so, and cheering erupted from the troops behind us, quickly spreading to the entire formation. The God Queen had arrived to lead her army into Ragnarök. I felt more like an impostor than ever. "I was born for this day."

CHAPTER TWENTY-SEVEN: THE GOD QUEEN'S

FINAL BATTLE

Amir had been excited to hear that we were going on the offensive. That last desperate chance, which made the pit of my stomach sink, was to him the chance he had been waiting for. "We have been fighting this war for too long," he said. "It will be good to finally put it to an end."

"I have never heard you wish for an end to fighting before," I said.

Amir stroked his beard. No longer an affectation, it had become his natural manner. He still wore leather bindings around his wrist, which had never recovered its strength after his duel with Old Harsis.

"When they killed my father, it broke my world. All I could think to do was to fight, to get revenge. When I met you, I was a man starving for revenge." He smiled, almost wistful, at his youthful self. "A brave, foolish young man! I feasted on revenge, every day, and it felt good. It still feels good, every time we destroy one."

His eyes met mine. "We have had a good war, Yishka, you and me. But before, when I was a boy, there was a raid or two every month. I hardly saw a killing. In the last five years, I have fought every day, and

I have seen men die every day. It is enough blood. Enough war. It is not even mine now, with your General directing everything."

"I am not sure about this plan, whether we can win," I said. "After the last battle…"

"You say we should attack, and the goddess has never been wrong." Amir was as trusting as ever. It was heartbreaking.

"I have been wrong many times. But on this occasion, I think we have to do or die."

"Death in battle is glorious," he said, lacking the old conviction. "To destroy those things at last and avenge my father will be more glorious still."

"And afterwards, you can enjoy the fruits of peace."

He sighed and shook his head. "The world has changed."

There were fewer roaming bands and more settlements now. Farms and hamlets dotted the plains. The days of raiding parties burning villages and attacking caravans were gone. Now there was law on the grasslands, and its chief instrument was Amir himself. The settled bands, with their scrappy fences, makeshift irrigation, and ragged fields of crops, were thriving. Those who kept to the old ways—herding their goats from one place to the next, with only what they could carry— were starting to think themselves poor. And once the burden of the war was lifted, the people of Wintertown would really start building, assuming Stone did not take everything.

"It will be a wonderful new world."

"But you will not be in it," he said.

He had never forgotten. I had not spoken about going back to my own country for years. None of the other women ever seemed to think it was a realistic prospect, and the subject had not come up. They all seemed happy enough to make their lives here. But it was true I had never quite abandoned the idea of returning to London and to 1927, to the green fields and the grey buildings, back to steam trains, red buses, and black taxis, back home to my family and people who loved me.

"We will have to see. Until we can crack open the creature's citadel and destroy them, any plans for the future are moonshine."

"We will win," he said, something of the old fire lighting his face. "It will be the biggest, most glorious, most victorious victory in the history of the world. We will build the biggest memorial ever. Men will talk about it until the end of time." Amir had never lacked self-confidence.

Izabel too had brought up the subject of my going back home. She was still the same Izabel and still spoke to me in English, but she too had changed. Like Amir, she had lost some of the joy of battle. War weariness was affecting all of them.

"You're going back up the rabbit hole then?" she said. "I'll miss you."

"It may not be that easy," I said.

"True that." She hesitated. "I just had an idea… if you fall."

"What do you mean?"

"If you try to climb up, and you fall down. Back into the pool. I'm guessing you'd go back."

"Back? Back in time?" I had never considered the possibility, but of course it made sense. This was not necessarily the furthest back that it reached. "You mean back five years ago to when this started?"

"Further back. Maybe fifty years back. Then you'd be like this strange woman coming out of nowhere like nothing the nomads had ever seen." She looked me in the eye. "You'd have to start all over again."

"You mean… I would be the original goddess? The one who became the High Priestess." I laughed then stopped. I was sure there was some flaw in it. That wizened old woman could never have been me. She was much too small, for a start, and I would surely have recognised myself. I tried to remember what colour her eyes were.

"This place will do for me, especially when we wipe out the Spawn," Izabel said. "We could go with Timi's caravans, see the world. I'm not messing with time travel."

"Are you trying to dissuade me from going?"

"It was just a stupid idea," she said.

I wanted Amir to come to our pre-battle gathering with Marie-Therese and the rest, but he preferred to be with his warriors. They would share a flask of something, joke about who would kill the most, and slap each other on the back. It was where he belonged.

The night before the battle, I had dreamed of my friend Daniel as I had not done in years. I sat up in bed. It was full morning, and Daniel was sitting on the stool opposite. His fist was held out in front of him, and a fine trickle of sand ran from between his fingers.

For a moment, I was completely baffled, then the penny dropped.

"Daniel," I said. "This is a dream. I'm having that dream again."

"It is more or less inevitable that humanity will be superseded, sooner or later," he said, watching the sand, which fell in a perfectly straight column. "Just a matter of time."

"Are you trying to tell me something? I assume you're some part of my subconscious mind, full of suppressed knowledge."

"That's not really terribly flattering." He looked up with a quick smile to show he was pleased to see me.

"You haven't changed a bit," I said.

"There are many things that blow into Earth on the cosmic wind, things with more complex spacetime geometries than our own. Things we cannot begin to understand."

"You mean Cthulhu?"

"Not being adapted to conditions here, it makes sense for them to absorb or assimilate mankind rather than destroying it," he went on. "They can then percolate back through time from their landing point, rewriting history."

"You do sound very like Daniel." I was drinking in the sight of him, the badly ironed shirt, tie knotted in a complicated way that only he understood, the grubby glasses, and everything that made Daniel Daniel. The strongest wave of nostalgia rushed over me. "I always take seeing you as a good omen."

"An omen is information travelling through time," he said. "But of course, it does not necessarily mean you changing the outcome."

Where the stream of sand reached the floor, it was not falling into a formless heap, but each grain was dropping into place, forming a miniature sandcastle.

"That's clever," I said.

"Entropy," he said. "You're used to seeing things go from more ordered into disordered states, but manipulating time makes the opposite equally possible."

"Is that how the Spawn regenerate? Can we stop them? I wish you could speak plainly instead of always lecturing about polydimensional thingamajigs—but then you're Daniel, and this is what you've always been like."

He said nothing but poured sand endlessly from his hand.

"If you were real and not just a dream," I said. "I'd ask you to give a message to William for me. It's just, it's been so long… I've no idea what to say to him anymore." I thought about saying that I would see William soon, but that would have jinxed it.

"Don't worry, Jessica," Daniel said, fire running across his chest and obscuring his face, blurring his final words. "William knows."

When I woke up, I wondered if dreams of Daniel were brought on by stressful events or whether they happened whenever the force that motivated the Spawn was at its lowest, just as some had visions of Cthulhu when his power was at its height. Why I should see Daniel, though, was another mystery.

As we rode towards that final battle, Amir was as brash as ever. The General appeared quietly confident, and Crow—Lord Crow—whose judgement I also trusted in military matters, seemed eager to join in the fray. He had brought with him a vast contingent of hunters, calling back some who had retired or taken up other occupations, all summoned for one final and profitable blaze of killing. Lord Anbu, who commanded the crusader contingent, would have followed me to the gates of hell and beyond, and he anticipated the final battle with the grim satisfaction of a Christian riding to Armageddon.

The usual pall of smoke lay low over No Man's Land from the burning. There were patches of vegetation, though, with bright splashes of red poppies amongst the green.

"The enemy is torpid today. Even asleep," the General said, as a messenger relayed another report.

We ran into some groups of Spawn, but they barely delayed us. They fought piecemeal in fours or fives, slow and confused. Pike and halberd soon dispatched them. The exorcists disintegrated them without difficulty. I did not even get to the spot before they were dispersed.

"I hope they stay asleep," I said, looking at my watch.

The conjunction or eclipse—the astrological signs were imprecise, at best, and probably meaningless—would last half the day, which I assumed was twelve hours. Assembling our forces had taken longer than expected. I'd planned to start out well before dawn, and now we only had ten hours to go. Surely that would be enough time.

"The enemy does not offer battle," the General observed as we approached the creatures' encampment. He kept scanning the grassland in all directions, but the only movement to be seen were squadrons of Amir's scouts.

Previously, any approach had been met with large numbers of the Spawn coming from the stronghold and spreading out, forcing the attackers to beat a retreat before they were surrounded. We had fully expected another battle before we reached this point. Today, the defenders were lethargic, drugged by the influence of cosmic forces or perhaps gasping for the ethereal air that sustained them. We had expected to have a pitched battle here, one in which we could finally inflict a crushing defeat on the creatures. Surely, they would try to stop us before we stormed their citadel.

We reached the perimeter wall, and the army halted. This was as far as we had ever come. I had never seen their wall so close. A dove-grey coral reef eighteen feet high, it stretched out of sight in both directions in a long arc. It was made of intertwined strands of hard material the thickness of an arm, seemingly melted together. I had expected something like mortar or cement, but instead, it reminded me of weathered bone, as though the entire wall were a colossal, open-topped skull.

Nothing grew on the wall: no lichen, moss, or grass. Nor did any insects crawl over its surface. There were no birds here, and the only sound was the wind over the wall. I reached out but withdrew my hand. There was something disgusting about the thought of touching it, as though it was contaminated. Unclean, in fact,

Narrow oval holes, too small to crawl through, perforated the wall at irregular intervals. In places, there were four or five of them together. These were the entryways for the Spawn. They could squeeze though them with surprising speed, and soldiers surrounded each exit as though expecting Spawn to emerge at any second.

From a distance, we had been able to see narrow spires projecting high above the centre of the citadel, but closer up, the curve of the ground and the presence of the wall made it impossible to tell what lay beyond. Originally, their city had been reported as being less than a mile in diameter, but now it looked much bigger. Illi had said it was growing.

There were figures walking on the wall: Illi and her ghost scouts. They had a quick conversation with the lead riders, and the report came back that there was no sign of the enemy on the other side of the wall. Scaling ladders went up, and men joined them. Then Illi and her women threw down ropes and disappeared behind the walls. That would do as an entry for lightly armed scouts, but not for an army of pikemen and cavalry.

"This is it," Izabel said.

"If the army enters the city, we will not be able to co-ordinate," the General said. "It will be impossible to manoeuvre, and units will be separated. Gods know what the hunters will do, looking for loot, never mind the crusaders."

"We've been through this," Izabel said. "If we have to go inside to kill them, we do it. We've got the equipment."

"The creatures are feeble today," I said. "They are hiding behind their defences, as we would do if we were weak."

"The enemy likes ambush," the General said. "It is his favourite tactic. Inside may be one giant trap."

"Nobody said it would be easy," Izabel said. "But it's the best chance we've got."

Even then, they did not seem quite decided, so I weighed in. "Either we give up now, or we attack." I pointed to the wall. "The way to victory lies through there."

"Very well," the General said. He would not see Stone again unless he won here. "We will proceed with the assault."

The men on the wall were shouting down to the scouts inside and indicated to the General where the picks could be best deployed. The picks were like medieval battering rams, tree trunks wielded by twenty men each. Instead of the blunt head of a ram, though, the picks had sharp chisel heads, works which had cost Turm a grievous amount of good bronze. He had forged them well; every blow went deep into the barrier, sending explosions of fragments flying everywhere with great clouds of powdered rock. The barrier was only two feet thick, and they broke through in two places almost immediately. After that, it was a matter of widening the gaps.

Crow and a score of hunters stood ready. They would be first into the breach, ready to break through any defenders. He was unarmoured, as usual, but wore a green amulet around his neck, supposedly a protective charm. They were available for purchase in the market now.

"See the clouds?" Damki asked. Clouds had been gathering to the south. Big swirls of ink in water, they formed out of nothing, unlike any clouds I had seen here.

"What do they mean?"

"I've never seen clouds like that," he said. "But there are riders underneath them. A dozen or so."

I strained but could only make out ant-like figures in the distance. The prescription for my glasses was years out of date.

"No spears," Damki added. "Those are big horses, not our ponies. The ones in front have black robes. And… they are wearing masks."

"Sorcerers?"

"They have stopped now. They are watching us."

"We need to send a messenger to them," I said to the General, who was watching with satisfaction as the picks chewed through the walls.

"They would ride here if they wished to talk," he said. "It seems they only wish to observe. Maybe they will join in the looting of the enemy city." This was his little joke. Sacking a city was usually an occasion for rich plunder. In this case, the only prizes on offer were the teeth of whatever Spawn they could slay.

"General!" one of the officers shouted, peering through the dust thrown up by the operations. "The opening is wide enough to proceed—sir!"

"Carry on, Lord Crow," the General ordered.

Two hunters with round spiked shields went through first, followed by Crow, with a drawn blade and hatchet, a tall black plume in his hat, and a dozen of his picked men. This advance party disappeared from sight. Seconds crawled by. A cohort of pikemen formed into a column with their weapons, ready to follow through the opening.

The picks continued their work, widening the gap with every blow, throwing up so much dust that it was impossible to see beyond. There was shouting from the men on the walls.

Crow reappeared from the cloud, beckoning. "Come on you fools, come on!"

"Advance!" the General ordered, and the drummer started up. "And move those picks thirty paces left and get working on a larger breach. "

The whole army had formed into a snake behind us, like a queue waiting to get into a football match. After the first cohort was through, the General and I moved forwards. His aides and advisors followed, and Damki was close by my side. Half an hour after arriving at the citadel, we lowered our heads and stepped through the opening for our first sight of enemy territory.

It felt strange, forbidden. This was the secret place we were not meant to enter, a place I had for so long wondered about. It did not seem possible that I was finally setting foot here; I half-expected to see another wall or some other obstacle in front of us.

There was a fight in progress, but it was one-sided. The pikemen had forced four Spawn back against the side of a building, where they were pinned in place by a dozen shafts, as halberdiers chopped away at their writhing tentacles.

The buildings, or structures, or sculpted shapes around us drew my attention. My first impression was that everything was out of scale, like we were standing on an Alice in Wonderland tabletop surrounded by giant cups, steaming kettles, butter dishes, and huge cruets of pepper pots and saltshakers. The impression vanished, though, as soon as I looked at anything. It was a junkyard, everything jumbled together without rhyme or reason. There was nothing that looked like a house exactly. It all seemed somehow fragmentary. If I had to put an architectural name to it, I would have said it was Futurist—mainly because it did not resemble any historical building style.

The four creatures succumbed in seconds. Noora dispersed the remains of the final creature, and the General ordered his men to leave off gathering the teeth and form up.

"There will be plenty more," he said grimly.

The nearest structure, the thing that had reminded me of a saltshaker, was a circular pillar eight feet in diameter and twenty feet high. Its entire outer surface was pocked with dozens of cubbyholes. Metal gleamed from some of them, and I found a spearhead in one, a barbed arrowhead in another, and a second spearhead, a harpoon head, and a knife in a third. There was a whole compendium of weaponry, some intact, some broken, not in any order I could discern.

The buildings had no regularity, no pattern for the mind to get hold of, either. The thing that had struck me as a butter dish was more like a rectangular blockhouse on a low platform, with dozens of different-shaped windows or shafts cut at angles in its thick wall. The inside space was small due to the thick walls, and mostly taken up with a polyhedral chunk of stone—worked stone, not the mortar-concrete that made up the other structures.

What could have been a slice of giants' cake was an angular wedge, just two walls meeting together in a V-shape with nothing inside—nothing except a creature, which turned from the colour of mortar to albino white as it moved. It stretched as though waking from sleep, extending tentacles. The pikemen hurled themselves at it, pushing past me and impaling it instantly.

Afterwards, I spoke the words as easily as singing, and the noxious steam whooshed away in a dozen small cyclones. The soldiers were already leaning their pikes against the walls and filling their pouches with its teeth.

"Be careful," Damki told me. "There are Spawn everywhere."

The General had ordered the two hundred men of his lead cohort to spread out in a broad front, maintaining contact and clearing everything as they went so that there were no enemies left behind us. Crow led groups of hunters through our line, eager for prey.

The General let them go, showing disdain for their lack of discipline. "Stay in contact! Keep the line!" he bellowed to his men in the language of Stone. "Otherwise, you'll have tentacles up your arse."

The soldiers advanced cautiously, poking every new opening with a sword or pike. They explored every space and tossed lighted torches into dark cavities. That soon became impossible; the men would have needed to be monkeys to get into the towers, and many of the structures, if they were structures and not just blocks, had no entrances except narrow holes or slots. I watched one soldier walk by a head-high porthole: as he peered in, something grabbed him and tried to drag him through. His neck was broken before others could help.

Sometimes Spawn emerged from unexpected hollows or dropped down from plinths, all of them turning as white as snow when they started moving. There was no co-ordinated defence, though, and everything that came at us died.

The place should not have been called a city, but there was no other word for it. The others seemed less confused than me, though. To them, it was simply a landscape. They were not struggling to find sense in it or to see the meaning of that squat, smoking silo with curved sides that had reminded me of a teapot. The cloud that issued from it was not smoke or steam, but dust, and the vibration suggested something grinding inside, but there was no entrance.

Pillars and towers were the dominant architectural form, from warped cubic plinths to twisted spires like unicorn horns. Some of them could have been chimneys. Others were more like radio masts made of stone scales. No two structures were alike.

"Strange, isn't it?" Illi asked, appearing by my side. "The Spawn are mostly asleep. It is a confusing place, but we are finding the way through to the middle."

I advanced with the pikemen through a forest of giant strange-smelling headstones. Each was studded with hundreds of projections that oozed dull-red liquid. Masses of flies, some still alive and buzzing, stuck to them as if they were giant flypapers.

"Fly farming," I told Damki. "There is no game for them to kill, but they can attract insects." Could they realty gather enough insects to feed themselves? Given the vast clouds of flies that accumulated around dead bodies, maybe they could.

Damki nodded dumbly. He crouched as though the place oppressed him.

As I rounded one of the headstones, I found myself face to face with a naked man. He was picking beetles off a trap and eating them one by one. He looked at me with dull, idiot eyes, and Damki ran him through with a spear before he could react.

"He would not have told us anything," Damki assured me.

We entered a plaza, where squat pillars supported a latticework roof overhead. What looked like clouds of white mist from a distance proved to be something else. Thousands of bones were suspended at eye level on threads. As my eye wandered over them, I started to make out entire skeletons, exploded anatomies—a goat, a horse, a dog, a snake… and a human. Skull bones and teeth orbited together. Each hand and foot had been separated into individual bones, all of which dangled within a few inches of each other. It might have been an art gallery, a museum exhibit, or a scientific demonstration.

There was movement at the other side of the bone plaza. Dozens of small Spawn were slithering and swimming towards us. The sergeants barked their orders, and the pikemen formed up in rows, with the points from the ranks behind projecting out in front of us. The Spawn came on like a swarm of malicious imps, heedless of any damage. I must have dispelled ten, one after the other, but there were far too many. We left the plaza full of bodies pinned to the ground, several skewered on pikes like grotesque kebabs, held in place with knives or swords as crossbars.

"There are too many," the General said when I caught up with him a few minutes later. "We have sealed some of them in their lairs, but we need hundreds more exorcists, and it would still be slow going."

"What about the men who were setting a fire?" I asked.

"Nothing to burn," Izabel said.

"This is no human city," the General said, looking around distastefully. "No wood, no cloth. Just this damn mortar."

I had relished the thought of seeing the whole thing consumed by flames. It was not a real city, but a facsimile of one.

"We're slaughtering them," Izabel said. "But it's like one of those guys who gives you a free punch, and he's so tough you can't make a dent."

The General revised his plan. Two cohorts would remain immediately inside the breach, maintaining a perimeter, with the soldiers from the town outside as a reserve. Meanwhile, the lead unit would adopt a close formation to march through to the centre. The hunters, nomads, and crusaders would roam at will, out of his control.

"I fear the opposition ahead," the General said. "Incidentally, your friends have advanced." He pointed to one side with his sword.

Five dark-cloaked figures stood on the wall. The sorcerers had taken the opportunity presented by our advance to see the place for themselves. Surely, they could have advised us how to proceed or how to destroy the place… unless they were not as omniscient as they pretended.

"What are they doing?" I asked.

"Signalling to something in the clouds, I think," he said. "If it is magic, I hope it is benign."

Behind us came the clank and rumble of collapsing masonry. We looked back as a cloud of dust rose above the point where the engineers had succeeded in bringing down a section of wall. The sound had barely ceased before excited nomad warriors were yelling at the tops of their lungs, urging their horses over the rubble rather than waiting for a path to be cleared.

"This is no place for cavalry," the General said. "But Lord Amir will not be denied his glory…" He rattled off orders in his own language to a sergeant, and gaps were opened in the ranks of pikemen to let the horsemen through. "We can let them ride ahead and find the ambushes."

As the riders urged their horses through the passage between the infantry, I scaled a low plinth to get a better view of what lay ahead. The highest spires must be the centre of the citadel. They were mainly circular or hexagonal pillars, some a hundred or more feet high, each with a creature squatting on its summit, like Simeon Stylites the other ancient pillar-saints, marooned above ground to be closer to god. Beneath the gathering dark clouds, they looked more like gargoyles.

"What are they doing up there?" the General mused. "How did they get there?"

"They're big," Izabel said. "Those ones on the towers."

"They are," I agreed.

Without anything to estimate by for scale, it was hard to tell. But the pillar-sitters looked easily several times bigger than any we had previously encountered. Were they there to scan the horizon and signal, like our watchtowers? Or were they communing with Cthulhu? I could not begin to guess.

Some of the structures were buildings, but others were more like sculptures. One street was lined with elephant-sized objects which suggested whirlwinds or dust devils with finely contoured surfaces. It was impossible to tell whether all the minute detail was the result of intentional craftmanship or if they were as meaningless as the shape of a stalactite.

We advanced through a maze of ribbed concrete mushrooms eight feet high, packed so closely that their rims touched. The ground was scored with deep troughs or open pipes, but they were empty, and there was no sign what this place was used for. We came across a long cylinder, the size of a train carriage on its side like a fallen tower, honeycombed with holes. As though someone had touched a tripwire, four Spawn emerged simultaneously from different entrances, unfurling their tentacles. There were four more behind them, and another four after those. I slipped back through the ranks as the pikemen took up a hedgehog formation.

"They could climb above us," the General said, looking up.

"I'm there," Izabel said, handing me her halberd and clambering up to the surface above.

"What can you see?" I asked.

"Gravel," she said. "These things are all covered in different-coloured rocks."

"Any enemy?"

"Not yet. The ones on the towers are watching us, though."

The threat did not come from above, but from below. Long tentacles snaked up from the pipes in the ground, dozens of them. They were slow and clumsy, but they grabbed many men, twisting and tearing off limbs. I drew my sword and fended off those that came close, then stepped in to exorcise the emerging creatures when the halberdiers were able to hack at them.

When all of the Spawn had finally been cut down and dispersed and our wounded tended and sent back to the breach, the battle-situation had become more complex. The General's men no longer formed a continuous line. A contingent of hunters battled something at the end of a street between boat-shaped buildings ahead. Riders hurtled past on our left and right.

"There's no organised resistance," Izabel said, jumping down beside me. "There's just a lot of Spawn."

As we continued, we came across more and more Spawn, mostly smaller than the adults we'd seen on the outside. They were mainly inert, barely stirring unless they were disturbed, then they came to life. Inside wells and cisterns, they bobbed about like olives in a jar. An opening at the base of a tower showed a row of them roosting like bats on a spiral rail disappearing out of sight. A giant stone beehive had one crammed, sleeping or comatose, in every cell.

We could not kill all of them, and we only fought those that moved. Every so often, they flopped down on us from platforms or surged up through manholes. Tentacles suddenly felt blindly over the top of a wall. It felt good to destroy so many, and today, exorcism was easy. The words almost seemed to be sucked out of my mouth rather than needing to be spoken. But if I carried on all day, I would not get all of them. I had not even tried to estimate how many were in the towers and tunnels we had passed.

The soldiers halted by a row of spherical stone cages. A bald, fat woman stared sullenly from the nearest. I did not know what the soldiers were staring at until I saw she was reaching out through the bars with a tentacle instead of an arm.

"Kill them," the General said.

Shaken, I did not argue. The caged things disintegrated as they died, and when I pronounced the incantation, they left crumbling brown skeletons which were nothing like human.

The exorcisms were easy, but even so, I was starting to feel a little lightheaded from doing so many.

The next plaza was sculpted into a concrete seascape, where the waves rose to storm height towards one corner. The waves were too high for us to climb over; a Spawn wandered between them, turning to face us. It was big and globular, but slow.

It was white, as they all were today, but as the nearest one faced me, it darkened. Patterns flickered across the creature's skin as though it were a movie screen, showing a city burning, babies on bayonets, crucified children in the street, my own screaming face magnified. Izabel and Damki hung back, wary that it might start lashing out, but a pack of hunters appeared, birdcage helmets gleaming in the sun. The men rushed the creature with short, double-headed axes. They did not seem to fear getting close today but made short work of the butchery.

"What was that?" Izabel asked, and I shook my head.

"Highness—if you please," the nearest hunter asked in strongly accented Language. "Our exorcist," he panted. "Back there. Busy somewhere."

I completed the task as easily as reciting the alphabet and left the hunters happily scrabbling for teeth on the ground. There was a commotion away to one side. Voices shouted at the other end of a narrow alley between rows of slanted chimneys. I recognised one of the voices and went down the alley, Damki and Izabel close behind me.

We came out into an open space or courtyard and founded Nergal being dragged by his arms by two brawny hunters. Unhurt, but disarmed, unhorsed and confused, they were hauling him to an oval hole like a well-mouth.

"This does not concern you, Highness," Crow informed me.

I stopped, Damki and Izabel to my right and left. There were six hunters, counting the two holding Nergal. They had not encountered Nergal by chance on the battlefield. Separating one victim out from the pack was what they were good at. Nergal's demise would clear the way for Crow to become the ruler of Wintertown. This was his whole reason for being here today.

"Don't kill me," Nergal begged.

"It might have slipped your mind, but you once condemned me to death by one of those creatures," Crow said. "I am returning the favour."

"Please!" Nergal said.

"Don't kill him," I said.

"What?"

"I beg you, Lord Crow. This is not worthy of you."

Damki moved protectively in front of me, spear lowered.

"I am owed my revenge," Crow said reasonably. "I've waited for this."

It was the sort of argument nomads understood, but Damki showed no sign of relenting.

"Damki, stop!" I said.

One man kept holding Nergal in an armlock while the others spread out, flanking us. Whatever authority I might have meant nothing to them. Izabel took a step sideways, halberd lowered, facing the nearest hunter. I did not draw my sword but kept my hands high.

"It might have slipped *your* mind," I said. "But when you were condemned to death, Crow, you were saved by the intervention of a woman. I ask only the same for Nergal. Please, we can settle accounts tomorrow after all this."

Horsemen rode by on the other side of the buildings. Crow weighed matters up. Honour, or politeness, won out. His plans were being disrupted, but killing Izabel, Damki, and me might complicate matters too much.

"You live 'til tomorrow, worm," Crow said. "Enjoy it. And you"—
he addressed Damki—"also owe your life to a woman."

"Thank you," I said. Nergal, released, hurried past us and back
towards our lines.

"And so we have *fair play*," Crow said. "Remember this, Highness."

"Good hunting," I said and turned to go.

"This is not a hunt," Crow said. "We can kill as many as your
exorcists could dispel back there without coming this far and risking
our lives. This is futile. What is the General looking for?"

"We need to destroy them."

Crow had been at the council of war before we set out. He knew as
much as I did. And he knew that by this stage, we were proceeding
blindly.

"My men will not go much farther," he said. "A good hunter knows
when to call it a day. More of the Spawn are waking up, and for myself,
I would prefer to get out alive."

I rejoined the General with his cohort of pikemen. Their numbers
were noticeably diminished. Only about a hundred fifty remained.
From the way they looked about them, I could tell the remainder were
wondering why they needed to go farther and when they would be
allowed to retreat to safety.

I was getting disorientated. None of the streets ran in straight lines,
and I could no longer be sure which way the centre was. The only way
to navigate was by the spires, and we were starting to pass the
outermost of them now.

"This is the centre of the city," the General said, as we came into
an irregular plaza.

A troop of nomads crossed in front of us, in pursuit of who knew
what. In the middle of the plaza was a circle eighty feet across,
surrounded by a ring of stones the size of footballs. There were no
Spawn in sight.

"I recognise this," I said, as the sculpted topography inside the
circle registered.

It was our sand table, or a larger version of it, an exact map of the surrounding area centred on the inhuman city. Polished pebbles of different sizes and shapes must be the markers showing where forces were.

"There is nowhere else to go," the General said, eyeing the buildings. Like me, he was looking for a ruler's palace, a military headquarters, or some kind of centre.

"There must be something," I said.

I don't even know what I was expecting to find. A delegation with a flag of surrender? A crystalline heart-stone we could shatter, causing the whole citadel to crumble into dust? An octopoid ruler on a throne, one who could be slain to end the war?

"We should look to our return," the General said.

I stepped into the circle of stones and kicked at a model wall experimentally. It crumbed easily enough, dry clay rather than mortar.

"Tell your men to destroy the map," I said. "There must be something else we can break."

As if I had summoned her, Illi was running soft-footed towards me, signalling urgently. "This way."

I followed her, Damki and Izabel close behind, though Illi said there was no danger. One side of the plaza was a wall made of rows of chimneys or organ pipes. It looked like a continuous barrier until we were close enough to see gaps between them. Beyond were a series of pools. In a dizzying moment, I recognised them. This was the place where I had first arrived. Not fifty yards away was a stone outcrop, now almost buried under curious excrescences, but the shape of the cavemouth was unmistakable.

"Fount-of-monsters," Illi said.

The pools were full of dark liquid, moving restlessly. They were arranged so that water flowing into the top one would divide and cascade into many pools below via different routes like a series of ornamental ponds. By the top pool was a spreading fan of slender metal leaves, each taller than me. Their edges were sharp, like razor

WAR OF THE GOD QUEEN

shells. The liquid in the lowest pool seethed with life, rippling like carp ponds at feeding time. The acrid stench would have told me exactly what was in the pool, even if I had not already guessed.

A breeze blew over the stone organ pipes. The air made a low sound like breath over the top of a bottle. By some hidden means, the note changed, low, then high, then low again. I looked to Illi, who had frozen in place, eyes wide. The sequence completed and died away as the wind fell. But there was no mistaking the rhythm of the chant which summoned the spawn of Cthulhu. Captured from the wind, like a Tibetan prayer wheel, it spun in the wind, repeating its charm again and again.

It was a factory for multiplying monsters. A Spawn would sacrifice itself by hurling its body into the fan of blades, an apple sliced by a mandolin. Segmented apart, it disintegrated, and its remains fell into the first pool, where it was diluted and divided, again and again. Rather than regenerating into a single individual, the slime would reform into several smaller versions, when the wind was strong enough and when the stars were right.

"We have to smash it." I was looking at those blades, the only metal we had seen. I would have bet that those had been fashioned and set in place by a human, not one of the creatures. They would not be easy to replace.

I was already looking beyond the fount-of-monsters. The arrangement of pipes was complex, and there must be some intricate mechanism controlling the sequence of notes. Breaking that would be a setback to them too. Losing their map might be a more serious loss. I did not think they had a copy sketched on a goatskin somewhere. But I wanted more.

"What do we do?" Damki asked.

I had never thought before that the Spawn faced the same challenges we did. The enemy was always faceless, all-seeing, effortlessly threatening, never feeling pain or loss. They were fighting a war of attrition just like us, against an enemy who was never worn down. Maybe they were in as bad shape as we were. Like us, the enemy had to co-ordinate their forces, communicate with them, and direct them. Maybe they even had to educate and motivate them. I had always assumed some sort of telepathy was at work, that the whole thing was under the control of some remote brain.

But what if the brain was all around us in material form? What if all their power of co-ordination, of planning and memory, were laid out here? The cranium-wall was there to protect something, something that could not be easily restored. Like our city, much of theirs would be taken up with things which were not essential. But there must be something vital. Some of this might be badminton courts and war memorials, but something here must be essential, irreplaceable. We had drilled a hole into its skull. Where was the most vulnerable part?

I took off at a run. I did not know exactly what I was looking for, but I knew it must be somewhere here at the centre, and I would know it when I saw it. I ran past a spaghetti-tangle of open pipes, a squat pagoda of triangular slabs welded together, a pyramid of stacked human-sized globes that glistened wetly, and an oval swimming pool half-filled with glass scales. I had almost completed a circuit back to the fount-of-monsters when I saw it.

The arrangement was like a Roman amphitheatre—a hollow painstakingly scraped out of the earth, with six tiers going down. Sunk into each tier were hundreds of stone basins of different sizes, each one a miniature amphitheatre in its own right with dozens of smaller bowls, some no larger than teacups. Each contained a number of polished pebbles the size of grapes—black, brown, and grey. A few were white or red. I picked up a handful; some of the pebbles had notches or markings on them. It seemed like a many-dimensional version of the wooden boards with holes that the merchants used to make calculations.

The General was with his men, pikes pointed outwards in a defensive formation next to the map, now trampled flat. They had advanced as far as they could and taken their objective. They had nowhere to go. He was only waiting for my approval before sounding the retreat.

"General," I said, "get your men to destroy the fount-of-monsters over there, and go into the amphitheatre and throw all the pebbles into the middle. Then we can go."

Two detachments were sent to carry out the vandalism, wary but eager to get the endless mission over with. As they battered and chipped at the fount-of-monsters and the handfuls of pebbles started rattling on stone, the whole citadel seemed to hiss. The soldiers stopped their work, and the General urged them to continue. The metal fan blades were broken loose and cast aside. The soldiers scooped pebbles with their helmets and baled them furiously.

I sensed the movement before I saw it. The building I was watching. The pyramid of globes erupted as white Spawn squirted out of the gaps like toothpaste from a tube. Like ants whose queen was being attacked, the entire population had been galvanised into action. They were sluggish, but they were everywhere. They had not wanted to come out and fight, but now they had no choice. I actually laughed aloud. That could only mean that we were doing some real damage—serious, irreparable brain damage.

"Exorcist, here, here!"

I moved to perform the rite as creature after creature was struck down. There were too many to keep at bay with pikes, especially the small scuttling things boiling out of the fount-of-monsters. One slithered along the length of a pike towards the horrified face of a soldier, reaching out at his eyes with spaghetti-like tentacles. He threw down the weapon before the thing reached him, but another was already clamping onto his leg. As he shouted and struggled to dislodge it, the first one reached him, and he fell over in a spray of blood.

"Gods," the General said then snapped an order.

The drummer started beating, and the soldiers regrouped into a single unit, forming back into a rough circle interspersed with a few blue-clad exorcists. They fought off the wave of Spawn with their short sickle-shaped swords, and I had drawn my own blade. This was mainly to fend off severed tentacles that tried to attach themselves to me, but also to administer the coup de grace. Damki stood at my back, fighting the onslaught from his side and protecting me as I spoke the incantation again and again. Izabel was battling away on the other side of the group.

As the fighting subsided and the exorcists destroyed the last of them, Damki tugged my shoulder and pointed to one of the spires. "Look!"

The Spawn squatting on their columns were moving, stretching, and unfolding giant bat wings. They did not fly, but they started to lower themselves on thick ribbons of gluey membrane.

"To the left!" the General shouted. "Gather pikes and halberds! Form up!"

A parade of monsters, full-sized Spawn, was advancing down the avenue towards us. The slug-white mass advanced slowly, as remorseless as a glacier.

The General was scanning in all directions, but one by one, the streets were filling with Spawn, leaving us no clear line of retreat. The General's other cohorts were far behind. The cautious approach of only advancing with his best unit had left him stranded.

Others had seen how the Spawn had been suddenly animated, though, and where they were converging. I could hear a distant thundering of hooves, and as the main body of creatures emerged into the plaza, it became louder. A nomad cavalry charged into them, with Amir's banner in the lead. Amir's leopard skin flashed past and disappeared as more horsemen poured by.

With a crack like a whip, green lightning licked down from the clouds. It lit everything with a weird light, making it all bottle green. One of the huge descending Spawn fell into a smoking heap. The lighting struck again, and another Spawn fell from its column.

The General was preparing to advance into the melee ahead of us. At least half the nomads were fighting on foot now, intermingled with the creatures, clutched at from all directions like men wading through brambles. I saw Amir whirling around, a curved blade in his good hand, ducking and slicing, grinning fiercely all the while. His men were more than holding their own, but they needed help.

Izabel shouted a warning, and I turned to see a churning mess of half-living material flopping and oozing out of the fount-of-monsters. It was semi-solid, one part disintegrating and sloughing off even as another part coagulated. It should not have been able to live; only willpower was propelling it. The thing rolled into a single snakelike form. Izabel hacked at it. The blade of her halberd disappeared into the mass. Then it flexed, batting her and two soldiers aside like skittles.

The giant inchworm doubled and flexed again. Green lightning lashed down deafeningly, and part of it exploded like a shrapnel shell. The thing arched, exposing a cauldron-sized cavity of charred flesh, but the wound closed over again like an eye blinking.

The men around me were scattering as they saw the creature was headed directly for me, like an oncoming express train. I hacked at it with my sword, but the chant was my real weapon. The words formed themselves into a blade, a guillotine which rose, fell, and chopped, slicing through the softer reality of the creature. It coiled around me, smothering me and blotting out the daylight.

Roaring filled my ears. The pulse surged through alien veins, but somehow, I was able to keep chanting. This was our day; the stars were with us. The mass of jelly could not animate itself. It was fractured and incoherent. It fumbled at me with clumsy, benumbed limbs and bit at me with unformed mouths. I hung on, chanting it away, unravelling its being syllable by syllable.

I felt like I was swimming across an endless black ocean of warm water. I just had to keep going for as long as it took, which was forever. I kept going, even after I could not remember where I was going. *Keep going, Yishka. Keep going, Jessica.*

A warm, thick smoke enveloped me. Blinded and panicking, I flailed my arms, rolling and trying to regain me feet. I found a bubble of blessed pure air. The smoke was already dispersing, folding back in on itself and melting away into the atmosphere in a thousand tiny swirls.

When I came to my senses, the fighting had receded. I was not even sure if there was any fighting. The roaring was fading, but I was seeing and hearing everything from a great distance. The world around me was hazy, muffled, and dreamlike. I had just downed an entire bottle of champagne, and it had gone right to my head.

A green flashbulb went off in the distance. I did not see where. The dark cover overhead had broken up into smaller clouds which roved over the city like marauding zeppelins, flashing down green fire. There was no sign of the sorcerers; that section of wall seemed to have been demolished.

I turned in slow circles, trying to take in the scene. Dead men lay all around me. Nothing was moving, no Spawn. There was the General's drummer boy and two of his officers. They had all died together as if stamped by a giant boot, perhaps in the thrashing of that worm thing.

"Hello?" I said, but nobody was there. Two riderless horses cantered by then veered down a side street.

I could not see the General or Damki amongst the dead. There was a blue tunic seared black amongst some nomads. I recognised her face, but could not recall where I knew her from. Then it came back to me: she had been one of the little girls who sneaked into the tent to listen to me telling Rachel nursery tales on her sickbed, five long years ago.

The lightning had struck many times. As many of the dead seemed to have been killed by its fire as any other cause. Nergal's half-blackened body, still wearing his fine governor's robes, clutched a spear awkwardly in one hand.

"I'm sorry…" I could think of nothing else to say.

Not far away I found Amir, or what was left of him. He looked as though he had fallen or been thrown down, head-first, from a great height. His cloak trailed behind him like the tail of a meteor.

He'd wanted a heroic death while avenging his father and defeating the enemy. It was exactly what I should have expected. It was impossible to believe I would never hear his voice again, always gently assuring me that if the goddess wished, it would be done. His smile, so easy and so familiar after all these years, and the look in his eyes that said he trusted me, would follow me to the ends of the earth, whatever my latest crazy idea was.

I wanted to apologise to him. I needed to explain that this was not how I wanted it to end. I wanted to defeat the Spawn with as few casualties as possible. But maybe if we had been bolder, if I had listened to him more, maybe we could have grasped the nettle and attacked earlier. No, it could never have happened like that, but I wished that it might have.

I wanted to thank him. I never had thanked him properly for all he had done for me. Without him, I would have been just a strange woman from an unknown tribe with no man to protect her, a night's entertainment for his warriors. Amir had a nobility of spirit, which I had always taken for granted. That was Amir: always brave and unselfish.

Green light flickered all around. There was no other movement. As I straightened up, all the emotion I should have been feeling was gone. I did not feel sorrow or anything. I was past feeling. Without Amir, none of this meant anything. This was not my world. My world was somewhere totally different to all this.

"I'm so sorry. It's been lovely, but I simply have to go now," I said to nobody in particular then wandered unsteadily towards the cave mouth.

I had done my bit; the war was over. The amphitheatre was wrecked, with puddles of glass from a dozen lighting strikes. The Spawns' brain centre was beyond repair. Surviving individuals could be hunted down and killed one by one, however many weeks or months it took. They would not recover; they would not multiply. Mopping up operations would continue, but the war was over. Cthulhu's seeds would not take root here.

I could go home at last. Home at last.

The first thing I wanted was a good long soak in a hot bath. But I also wanted to listen to an orchestra playing Mozart, to eat hot buttered crumpets by the fireside, to lounge on a sofa and leaf through magazines, and to hold normal English conversation. Back where I belonged, there were no savages with spears or monsters. The bus would speed by and splash me with water from a puddle and leave me with wet feet on a dull Thursday morning. I just wanted to go back to my home, my friends, my parents, my life, my England, and my everything. They were all waiting in that cave.

I did not think I would need a ladder or a rope. I felt I would be able to float upwards like a balloon, rising higher and higher until I reached 1927 and London. Or perhaps 1932, as time must have passed there too.

The cave was smaller than I remembered, but the pool, the steps, and the shape of the cavemouth were all unmistakable. I was not afraid there would be more Spawn lurking in wait. They were in eclipse now.

I squinted at the cavern roof, tying to make out the shaft through which I had fallen. There was nothing there. The ceiling was smooth and unbroken. The shaft which connected this world with the one I had come from had vanished back into some Einsteinian fifth dimension.

My dreams of going back to England drifted away and faded like the dispersing fog of those vile creatures. I was too stunned to react, too numbed by everything that had happened.

"Yishka, are you here?" Izabel asked from the cavemouth.

"Am I here? I don't know where I am," I said distantly. My mind was, mercifully, a complete blank.

Izabel looked dreadful. Her face was covered in dried blood, and her right arm hung limply by her side. She carried a sickle sword in her left hand.

"Amir's dead," she said then swallowed. Her lip was trembling.

"I know. Everyone's dead. This is the end."

I looked at the blank ceiling again as though it might change at any second. Everything had been leading to this and now there was nowhere left to go, nothing left to do. The waterwheels of thought, which had been so busy with so many details for five years, were going round empty now, coming up with nothing. I was a runner who had sprinted off the edge of a cliff and whose legs continued to flail, gaining no traction on thin air.

She looked up at the featureless surface. "Yeah," she said, more to herself than me. "Game over."

CHAPTER TWENTY-EIGHT: AFTERMATH

I HAVE NO MEMORY OF what happened afterwards. Apparently I just stood there, staring upwards for some time, while Izabel dove repeatedly in the pool. She swam down to search through the sand at the bottom with her fingers. She came up with combs, purses, even my original spectacles, and eventually found what she was after.

The malevolent lightning continued to rage, but had dispersed and moved outwards, and somehow failed to strike us. After Izabel got us back, they put me to bed, and I was unconscious for two days, falling into a wordless darkness. After that, I remained bedridden.

It may have been a combination of physical and emotional exhaustion, perhaps with added psychic stress from carrying out so many dispellings in such a short space of time. To be frank, though, it would have been more accurate to call it a nervous breakdown. I could have crawled out of bed, but I did not want to. I had no wish to face my people, especially the women. All the widows.

I did not want to know who was dead and who was alive. It would be too upsetting. We had fought, and we had won. Although from the perspective of my sick room, it seemed as though the real contest had been between the desert sorcerers and the spawn of Cthulhu. We were cannon fodder, pushed forwards to thin the ranks of the enemy and keep them distracted while the sorcerers wheeled up their heavy artillery. We were the irritation that forced them out of their bunkers so they could be destroyed by bombardment when they were at their weakest. And if we were in the target area, it did not trouble the sorcerers' calculations.

About the only person I could stand to see was Illi. She never spoke, just sat quietly beside the bed. I sometimes heard others—Marie-Therese, Izabel, and Inzalu—talking outside my room in low voices. I glimpsed Dota every time the door opened, sitting on a stool, a blank tablet on her lap, waiting for orders.

The activities of Wintertown continued, too, beyond the walls. Gangs of chatting women wandered by. Vendors pushed creaking handcarts by and shouting the prices of their wares.

I realised gradually that the high tide had passed, and there had been no assault on the city. We really had won.

The flies buzzed in circles and crawled across the ceiling. The ceiling was coarse and unfinished; I had never bothered much with ceilings, just thrown everything together any old how to get the job done. Someone had put a vase of flowers on the shelf opposite, where I could see them. They were lovely, but they were not English flowers.

This place had been tolerable so long as I could convince myself it was temporary. A person could put up with anything for a short time, even if that time got longer and longer. But now there was not even the illusion that I would be going home.

I refused to see anyone else, but I could not keep out Lu Zhu. As physician, she could overrule her patients. She came and went, examining my eyes, my pulse, and the inside of my mouth, but she did not attempt to talk to me. Her expression was patient and professional, but not warm. I could only guess how many injured there would be, how many maimed in body or mind. Marie-Therese would have cleared out buildings to make hospital wards, and Lu Zhu would have done the rounds. And she would hold me responsible for all of it.

"I'm sorry," I said eventually, just as Lu Zhu was about to leave. "About everything." My voice sounded strange after so many days without speaking.

"You did what you thought you had to do," she said, more weary than angry with me.

"Should I have behaved differently?"

She came back and sat by the bed. I thought she was going to chide me about how I'd mismanaged the war. As usual, I'd misjudged her values.

"I don't know. It has been hard for the women. They have carried so much of the weight these last years."

"I know, but—"

"You never really talked with them," Lu Zhu said. "Only with the men. Amir and Nergal and the General. If you had involved the women, maybe you would have found another way. I cannot say. It is too late to know now."

"You've done a lot for the women, though."

"A very basic medical system, a little education. They are learning—they want to learn. But things are still very bad." There was an implied criticism, but she would not give voice to it.

"If there was something you wanted me to do, you should have said. I was always open—"

Lu Zhu raised a hand impatiently. "Be quiet. I will not argue with you now. Not after all this time. You defeated the Spawn. Now, you must rest and eat the food brought to you. I will come back tomorrow."

Everything was over. The war was over. Amir was over. My only purpose here was to get home, and the way back to my world was forever closed. I had nothing to live for. Nothing to look forwards to. No reason to get out of bed.

Children played in the street. Illi stood at the window, well back from the slatted shutters, watching the game with a critical eye as the children prepared to hunt, organised by what sounded like the oldest girl.

"I want to be an exorcist."

"You can't, Sabian. You're a *boy*. You can be a harpooner."

"Can I be a scout?" a girl asked.

"Yes, but scouts have to be silent."

"I'll be silent!"

"Shush then. Murrim, you can be exorcist. And, Alshu, you're the monster."

"Let's hunt the monster!"

I heard the whole process of stalking and battling, the shouts, the cheers, and the gurgling melodramatic death of the monster. And then one of the girls recited a nursery-rhyme chant, how they thought dispelling should sound. More cheers followed.

"Get the teeth," the older girl ordered. "They're valuable."

"Yes! Yes! What shall we buy?"

Sooner or later, people would come for me. Marie-Therese or one of the others would be unable to decide what to do without my advice. Maybe I would be drawn back into involvement with the town. I could feel ants of curiosity wandering around me, starting to want to know what was happening with my buildings, my plans.

I would not return as a goddess. Not that! But I would not be able to resist putting things right and doing what needed to be done. Someday, I would have to steel myself and engage once more with this world. I would have to find out who was in charge of Wintertown now and where we stood with Stone, whether the economy was holding up, and what was happening with all the hunters who found themselves out of a job. There would be much to do, so very much to do.

I resented it all. I had done my bit. I deserved to go home. "I just wanted to go home." In my own ears, I sounded like a spoiled child. "Home."

"You are home," Illi said.

EPILOGUE: DULWICH, 1928

CRISPY HAD DOZED OFF IN his chair while I was reading, and when he awoke, he found me still staring at the last page. The walls were illuminated by the grey half-light which precedes dawn proper. Bunny snored softly from my bed.

Crispy coughed. "Quite a tale, ain't it, Bill?" he said quietly. Sober, in the light of morning, Crispy was a different man to the boisterous drunkard hammering on my door in the early hours.

"It is," I agreed.

"We had our doubts," he said. "Of course we did. Whole thing is ludicrous, in the light of day. Not so ludicrous in those caves, though. We saw things."

"Why did you bring it to me?"

"There isn't really anyone else we very well can show it to," he said. "Mainly, though, she mentions you, Bill. Obviously had a soft spot for you. Thought you'd like to know… what happened."

"Thanks."

There was a moment of quiet, and Crispy cleared his throat then carried on briskly. "Not that we get the end of the story. I suppose they killed off all the monsters. After that, hard to tell. Happy ever after, I suppose."

"What happened to the city?"

"'Nothing beside remains,'" Bunny quoted, awake after all. "'Round the decay of that colossal wreck, boundless and bare, the lone and level sands stretch far away.'"

"Cities disappear. Half the cities mentioned in the Bible can't be found," Crispy said. "Time swallowed them all up. Ripples disappeared in the sea of history."

"Did you tell him what we found?" Bunny asked.

"Not yet," Crispy said. "He's only just finished reading."

"What did you make of it? Did it ring true to you?"

I was silent, touching the pages in front of me. "Entirely true," I said at last. "Those were her words. I don't doubt any of it." My visitors waited for me to say more, but my lips were sealed.

"You know more than you're letting on," Crispy prompted. "About... about Cthulhu."

"Maybe I do," I said.

"One thing I meant to ask—that other chap she mentions... Daniel? Isn't he another one of your friends, that funny little mathematical chap?"

"He was. He's dead," I said. "Another victim of the Horror. In a fire, as it happens."

Another pause.

"Well, your business is your own," Bunny said. "If you prefer not to talk, we understand. We just thought we'd let you read it."

"Quite right," Crispy said. "We won't ask you another thing. And you'll stay mum about all this, of course."

"We don't want to look any more like prize chumps than we already do," Bunny said.

"Another day dawns, what?" Crispy said, stretching and rubbing his eyes. "Back in Blighty."

Outside, grey clouds brushed the rooftops, and drizzle spattered the windowpanes. It was just the sort of English weather that Jessica had dreamed of. Or that she was still dreaming of, somewhere.

"We'd better go out to forage for breakfast, I suppose." Crispy took the drift of papers from in front of me, squared it up, and stuffed it back into his bag. "I'll see you get a copy, in due course."

"That's very good of you."

"We ought to see if the trunks have arrived from Southampton," Bunny said. "And then we have to see a man about a book."

"What are you two going to do now?" I asked.

"Oh, I don't know," Crispy said. "On to the next adventure, I suppose."

The two exchanged a look.

"I have had enough adventure," I said.

Like Jessica, I had won my battle against the forces of R'lyeh, and it had left me drained. I had recovered to some degree and made a life in the world left to me without my friends. At least I did not need to mourn Jessica any longer. She was gone, but her death was no longer on my shoulders.

She would probably do better than I had. Odd to think of her, four years older than me, tanned by the Persian sun, grown into a ruler. I hoped she would settle down to the business of organising her city-state and get the roads paved and the ceilings plastered to her satisfaction. Maybe she would find herself a decent husband with whom she could play badminton, invent cocktails, and watch the sunset.

"If you say so," Crispy said. "But you'll forgive us for thinking that might not be entirely true."

We shook hands and promised to keep in touch. After our adieus, Bunny paused in the doorway for a significant moment. "Time travel, eh, Blake? There's a thing. *Quite* a thing. All sorts of possibilities, what?"

Then they were gone.

It still was early, but I could not think of going back to bed. I lit the gas ring, put the kettle on, and started to get ready for another working day.

This concludes 'War of the God Queen' – but Jessica's adventures continue in 'City of Sorcerers', the second in the series, due out in 2021

If you enjoyed this story, why not post a review on Amazon? You'll be helping others discover a new writer and share the pleasure.

And don't forget to visit the Shadows from Norwood Facebook page
www.facebook.com/ShadowsFromNorwood
For the inside story, links, photographs, interactive map, videos and more about the writing of the stories in this cycle.

How Jessica Merton came to be sent back in time is recounted in the novella 'The Dulwich Horror of 1927' available as an eBook, and also as the first story in 'The Dulwich Horror and Others', a series of linked tales set in South London.

Jessica's circle are linked to the Harry Stubbs series, in which a former heavyweight boxer and sometime debt collector finds himself tackling horrors beyond imagination in 1920s London:

The Elder Ice
Broken Meats
Alien Stars
Master of Chaos
Destroying Angels (due 2021)

All David Hambling's books are available from Amazon:
Author.to/DavidHambling

Printed in Great Britain
by Amazon

27937997R00220